A Wreath upon the Dead

*The publishers gratefully
acknowledge the support of*

An Chomhairle Ealaíon
The Arts Council

and the Arts Council
of Northern Ireland

A Wreath upon the Dead

BRIEGE DUFFAUD

They put a wreath upon the dead
For the dead will wear the cap of any racket

PATRICK KAVANAGH

POOLBEG

First published in 1993 by
Poolbeg
A division of Poolbeg Enterprises Ltd,
Knocksedan House,
123 Baldoyle Industrial Estate,
Dublin 13, Ireland
This edition 1994

© Briege Duffaud 1993

The moral right of the author has been asserted.

A catalogue record for this book is available from the British Library.

ISBN 1 85371 328 7

Cover painting by Micky Donnelly
Cover design by Poolbeg Group Services Ltd/Red Dog Graphics
Set by Poolbeg Group Services Ltd in Garamond
Printed by The Guernsey Press Ltd, Vale, Guernsey, Channel Islands

To my children, Patricia, Penelope and Ronan Duffaud

My sincere thanks to Joe Canning of the Southern Library Board, to the Ulster Folk Museum, to Kevin McMahon, to Michael Finnegan and my mother, Mrs May Finnegan, who were all very helpful with documents about life in nineteenth-century Ireland.

CHAPTER ONE

MAUREEN

The Laurels,
Belfast Road,
Claghan.
1 March 198-

Dear Maureen,

. . . but she and Cormac O'Flaherty both died on the voyage to America, so I can't think how you're going to wangle one of your famous happy endings there! And I must warn you too that Marianne McLeod's diary stops well short of the Irish Famine so it may not be of much use to you in any case. However (after those discouraging remarks!), we did finally get it photocopied for you. No, don't bother about paying for it—actually, Eric press-ganged a couple of boys into doing it on the school Xerox. At Thatcher's expense, you might say! Incidentally, I can *not* get over your saying you voted for the woman: no wonder you had to leave the country. I hope it was only some kind of kinky idea of striking a blow for feminism? If I recall rightly you used to be quite left-wing, as bolshie as

1

any of us really! Those dear dead days in Claghan Jazz Club. Do you remember the weekend we all descended on Belfast to campaign for that Labour man? The awful scruffy pub down by the shipyards (did you know that John Betjeman got up a petition later on to have it made a national monument like the Crown in Great Victoria Street? Only I believe it's been bombed or burned down or something since). Will you ever forget when Eric got a bit carried away about the monarchy and this dirty great docker leaped up waving a broken bottle and yelling: "You keep your stinkin' papist hands off our queen, Mick!" As if only RCs could be socialist! But I remember your saying at the time that your parents were convinced that all communists were Protestant. Poor benighted Claghan, even then! But could we ever have imagined when we were seventeen that things would turn out as they have?

Did you know, the girls and I spent two wonderful weeks at Greenham Common last autumn? Really rough but what an experience it was! We did really feel as if we were doing something positive at last—all pushing together, as it were, to try and turn the world a little bit in the right direction. Here in Ulster, of course, nothing positive seems remotely possible now—we are all congealed in our little predestined roles, programmed to keep on marching forever to the same tune, if your literary mind will pardon the mixed metaphor! In Eric's and my case naturally the tune has to be "The Orange Sash." Not that I would want to change it for "Faith of Our Fathers" or "Bould Cormac O'Flaherty," as interpreted by our local bard, Cuchulain McCool, but it did at one time seem possible to force ourselves out of step and create an alternative. I suppose I just mean skipping along to "We Shall Overcome" or, good heavens, even "The Red Flag" would have been an improvement! But all those hopes have been blown sky-high long ago. It's so disillusioning for those of us who were young and full of hope in the Sixties. But you'd already left Ireland by then, hadn't you? One forgets how very isolated you must be from all these local problems. Or do your parents keep you in contact with all that happens? In a way I envy your having such an opening on the great wide world—not to mention lovely French food!—though I'm not sure *I* could bear to live abroad. Only it is so frustrating here. Eric tried to stand for parliament, you know, as a Greenpeace candidate the time of the last election and they wouldn't let him! All the powers that be on our side treated him literally as if he were a silly child trying to interrupt an important adult conversation, the more extreme Paisleyite element gave him a mixture of friendly persuasion, subtle menaces and downright bullying, and even the stupid (sorry, but it *is*) Roman Catholic rag had a silly cartoon of him with his head buried in a child's sandbox hunting for a toy bomb while the town was in flames around him! The mentality! In the end he stepped down and left the field clear for the official Unionist candidate because we did basically agree that it would be very negative on his part to split the opposition to Sinn Féin. So at least the town is kept safe to that extent from being a terrorist stronghold. And the only gratitude they had was to tell him that no one would have voted for him anyway! Do you realise, Maureen, this immense nuclear threat is getting more and more thinkable, closer and closer to us every day and over here it's simply brushed aside as a child's gimmick: Claghan has more important things on its mind than a nuclear holocaust! We both try, of course, to make our pupils even the slightest bit aware, but it's hopeless. They're brainwashed from birth.

I'm really curious as to what kind of book you're writing this time: it does seem like a new departure if you're bringing the Irish Famine into it—I hope it's not going to be wildly sectarian??? Though you don't really write serious books, do you? I got *Scent of Hibiscus* from the library, you'll be glad to hear. Bit too lovey-dovey for me, and of course I don't get all that much time to read nowadays.

Anyway, here's our famous ancestor's diary and a couple of dry-as-dust historical documents written by clergymen, and some letters from the "family archives." A few hair-raising items too—just take a look at the recipe for using dahlia roots as a potato substitute! How many starving peasants can you picture doing the Percy Thrower bit?! However, do your worst with them and best of luck.

Luv from Myrna and Eric McLeod

Claghan Museum of Local Culture
21 March 198-

Ms Maureen Murphy,
Château de Lapire-Vacherie,
Finistere,
France.

Dear Ms Murphy,
I have received the letter in which you ask for information about Cormac O'Flaherty. I am interested to know that you intend writing a novel about him but fear that I can add little to what you already know. I can, however, let you have a print-out of the evidence given by the then parish priest of Claghan to the Select Committee on Outrages which reported in 1852 on the agrarian disturbances in south Ulster. This does touch very closely on the subject of your proposed novel and may be of help to you.

I enclose a photocopy of some pages from Flowerdew's book about Ireland written five years before the Great

Famine, in which he treats at some length of the conditions in which tenants lived on the landed estates around Claghan.

I would draw your attention to a useful booklet by the late Peter Maguire, former principal of St Ronan's Primary School, published in the 1930s by the Catholic Truth Society of Ireland. It has, of course, been out of print for many years but you may be able to obtain a copy from acquaintances in Claghan. The booklet was largely based on personal interviews by Mr Maguire with a selection of the town's "senior citizens," many of whose parents would have been contemporaries of Cormac.

As you have been out of the country for some years you may be unaware that Dr Martin McCormack of Claghan is an acknowledged expert on local history. He has given many interesting lectures on old buildings and monuments and on the great Gaelic families of the region and, though I fear the nineteenth-century agrarian troubles are outside his field of interest, it might be worth your while to contact him.

You mentioned a contemporary memoir by Mr Thomas O'Flaherty published around 1860. This was indeed reissued recently and you may obtain a copy by writing to the Public Record Office of Northern Ireland. The address is 66 Balmoral Avenue, Belfast. I must point out, however, that this document is generally considered to give a biased and distorted version of the facts. It might, however, be of interest as a source of background material for a work of fiction.

I hope this information will be of assistance to you and I sincerely look forward to reading your novel when it is finished.

J P Hale
(Curator)

Extract from The Beauties and Miseries of Our Sister
Isle
by Reverend Richard Flowerdew, BA (1840)

Everywhere in the region the land was discovered to be
of a most inferior nature, in keeping with the ridged
and rocky aspect of the landscape. In spite of this fact
cultivation is carried on almost to the very summits of
the mountains, the potatoes and oats there produced
being of far from the highest quality. It is indeed a
credit to these unfortunate people, that by unremitting
industry they have been capable of bestowing even this
small semblance of fertility on such barren land. It was
not always so indeed. We spoke at some length with a
Mr Robert Lockhart who manages the estate of the Earl
of Baudry (now resident in France) and who appears to
hold no high opinion of the worth of the indigenous
population. He informed us that, even as late as the
seventeenth century, the native Irish preferred to live by
rebellion and plunder, had very little ground under tillage
and, when occasionally they consented to bend
themselves to labour, their ploughing was performed by
horses yoked and drawn by their tails! According to this
Lockhart, if the peasants are industrious now it is solely
thanks to the quality of the instruction and example they
have received from the Scots and English settlers who,
during the plantation eras, were established in the country
in order to secure the peace of Ireland and to retain the
island securely thereafter under English government. It is
no part of my mission to decry the Cromwellian
confiscation of Irish lands—every schoolboy knows that
for centuries, in spite of the most solemn treaties, native
chiefs and landowners seized every opportunity of rising
up against the Crown in open acts of hostility and
rebellion—but in all honesty I must record that our

observations throughout our tour led us rather to form the opinion that, if the peasants are industrious, it is from a most natural and human desire not to perish untimely. Without constant toil they would simply lack sufficient nourishment to remain alive. Here are no kind landlords to watch over their well-being, no benevolent ladies to carry comforts to the poor, no manufacturing industries to provide employment: they depend entirely on the produce of their mountain fields to feed and clothe their families and to pay the rent of their miserable cabins.

This conclusion was further corroborated by a conversation with Mr William Gardiner, a schoolmaster in one of the National Schools, and a most cultivated gentleman of English settler stock. He informed us that with a few exceptions the condition of every man in his district is that of a labourer, there being no alternative employment available; that the yearly wage of a labourer in full employment (and the majority are employed on but rare occasions, for harvesting and road-mending) cannot exceed eight pounds; that the rent of the poorest sort of cabin is around two pounds; that if the population did not subsist so entirely on potatoes, it would require a further five pounds to provide one grown man with a year's supply of the roughest kind of food—thus leaving one pound per annum to support a family! For, in addition, these people are prolific breeders and there is little paid employment for women and children in the region. With these facts and figures at our disposal we found it difficult indeed to accept that the native Irish have need of Scots example to spur them into industrious habits!

It proved impossible to hold converse with any English landowner, though the region is divided up into several medium-sized estates and two or three large ones. Only one landowner lives on his demesne, the Hon George Mead, and he happened to be travelling on the Continent at the time of our visit. All the rest are absentee, though one or two pay occasional visits of inspection. Lord Baudry has never been to Ireland, nor has Mr Thomas Watterson. We must conclude therefore that these gentlemen have no idea of the appalling poverty in which tenants live upon their estates, and indeed that they do not give the matter much thought. Mr Watterson, for instance, at the time of our visit in 1839, had given *carte blanche* to his agent to evict as many peasants as he thought necessary in order to innovate a more lucrative method of farming the land. The prospect of widespread expulsion was, we were informed, causing much unrest and unease upon the Watterson estate, many families (already reduced to misery by a succession of bad harvests) living in a condition bordering on despair, knowing not what their future might be . . .

"Hello, is that Dr McCormack? Oh good! Maureen Murphy here . . . No, no, I'm not a *patient*. Well, I suppose you'd know me better as Mary Brigid . . . that's right, a daughter of Jamesy Murphy. I was at school with Nuala actually . . . Oh you do, that's nice . . . Oh did he? That was kind of him. I didn't even know there *was* a museum in Claghan, actually, until Myrna told me, shows how out of touch I am! Oh, I wouldn't say that exactly, not turned my *back*, after all I *am* writing a book about the place. No, in France actually nowadays. Listen—this Hale man, the curator chap, would he be a brother of that MP whatsisname, Harry Hale, the guy that got blown up, some relation of Eric McLeod? . . . Oh the Catholic Hales, oh of course I remember, that big farm. I only wondered, but of course it figures now why he never mentioned the diary and then he was a bit funny over this other document I've . . . Marianne McLeod this ancestor of

8

. . . she kept a diary and Eric and Myrna had it photocopied for me . . . Well, the McLeods of Claghan, who else? . . . Oh well, more just Christmas card contact really . . . No, it's fine, the diary, only it stops well short of the famine and I do *want* to bring in the famine and the emigrant ship and all and I can't find a thing about it, that's why I thought you . . . Yes, oh gosh, that would be fantastic. And newspaper cuttings of the period? Super! . . . No, I've got old Maguire's book, thanks, found it in my things when I was moving house actually, that's partly what gave me the . . . Bit yucky though, isn't it? . . . Oh, I'm not questioning, yes I'm *sure* he got the facts right, it was just the style that I . . . Yes, yes, I know it was sincere and . . . Yes, of *course* I'm aware of the injustices and the eight centuries of . . . Yes, but I do want to tell it from both sides, naturally, and . . . Oh, I don't see that, I don't see why I *can't* tell it from both sides . . . I know I'm a Catholic, yes, but . . . No, I'm afraid I *don't* see where disloyalty comes into it, I haven't the slightest intention of writing a sectarian tract just because things happen to be . . . How do you mean, a forgery? As far as I know the original diary's been in the hands of the McLeod family ever since their ancestor skipped with this Cormac guy, so how do you mean, later date? . . . No I never heard of any old drunken crook in the McLeod family, must have been before my time! . . . Yes, of *course* I'm researching seriously but I haven't had much time yet to . . . Well, thanks anyway for the warning, I'll be sure and bear it in mind though I still think . . . No, what you tell me of those cuttings they sound just great, just what I . . . Oh yes, indeed I would! Contemporary poems about him! Gurreat! Thanks a lot, Martin, you've really been a fantastic help. I'll be sure and shove you in among the acknowledgements in the front of the . . . *What?* How do you mean? . . . Yes, well thank you very much for your help, Dr McCormack. Goodbye!"

What *did* the bastard mean? "I'll be dead and buried by the time this book gets written." So coldly. Such, such contempt even. He wasn't joking, not a laugh, I'll be dead and. The most extraordinary. I mean, why snub me like that? Someone he hasn't seen for—what is it?—must be seventeen or eighteen years. I shouldn't have let on, should have made a joke of it, gosh I didn't even know you were sick, Martin, something like that. Pass it off. Maybe I shouldn't have called him Martin, maybe that's why he. Too familiar. But God above, wasn't I at school with him, sat just across the. And at the convent with Nuala. Was I being too gushing or what, Trevor always says I. Yes, but someone I knew from years back. I suppose he's a big man in Claghan. Yes, but we could buy and sell him, Trevor and me. He doesn't know that. Maybe it's just he looks down on the sort of thing I usually write, I mean maybe being a historian and all he thinks I'm not up to. Maybe he doesn't even know I write? How would he know, I keep thinking everyone knows but I mean, I can't imagine the McCormacks and that crowd getting all steamed up over. Over *Scent of Hibiscus*. Well. So what? You never *took* yourself for James Joyce, did you? And what's so great. I mean, what's so different about the great Gaelic families of Claghan? Pure escapism too, I mean, there weren't any after about sixteen hundred or something; what does he think he is, a bloody Inca? He wouldn't know I write, probably thinks I'm stuck in a council flat somewhere married to a Renault worker. He probably wouldn't know anything about me since I was about sixteen or seventeen. He saw himself talking to (what was he seeing on the other end of the line?), he was seeing himself talking to one of Jamesy Murphy's gawky daughters from over in Claghan Bog, that's what it was, the stuck-up mealy-mouthed prick, and that's all any of that breed ever was.

He wouldn't know anything about me since I left Claghan, our ones don't exactly mix socially with. He's a big man probably, probably drives a Volvo or something, must have got a big lump of insurance the time the place got bombed, as well as being a doctor and all. A doctor in Claghan, what's a doctor in Claghan? Made a right old eejit of myself anyhow, super this and super that as if we were. Ooh thenk yew soo much Martin, as if we were equals or something! We *are* friggin' equals, catch yourself on. Chatting away as if Nuala and I used to be best friends. I used to wear Veronica's cast-offs at the convent and Nuala made damn sure everyone knew it. I was lucky to get them, saved Mammy a fortune. It was only because Aunty Agnes worked there, old Mrs McCormack thought the world of her. She was one of those big Hales, wasn't she old Mrs? That's it; they run half Claghan between them. Pay no heed to Thomas O'Flaherty's memoir, he said and it's easy seen why. Big revelations on the origins of one of our great Gaelic families—roll up, roll up! Gombeen men and racketeers from way back, bet they had a gun to old Peter Maguire's head back in the Thirties when he was writing his rubbish. The maid's niece, that's what I am. Bloody hell, Maureen, catch yourself on, you're out of Claghan these twenty years or more. How could I have forgotten Claghan, the mentality! God, I used to know that mentality inside out, how could I have forgotten it? All their wee clans and cliques and dramatic societies and what not. A right bloody exile I've turned into, all the sentimental clichés. Nice smiling classless society, poor oppressed mass of Catholics standing hand in hand against centuries of Orange tyranny. Must have puzzled him that I knew the McLeods all the same. Wonder if *they* still do? With the troubles and all I expect they've. Probably they've drifted apart.

"Claghan: A Divided Society." You're telling me it's divided! Only not maybe the way Time magazine meant. Must ask Myrna if they still. Remember how they used to lick round the McLeods and the Watsons and that, before it got fashionable to be an oppressed minority. Great big status symbol, having Protestant friends. Well, nice *professional* Protestant friends: as far as I know there was no great rush on the labourers out of Lewis's factory. Oh go on, be honest, Maureen. Weren't you as bad yourself? Why else did you join Claghan Young Socialists and start hanging round Myrna and Eric and that crowd, only to crawl out from under your galvanised roof and join the middle classes? Spoiled wee gets from big houses up the Belfast Road playing at being a mixture of Satchmo and Fidel. That's why they accepted you, make no mistake about it, they probably thought under the convent uniform you were black and barefoot and sang like Bessie Smith. One thing sure, you wouldn't have been let so easy into the *Catholic* middle class. Will you ever forget them at Mass, shut away from the rest of us up on the front gallery, doctors, teachers, solicitors, afraid of catching our nits maybe, clattering down to go to Communion when the rest of us were getting ready to stand for the Last Gospel. It half-killed that crowd to have to as much as share a God with the commonality. I wonder if it was like that in Cormac's time? Probably was, why not? All these well-meaning Flowerdews and that, seeing it all from the outside.

Like Madame de Lapire-Vacherie. Now where could I find out details like that? Ulster Folk Museum might be a good place, that man, whatsisname, Crawford, very keen on the sociology of. Nuala couldn't be stood the time the McLeods asked her parents in for a drink, God you'd have thought it was a royal garden party. Still, if he sends me those newspaper cuttings, who cares? I'm *worse* than the de Lapire-Vacherie woman: such a friendly spiritual people, Madame! The picturesqueness of their struggle, the simplicity of their values! Simplicity of their bloody balls. Claghan brings out the worst in me. Imagine forgetting the awfulness of it. All misty-eyed. Whitewash and thatch like a Yank; it's eejits like me send money to Noraid. Probably laughing at me now with Nuala and his wife and all, who's this he got married to? Philomena Larkin wasn't it, the solicitor's sister? Oh pardon *me*, Philomena

Ó Lorcáin, thank you very much! Pardon me for grinnin' but there's something needs a pinnin', daft the things that come back to you. They got aware of their ethnic roots sometime in the late Sixties, only how do you say Philomena in Irish? We used to shout that after posh women going to Mass, make them think their slip was showing: Pardon me for grinnin', but there's something needs a pinnin', there's a sample of your linen hangin' down. I suppose we *were* as common as dirt when you think of it. The day the carload of English tourists threw a bag of food like we were monkeys or something. A paper bag of broken buns and half-eaten sandwiches, oh the dear little peasant girls and their poor bare feet, here catch! We flung it right back in their faces. No, that's a lie, Maureen, we did nothing of the kind. We turned and ran and then, when I was in on our lane, I heard Peggy, my friend Peggy, away up the road again like a hare to get the buns. It might be all they had between them and hunger, Mammy said. The mother was dead and the father away labouring someplace. The McCormacks kept to themselves, wore shoes to school. Some of the other shopkeepers' children used to take them off going up the road to be like the rest of us. Necessity the mother of fashion. Going barefrit we called it, bursting tar-bubbles with our big toe nails. The McCormacks never. All right till you crigged your toe on a lump of gravel. Racing along as happy as Larry and then agony. Hubris and nemesis on the Bog Road. That's where the O'Flaherty murders happened, one of them anyhow. Dobson the land agent. The other in McCormacks' hotel that got bombed. Claghan Hall. I crigged my toe all right on that friggin' phone today! Can't you just hear them: know the latest? Poor old Agnes's niece is trying to write a book, Merry-Brudget Murphy, to be *sure*, you remember, at school—don't you remember?—with the nits, we weren't let sit beside her, remember Mother made a big fuss and Miss Feeney ended up crying. Well anyway, she's trying, I had her on the phone today, she's trying to write a book about Claghan! Did you ever hear the! Jumping on the bandwagon and she can't even ride a bike! Har Har big joke, who does she think she is?

Who do *I think I am, Maureen wonders, well* who *after all?*

We took the opportunity of visiting several native dwellings, of the poorest as well as of a less humble sort—though all indeed provide only the most rudimentary form of accommodation. Most have neither window nor chimney; they are mere shelters of rough stone, hastily built, of one room only about twelve feet square where a whole family sleeps in promiscuity upon a heap of straw and rags. Yet the inhabitants were smiling and hospitable, invariably offering us refreshment from their small store of potatoes, which it would have been thought most unmannerly of us to refuse. Their drink for the most part is water, coloured with a little milk when available. We have been told that many fall into debt on the occasions of marriages and funerals, as the unfortunate custom is to provide vast quantities of ale and spirits at those times. It is difficult to remain for long inside a cabin as the atmosphere, thick with turf-smoke and the various odours of poverty and overcrowding, is painful to unaccustomed senses. Some of the ladies of our party came, indeed, close to fainting at times.

The better sort of cottages have chimney and window, with sometimes a rough partition to separate the sleeping-quarters from the rest; though even here the inhabitants fear to make further improvement which might increase the value of the property, it being the common practice for agents and middlemen to seize on just such a pretext to raise the rent, or even to evict and relet. We visited one such cabin on the insistence of Mr Gardiner, who was anxious that we meet with a superior type of peasant family as well as with the usual run of labourers. The

O'Flaherty father, dead in the cholera epidemic of 1832, had been horse-trainer to the late Mr Henry Watterson, brother to the present landlord; the uncle is a locally-renowned cabinet-maker (Mr Gardiner spoke of an Irish Chippendale but we assumed he had fallen into the native habit of exaggeration!), the son and daughters are said to be endowed with more than average wit and intelligence. The wit we were left to guess at for, on seeing us (no doubt to their simple minds a party of elegant English gentlefolk!), they were seized with a great bashfulness and could only smile and smile. The son, a well-looking young man, did at first make some attempt to converse with us but, on my making a harmless pleasantry on the subject of his pronunciation, he speedily became as tongue-tied as the others. Happily, Nicholas Fielding, a Belfast divinity student who accompanied us, is making a study of the native language and was able to communicate adequately with them in both tongues. Of their intelligence it is difficult for strangers to judge, their awkwardness of manner predisposing one to address them as if they were small children which, honesty compels me to admit, is perhaps not the most efficacious method of gaining their confidence. The uncle is certainly a man of some education, though heavily pedantic in speech, and evidently unaware of any English author of a later date than Goldsmith!

We met also with an abundance of farmers of Scots descent, pious worthy Presbyterians for the most part, industrious indeed and with a comfortable enough style of living. Many own their own houses and land and some few are in a way of aspiring to a higher status as minor landlords and gentlemen farmers. It is in the main to these people that the young native girls are hired out as domestic servants.

It has been pointed out to us by Mr Gardiner and others that, at the time of the Cromwellian transplantation, the whole Gaelic and Norman population was either exterminated or exiled to the wild undeveloped regions on the far western coast of the island, with the sole exception of the mere tillers of the soil, allowed to remain in place to labour the land for the settlers. This theory is, however, disputed by Roman Catholic leaders, and indeed the parish priest of Claghan village, Rev Joseph Molloy, was at pains to demonstrate to us that many of his parishioners are in fact descended from dispossessed Irish landowners. In a few cottages we were shown ancient legal documents, now valueless, dealing with the former tenure of large holdings of confiscated land. Nevertheless, and in spite of many other supposed proofs of erstwhile substance, we feel that descent from poor stock does in part explain the meagre physical appearance and lack of spirit that we constantly observed in the native people throughout our tour of this southern part of the province of Ulster.

Maureen wonders if the Reverend Mr Flowerdew, on his travels, ever strolled over the Bog Road, up the lane and into Murphys' own street, well-meaning liberal with a white hanky pressed to his nose, and been offered refreshment of potatoes and water by her own . . . her own what? Grandparents maybe. Let's see—Daddy was born in 1899, youngest of fifteen children, so *his* parents in 1840. No, Granda would have been in the cradle and Granny not yet born; Maureen's *great*-grandparents no doubt saw the English writer, they lived near enough the main road, were well-established tenants of Lord Baudry. So Granny's mother would have stepped forward with fine gracious courtesy, hands stretched out in welcome: Won't you come in out of the rain now, Reverend Sir, and take a bite to eat with us. No, to be *sure* it's no trouble! Best stool drawn forward; Minny would you run out to the well for a jug of fresh water; Brigid like a good girl throw a few spuds in the greesha . . . and the weather we're having, sir, wouldn't it walk through you? Sit over to the fire now, you must be perished, sir. Sadie, the tablecloth, child, out of the chest (good white linen tablecloth kept for priests' visits, deathbeds, weddings), and what do you think of this country of ours, sir? No, no, don't stir. You're not in the way at all. Sit your ground now, sir, and why don't you hand me that coat of yours, you'll feel the benefit of it when you. Only all of this would have gone on, naturally, in a guttural-sounding direct translation from Gaelic so the poor woman would have been perceived, not as the gracious well-mannered hostess she thought she was, but as a smelly peasant in a red frieze petticoat, gesturing with shy grins and uncouth mouthings, to be noted in a line or two: simple hospitality of bog-dwelling natives or whatever. And she'd have felt so violated by the impertinent pity! Can't you just *see* them, see Cormac O'Flaherty hating, cringing away under the whiplash of kind uncomprehending words. As *I* cringed, Maureen recalls. I'll have no trouble anyhow creating nineteenth-century peasants —they were there all around me, inside of me, in my childhood. Nothing had changed in a hundred years, nothing has changed now: who do I think I am, she wonders, who did I ever think?

29 Heathfield Rd
London, NW6

Dear Maureen,

God above! And there I was thinking you'd improved with age. No, I *don't* know anything about Cormac O'Flaherty. Nor about Adam and Eve or any other of my VIP ancestors. And I don't much care either. That was my old dad's department—remember old Pakky at home in Quarry Street? You should have listened to him at the time: "Shiploads of grain and beef sailing into English bellies while the poor Paddies starved," wasn't that his line? He's dead too. They're all dead, Maureen. What do you want to go digging them up for? Who do you think you are, anyway: Cuchulain McCool the folk-singer? I thought you were meant to have escaped from Claghan. Stay escaped. Sorry I can't help you, old chum! If you *must* write about Ireland why not the divorce laws or the abortion referendum? See you sometime,

Kathleen O'F.

CHAPTER TWO

MAUREEN

Who *did* she think she was?

She was wee Maureen, that's all she thought for a long time. They said it incessantly: wee Maureen, ah, the wee ba, the wee darlin'. Incessantly she was on knees, on shoulders, held safe on the horse's warm damp back while he dragged a cartload of hay to the haggard. She was surveyed, she was measured, she was bathed, she was curled, every smile was an exhibition, every cry brought a regiment running. Two died before her; that was in her consciousness along with the story of her daddy riding over and back the four hilly miles to see her in Claghan hospital. She was named after the two grannies but her daddy was the only one who kept to that: Mary Brigid he'd call her, Mary Brigid. Anxious not to favour one side or the other. His mother lived in the house with them, a white-headed monument of a woman with black satiny skirts to the floor and strong men's boots with toecaps. She was Brigid Murphy and she was well over the eighty mark. Her husband, Jamesy the thatcher, had died a few years earlier, leaving the way free for his forty-year-old son to bring home a young wife. All the rest were in America this years and years, a big family of ten daughters and five sons of whom he was the youngest. The one whose duty it was to stay at home with his parents instead of getting on the emigrant boat at fourteen or fifteen like the rest. He would have preferred to go. He was a small studious man with fastidious manners who would have done well in an office or bank had he not been forced by circumstances into manual labour. All his life he would harbour the resentment, along with a shamed sense of inferiority that he unconsciously ingrained into his children as they grew up.

His mother was Granny. She leaned her white smiling head over the cradle, smelling of grass and nettles and turf-smoke. She loved and was loved. She made blonde curls in the baby's hair with a finger dipped in spit: wee Maureen, ah the lovely wee ba! She was up in the morning first thing seeing to the fire, milking the goat, warming Maureen's bottle, hanging the kettle on to boil, leaving the young couple to rest a bit alone in the room. There was just the one room besides the kitchen. There were two double beds with a narrow passage in between, a press full of Yankee clothes, one small sash-window. Three holy pictures, a statue of St Teresa and another of the Divine Infant of Prague. Wee Maureen slept in her cradle above in the kitchen, warm beside an open fire that had never gone out in the history of the house. Last thing at night, after the Rosary, Daddy clamped it up with damp sods, put an iron lid on top, leaving it to smoulder warmly through the darkness.

The old woman and the young got on well, there were no jealousies, none of the wild screeches you heard in other families. Jamesy Murphy esteemed himself happy in spite of everything. The three of them existed, smiling and united, to be at the service of Maureen, the queen of the house, the wee gift that God sent them after so much hardship and disappointment.

Mammy was a stranger to Claghan: she came from away

over in the Free State and knew how to sew the lacework for the Carrickmacross nuns. She never had a minute. It was Granny took Maureen down the fields and across the kesh and showed her Claghan Bog whose bottomless pools were stiff with dead men holding pikes and scythes and pitchforks from some old battle. "It was th'oul' English, darlin', drove them backwards into the bog and them after surrendering, rode them down screeching into that bog there, white flag and all, Cromwell's mad dogs of Protestant soldiers, aye and it was them same soldiers was given the poor Catholics' land after, in place of wages."

The townland they lived in was called Bohamamuc and when Granny took her walking to Mass in Claghan the bog stretched alongside the road for nearly a mile, nearly as far as McCormacks' big house, Claghan Hall, that used to be the home of a beautiful noble Scotch lady, only she sacrificed home and wealth to marry a brave Irish hero and devote her life to the one true faith. Claghan Hall was famous long ago because shocking murders were committed there at the time of the Land War. A murder happened on the Bog Road too, not far from Murphys' own house, a bad man was knocked off his horse and beaten to champ with a blackthorn stick the time of the famine. Granny's own father had often recounted how he was one of the first to come on the corpse, God bless us and save us, and the state it was in and the scawl-crows busy feasting themselves for God knows how long before anyone passed up that road. And later on poor Micksey Malone was shot coming out home from McCormack's bar at twelve o'clock at night by the Black and Tans. "And the poor fellow stocious."

There was nothing only murders and death in Granny's stories of Claghan but Maureen at the time didn't think it strange, or even frightening. It was as ordinary as anything else in her life. Death came into every story she ever heard, at home, at Mass, or even when Daddy turned on the wireless.

And when Mammy, sewing on the doorstep, told her stories, they were about a man being flogged with whips till the blood ran out of him and made carry a big heavy lump of wood up Mount Calvary which Mammy said was like Claghan mountain only twice as high and the sun ten times as hot and the Roman soldiers jeering him every step he took and then being nailed to it with six-inch nails and left to die in the sun and the stinging flies, while Cromwell's iron-headed soldiers stripped every stitch of clothes off him and played dice over who'd get his coat.

Mammy's hands flew white and soft over the wisps of white net and muslin, over the delicate tracery of roses and shamrocks and harps, and she told Maureen how the blood ran in rivers and caked and matted and blinded and the blue flies buzzed and the scawl-crows waited on the bushes and them big long thorns pressed into him and Hitler's soldiers laughed and booed and he died there drinking vinegar in the parching sun. "That was your fault, daughter, your fault and mine. The whole lot of us had a hand in it. If we were to flog ourselves like poor Matt Talbot our whole lives long it wouldn't be enough to atone for that death." Mammy showed her the crucifix on the end of her rosary beads and told her to kiss the poor man twisting in pain and when she kissed it she tasted blood but it was only her own lip that she was biting hard, trying to be like Matt Talbot and atone for Our Lord's death. Our Lord was a holy Irish martyr and that's why the English killed him.

Maureen got a sty on her eye and Granny took her over to a field behind McCormacks' where there was a big stone with a holy well in it. The well was the shape of an eye. A virgin saint long ago disfigured herself on that spot sooner than put her chastity in jeopardy. Granny made Maureen walk nine times round the stone saying Hail Marys and then bathe her eye in the blessed water of the well. The water never dried up, the hottest day in summer. Granny took a

present of half a dozen eggs to Mrs McCormack, to be let visit
the stone. It wasn't a *payment*, don't think that now, Mrs
Murphy, only we can't have the whole country traipsing free
gratis over our land, now can we? Martin and Nuala and
Veronica McCormack all stared at her and Granny and followed
them up the avenue and round to the kitchen door with the
eggs, snorted and skiggled and pointed at Maureen's bare feet
and Granny's long black skirt and laced men's boots, pointed
at Maureen's eye and bee-uched and snorted. She hated hated
hated, wanted to see them dead with thorns matting blood
into their clean blond hair, dead standing up in a boghole
with pikes eating their eyes. New people, new ways, Granny
said; in poor Matt O'Flaherty's time there was no such thing
as having to pay to use the saint's stone. Weren't you as well
going in to Doctor Brady and paying your fee and have done
with it, and isn't it easy seen there's gombeen blood in every
one of that breed? Claghan Hall used to belong to the
O'Flahertys who had to live in a wee house in Quarry Street
now because they drank themselves out of it. Kathleen's
granda drank them out of it, Granny said. "You mind wee
Kathleen, darlin', your wee friend Kathleen that we went to
see in the town?"

(Kathleen O'Flaherty played marbles on a clean white
doorstep while Granny drank tea with big people inside the
dark house. She stuck out her tongue and shook her black
ringlets and wouldn't let Maureen play. Children came out of
other dark doorways up and down the street. They sang:
Mucky-feet, mucky-feet, dirty wee get, barefoot, barefoot in
from the bogs! Maureen ran in terror away from the dazzling
doorstep, into the dark kitchen where the big people drank
tea out of flowery cups and muttered and laughed. Drank
themselves out of it, Maureen whispered, drank themselves
out of it. But no one was listening and Kathleen made faces
in past the doorpost and ran away skiggling up the sunshiny
street, shaking her black ringlets. Maureen was a heavy barefoot

lump left sitting useless among the old women's knees.)

Before the O'Flahertys came home from America, Claghan Hall belonged to Protestants called McLeod. The beautiful Scotch lady was called Marianne McLeod and there used to be a song sung about her and her hero Cormac O'Flaherty only Granny couldn't remember the words. If there was murder mixed up with the McLeods and O'Flahertys both, there was worse than murder in the McCormack crowd. Only what could be worse than murder, Maureen wondered. Filth and adultery and getting fat on other people's misfortunes could be worse, darlin'. "And what did they do with the eye, did they bury it? And did the girl die when she pulled it out?" She must have, surely nobody, saint and all as they were, could have survived that? But no, she ended up as a nun in one of St Brigid's convents and lived to a great age and Granny wasn't sure but the eye was likely preserved as a relic and people came from all over to touch it and be cured, unless she was mixing it up with something else.

Maureen's sty went away within a few days and she said a prayer of thanksgiving that Granny taught her. She was four years of age. The Germans bombed Belfast and London again on the wireless and then Irish men went over to England and put other bombs in the saddlebags of bicycles outside of grocer shops where people were lined up to get their rations and a whole lot of mothers and children were blew to ribbons. Granny and the big people talked about it when they took Maureen in visiting to Quarry Street, some for, some against, a shocking thing to do, a shocking thing to do, but Kathleen O'Flaherty's father stood up and shouted that innocent children or no innocent children the English was every bit as big a huers as Jerry and always was: Cromwell and the Tans, and the priests hunted like wolves and people left to die in the ditches round Claghan while shiploads of oats and beef sailed out of Portnafinn harbour only eight miles away. And Maureen fell asleep on someone's knee to stories of death and hunger and blood running, was carried home in a half-dream of dead broken children to sleep in a room walled with crucifixes and bright painted images of God with his heart torn out dripping big scarlet drops behind the picture frame and Our Lady looking sad and tired and ashamed of the people's sins, pointing to her own broken heart: it's your fault, Maureen, you drove in the nails so you did, you dirty wee get, you! Woke to Claghan Bog outside the window with Cromwell's victims lined up stiff in the bogholes, miraculously preserved intact, poor pathetic weapons and all, across three centuries. Woke to the dusty street and the pighouse and the five acres of humpy fields rising up towards Claghan and the mountain, slow thick hedgerows crawling upwards from the bog, hawthorn and briar and wild rose that had been already there growing in the old murdering landlord days, no different. And the people no different.

It was Granny told her that long ago, when *she* was a girl, the pighouse was a one-roomed dwelling with mud floor and glassless window slits; whole generations of families were reared in it, the barn the same and the byre and the henhouse. There was a whole lively wee claghan of houses around the street that time; the children, dozens of them, swung on the sycamore trees and played hide-and-go-seek round the hedges and kicked an old ball through the dust of the street. All died away, Granny sighed, into famine and hardship or away lost in America this seventy years or more. I had ten wee girls myself, she said, and before they got a chance to grow up right they had to get on that boat and go away from me. There was nothing for them here only want, and some good came out of it in the latter end, for when old Baudry was forced to sell off his land to the tenants it was their dollars paid for these few wee acres. Lord Baudry was a bugger, Granny said. The time of the first famine and he only a young man, he had the people out building a high wall round his estate and them half-dead of hunger and disease, getting the last ounce of work out of them to pay the gombeen man for the wee grain of Inja meal the Yankees sent over to be handed out free to the starving. "One thing sure, Maureen won't have to go," Mammy said. "There'll be no emigrant boat for you, Maureen, I'll guarantee you that." And her needle flew winking in the sun over the baskets of lace roses. "With the help of God, Maureen'll die here in Claghan among her own."

Death and Claghan were mixed together in Maureen's mind. Violent death and saintly death, a thousand frightened ploughmen ridden into bogholes, living skeletons moaning under the wild rose bushes, a landlord's agent smashed into the dust and stones of the Bog Road. Death hung over Claghan as the solid mass of blue-green flies hung over the dunghill in the haggard. And every death had its guilt: we sinned, we betrayed, we sold ourselves into slavery. A lifetime of sacrifice and hate wouldn't be enough to atone for it. Jesus and the martyrs died to redeem us. Pearse and Tone and Cormac O'Flaherty died to redeem us. Later, at Boharnamuc primary school, Miss Feeney and Mrs McCreesh would teach her that she must always be prepared to lay down her life for Ireland or for the one true faith if the opportunity arose; there could be no higher destiny.

Only by then Maureen had stopped listening. Granny dropped dead one day without any warning at all. The blue-green mist of flies that buzzed over Claghan turned suddenly and buzzed over *her*. Death was not something in a story. Death could come buzzing at any time, over Mammy, over Daddy, over Maureen herself. She wanted nothing more to do with death or stories of death. Nobody noticed her shock: the old woman had been coming up on the ninety, you couldn't expect her to live forever . . .

More children were born into Murphys', Maureen was no longer the queen of the house. She was no longer even Maureen. After Granny's death they began calling her by her baptised name, Mary Brigid. Maureen was in no Litany of the Saints though they'd humoured the old woman over it the way they humoured her about her yarns of famine and murder and landlords dead this sixty years and more. Mary Brigid was reality: it was Our Lady and Ireland's patron saint leagued together to watch over her and keep her pure and good. There were no more stories to listen to; the visits to Quarry Street became rare. Daddy said the O'Flahertys were too carried away in themselves. We're an ordinary decent class of people, he said, and always was, and we have no call to be getting ourselves mixed up with that crowd of mad-heads.

Mammy no longer had time to instruct Maureen, with all the new arrivals to be attended to. She sewed with one foot rocking the cradle and one eye following a staggering toddler through the hazards of the street. In the long run Maureen came to see the crucifix as no more than a handy bit of metal to chew on to keep her awake as she daydreamed her way through the endless decades of the Rosary.

Mammy's sister Agnes came to live with them to be near her boyfriend, Big Jim Malone, who worked in Meegan's Garage in Claghan. He'd been a corporal in the war and was mad daft about cars. When he got his own wee business together they'd get married, he told Agnes, and Mammy watched them like a hawk: a British soldier that was out foreign for years; now watch yourself, Agnes, and stay pure and good and have respect for yourself and for Our Blessed Lady. Agnes went into service in McCormacks'. She got up at six to walk to her work and came home at eight o'clock at night. Maureen shared a bed with her and the room smelt of face-powder and Devon Violets. Big Jim bought her a second-hand gramophone and a stack of bargain records in Smithfield Market in Belfast. Everybody listened to the records. Mammy sewed away humming: "I Was in Havana for a Night," and "On the Road to Mandalay Where the Flying Fishes Play." Maureen used to skiggle in to herself when she heard: "Come

27

you back you British soldier; come you back to Mandalay!"
thinking of Agnes and Big Jim behind the sycamore trees
when Mammy wasn't watching. In bed at night, squeezed in
between snoring Agnes and the damp wall, she used to lie
awake in a scarlet satin ball-gown and peeptoe sandals dancing
and dancing under the orange-blossom while guitars played
and a dark head (Brylcreemed and waved like McCormack's
barman, seen across the aisle at Mass) bent whispering tender
vows of love, for it was fiesta and we were so gay, South of
the Border down Mexico way.

South of the Border was really the Free State where de
Valera was king and they had the best of everything:
neighbours made a fortune smuggling soap and butter and
beet sugar and sweets, but Mammy and Daddy were too
honest to smuggle because Canon McGinty said it was a sin.
Thou shalt not steal and wealth is not everything and it's hard
enough to get through the eye of that needle without having
to pull a cartload of smuggled bacon through it along with
you! We'll see how these smart ones fare at the Last Judgement,
Daddy said. "Honour thy father and thy mother!" Canon
McGinty shouted off the altar. Which in this particular case,
he explained, means also the King of England and the Stormont
government who, for the time being anyhow, are our lawfully
appointed rulers and let none of the young men of Claghan
forget that, under pain of excommunication. Everyone knew
he was talking about the IRA as well as the smugglers. He
doesn't mean a word of it, Pakky O'Flaherty said outside the
chapel; no stauncher patriot than the Canon; it was Cardinal
McRory made him say it, sure isn't he under orders from his
boss like any other man?

Daddy built a second bedroom, installed a hygienic dairy
for sending milk to the creamery, grew potatoes and oats to
feed the poor English, half-dead of rationing on the wireless.
Mammy sewed furiously, wedding veils and christening robes
and New Look evening dresses, to save her children from

the emigrant ship. But dreaming Maureen as she kissed on the Isle of Capri knew inside of herself that *she* would never be one of the countless martyred millions Miss Feeney talked about in school with fierce ecstatic face and staring eyes, who over the centuries died for Claghan and Ireland. Or, for that matter (Hawaiian guitars twang-twang-twanging away in her head, Miss Otis regrets, Miss Otis regrets), one of the countless decent class of Murphys who died *in* Claghan or *in* Ireland.

CHAPTER THREE

(PAGES FROM
MAUREEN MURPHY'S NOTEBOOK)

Dreams of a Claghan Child:

I 'll be a fairy princess and live in a castle, marry a prince.
Silk frocks and jewels and long golden hair, the prettiest
in the whole world I'll be. Santy's going to bring me the big
plastic doll in Campbell's shop window: glass eyes that open
and shut, that says Mama, blue satin dress and knickers with
lace and a pram to wheel her in.

(Who did you think you were? Santy brought you: *Tales
of the Irish Saints*, a pair of knitted socks, six wax crayons
and an orange. That doll was for Nuala McCormack.)

Yes but then:

Miracle!

The Yank O'Flahertys sent a Yankee doll. Glass eyes and
nylon hair and everything.

(There was three pounds customs duty but your parents
paid it. Scraped and borrowed but wouldn't let you down.
Your own's all you can depend on in the long run.)

Just proves that *anything* can happen! If you want it
enough, *anything*!

Dreams of a Claghan Teenager:

I'll be a film-star, sing on Top Twenty, Radio Luxembourg, the sponsored programmes. Red velvet dress and a bust like Jane Russell, legs up to yonder like a Derby winner. I'll win the Irish Sweeps, be a millionaire. People do, people do, makes no difference *who* you are, *you* can wish upon a star. I'll marry Clark Gable, Slim Whitman, Lee Lawrence, Gigli, one of the Inkspots. All of the Inkspots. I won't marry anyone. I'll be someone myself. I'll be everyone. For the *way*-ward wind is a *res*-tless wind . . . I'll be a ballet-dancer, concert-pianist, act Shakespeare with Micheál Mac Liammóir. No I'll ride in the Dublin Show, gold medals and a cheering crowd, climb Mount Everest, win the Grand National, explore the Sahara in long Arab robes . . . And ah wuz *bo-o-orne* on the wayward wind . . . I'll fly planes, be a fighter pilot, be a nurse with Doctor Schweitzer, a nun like the Little Flower. Wear thorns and a hair shirt. Die for Ireland.

No. That's kids' talk. I'll do something possible. I'm bright. Top of the class. I win scholarships.

I'll be a doctor myself.

Big house in Claghan or a leper's hut?

The gutter or the stars?

Or I'll be a solicitor, barrister, first woman judge in Northern Ireland. Be an MP, be Prime Minister, rule the roost from Stormont Castle.

What's to stop me? I'm bright!

(Who do you think you are? You're bright. So you'll be an elementary schoolteacher and get a wee job in Boharnamuc, a safe decent job with a pension. Safe from the dole queue and the emigrant ship.)

I won't be a teacher. I'm going to be a doctor or a. (Seven years without earning! And who's to buy you a practice after? If you think Catholics gets took on in the hospitals. Eight long centuries of.)

Well I won't be a *teacher*. I'll go to university, read

literature, science, languages, sociology.

(Never see all them Catholic graduates behind the counter in Woolworths?)

I *won't* be a teacher. I'm good at French. I'll take up Spanish, Italian, German, go and work in the Foreign Office. Be a consul, diplomat, ambassador, be an international executive. Work for MI5. Travel for the British Council, carry our culture to the ends of the earth!

(A *Catholic?*)

I won't be a teacher. A journalist, that's it! I'll go to London, write for the *The Observer*, be a famous correspondent. Travel.

(*Emigrate?* After all our . . .)

I'll go to Belfast, then, join the BBC or the Civil Service. I'm bright. I'll get promoted to the very, very top. I'll be a—

(You're a *Catholic*, remember.)

Well I won't be a teacher. I'd rather sign on the dole.

(After all our sacrifices! You can leave the convent, then, and go to the tech. Do shorthand and typing. Get a job in McCormack's office. Your auntie Agnes'll put in a word for you.)

Get a job in London! Paris! Hollywood!

(Emigrate! The shame of it!)

Mario Lanza's secretary, marry the boss! Marry a Rothschild, marry a merchant banker, marry an Arab sheikh!

(Non-Catholics, may God forgive you, and the way we suffered for our faith. You'll marry a decent Irish working man like everyone else!)

Well I'll do *some*thing. Marry *some*one. Get out of Claghan anyhow!

(Turn your back on your homeland? Break your poor mother's heart after all her.)

Adult Realities:

I went to the Tech, became a teenage rebel.

(Wonder who you thought you were with your white lipstick and your hair to your knees and your bunch of Protestant friends?)

Dropped Boharnamuc and Quarry Street and Kathleen O'Flaherty and the parish dance-hall. Joined Claghan Jazz Club, met Eric McLeod and his sister Debbie and their friend Myrna Watson. For two whole years we were inseparable: cheered for Cuba, wept for Sharpeville, read Salinger and boycotted Cape oranges.

(Canon McGinty used to stop you on the road and roar at you about occasions of sin and the risk of mixed marriage. Making a show of you in front of the.)

I dropped my awful name, chose Maureen instead.

(You didn't *choose* it: it's what your poor granny used to call you.)

By the time I learned *that* I was stuck with it. If Maureen hadn't been floating in my subconscious I'd have gone for Victoria Caroline Scarlett Arabella . . . Anyhow, I got my diploma and cleared out to lovely London.

(Took the emigrant ship!)

Typed in a Carnaby Street back shop. Wrote love stories in my spare time.

(Adult fairytales, to sublimate your failures—what happened to the first woman judge in?)

What happened to Northern Ireland? *I* married the boss.

(Married for money, ye huer, ye!)

Married for background. Married romance.

(Some fairy prince! East End delinquent made good! Where's Mario Lanza then?)

He had a chain of boutiques.

(Not Mary Quant. Not Laura Ashley. Not even Chelsea Girl.)

But the time was right. London swung. Trevor branched out.

(Swung from branch to branch, by the looks of him now!)

We were happy. Had fun. Sybilla's, Annabel's . . .

(And never went near an Irish club! Turned your back on your homeland. Wealth isn't everything.)

No but it's plenty.

Then London wobbled. The world wobbled. Even Claghan wobbled. But my books sold.

(Rubbish and all as they are! Everyone suddenly had to start sublimating their failures.)

London became a bore, full of unemployed muggers and the streets filthy.

(And you were too old to be a Sloane Ranger.)

We bought a château in France, Trevor and I. I *made* dreams come true: I live in a castle!

(An old ruin.)

But it once belonged to Lord Baudry. You could say I've turned the tables on history. And I'm safe now, from the dead men in bogholes, the evicted starving under every hedge, priests hunted down like wolves. I'm safe from the past. I've escaped from Claghan, it's just a place in my next romantic novel. I've chopped off my roots. I'm not a persecuted Ulster Catholic. I'm me. *That's* who I think I am. That's who I've wanted to be since I was five years old.

(So why don't you quit having this wee dialogue with your hang-ups, and get on with your flamin' novel!)

CHAPTER FOUR

MAUREEN'S NOVEL - CLAGHAN
1840

F rost in a thin sun: November. A fat crow heaves itself off the graveyard wall and trails aimlessly into grey shabby sky. Its empty shout could be derision, could be Sunday boredom, might even be some awkward-sounding joy. A poet might know, might flap down with sure beak and pick the one live wriggling word out of the great useless heap of carrion words. Crow. The emblem of these hungry townlands. Crows eat carrion, crows eat death. Crows gorge themselves on desolation. Last winter the crows must have feasted. It's not a matter anyone would like to mention, but why wouldn't they have? And this coming winter? No word of evictions lately, that's one good thing came out of old Dobson's death. So why then do I feel that I have placed myself outside of all decency? I am alone, completely alone now. Oh I'll go up to Jem Mullen's tavern tonight when it's all over and I'll say to the boys: "I got rid of that huer all right!" and their poor limited minds will hear only the words. They'll clap me on the back, a hero Cormac, you're a bloody hero, man, the way they did after Dobson but behind the words, theirs as well as mine, I alone will hear anguish. Anguish because long before I push open Jem's door this evening I will have taken one more step away from humanity. Baxter will come stepping along this road in the next half hour or so, stepping out with his righteous Sunday walk, afraid of no man. He got his letter all right, the same as Dobson, a letter with a picture of a coffin drawn on it, a real work of art begod! You murdering scoundrel. We make you a present of your last overcoat. Take warning—signed—The People. It never took a feather out of Dobson, the old scawl-crow. He went swaggering around the country just as bold as ever, an easy target. And what is this other boyo thinking? Easy enough to swagger at a bar counter with your friends around you, I know that myself now. It's when you're on your own again. Does anguish sometimes take him by the neck and shake him senseless? But then, what human feelings can that class of a man have? I myself now, I cannot make a claim to innocence. How can I ever again have a heart full of joy at a child's laugh, a cherry tree in blossom, a young girl's kiss? Wouldn't my love only soil and disfigure those things now? I know what I am capable of. And I am alone. Silence or boastful words, them's my choices. There's no one at all to speak the truth with. A while past, I could talk with Mother: I was the head of the house, her big clever son that'd do well in life, the one she depended on. Now I have to go masked before her, examine every word before I utter it. That poor pious woman would be broken to bits at my crime, would urge me piteously to confess to Father Molloy and do penance, would pray evening after evening, humbly on her knees on the damp clay floor, crying out for mercy to a distant bearded gentleman in long foreign clothes, to a lady with a smooth smiling face like a landlord's daughter. A face that never had to bend red and sweating to blow up the fire round a pot of wormy potatoes: what could the likes of them know of us or our troubles? He was a tradesman they say, a bachelor carpenter with a bit of an education. Like old

Uncle Thomas begod! He got nailed to a cross, flogged and all the rest of it but He rose again. That's the whole difference: He came to life again. May Byrne will not come to life again, no, nor any of them. They say He will forgive us our sins if we are truly penitent. Just words. Priests' words. You learn it by heart, what choice have you, and if the square on the hypotenuse is true why wouldn't that be true just as well? But I am not penitent. I am not sorry that I killed Dobson. Oh I'm sorry all right for the poor human thing that twisted in the July dust of the Bog Road and would not die. I'm sorry that I had to keep on beating and beating for, how long, hours was it? Hardly. It was more like minutes, five or ten minutes at the most, it was. Inflicting pain upon pain, and in the latter end I had no thought of vengeance or our oath or of doing a brave deed or of ridding the countryside of a tyrant, none of that sort of stuff at all. No, in the latter end I struck basely, fearfully, in blind selfish cowardice so that he would die without mentioning my name. So innocent I was to begin with, so little I imagined the reality. A blow, I thought, one swift sharp blow across the skull and he will fall down, instantly without life. A tyrant dead. Such a clean abstract thought. No blood, naturally, nothing as dirty as blood! But how he fought and panicked and hated. Thrown broken in the dust, how the bastard still protested against this death! And I had to keep striking like a savage randomly, half blinded with sweat from the effort. And with his red splashing blood. I remember once trying to crush an earwig on the kitchen floor. When I lifted up my clog the thing was bruised, half flattened to the sole but still living. I rasped my foot along the floor twice, as hard as I could, and by God it was still alive. A warrior. I ground it to nothing among the dusty earth of the floor, in a mad blind fury to annihilate it and its pain, and my guilt in its pain. Only was there something invisible still alive there, still screaming without sound? And was there with Dobson too, when at last I left his brains

37

mixed to a paste with the summer dust? For that I am sorry.
For that I would do penance. Shall do penance whether I
want to or not, night after sleepless night tossing on my straw
mattress sweating. Reliving the horror of that still afternoon
working away alone there between the hedges of hawthorn
and briar. At one moment I thought it was finished, straightened
up to breathe the clean air free and guiltless. I looked and
saw blackberries already formed green on the brambles and
I thought in a month or so the children will be out gathering
along this road and there will be no trace left then of what
I have done or of Dobson, and the small boys will keep
throwing excited half-frightened side looks at the ground
hoping for tracks, lingering stains, but there will be nothing
for them to see. It will be as if nothing had ever happened.
The road will be clean and dusty again, these berries will
have serenely ripened as though no horror had taken place
around their roots. I could picture it. I could clearly see the
road empty and clean again. For an instant I was weeks on
in the future, confessed and pure and clean as the summer
road. It's over, I thought, and I am free of him. And then he
groaned and I looked down and the mess was still there and
he lying broken in the middle of it and nothing was over. I
was condemned to go on killing him. When I wake up in the
night he is no longer the cruel agent of an absentee landlord.
In the night he is only that poor broken thing that I am
endlessly destroying in the thirsty glare of the Bog Road. In
the daytime it is different. In the daytime I can proudly meet
with others who know of my act, who have sworn the same
oath. In the daytime I can even say to myself with triumph:
I got rid of old Watterson's agent all right! And I know that
the daytime thoughts are real and valid. In the day I am a
man, in the night a wee child whimpers away inside my head
crying for its mammy, weakening me with its foolishness. Ten
months ago that bastard evicted a hundred families off
Watterson's land. Some of them are in the workhouse this

minute with a roof over their heads and a bite to eat, but with wives and husbands and children separated for ever. The majority of them are still walking the roads begging, or trying to survive in roofless burrows scraped out under a hedgerow. I see the odd one now and again on fair-days and I get scattered bits of news. I know for certain that thirty of my neighbours, people of all ages I used to bid the time of day to or kneel beside at Mass . . . and that nice wee girl May Byrne that I courted at Sean Maguire's wedding . . . all died last winter at the backs of ditches or huddled in the straw of strangers' outhouses. And likely a lot more that I'll never hear tell of. It was a most shocking winter to put people out of their houses to wander the frozen countryside, sure birds and everything was falling dead last winter, not even as much as a bunch of haws left on the bushes. Dobson said he needed the land cleared in time for the spring ploughing. I know the most of them were squatters and paid no rent, I know the rest couldn't meet the big rises and were of no benefit to the new landlord. I know the estate is still deep in debt from Mr Henry's racehorses. But all the same, to put people out in the weather there was last winter! Mr Henry, lord a mercy on him, never put no one out. That was the trouble, Dobson claimed, they came from near and far to build shacks on the estate because Mr Henry had the name of being too kind, or too lazy, to bother his head with evictions. He liked a quiet life, Mr Henry. Fast horses in the stable, a servant girl in his bed, the fill of his belly to eat and drink. A lecherous sort of an old blackguard that you wouldn't want your sister to as much as bid the time of day to, but he wasn't the worst of them. The brother is a different matter now. The brother stays warm and snug beyond in England, never clapped eyes on one of us. We are not human to him, we are only figures in a rent book, dots on the landscape. You take a bit of a rag and wipe us off the way you'd wipe fly-shit off a map. Plant wheat in the place of us. Graze herds of cattle. But Dobson knew us all right. He grew up among us. We were flesh and blood to Mr Dobson all right, and still and all he set fire to our thatch and turned us out into the winter roads. Not me nor Mother. No, not us. We're the lucky ones. We can manage the rent and the girls are in service with Protestant farmers and, come a bad harvest, we have Uncle Thomas to help us. But our day might come for all that. The likes of us have no security, we are perched on the crust of the land without roots or foundations. And, blast it to hell, them's only words! I'm making up fine phrases now to excuse myself. What excuse do I need? Sure even if our day never came, even if they left us quiet for a century with our strong cabin and our few acres of ground, there isn't just us, we're not alone in the world are we? They were our neighbours that died last winter of cold and hunger. Minny Hearty and old Sarah Kavanagh and May Byrne. I had a good hoult of May Byrne the night of Maguire's wedding and now she's dead at the back of some ditch. They were my own neighbours, and I was right to get rid of the bastard. It put the fear of God into old Watterson anyhow! Mr Lockhart was saying he was like a hen on a hot griddle till he coaxed this Scotchman into buying the place. Desperate to sell, desperate to be shot of it all. Sending messengers over on every boat. Old Lockhart himself is a bit jumpy this last while, maybe thinks he's next for the picture of a coffin. But Lockhart needn't worry, he'll die in his bed all right. People know where they are with Lockhart. He's a contemptuous old so-and-so that thinks we're no better than pigs but he does his job and that's it. No zeal about Lockhart. He does what Lord Baudry tells him and he does it hard, but he doesn't do it with brutal evictions and squads of English soldiers to harry the people. The one that bought this place though, this McLeod man, he may look out for himself, we're started now and we'll go on with it. Let this deed that I'll do today be a warning to them all . . . Watterson's agent is gone the long road and with the help of God Watterson's driver

will follow him before an hour is out! I'm posted here like
Death behind the graveyard wall. A black streamer of ugly
old crows flaps throughother up the Sunday sky. Let you pray
for your soul, Bobby Baxter! And pray for the soul of Arthur
Dobson while you're at it! Ah what good will it do, what
good? Aren't we only fooling ourselves? They have the power
to starve us by the thousand and ill-use us and send us out
at a whim to beg the roads in the dead of winter, and now
and again we get rid of some miserable get of a paid servant
that carries out orders while his master stays safe in England.
That's all we are good for now, trampling on earwigs.

The time of rebellions is over. Our great families, bad luck
to them, fled long ago with their wealth to France and Spain
leaving the weak as usual to soldier on on their own. That's
a thing, if I said it out loud, I'd be stood up against a wall
and shot for! But it's only the truth. And Bold Robert Emmet
and Wolfe Tone died thirty or forty years ago, that's if they
ever existed outside of public-house songs.

Sometimes I believe the heroes and the chieftains were
invented like a drug to keep us enslaved, a lying promise to
fool poor eejits! Like Jesus and Mary and St Patrick, a foolish
hope put out by the priests. Starve for a hundred years more
and then maybe if you're good a great leader might rise up
and free you. Or a saviour might come and carry your poor
stunted carcase away to live in a Big House in the sky with
a garden full of apple trees and someone else to dig the
potatoes. Foolishness. But I do not know what else to believe.
What is there for the likes of me to believe? What do all the
rest of them believe down inside of themselves? Have they
some sort of a rock to grip on to behind all the holy pieties?
My uncle Thomas now, a well-educated man, houseful of
books, well in with the high-ups, now how could a man like
that have the self-same beliefs as my poor mother? And Father
Molloy, nicely spoken, trained in a French college, what does
he believe when he's down off the altar and alone with

41

himself? Questions a body would never ask for fear of being cursed. An Eye watching you, Ear listening, Judgement waiting. That flat stone in our middle field, eye-shaped hollow scooped out, full up of water on the driest day . . . how do you account for that now? You dip in and cross yourself passing it, mutter prayers while you plough the field around it, taking great care the coulter doesn't rasp the holy stone. A pious young virgin tore an eye out once. Imitating Brigid, disfigured herself to keep her chastity safe for Christ, who rewarded this mad act by providing an eternal scoop of blessed water for the salvation of Claghan. Aye but would any girl in her right mind do a thing like that? A saint. Is it all just priests' talk? Mother swears by it. Aye but my old mother swears there's a fairy in Callan's thorn bush and that Finn McCool walks on the top of the mountain yonder, and that Peg Cassidy could turn milk if she took the notion. A quare crafty old faggot, Peg! must make a fortune out of all the wee presents the people give to sweeten her. Mother stays old-fashioned. There's roads and railways and canals the whole length of this country nowadays, there's English and French and German scholars busy tramping the mountains with notebooks to put us into histories and guide-books, you can walk into Campbell's grocery and buy tea and coffee and oranges from the far ends of the earth . . . and still Mother's daily life is some dark unholy mixture of the druids and Saint Patrick. What'll they make of *her* at the last judgement? Good God, what will they make of me? If there's a hell will I deserve it? Only what is there for a fellow like me to believe? A jug of poteen, a horse to ride whenever they give me a chance, that nice golden woman to love in the dark of a barn. And now this thing that we're swore to do. That's all I have to believe in, a thing that a few rough labouring lads swore in idleness one night in Jem Mullen's tavern. And if Mother and them are right and it's me the poor eejit . . . I am alone. If Henry Watterson had to live I'd be a big man now, riding his horses up and down the country, holding my own with the best on the Curragh of Kildare, fine city ladies sending me love-notes. I had no heed in conspiracies them times, nor in foolish thoughts about God and death. I skimmed happy as a dragonfly over the surface of life. Now with no occupation and no future, I have to think, I have to question, I have to suffer, I'm torn into fifty pieces with doubt. Uncle Thomas might be a good man to talk to, might be the man to understand what I mean, They say Thomas fought in a rising once. They say. But Thomas thinks I am a poor ignorant lout.

Thomas gave me up long ago for a hopeless case. I'd say in his own way Thomas is as limited as any of the lads I drink and conspire with in Jem Mullen's. I was a great fellow as long as I went over there of a Sunday to read his books and learn the bit of Latin. He'd have liked to make a priest of me. Or a schoolmaster anyhow. It must have broke his dry old heart that day I told him the landlord was training me up to be a jockey and that that was all I myself wanted to be. And that to crown it all Mother agreed out of respect for my father's memory. A dead father has more pull than a live uncle, scholar and all as he is. Thomas cannot understand that a lad who likes reading is not always a lad who wants to teach school. Amo Amas Amat fair enough and the Faerie Queene but that doesn't mean I want to spend the rest of my days in a draughty barn teaching Euclid to dunderheads. Or in a confession box exciting myself with young girls' sins. I want to commit my own sins. The faces of Thomas and old Molloy when I came out with that one! A pair of dry dusty old twins . . . begod I think the Greek grammar must have nudged up too close to the Latin one some night and spawned the pair of them. No but if that's what teaching does to a man . . . Thomas never understood that what I got out of his books was a dream of lovely rich women in silk dresses and tall rooms and laughter and the slash of whiskey into glasses and horses galloping galloping . . . A school-master's no closer to those things than a peasant. He is further away from them. He's set himself limits, low safe limits. I wouldn't jump a horse over a schoolmaster's limits . . . too damn middling and cowardly! The time was I set myself no limits, high or low. When I was sixteen it was the gutter or the stars, and now . . . For all my jockeying came to in the long run I might have been better off teaching school. *Would* have been better off without a doubt. I am a small farmer for life now with the rent-man's boot always within an inch of my arse. And the constables and the rope and the bleeding ghosts of . . . I will not think of that now. I am a man. If Thomas had any sort of nature he'd have spoken to Mr Mead for me, got me into the stable there. He is well in with Mr Mead. But no. He will hold his disappointment against me forever. And yet I do believe he would be the one to understand if I got a chance to speak of my anguish to him, of all these different parts of me that are constantly at war. The hard thing is to get that chance now. Some old shyness, some backwardness in me. I walk over there to his cottage time after time and I push open the door upon neatness and books, upon a swept hearth, tranquillity. Thomas looks up and his very glance of mild enquiry turns me straight away into a yokel, frequenter of taverns, enemy of reflection. Here am I Diddley Doubt with the tail of me shirt hanging out, as the mummers say. I feel I'm trailing muck and dirt from the fields unto Thomas' civilised floor, my face flames scarlet, every freckle standing up like a wart, big flaming thatch of yokel's hair. Now, I'm the best-looking lad in the barony, I've read the English poets and bits of Homer too, I sit a horse like a gentleman. Alone, communing with myself I *am* a gentleman. Faced with Mead or Lockhart or the student last year that was writing the history book I'm only an ignorant lout. One kind smile from them and my tongue thickens in my mouth, my nice long English words scamper away like mice into corners, I babble tavern Gaelic, clown's arms swinging awkward around knobbly knees. And it's the same when I'm with this scholarly uncle of mine and his schoolteaching priestly friends. There's other things, sure I know well there's other things besides women and whiskey. Time after time I go running over there to be let take part in their talk. To be let join them in some quiet place where men talk about other things besides drink and women. And time after time they exclude me, their prim voices turn me into a jeering clod. I crack a few raw jokes and go home despised. And yet surely if I got half a chance. Surely a man of Thomas' learning could take all the different bits and colours of me that are whirling round broken and meaningless now and fit them together to make some sort of pattern? To make the human being called Cormac O'Flaherty? Because Thomas is not like your ordinary village tradesman. Thomas has an education and a past. A past that he won't talk about. They say Uncle Thomas fought in a rising. They say he came running up here from the South with my father that was only a wee gassan then, and the hangman hot on their heels. They say. Thomas doesn't say. Old Maggy McCreesh though used to swear he told her all the ins and outs of it years ago when he was courting her. It seems he was dead set on marrying her when he was a young man and never overed her refusal of him. He must have had a brave peculiar way of courting if all he could do with a girl was put the fear of God into her with wild tales of slaughter and butchery down in Wexford. "Where *is* Vinegar Hill?" Maggy used to ask us in her wee quavery voice when she was telling us, "Is it out foreign? Is it away out with Napoleon Bony Parts Thomas was?" Troth and it's quare bony parts he must have himself, we used to say, teasing her, and did you get ne'er the wee squeeze out of him at all at all? "Ach musha, gassan dear, sure a fine respectable man like your uncle would have no heed in hugging and squeezing, sure isn't that only for the poor glunthakamays like yourself!" And away with her into screeches of laughter. Though on the other hand you could never believe one word that woman ever said. To listen to her every man-jack in the country was mad after her when she was a girl so maybe Thomas was all in her head, Vinegar Hill and all. He never got married anyhow and if he had we'd have been in a queer fix when father died of the cholera, out on the roads like many a one only Thomas stepped in and reared us. Out on the roads like poor Maggy herself after McCreesh died and she couldn't manage the rent. Who is there to look after the likes of Maggy? That's why I can't repent over Dobson, or over this other huer of hell that'll be stepping along the road any time now for his Sunday walk . . .

So simply it all began last springtime. It came like an offer of work, a message that Jem Mullen had a job for me. We thought it was to help in the business, Sheila and me, thought he needed a smart man to read and count for him and work out the interest on loans. Sheila lying back on a stack of fodder last April, holding out the apple in her white shapely hand. I had no wish to work for Jem Mullen. "But picture it!" she said, tempting me, "Every single day of our lives, Cormac, we'll be under the same roof and a grand feather bed ready to bounce into as soon as he goes off on his rounds. Better nor an oul barn full of hay, Cormac!"

"Aye but what about Jem?" I asked her, "He only wanted me to work for him, not to take a wife off his hands. We'd be destroyed, Sheila, Jesus he'd be watching us like a hawk, any right man would."

Rain running in rivers off the slated roof, enough glimmer of light to show her flung down on the hay like a sprawled white shadow, like the careless ghost of some young queen, crown and raiment thrown aside for an hour's abandonment. Aye, but all the same we weren't in Troy. Nor in Camelot either. We were in a barn at the back of Mullen's tavern in Claghan. If anyone saw us we'd be destroyed. They'd run us, they'd stone us out of it! Father Molloy of a Sunday: Erin's greatest treasure the chastity of her girls and women. "For God's sake, Sheila, would you throw a few clothes on you!" And woe be on our land if we wantonly let tarnish that treasure. "You're an awful oul shibby, Cormac, sure who do you think's going to come in here? The priest?" "Jem might." "Aw-haw no fear! Can you picture that man of mine leaving the bar without a boss at this hour?" No, I couldn't. Jem Mullen's wide red jowls would be wobbling apart in laughter behind the counter; that big ignorant tub of lard shaking and heaving with faked jollity. Great fellow, Jem, always the laugh and the joke and the big warm shake-hands. As long as you pay for it. You pay well for anything you take in Jem Mullen's. Here am I, Johnny Funny, I'm the man that makes the money! And as long as there was a client to be coaxed, a bit of business to be settled, some poor sod talked into taking out another wee loan now to get him past rent-day (and sure where would you be without your bitta land, Pat, nothing else between your childher and the workhouse and I swear by the saints that as long as big Jem has a few pound to lend ye need go in no fear of eviction), as long as there was all that to hold him Jem wouldn't leave the tavern unattended to go searching the outhouses for a stray wife. Ripe fruit of laughter, hot lightening thrust of spirits, song and talk to send a poor fellow out with his mind in flames, an hour or so's soft pleasure in a barn of hay. It's all yours if you pay the price. In the long run what are any of us only a pack of poor mummers going where we're put, mouthing the lines they hand out to us? We dance our wee dance and we wave our wee swords and in the long run the Prince is victorious, not a thing we can do to change the play. Lockhart and Watterson, and Dobson kicking on the ground, and Sheila with her lovely body, and me here shivering behind a graveyard wall, in a hundred years time, in a thousand, it'll be the self-same play over and over and over again with another band of poor eejits playing it. So I said my lines like the rest of them. The endless length of her slim white body, red-gold hair, pair of long green cats' eyes shining up at me out of a tousled blondness of hay and hair: who wouldn't be a mummer?

"I'll go in with Jem," I said. A tin box bursting with mucky coppers still stinking of dung from labourers' hands, a knitted stocking under the mattress with a wee hoard of usurer's silver, mortgages on half a dozen bits of stony farms: I didn't much want to be mixed up in all that. But the white perfection of her body, all the beauty a man could hope to find. "I hear you were looking for me," I said to Jem. "I was, Cormac," he said, "Come on in here now to the back room and we'll take a glass together."

And it wasn't what I thought at all. He was looking for no book-keeper. Now what in the name of God took Jem Mullen into politics? What's in it for him? What does he get out of the maiming of landlords' cattle, out of the burning of landlords' crops, and now this last while out of the killing of landlords' agents? It's a mystery to me. He gets something out of it, that's certain sure. And he keeps his own hands clean. Jem swore no oath himself, not in front of us anyhow. There's Tim Murphy and Sean Morris and myself and a crowd of wild fellows from over beyond Claghan, fellows that was sick and tired of idleness and the grey waste of a labouring life. Fellows that had their souls hardened within them from they were children seeing their fathers flattened out of manhood between priest and poverty, crawling like quiet decent worms from womb to grave. Fellows that couldn't convince themselves a few stars and maybe an empty sky was future enough to look up at. There must be fellows like that everywhere, you come across them even in Thomas's books long ago in Greece and Rome and everywhere. Fellows with long robes or turbans or black faces or yellow ones, standing around with their tongues hanging out, longing to be told they have a part in the play. Here am I that didn't come yit, big head and little wit! No matter what class of a stupid eejit's play it is, there's fellows just waiting to have the words put into their mouths and the wee wooden sword shoved into their hand. And to convince themselves, that's the worst of it, to convince themselves in the long run that they made up the words themselves and that they have some sort of a choice which direction they wave the sword! That's why I swore the oath anyhow, I can't speak for the rest. It was only lately I started picturing the slow frightful deaths of all them people a year ago, May Byrne and the rest, wandering around without shelter in the black frost of last winter. And whatever profit Jem or anyone else makes out of it, I know there's families sleep warm in their cabins this winter because of what I did. So why in the name of Christ should I go and confess to some priest that I killed Dobson? And why should I even think about staying my hand against this bloody henchman of his when I can hear his boots ringing out now on the frosty road? Even if I'm only a poor fool of a mummer, well, so be it, let me do what I have to. Come on now, Baxter, come on ye boy ye! There's a coffin ready and waiting for you behind this graveyard wall. I am not sorry I killed Dobson and I would be committing a shocking crime against my own people if I repented of that deed. Only always in the night I see him lying there, the half of him flattened into the roadway and the other half, God bless us and save us, trying to rise. Trying to crawl away from me and only managing to crawl deeper and deeper into the sticky dust.

CHAPTER FIVE

MARIANNE MCLEOD'S JOURNAL (1840-1842)

15 June 1840, Edinburgh

I am seventeen years old today and Papa has very kindly offered me this book in which to record the triumphs and the tragedies of being at last a young lady. It is a very large book, like a family Bible, bound in blue leather and with a gold lock and key. This unnecessary description is meant as an aid to collecting my wits for I confess that I have not the least idea what I ought to write in a journal. My life is so uneventful—no triumphs, no tragedies, and I do not even feel that I *am* a young lady! I suppose I must be one, now that Miss Lawson's Academy has closed its doors forever behind me and that I must soon, according to Mama, be thinking of making a suitable marriage; but it seems such a joke that I am no longer a child and that I am at last allowed to think, and even talk, of grown-up matters.

But what *do* young ladies recount in their journals? Balls and assemblies attended, compliments received, happy or unhappy love? In all of these realms I am equally deprived. I have not yet been to any balls—my Argyll aunts are to bring me out this coming winter, in spite of Grandfather's grumbling, but last season I was still in the schoolroom. I have not yet loved or been loved. Nobody has ever paid me a compliment: what if nobody ever does? I am by no means a beauty; Mama says I am the very portrait of Grandfather McLeod, a rude self-made linen-draper who came here from Glasgow to seek, and in the event make, his fortune. I am short and plump with coarse curly hair and very pink cheeks. I can never aspire to true elegance. In years to come I shall certainly, oh horrors! be a stout old lady. *Tant pis*, as Mademoiselle Bouchard used to say. I shall have plenty of time to cry about that when it happens! All the same, I am aware of being a sad disappointment to poor Mama who loves to be surrounded by beautiful things and who had hoped no doubt that the aristocratic Argyll looks would triumph over the plebeian McLeod ones! But everyone I meet agrees that I am clever, and sometimes even amusing. This consoles Mama somewhat: she says that a clever rich girl will never lack suitors and that, once married, if I can manage to keep my husband suitably entertained I shall never lose his interest. She claims that she has not once seen a plain witty woman sulking in a corner while her husband flirts elsewhere, but she has seen many beautiful geese do so. Perhaps this is only because a plain woman does not dare show herself at a disadvantage, while a beauty feels free to indulge in tantrums, sulks and fits of passion, knowing that she will always be forgiven? Whatever the truth I admit this consoles me too: I want very much to be married and live in a pretty town house and give dinner-parties and have children, and how dreadful it must be to be sought *only* because one is rich. It would be delightful to marry a man who really believed I was beautiful, who saw in me what others do not—only, on reflection, what sort of creature could that be? Some poor clerk without ambition, some pitiful nonentity who had never dared to

dream of palaces and fair ladies, a man totally without
fantasy? No, I confess that I should not enjoy the society of
a young man who aspired to so little that he mistook me
for a beauty!

Now I have written a page of nonsense, uninformative
and not even very true. I am not at all saddened or embittered
by my lack of distinction though I do think it unfair that Eric,
who is only a man, should have inherited the Argyll beauty—
all legs and straight blond mane like a racehorse!

What I ought to have written about is Eric's great friend,
young Mr Watterson, who has been staying with us these
past three weeks and who seems prodigiously taken with
my cousin Emma, also here on a long visit. Mr Jeremy
Watterson is English; his father owns estates in Yorkshire
and Ireland, and at first Mama thought he might do for me.
She tried her hand at match-making for a week, happily
with great discretion so there was no embarrassment when
he was seen greatly to prefer Emma. Emma is completely
Argyll, in name and looks, so his people can make no
difficulty about the match as they would surely have done
had he wanted to marry me. Emma is an Argyll also in her
poverty so it will be a great relief to my dear aunt and uncle
that she has found a beau with a fortune! Though I wonder
how she will enjoy being the wife of a great landowner—
poor Emma so intelligent, so rebellious, so longing to travel
the world on a dromedary's back like those intrepid
Englishwomen, leaving behind her a trail of scandal and
bad literature! Will it amuse her to carry soup and improving
tracts to poor cottagers beaming their gratitude from the
doorways of their pretty toy houses?

But I fear these speculations have no place in a young
lady's journal. I must learn to record facts, otherwise I shall
have used all my pages in a week. "Facts!" Grandfather
McLeod likes to say to Papa, "Stick to hard facts, Georgie.
Yer fancy might have led ye to walk the wards of a slum

hospital wi'oot a coat to yer back but the facts are these: yer an honest merchant's son and yer worth a fortyin and if the nobs doesnae leik it ye can afford to spit in all their faces!" Poor Papa who is the gentlest of men wanting only to do good in the world and who has never, I am sure, aspired to spit in anyone's face! Unless perhaps Grandfather's? It is, I hope, some consolation to Papa that Eric at least is to be a doctor and help his fellow-creatures. And that I shall probably marry one because my brother has an abundance of student friends of good family, before all of whom I shall doubtless be dangled. It would be too much to hope for that he should ever succeed in luring another young landowner to the house!

7 July

How swiftly it has all been settled. They are to marry. Mr Watterson has made his declaration and been accepted; he and Emma have gone, presumably in raptures, to my uncle Argyll, permission has been granted. (Idiotic phrase! As if any of us expected my aunt Argyll to leap screaming in outrage off her threadbare sofa: "No you shall *not* have my penniless daughter's hand, you rich English squire!") Letters have been carried in haste between Edinburgh and York and back again: the Wattersons père et mère are expected in town within a few weeks. Happily it is summer and the roads in excellent condition—what a flaw in the romance of it all had they been obliged to flounder through hundreds of miles of mud to reach the happy pair. And then they had intended coming to Scotland in any case, as they do every year, to spend August in their summer residence on the shores of Loch Lomond, so Jeremy could not have fallen in love at a more opportune moment. Try as I may to find a touch of fantasy in this marriage, I fail. It all enters into the realm of the suitable, the expected, the convenient. Does Young Lochinvar *ever* come riding out of the West?

We shall meet the Wattersons, naturally, and they

will see that their beloved son might have done far far worse for himself! I am *not* jealous, though I should dearly have loved to marry a landowner with estates in two countries. Emma herself talks with irritating calmness about her forthcoming marriage and seems not at all impressed with her good fortune but, though naturally not deeply in love (he is shorter than she and his legs are rather spindly), she is fond of her Jeremy, who is a good-natured obliging young man (and the makings, Mama says with another disappointed glance at me, of an excellent husband). And in spite of her passionate speech last evening in her parents' drawing-room (to which her intended lord listened with gentle beaming indulgence) Emma is a sensible girl and has no doubt long since realised that it is not to be imagined of a penniless and well-born maiden that she should gallop the world on a fierce charger, tilting at windbags and liberating American slaves—that is her latest wild enthusiasm! She was taking herself so much for the conscience of the world that I could not resist teasing her, and as soon as she had done speaking I recited one of William Cowper's verses on the slave trade:

> *I pity them greatly but I must be mum,*
> *For how could we do without sugar and rum?*
> *Especially sugar, so needful we see;*
> *What! give up our desserts and coffee and tea!*

which made everyone laugh heartily as Emma is renowned for her sweet tooth. She was furious at me for spoiling her effect, though she claimed it was because I was so insensitive as to draw attention to myself by mocking misfortune. However, as she has a better nature than I, she soon joined in the laugh and we were friends again.

It is thought that old Mr Watterson will entrust his son

with the management of the Irish estate, now in the charge
of a land agent. And there surely Emma will find scope for
adventure and well-doing, for one hears that it is a savage
land full of ignorant and superstitious peasants.

12 July

Such an incredible event! Grandfather died, quite suddenly,
on the morning of the 10th, and is to be buried tomorrow.
We were all present because his heart failed him as he was
leaving the dining-room after breakfast to go to his study,
and he was dead in an instant. A shattering occurrence. One
moment there he was as usual presiding over the breakfast
table, giving his orders for the day, criticising the immodest
cut of my morning dress—and the next moment: nothing!
Nothing at all. Someone who had complete control over all
our lives no longer exists. He has become part of a ceremony.
The house is full of people coming and going, speaking in
hushed voices, wearing faces of sad circumstance. The blinds
are drawn, we tiptoe about in the dimness as though there
were something to disturb; even the servants whisper. It is
impressive and rather frightening. My first experience of
Death.

1 August

The atmosphere has lightened, one feels free to breathe
again. I speak, or rather write, flippantly now but I confess
that I too was for several days afflicted with the general
sense of tragedy. And yet, why? As this is a most private
journal and the key hangs always round my neck, I do not
mind admitting that I see more cause for rejoicing than for
sorrow. Naturally we must all spend a period in deep
mourning: this is civilised usage and has to be observed, but
what I *cannot* understand are Papa's tears. Still less Mama's.
Papa is forty-five years old and, until three weeks ago, spent
his entire life in chains, working under Grandfather's orders

like any office-boy and drawing a monthly wage. A generous wage, but doled out to him every four weeks as if he were a counting-house clerk and not his father's sole heir. And he hated the business! Rather I should say he *hates* it, because he is an old man now and what is left to him but to carry on as a merchant? It is too late to alter the course of his life. It were far better for all of us if Grandfather had died thirty years ago. There, I have said it and, sin though it may be, I am not sorry. Grandfather was a tyrant. He was also a most religious man, upright and strict, with rigid views on the keeping of the Sabbath and on the modesty of ladies' dresses but I ask myself: how could a Christian man, exercising honesty and mercy as we are taught to do, have amassed this fortune in one lifetime? Though it is not an immense fortune it *is* a tolerable one and I cannot help but question. I questioned nothing in his lifetime: he was there and his power was absolute. Perhaps that is why my parents cry, because now they must suddenly grow up and lead their lives and ask questions? What nonsense I talk!

6 August

We have met the Watterson parents; they are a charming couple, very English. Now what do I mean by that? Well of course their accent, but then also there is a lack of manner, a certain gruff simplicity that makes us—not only the Argylls but all Edinburgh society—appear slightly too rigid, too formal in comparison. I am sure this is superficial. I study them while they speak and it amuses me to find that behind the casual ease of their style, their standards are as high and their ideas as conventional as any one finds here. They would certainly have frowned most darkly had their son desired to form a connection with low trade! They drank tea with us yesterday afternoon, as did my aunt and uncle, and of course Emma and her Jeremy. Mama's first idea had been to give a grand dinner in their honour—full of elegant Argyll relations with their long legs in darned silk stockings and as few lowly rich McLeods as possible. But Grandfather, even in his grave, has not yet lost his habit of curbing her extravagance. Being in mourning we had to be content with an intimate family tea-party. For all that, we contrived to be discreetly merry in spite of our black clothes.

7 September

Papa and Mr Watterson have become very good friends, which is an astonishing thing in two men of such opposite background and temperament. Immediately after our little tea-party the Wattersons travelled with Emma and her parents to Loch Lomond. Amazingly *we* were given a most cordial invitation to join them for a week or ten days. Mama was afraid it would not look well as we are in mourning, but Mrs Watterson persuaded her that a few days' enjoyment of country air would do her a world of good after the painful ordeal she has so recently endured. I cannot see why it is so painful for Mama suddenly to find herself rich and independent, but perhaps Mrs Watterson was referring to the death of a beloved father-in-law! I was not allowed to go to Loch Lomond. I stormed and raged but Mama was firm—I had a previous engagement to visit my dear schoolfriend Caroline Duncan at their house in the mountains, and apparently it would have been the height of ill-breeding to attempt to break it. Well of course Mama was right, but I did think it hard.

In the event, however, I was glad she insisted. The magic of it! I spent two most delightful weeks with the Duncans, picnicking and going for long expeditions into the hills. So different from Edinburgh. I did not at all feel conscious of my lack of elegance; my pink cheeks were for once not out of place, and the wonderful thing about rough curly hair is that it can withstand any amount of violent exercise. After an hour in the mountain breezes poor Emma would have been a tousled mess, her blond-complexion sunburned, her combs and ribbons flying in all directions. On reflection I wonder that she could ever have dreamed of adventuring through desert and jungle: the poor girl could never have borne it; she would have been dead inside a week. I am sure she will be far more comfortable as a rich man's wife!

As for me, I may one day soon be a *poor* man's wife! Caroline's brother Alastair is charming. Much much more than charming indeed, but I must begin to practise a decent reserve—I *am* a young lady after all. Though who could have guessed it this past week? We ran races in the heather, my skirts tucked up, and no silly Edinburgh nonsense about chaperons. He paid me funny compliments, said I was like a tough little mountain pony. I was cross at first but when I saw some hill ponies I realised what attractive creatures they are, and could not be angry any more—while wondering all the same if any sane man would ever be moved to *kiss* a mountain pony! I was soon left in no doubt of that and, though I have been visited with feelings of guilt and inquietude over my imprudent behaviour, I feel this may be due simply to the strictness of my upbringing—after all, it would have been quite ridiculous and missish to affect a coyness I was far from feeling! We walked for hours on end beside tiny rippling streams, leaving Caroline to sit in the shade with a book, while we feasted on wild berries and talked about life and about our hopes and fears. I did not tell him how I envied Emma her good fortune because he might have formed a mistaken idea of my character and thought me mercenary. Though their ancestors were Highland chiefs, and some say kings, the Duncans live very simply. I was amazed at the poverty of their house, so very bare compared with our own, but of course I did not make any comment. Old Mr Duncan is a professor and also a poet. I do not suppose there is much money to be made at either of those things. Alastair is to be a doctor of medicine like Eric. They are in the same college. I wish Eric and I were better friends. Then I could talk to him of Alastair, but I am afraid of his cold sarcasm. Am I in love? Of that there can be no question! I have never before met another human being with whom I can talk of things that are close to me. I believe he has a similar feeling about me. He spent the greater part of his time in my company and seemed so happy to be with me. Indeed I hardly found time to speak to Caroline, who was my greatest friend last year at Miss Lawson's. I found her indeed very much changed: she has become cold and ladylike. I believe she found my behaviour childish for she rarely consented to join in our romps!

In Edinburgh I found Mama and Papa much refreshed and full of delight at the Wattersons' hospitality. Such luxury, they say, for what is a mere summer residence, such food and such elegant society. Mr Watterson, it appears, was rather downcast at first, having received word that his Irish land agent was killed in a duel, and being fearful that he himself would be obliged to go over there to deal with his affairs. How romantic to fight a duel in this day and age, but also how very silly—did the poor man take himself for a Byronic hero? And what an extraordinary country that must be where estate agents fight with pistols over a lady's honour! In the event, Mr W was not obliged to cut short his stay in Scotland; his friend the Earl of Baudry who owns the adjoining lands has kindly lent him the services of his own agent, who is looking after the estate temporarily and keeping Mr Watterson informed. He talks seriously of selling the place if he can find a suitable buyer. He says that with his lands and tenants in Yorkshire he is already overburdened with work. The Irish estate came to him only a few years ago from a brother who died without heirs and, though it is a flourishing property covering many miles of the countryside and yielding excellent rents (so says Papa), he would prefer to be quit of the responsibility. I fear Mr Watterson is a lazy man who prefers his own pleasures to the care of his tenantry!

14 September

My father has gone insane! He is completely out of his mind! At midday he left the house to meet Mr Watterson at a gentlemen's club in the city. He returned at five o'clock in the evening, summoned Mama from the tea-table, and was closeted with her in his study for almost an hour. When they emerged, Mama was red-eyed but seemed happy, even greatly elated. Papa too was in a state of excitement, not at all his usual self. Eric and I were naturally in great pain from suppressed curiosity. Then Papa announced (and announced as though it were something wonderful!) that he had bought Mr Watterson's estate in Ireland. It seems that the possibility has been discussed many times, unknown to us, both in the course of the visit to Loch Lomond and since, and today it has finally been decided. It is even now too late for a change of mind: the contract has been drawn up, signed and witnessed. Nothing remains but to sell the shops and house and to realise our capital. I say "our" but of course it is Papa's capital and Papa is mad. He actually intends to tear us away from Edinburgh and our friends and make a home for us in that dreadful dreadful country. Well, I refuse to go to Ireland! I refuse to leave Edinburgh! I will become a governess. I will kill myself. I will run away to Alastair and we shall live together in a croft in the mountains. Papa is mad. An old man to sell all he has and go adventuring in a wild foreign country! It resembles an idea of Emma's, but even Emma has grown up to good sense. Oh why did Grandfather die?

15 September

Mama has spoken to me with great cruelty. She said it is not only in looks I resemble Grandfather McLeod. She accused me of having a mean huckster's soul, content, in spite of my excellent education and talents, to live and die in a back-shop. Which is a ridiculous exaggeration because we have a commodious house in a most beautiful district of the city, far from the vulgar commercial quarter. She said she had rather be childless than have a daughter so lacking in fantasy, so devoid of the spirit of adventure, so content with mediocrity. I did not attempt to defend myself because she would not have understood. When she gets carried away by her disappointment in me she never listens to reason and she is even less likely to now that she is crazed with this mad scheme. I will speak to Eric today. *He* will certainly not go to Ireland. His career and his future are here. I will ask him to persuade Mama to let me stay and keep house for him. That would be an entirely respectable solution as my aunt Argyll shall be free to look after me now that Emma is off her hands. And no doubt it shall not be long before I too marry, and then I will be independent. If only Alastair had made some definite statement of his feelings, how much easier it would all be! I have gone over and over all our conversations and although I know there was much spirit of affection there were no actual words spoken with which I can confront Mama.

I have not yet received a reply from Caroline. Papa I have not seen since his announcement of last evening, nor do I wish to see him. I cannot understand what has possessed him, but suspect that he has been so carried away by his new-found freedom as barbarously to betray the best interests of his family. Mr Watterson has shown himself to be a most dishonourable man. Naturally this is why he cultivated Papa so assiduously: an innocent shopkeeper with a fortune to squander! Whatever its defects, Miss Lawson's Academy at least taught me to know my place, and from the first I was astonished at their friendship. Now this! Linen-drapers do not turn gentleman farmers or country squires on a sudden whim—we shall be ridiculous among the other landowners. Supposing they laugh at us? No, I cannot go. I will not go. I shall stay here with Eric. If Papa would only decide to employ an agent I should not complain. We could live very well in Edinburgh on our Irish rents. It is what most people do. But to go and live there—madness!

16 September

Everyone betrays me. Eric thinks this move is a wonderful idea; by next summer he will have qualified as a doctor of medicine and intends to go and practise in Ireland. An adventure, he calls it, and a chance to devote one's life to doing good! That odious Mr Watterson encourages him, speaking of the opportunities that exist over there for a skilled and energetic young man. Eric has of course inherited much of Grandfather McLeod's evangelising temperament and I really believe he has it in mind to convert the heathen natives with pills and potions!

Emma, though she pities me from the bottom of her heart, yet tries to cheer me with second-hand accounts of the gaiety of Irish life—the profusion of English and Scots neighbours, the balls, the hunts, the hundreds of servants recruited cheaply from among the peasantry. As if I cared. I want only Edinburgh and the love of Alastair Duncan. I dreamed last night that we had wandered away together along a mountain stream as we used to do only a few short weeks ago, that we stood for a long moment embracing by the side of a waterfall, bathed in its cool spray, and when I awoke this morning (oh so full of warm affection and hope!) I remembered that I must go, and the thought was terrible. And Caroline has not written. Not once since I returned home, which is very strange.

We are to go to Ireland next spring, not before because of the danger of rough seas, so that leaves me six or seven months. Emma's engagement was concluded within a few

weeks. But then, it is true, they were living under the same
roof, meeting daily. If I can persuade Mama to write and
invite the Duncans on a visit . . .

17 September

Papa came home for tea and sat with us in the drawing-
room for hours enthusing over our altered state. Mama and
Eric were full of slavish acquiescence and indeed appeared
at times to be as flushed with foolish anticipation as Papa
himself. I listened in perfect silence and with a stony heart,
which was noticed and caused Papa at last to address
himself almost exclusively to me, pointing out the great
elevation we are about to make in our social position. "In
Edinburgh," he said, "we are nobody. Even with father's
fortune we can never spread our wings here; they all know
me as a mere linen-draper's son. In Ireland, my dear, we
shall be landed gentry and keep our own racehorses. And
you, Marianne, shall have the sons of the nobility to choose
from!" I almost retorted that I wanted no Irish noble's son
but only the son of a Scottish poet, but judged it more
prudent to keep my peace. I listened with tolerable patience
to Mama's sentimental imaginings of a smart carriage (ours)
driving up a vaulted avenue of ancient limes (ours) between
rows of pink-cheeked beaming tenants (ours), of tall ordered
rooms with discreet silent footmen ministering, of neat
housemaids dressing us for a ball, of a retinue of devoted
native servants—all ours! I know that thereby poor Mama
hopes to recover the lost legendary grandeur of the
impoverished Argylls. For a moment I pitied her—had she
owned an Irish estate in her girlhood, drunken old Granda
Argyll would not have forced her to accept the first rich man
who offered, even if he was only the son of a Glasgow
shopkeeper! But then I reflected that she does not need my
pity: she and Papa love each other, it was not solely a
marriage of interest. Perhaps in that case they will be all the

more ready to help me further my own hopes? Tomorrow I intend to speak to Mama; I can put it off no longer. She may scold me, but her sense of duty will surely oblige her to find out discreetly from Mrs Duncan whether Alastair has any serious thoughts of me. Or at any rate she may think it wise at least to invite Caroline and her brother here on a visit. Lovely tomorrow! What happiness it may bring me!

1 January 1841

I vowed two months ago that I would never write in this journal again. My spirits were so low and my soul so sunk in humiliation that I did not even wish to live. That is an exaggeration: I am quite sure that I always did wish to live, and I must take care in my journal to forgo all such empty and dramatic utterances. After all, if I cannot be honest with *myself*! And in this New Year, with all the changes and uprootings it is going to bring, I have determined always to be honest with myself. Thus I am going to write a true account of all that has occurred since October. I would by far prefer to draw a veil over it and endeavour to forget, but I *must* record it as a warning to my future self! Indeed it is not so very much, and not at all such a great tragedy as I had persuaded myself.

So: the Duncan parents, having observed me closely during the two weeks I spent with them, have decided that I am an unsuitable companion for their daughter. They were shocked, as was my dear friend Caroline, by what they termed my hoydenish and immodest conduct. All that innocent wandering in the hills, those harmless races and games which for me were simply a prolongation of childhood until Alastair's kiss (and such a small chaste kiss it was!) have been given a most shameful construction. I pursued their helpless son like a common flirt! I betrayed my low shopkeeping origins! They have, it seems, always had reservations about my friendship with Caroline. I,

stupidly, had believed it was Mama who objected because
of their poverty, and have often bitterly blamed her for
refusing to ask Caroline to stay. But no. The Duncans,
while allowing the friendship to progress safely under their
eyes, have always thought it unwise to let their daughter
spend any length of time among people with whom she
might be in danger of forming an unsuitable alliance. They
mean Eric! As if my brother would even *look* at that gawky
Caroline! As for their poverty and simplicity, how I have
been misled. They play at the simple life, spending several
months each year in that bare little house in the mountains,
but in reality they are the most arrogant family in Scotland.
Their simplicity is a pose, a fashionable affectation, as is
their concern for mankind, their devotion to education,
their refusal to hunt or shoot game. And Alastair is to marry
some aristocratic cousin, an engagement entered into almost
at birth. I was supposed to have known all about this and
to have yet tried to lure him with my wiles! What wiles?
I behaved with simplicity, even if nobody else did. But that
is no excuse. I have been very blind, very stupid. Fancying
that young man was in love with me when all the time he
was profiting from my ignorance, amusing himself. I had
no right to be so ignorant. That is the unforgivable thing:
I could think far better of myself had I really behaved like
a shameless flirt. It is being such a goose . . . Caroline
would not have been so silly, nor would Emma. They
would have kept a decent reserve. I can never think well
of myself again, forced as I am to recognise that the Duncans
are right in their condemnation: I do owe much of my
character to my McLeod connections, I lack gentility. Only
they need not have expressed themselves with such cold
cruelty. They might have allowed something to youth and
innocence. And Mama need not have been so coldly cruel
in her disapproval of me. Papa is right and people such
as we have no place in genteel Edinburgh society. I begin

to long ardently to be in Ireland!

❧

"Does it sound likely to you, Trev? That this diary's genuine? I mean, just supposing a sister of yours had perpetrated some dreadful scandal when she was a teenager, got involved with one of the Kray gang, say, and written all about the fellow in a diary . . . "

"None of my sisters would have kept a diary, love. Bleedin' illiterate, the lot of them!"

"No, but supposing she *had*, and supposing your parents had been murdered by the guy, I mean would *you* have piously preserved her diary for posterity?"

"I personally wouldn't have touched the thing with a forty-foot pole, but then I'm not an aristocrat."

"The McLeods were never aristocrats!"

"They were, compared with Paddy. That sort of people always did piously preserve their family scandals for posterity, the way our sort preserved the family china."

"*My* family never preserved anything. The family china was jettisoned as soon as they could afford synthetic stuff! All my lovely old seventy-eight records that I'm always on about! I went back looking for them years later you know, and found that my parents had only left them dumped in the corner of a shed until the sow ate them."

"As I keep saying, that's the Irish for you, Maur! And, speaking of which, love, I just bought one today."

"A *sow?*"

"A shed. Fifty metres long, structurally perfect, with this lovely authentic grain-loft on top and half an acre of ground. Five thousand quid!"

"That's the third shed in a *month*, Trev, plus those two labourers' cottages. What do we *need* them for, darling?"

"Paying peanuts like that, how could I go wrong? I'm

going to make one big clean-up eventually, you'll see. The old pendulum's got to swing away from bungalows one of these years and when it does, wham! Smart little Trevor Watts will be standing in the breach as always! Do you know, Maureen, there's this most fantastic . . . "

She can see Trevor is only politely interested in her new novel. He's fallen upon France like a fabulous new game of Monopoly, full of things to buy, things to sell, things to make him richer, cleverer, the best. Being a country gentleman could never have been enough for her husband. Trevor is on the move again, albeit in a slower, more countrified way nowadays. Tramping Brittany in a Barbour jacket and green wellies, haggling over ruined farmhouses, is perhaps a shade more relaxed, Maureen agrees, than planning crafty takeover deals at power breakfasts, and if it keeps him happy . . . But it irritates her, when all she wants to do is sit still in her lovely new château and ponder the past.

"I'm sure you're going to make us a bomb, ducky!" she smiles dutifully, and reopens the diary.

10 April 1841, Claghan
Well I have my wish and shall henceforth write in the blackest ink I can procure! This is Ireland. We are here. We have been here for ten days. And how shall I begin to describe it? So easy to make a list of abstract nouns: horror, disillusion, shock, etc., but what good? This is my life now and I cannot live it in distressed exclamation marks! So . . . we arrived by ship from Scotland, dear dear lost Scotland! The voyage was delightful, the ship's officers handsome and very charming, the heaving and tossing of the vessel great fun, the waves most impressive. Huge weather-beaten sailors kept tugging and straining at ropes, all the while bellowing at each other the most incomprehensible instructions. We

had delicious food to eat at the captain's table, plates and glasses dancing madly the while—and so many empty places! *I* was not in the least seasick but Mama, Papa and the servants were literally swimming in sal volatile and paregoric, poor things! It all passed far too quickly. I should *adore* to embark on a really long voyage—to America perhaps. Weeks and weeks at sea, such fun!

But we arrived. Our neighbour, Mr Lockhart, who manages Lord Baudry's estate and is in consequence very much taken with his own importance, kindly met us at the port and conveyed us home. He is a taciturn old bachelor, hardly brimming over with *joie de vivre*. We drove through the rain across a landscape of small rounded hills (nothing at all like our dear mountains at home), lakes and dreary-looking boglands. Scarcely a tree to be seen. Mr Lockhart told us that the woods were cut down centuries ago because rebels and popish priests used them as hiding-places, and that nowadays nobody plants trees because they are a waste of good farmland. Alas for Mama's dream of a vaulted avenue of ancient limes! There is not even an avenue, just a rutted lane. And alas for the beaming tenants. In spite of the rain we saw vast quantities of clownish misshapen creatures in the most extraordinary rags but they showed no sign of beaming at us. They all looked half-starved. They *are* half-starved, Mr Lockhart told us, their rents and taxes are so high that they are obliged to live on potatoes and water. Just as well, he said, they are no longer in a condition to rebel against us! Papa was shocked. Well we all were. Papa said as Christian people our first care must be to lower all the rents so that these poor wretches may begin to live decently. Mr Lockhart retorted very coldly that if Papa lowered the rents he would be bankrupt within a year; in fact he probably would be anyway unless he evicted half the tenants and turned the land over to cattle. That had been Dobson's plan, he said, and a very sensible plan it would have been too if he had not been living among savages. Poor old Dobson had been brutally murdered for his pains, he said with a dry laugh. Papa said: "Oh no, we know that is not true; Mr Watterson himself told us that Dobson was killed stupidly because he insisted, while drunk, on fighting a duel!" And Lockhart laughed again and said: "Aye, a duel with a gang of peasants armed with clubs!" We were most shaken. The hateful Mr Watterson had been in such haste to rid himself of a troublesome estate full of murderous tenants that he lied most dishonourably to Papa. What a dreadful beginning to our new life!

The house! Huge certainly but more like an overgrown farmhouse than a mansion and very much run to seed. The best rooms overlook the stable yard. Mama says the gardens are in a shocking state, and although some repairs and cleaning work had been done before our arrival, poor McGregor threw up her hands in horror and said before we could eat or sleep in any safety she would have to engage an army of scrubbing-women. Presumably she has done so, because for the past week the house has been filled with shrieks and laughter and what can only be curses in the most uncouth language one can imagine!

15 April

Mr Lockhart has been to see us twice and has given us masses of information, most of it appalling. Apparently Mr Watterson lied to Papa on many counts. The estate is by no means as flourishing as he claimed. His brother, Mr Henry Watterson, lived for many years in a state of continual debt, caring only for his racehorses, keeping no record whatever of rents owed, allowing all comers to settle freely on his land so that it was impossible to farm it productively. Poor Dobson, the agent appointed by *our* Mr Watterson, was expected to put all that to rights as speedily as possible. He seems to have been a very stupid man and simply swept hundreds of people off the land as one would sweep dead leaves off a path! No wonder he made enemies. When I said that, Mr Lockhart looked at me as though I had no right to meddle in gentlemen's concerns: "One cannot treat these yokels as if they were reasonable beings, Miss McLeod; if we show them the least kindness they will take advantage of it to destroy us."

"But that is ridiculous," I said imprudently, "because Mr Henry Watterson, according to you, was too kind to them and yet they let him live in peace. The one they destroyed was Dobson who was not kind at all!" Papa in some embarrassment told me quite sharply to hold my tongue and go and ask one of the servants to bring some refreshments.

20 April

I am sorry that Mr Lockhart is our nearest neighbour because he is a most disagreeable old man. But then he has lived here fifty years—fifty years!—and he must know more about the country than we do. We know nothing and we do find the natives frightening. If only they spoke English we would think them no more strange perhaps than the beggars one sees in the streets at home. But it is as though they were continually conspiring against us. The two maids Mama brought from Scotland have completely lost their nerve and insist on going back by the next ship. They are young city girls and one can understand how lost they feel. How I wish I could go with them. Even good stolid McGregor confesses that it takes courage to walk into the kitchen and give orders to that sullen-faced Kathleen O'Flaherty who speaks English so uncouthly, who cooks with such careless gestures, who seems not to have the slightest idea that there is a difference between dirt and cleanliness, between truth and falsehood. Indeed they all lie most shockingly. Today, for instance, McGregor complained that a pie meant for our luncheon had completely vanished. When Mama went to investigate she was met with a wall of innocence: "Och yer ladyship, sure it must have been one of them big stable cats got a hoult of it, sure it's divils they are for the bitta mate!" And we know, we *know* that the stable cat in question is the kitchen maid's cousin or lover or grandmother but what can we do? The one thing to avoid is direct confrontation for where might it not lead?

It is ridiculous! We are hypnotised by our own servants; we can think and talk of nothing else! Is it poor Dobson that makes cowards of us? We are hypnotised by him too, by this man whom we have never seen, of whom we have not the least description, whose most important characteristic— his *only* characteristic—is his death! But we are right to be frightened of them: Dobson's has not been the only murder. And the frightful things they have done to farm animals! At first I welcomed the dreadful things Mr Lockhart told us— I hoped they might induce Papa to give up the whole idea. But there is no question of that. More than Papa's fear of the natives is his fear of being the laughing-stock of Edinburgh. And then who would buy if he did want to sell? Only an innocent would buy this place. He will not hear of being an absentee landlord either. Papa is a moralist and we must all suffer for it! The only reassuring thing is that the native servants we have were all recommended by Mr Lockhart and according to him are from the most respectable tenant families. The O'Flaherty woman cooked for years for a very decent Scottish family who have gone to settle in Canada, her brother farms a few acres nearby and was apparently the precious right hand of Mr Henry Watterson, and the uncle who is in charge of the restoration work in the house is on terms of trust with the best families in the country. The others too—housemaids, stable-boys, kitchenmaids—were all handpicked by Mr Lockhart and his sister from a vast body of applicants, and Mr L naturally takes offence at the slightest word of criticism. We ought to feel safe but we do not.

30 April

We have been here a month and it seems like a century. A foggy rainy century. But there are leaves on the bushes now and daffodils in the overgrown park and some kind of white blossom in the hedges. No one calls but Mr Lockhart; I believe there is no one to call. He has a sister but she spends much of the year in Dublin and we have not yet met her. I imagine a grim-faced spinster, Mr L in skirts. We have neighbours at a distance of six or seven miles but they have given no sign of life. I shouldn't imagine they ever will. They are titled people; their estate is immense; they have a large stable of racehorses—so why on earth should they want to know *us*? Papa talks of buying a steeplechaser and intends to ask the advice of this Hon Mr Mead, so perhaps we might contrive to scrape an acquaintance with them in that manner and get a grudging invitation to a yearly ball or something of that kind. The McLeods as social climbers— so much for the gracious life I was promised!

Otherwise there are the Hales whom we meet at church and who have accorded us solemn handshakes. They have been here since King William—that was the first thing they told us! *Not* the Conqueror, they mean that dreary little Dutchman who beat Bonnie Prince Charlie. I think. I shall have to learn some history if we are going to live here; they talk of nothing else. Even Mr Lockhart never stops boring us with Cromwell and people like that! The rector has called on us, of course, also Mr Fielding the curate, a rather scrawny evangelical man who collects weeds and butterflies and puts them in books. He explained to us (at length) that this pastime is also an occasion for carrying out the Lord's work as it gives him a chance to pounce on peasants while he's prowling about their fields, and talk to them of the Redeemer.

Perhaps he did not use the word "pounce" exactly. He is
said to be a very intelligent young man but one would
never guess at that quality. I am bored, bored, bored!

1 May

The funniest thing! This evening Papa rode over to see Mr
Lockhart on business, Mama and I were sitting tranquilly in
the small downstairs parlour awaiting our supper when
suddenly there was a wild outburst of screaming rage coming
from we knew not where. Mama turned pale and I certainly
felt pale, expecting at every moment a ravening mob to
burst in upon us. We could hear McGregor's voice raised
in outrage, almost drowned by high foreign screeches. "They
are killing poor McGregor!" Mama whispered, and we began
barricading the door with chairs, imagining knives, death,
a corridor running with our blood. And then just as suddenly
it was over; we could hear laughter, a sort of friendly
scolding in Gaelic, McGregor's voice still raised in a nagging
grumble; she grumbles even more than usual since we've
been here. We rushed down the passage towards the kitchen,
Mama furious, and there we found the cook standing with
her arms akimbo, a redheaded young countryman looking
extremely cross and, in the centre of the room, old McGregor
fiercely upbraiding two children in bright dresses who were
puffing with giggles as they listened. Mama sharply bade
them hold their tongues and they sobered for an instant,
then caught each other's eye and were off again. I could
hardly restrain myself—how well I understood them! What
it is to be twelve or thirteen and quite unable to stop
giggling. And how ridiculous grown-up rage always appears
when one is in that state!

"Let me speak to them, Mama," I said and I drew them
into the scullery and shut the door. After they'd calmed a
little I asked their names: "Fionnuala O'Flaherty and Teresa
Brennan, miss, and sure we only came to get Cormac and

Kathleen to take us to the dance and that oul' one lit on us and half-kilt us!" It transpired that the bigger girl is our cook's sister, the cross young man her brother, that she rushed up here in her Sunday dress hoping for fraternal support against their mother who considers her too young to attend the servants' May Day Ball in Hales' barn! The giggling friend came to give moral support. McGregor found the two of them sitting on the kitchen table eating wedges of currant cake and turned on them a broadside of Scottish wrath—not one word of which they understood! The squeals we heard came when she grabbed an ear of each, intending to throw them into the yard without ceremony; the shrill cries of protest from the unfortunate Fionnuala's brother and sister! How foolish we felt, Mama and I. "Savages! What savages!" Mama exclaimed, to give herself countenance as she chased them all home. But of course the point is that they were not savages at all—just two pretty girls in their best dresses longing to be grown-up and go to balls, a mother who does not understand (perhaps wisely, but still!) and a big sister who consoles them with slices of cake. And, to complete the cast, an elderly Scottish housekeeper, quite out of her depth, and two supposedly civilised ladies who ought to know better than to go looking for banditti under every bed! This is the first reassuring incident that has occurred since we left the ship.

1 June

Two months here. We have not made one friend but have acquired a humiliating nickname. All the fault of that dreadful Mr Lockhart. Apparently he thinks Papa is letting our side down, being a traitor to his class and so on. From the beginning, even though we rightly distrust them, we have made no secret of our pity for the poor peasants. The rents are exorbitant in comparison with their small means (Papa speaks seriously of lowering them as soon as the estate

74

begins to show a profit), the various taxes they pay are quite unnecessary and I think it a great insult to oblige them to give tithes to the Established Church, which they do not even attend! And it *is* their country after all. "It is *our* country," Mr Lockhart retorts. "We brought them our civilisation and our language, we dragged them out of savagery! They didn't even know how to farm until we came and taught them. The land was a wilderness!" Yes, but to farm for *us*, I would have liked to reply for I hate his flat cynical voice, we taught them to farm for *us*. However, I say nothing now. I hold my tongue for good manners' sake and because I know I should not be listened to anyway, but I feel an immense pity for these poor ill-grown people who own nothing, not even the huts they sleep in. Not even themselves. If I were a brave person I would bring soup and medicine and warm clothes to them in their cabins as, in the books I read, the squire's daughter always does in England. But this is Ireland and I am frightened. It is really best to stay away from their cabins, which resemble rather the shelters of beasts than the pretty rose-covered cottages the poor inhabit in Jane Austen's novels! After all, if *I* were obliged to live like that and a well-dressed young lady appeared on my doorstep bearing good advice and a bowl of soup, I should be strongly tempted to throw both in her face!

Well, Papa must have been reading the same books as I because he too is shocked at these miserable huts. Some weeks ago, driving around the estate in the rain with Mr Lockhart, he mentioned the possibility of replacing them with good stout cottages more suited to the climate and of providing decent furniture. (Some have no furniture at all, only a pile of straw to sleep on!) Mr Lockhart said, in the cold voice we have since come to know so well: "I pray you, do nothing of that kind, Mr McLeod; it would be an act of base treachery to the rest of us; they would begin to butcher us so that we too might provide them with mansions to breed in. Besides, they would keep pigs in your comfortable cottages and before long they would have burned your fine furniture to distil their alcohol. Give these people an inch, Mr McLeod, and they'll take an ell!"

I feel Mr Lockhart exaggerates in his measurement: it is surely if we give people nothing at all that they may kill us to get at our ell—after all, most poor people are quite content with an inch. (But then, is that *really* so, or is it only a piece of moral nonsense they taught us at school? I begin to be aware that in Ireland one can take nothing for granted—how fragile we, and our solid middle-class worth, seemed that evening of the kitchen quarrel!)

So! Now we are known everywhere as the Cottage McLeods. We learned it from the rector who, with great condescending kindness, advised Papa to wait until he was somewhat longer in the country before he attempted to meddle with local custom.

I am intensely lonely; at times I almost envy people like the Hale girls who, I am told, spend their days sewing patchwork, cooking and preserving. Their parents are only yeoman farmers turned landlord and have kept up an old-fashioned thrifty manner of living. Florence, Eliza and Susannah are some years older than I, rather large dull girls who do not inspire me to seek their friendship. But I feel I shall be condemned to it in the long run for there is no one else. I have nothing to do in the house; I hate embroidery and I am utterly unable to sketch or paint watercolours or arrange flowers prettily. All I have ever been good at is conversation and there is nobody to converse with!

Mr Lockhart's sister has arrived at last. As I suspected, she is a spinster of forty-five who talks of nothing but the idleness of the servants. How I long for Emma but there is such coldness between my parents and the Wattersons that I doubt if I shall ever see her again. I read and read, and when I am tired reading I walk in the park (which is really

only a great field, hardly landscaped at all) and in the lane
quite close to the house. It is impossible to walk to Claghan
village because one must pass by whole settlements of
squatters' shacks where the most incredibly ragged dirty
people live. Mr Fielding says the original name of the village
was Claghan MacEighire because of some rich native family
who had their demesne there, and he suggested we might
rename it Claghan McLeod! He was not joking because he
never jokes, and Mama thinks it a wonderful idea. I hope
she does not attempt anything of the kind. How the Lockharts
would laugh!

Sometimes, when I am more lonely than usual, I talk to
the servants and to some of the decent tenants, the ones
who live nearby and who keep themselves and their cabins
clean. I think they are safe and I am no longer frightened
of *them*. They always speak to me very kindly, in
extraordinary flowery English. I suspect it is a direct translation
from Gaelic, and I cannot imagine why Miss Lockhart makes
such unkind fun of them for speaking like that. It might be
amusing to learn Gaelic: perhaps I could pay some of the
women to teach me? They might be glad to earn a little
money. There is no work to be done in the fields now and
they are always, men and women, sitting in groups outside
their cabins, surrounded by children and hens, talking, talking,
talking!

15 June

My birthday. I am eighteen. Papa has given me a pretty little
grey mare and I am to have riding lessons. It is arranged
with the cook's brother who used to be a jockey and won
dozens of races for Mr Henry Watterson. He must have lost
dozens too, as they say Mr W was ruined by his racehorses!
Tomorrow I am to be walked along the lanes on a leading-
rein—or rather, the mare is to be walked with me on her
back. I have named her "Bonheur" because now at last I

shall have something interesting to do. Dear Papa, he hopes so much that I shall begin to like Ireland! Mama disapproves of the whole idea, naturally. She fears that I shall become more hoydenish than ever. *Her* present to me was a delightful lace shawl appliquéd with Irish designs: shamrocks and brambles and hawthorn leaves; she had it made by a woman in the next county whom Miss Lockhart recommended. It succeeds in making even me look fragile and feminine. Only, who is there to notice? If we had stayed in Edinburgh someone might have fallen in love with me by now, and I should be choosing wedding-clothes!

I had no proper birthday party this year—I have no friends to invite. But Mr and Miss Lockhart and the Hales and Mr Fielding all came to tea. They talked a lot of grown-up nonsense and I was bored as usual. Where is the delightful society Papa promised us? Where are all the noblemen's sons who were to come rushing to marry me? What disillusion it all is—we are just barely considered gentry. So many long pedigrees in the country and ours so short! Mama contrives to insinuate that if I were a great beauty that would not matter: everyone would want to know us. As if I *chose* not to be tall and elegant! I have grown an inch this past year—but perhaps Mama would have liked me to grow Mr Lockhart's ell!

Mr Mead, from whom Papa bought Bonheur, has kindly indicated that his wife may call on us when their married daughters arrive from England for the summer. But it seems there are no young people there either. Eric comes soon, and that is something to look forward to. Perhaps when I have learned to ride well we shall go together on pleasant excursions around the countryside. He will make friends for us. It is much easier for a young man. There has been little violence this year, the Lockharts tell us, and it is possible to go about quite freely. There are of course the usual crowds of beggars but one has only to ignore them. That is what they *say*, but how can one ignore so many hungry people? Every day they come in droves to the kitchen door to be fed, smiling their irritating slavish smiles, calling down the blessings of all their outlandish saints, addressing Papa as "Yer Honour," then turning away gnawing on their crusts like dogs, yapping and growling in their uncouth tongue, leaving wild yells of keening laughter drifting behind them like hate. For how can they *not* hate us? "You arrived at a bad time," Miss Lockhart says. "These are the hungry months when last year's potatoes are all used up and this year's not quite ready yet. They are always hungry now; they are accustomed to it."

"Some of them can afford to buy meal," her brother added. "The rest think they have a God-given right to live off us!" And do *we* not live off them? When I am feeling most irritated at their gracelessness, most disgusted with the awfulness of their country, some respectable bore speaks cruelly of them and I want to rush out and fire off pistols in their defence! I keep quiet, however, as befits my age, and listen. "Come September, Miss McLeod, you will feel less sorry for them. They'll have the fill of their stomachs and good fires for six months—what more could they want? *And* they'll spend the winter dancing and feasting; you'll be driven as mad as we are with their fiddling and jigging! Hallowe'en, Christmas, weddings, it's any excuse for a drunken orgy."

"Even funerals," Mr Fielding said with his most righteous expression, "even such solemn occasions must be desecrated with their merriment. It is quite disgraceful and ought to be stopped!"

"And I tell you," Miss Lockhart continued, sounding most grieved about it, "in winter their homes are much warmer than ours. Proper little hothouses! They exaggerate in everything, you know. Like the grasshopper in the fable!" Yes, but I've always thought the grasshopper much nicer than the dreary old ant, and in the meantime they don't get much at *her* kitchen door. The Hale girls said nothing, munched cake and looked large and virtuous. Thus passed my birthday.

16 June

My first riding lesson. Quite terrifying for the first half-hour: horses are so slippery! I kept clinging tightly to the pommel, making wild grabs at reins and mane, kicking when I ought to have sat still, sitting still when I ought to have kicked. In short, making a complete fool of myself! Cormac O'Flaherty, my teacher, says people do make fools of themselves the first time and that tomorrow I'll be trotting around like an Amazon. Easy for him, he can sit astride, which must be much more reassuring! He is the cross young man we found in the kitchen that evening, poor little Fionnuala's brother. I asked about her and apparently she is working now in the scullery: McGregor engaged her last week. But she's so young, I said to O'Flaherty, oughtn't she to be at school still? And he laughed! "What school does she want, Miss? Isn't she far better off learning to cook and keep a house! It was a great chance for her getting in there, so near home and all." So perhaps now she will be allowed to go to dances, I said. "Troth, and I wouldn't bet on it, Miss; the mammy's a shocking holy woman!" They really *have* such an expressive way of speaking English! Papa watched the lesson and says O'Flaherty seems a very competent teacher, firm and yet respectful at the same time. They had a long conversation about horses and forgot all about me; I stood holding Bonheur's reins, hoping she wouldn't decide to bite or bolt. Papa wants him to help choose and train a racehorse. Poor Papa! What could he possibly know about racing? Surely he does not intend to be another Henry Watterson?

15 July

Eric has arrived at last, a full-blown doctor of medicine. *Very* self-important and, I suspect, longing for an opportunity to pounce on everyone in sight with vaccines, leeches and bleedings! All is smiles and welcomes, Edinburgh gossip, drives around the estate. Caroline Duncan is engaged to be married to a laird. Eric says he is ninety years old and has buried a wife already; Mama says nonsense: he is a delightful man of forty who sustained the tragic loss of his first bride some years ago and is now ready to be consoled with a sensible and charming young girl. How funny grown-ups are—forty or ninety, what's the difference? It serves Caroline right! Emma and her husband are still travelling in France and Italy. Aunt Argyll sent us her love and a trunkful of presents. In short, Scotland survives very well without us. I am *so* homesick. I question Eric greedily for every single detail of what's happening in Edinburgh, but *he* wants to talk only of Ireland. When I told him how dreadful it all was he said I was probably approaching it in the wrong spirit, expecting to find a little Scotland wherever I went. Mama was quite cross with me and told Eric I have made no effort whatever to settle down or even to be friendly with our neighbours. She said I was most rude to poor dear Miss Lockhart and that, although there is a family of very suitable young girls nearby, I have always refused their offers of friendship. She meant the ghastly Hales! Mama really imagines I could bring myself to whisper girlish secrets with those great creatures! Papa surprisingly joined in the attack: he said I was ruining my eyes reading all day, or else making myself ridiculous mooning about practising bits of Erse on the servants, and that at that rate I would soon turn into a cross old spinster. He was half-joking but Mama was not joking at all. Eric said we must all go to Dublin to brighten my ideas—he has an introduction to some people there— and afterwards when he is established as Claghan's first medical officer he intends to make inroads into the best local society. He is going to get a great shock when he *sees* the local society!

20 July, Dublin

We have been here for two days. Compared with Edinburgh it is like a small town, but at least it is not Claghan! We had tea with friends of friends of Eric, the Pennyfathers. A very *grand* family, brimming over with judges and barons and Lord Chief Justices and I don't know what. The branch we met is rather churchy and I sat once again at an elderly tea-table listening to elderly conversation! The exception was a son, William, who is Eric's age and, naturally, a clergyman. He is as pious as Mr Fielding but far better-looking. He addressed me a few gentle remarks on the beauty of the Irish landscape and then launched into an account of his attempts to bring Christ to the peasants. It was full of quotations from people like Nehemiah (Grandfather McLeod all over again!) and, in between two bites of bread and butter, he told us a most horrific story about a Roman Catholic servant who was converted to Protestantism by her English mistress and then punished so violently by her family and neighbours that she has been bedridden for five years! How extraordinary! Imagine Eric and Papa bothering to set about me with sticks if I decided to change my religion! These people are really very strange and very extravagant.

One of the other guests said it is because they drink so much alcohol, and then they all began talking about a priest called Father Mathew who has been going about the country for some years advocating total abstinence. Apparently he is most successful, because the peasants are so superstitious they believe he can work miracles and they are quite happy to kneel before him and take a pledge never to touch their beloved whiskey again! In return he gives them a pin with his portrait on it to wear in their clothes. I had in fact seen these pins without understanding what they meant. Many of the servants wear them, so at least Papa will now be able to establish who does *not* steal his "dhrink!" Eric said the workhouses will be full of publicans soon, but the Pennyfathers see nothing amusing in all this. They think it a very good idea in many respects, while still vaguely deploring anything that might serve to unite the natives into a body. I have noticed that even well-established people, whom one would suppose have a certain power and influence, seem to live in a state of mild panic here. They talked a lot too about Daniel O'Connell, whom the Lockharts always refer to as a vulgar upstart and an example of what happens when papists are given an education. It was all very boring, apart from the bit about the poor little crippled servant. Ireland seems to be full of people who have never been young. But at least we are to go shopping tomorrow, which is something.

1 August, Back in Claghan! Home, and the Meads have called at last! We are to spend an afternoon. Mama and I have not stopped quarrelling these last two days over what I shall wear. Emma sent me, via Aunt Argyll, via Eric, a most lovely scarlet cotton which I think is wonderful with my dark hair and makes me look most interesting and exotic. Mama says the effect is wonderful indeed and that I should be a great success at a servants' ball. Why, she asked, do I not ask the cook to teach me a few jigs and reels as well as the idiotic Gaelic phrases I bore everyone with? *She* insists that I wear a disgusting maidenly thing in white muslin which makes me look duller than ever.

I can ride reasonably well now—at least well enough to chat with Cormac O'Flaherty as we trot around the lanes. He is quite knowledgeable and amusing for a peasant—

6 August

We spent the afternoon in Meads', having tea on the lawn. There was a large party and it was all terrifyingly grand. First we were brought on a tour of the house. It was renovated recently, at great expense, and is very beautiful, full of lovely furniture and light and pictures. Great big windows look out over a real park. There is actually a tree-lined avenue and a butler. The sort of establishment Mama thought *we* were going to have! I could see her turning green with envy. I have not forgiven her for the white muslin; I looked ridiculous and provincial. All the other ladies were dressed like fantastic tropical birds—naturally Emma wouldn't have sent me anything that wasn't perfectly fashionable and correct! I believe Mama is so terrified of my being taken for what I am—a vulgar shopkeeper's grandchild—that she overdoes the gentility. She said afterwards that all the other ladies were older than I and married, and that I was dressed exactly as befitted my age. When you have succeeded in attracting a husband, she said, you may wear what you wish. How does she expect me to attract a husband if I am to go around wrapped in white muslin like a great cheese?

The Mead parents are kindly bluff people, but the daughters are excessively smart and brimming over with the latest English slang and gossip. They can talk of nothing but balls and assemblies and watering-places and great matches among their acquaintance—I thought I had walked into a Jane Austen novel at last! They are *so* proud of having once stood at two yards' distance from the dear Queen and been allowed to participate in what must have been a mass curtsey—because I can hardly imagine that in England they are considered important enough to be granted a tête-à-tête with her! And in exchange for all these glories I could offer only second-hand prattle about temperance priests and ranting old demagogues, so I contented myself with saying nothing

only second-hand prattle about temperance priests and
ranting old demagogues, so I contented myself with saying
nothing at all except when I was asked a direct question.
I was, in fact, asked several: the Mead sons-in-law felt
obliged to address me with the usual polite remarks and
queries suitable to a young country miss just out of the
schoolroom. None of them appeared struck with my beauty
or seemed anywhere near the point of clutching me feverishly
to their manly bosoms and making away with me to some
retreat. Had they done so their wives would simply have
drawled "How extraordinary," and continued talking about
Queen Victoria's clothes. Not one idea was expressed by
anyone the whole afternoon but I was not bored at all
because their gossip was so droll and so malicious. At least
the younger ones gossiped—the Mead Mama can talk only
of her massed bedding plants, whatever they may be, and
her husband opens his mouth only to neigh. He and Papa
passed most of the visit in the stables, though he did very
kindly ask for news of Bonheur and my riding lessons.

7 August

Quarrel with Mama. I ventured a little parody of the Meads'
conversation, and was accused of being a savage unable to
appreciate decent society. How unfair, because I did
appreciate it and only wish we had more of it. But it appears
I have been insufferable these last months and have not
shown the least gratitude for anything that has been done
for me. All my misdeeds were paraded before me once
more: I laugh at poor Miss Lockhart behind her back; I
indulge in impolite argument with her brother; I turn my
back upon the Hales, and so on. But failing to find the
Meads entirely above mockery is my greatest sin so far.
Mama is sunk in admiration of these delightful people and
intends to do all in her power to further the acquaintance.
I believe the only shortcoming she admits in the family is

that they had not the good sense to provide a son to fall in love with me. I regret it too! How I want to be in love, how I want to be loved. Maybe now that Eric is here we shall go often to Dublin and I shall begin to meet young people . . .

14 August

Old Mr Hale has kindly provided a house in the village, at a peppercorn rent, to be transformed into a dispensary for the peasants, with Eric as resident doctor. There has not previously been a dispensary at under twenty' miles distance, which caused much unnecessary suffering. Eric's coming is seen as a great blessing. Cormac O'Flaherty informs me that his family and neighbours view the idea with great enthusiasm, while naturally blaming the legendary callousness of foreign landlords for the lack of such a facility in the past. I rather tartly enquired if, in the days of the native nobility he is always talking about, the country was overflowing with hospitals, schools, and an abundance of cheap food for the poor? He laughed and agreed that well no, those were shocking wild times, Miss McLeod, and the high-ups more interested in making war on one another, from what he'd heard. But, he said, there was nothing to complain about because at least the Gaels were free and among themselves, not dominated by strangers. I said sarcastically that I supposed he'd have *enjoyed* being a serf in a chieftain's army, and he replied quite seriously that *he* wouldn't have been a serf because the O'Flahertys were themselves a great family before their land was taken from them! As bad as Mama and the Argylls really, or as bad as the Hales and their Williamite ancestry.

I wish people were not so obsessed by the past: Mr Fielding told us a ridiculous story yesterday about a churchyard some miles away where until recently one could go and gape at the bones of a family called O'Neill, the last of whom died a hundred years ago at least. One skull has red ribbons through its ear-holes to show that in about the year 1400 it supported the flesh of a great prince! I shrieked with laughter when I heard it, and Mr Fielding was upset. He had been upset anyway to discover that the new rector of this place had walled up the precious skeletons, finding it indecent to thus exhibit human bones. I do believe Mr Fielding had intended to bring me there for a pleasant summer excursion! I must ask Cormac what colour of ribbons the O'Flahertys wore in their ears! He will be sure to see the joke. How angry Mama would be if she knew of our conversations, but it *is* pleasant to have someone young and intelligent with whom one can laugh. And he is most respectful. But to such depths am I fallen: friendless and condemned to share laughter with the brother of our cook and scullery-maid! What would Miss Lawson think? And Mamselle? Only two years ago they were praising me as a brilliant pupil: so refined, so clever, so well-read. And here I am now consoling myself with kitchen humour.

24 August

Hales, Hales, and more Hales! Eric has been seeing much of the family because of the dispensary business, and the three daughters and their Mama have given him an invitation to "drop in any time at all, you and your charming sister; we see so little of her. Don't stand on ceremony now; just turn up on the doorstep; sure aren't we neighbours?" They have this curious flat way of speaking which makes everything they say sound cynical and slightly defiant. Like a Scots accent with the life drained out of it. (Perhaps what happens to Scots when they've endured 150 years of this place?) All the Protestant farmers speak like that; native voices are more varied, lilting and rumbling and wheedling all in one phrase! But the Hales. We have been turning up on their doorstep, or they have been turning up on ours.

We have picnicked; we have had long humourless conversations. I have made a great effort to conquer what Mama calls my unsociable nature, but what is really an abhorrence of mediocrity. *I* should have thought it a virtue to despise mediocrity but no, I am told it is a great fault and that if I am to be considered charming I must stop mooning about the field like a peasant gathering flowers and waiting for a sublime being to appear whom I can honour with my acquaintance. I have never seen a peasant gathering flowers but I have learned not to expect logic in Mama's scolding. Or reason. After all, a few months ago I hated the fields and the peasants and everything Irish. I passed my days in sulks and tears and longing for home. Now I am contented and can amuse myself for hours riding about the lanes and talking to people. One would imagine that a fond mother might feel some delight in her daughter's ability to accept so gracefully a life that was forced upon her! But no. So I smile at the Hales whenever I am bid, and make myself pleasant to Mr Fielding, who has begun to make himself far too pleasant to me!

3 October

Papa's racehorse has materialised! We were all—Mama, Eric and I, and even the servants—summoned outside at ten o'clock on this misty moisty morning to see . . . something beautiful, chestnut-brown, swooping and glistening and gliding and flying across the wet grass of the park, rising like a swallow over a low hedge of laurel. This is Heather Bells, four years old, sire Bellringer, dam White Blossom, a million other details of that nature, but I wasn't listening because on this glorious creature's back was a laughing golden-haired cavalier, looking as proud and noble as I thought only cavaliers in books could look. Who on earth could it be, I wondered? Some young absentee squire unexpectedly arrived in our midst? The young Earl of Baudry? An aristocratic officer from some Dublin regiment? And then—from the sublime to the ridiculous! He rode up to where we were all standing in awed admiration, made an impertinent half-mocking bow, was acclaimed and exclaimed over by Papa and Eric and loudly cheered by the servants—and it was only Cormac O'Flaherty! But lifted straight out of the ranks of the peasantry by his manner of riding a horse.

I was furious with disappointment and could hardly bring myself to praise either the animal or the rider's prowess. How extraordinary to have mistaken O'Flaherty for a gentleman. And how extraordinary that I have seen him every day for four months, have talked and joked with him, have even regarded him as my best friend here and have never until today noticed that he is tall and handsome and has beautiful golden-red hair. I who had begun to pride myself upon seeing the natives as human beings!

4 October

Finding it unusually difficult to fall asleep last night, I relit my candle and read my journal over from the beginning. How I have changed! What a stupid child I was a year ago! As for imagining myself to be in love with Alastair Duncan—what folly that was. A silly boy fit for nothing but to play games in the heather while his parents arranged his future!

[There are several pages torn out of the journal at this point.]

(Letter to Emma Watterson. Found among the pages of the diary,—Myrna wrote,—so obviously never sent. Luckily for you!)

Claghan Hall
3 March 1842

Dearest Emma,

I take up my pen in a spirit of intense boredom! Nicholas
Fielding rode over in the rain and stayed to supper, bringing
as usual a great wedge of manuscript for our delight.
When Mama spied him ambling into the yard on his fat
little nag with this solid (how too, too solid!) parcel wrapped
in stout canvas against the weather, she flung herself on
a sofa shrieking with laughter. I cannot, Marianne, she
cried, I cannot bear it! Marry Lockhart if you like, marry
a peasant if you can do no better but do not, I pray, inflict
this dour evangelist upon me as a son-in-law. I was
delighted to reassure her, as you may imagine from my
last letter.

Marry Nicholas Fielding! Even this forsaken barony must
hold better things for me. What a dreadful place it is. But
apparently (well, according to Mr Fielding) it was far far
worse a century ago when our more settled neighbours
arrived. Listen, Emma, to this: "The district was, even in
relatively recent times, almost a wilderness, its inhabitants
living in clusters (or claghans) of houses surrounded by a
pound wherein they drove their cattle at night to protect
them from the robbers who abounded in the nearby hills
and who found shelter and an abundance of hiding-places
in the caves and glens of the mountain." So I suppose we
ought to count our blessings! I would have you know,
cousin, that we are served this kind of information twice
a week over the grilled trout which Cormac O'Flaherty
brings us occasionally, with Mr Mead's compliments, from
a local river. A far more acceptable present, you will
agree, than poor Mr Fielding's dreary manuscript!

This evening my supposed suitor regaled us with "The
Nature of the Soil and the Productions Thereof." You
cannot imagine, dearest Emma, the variety of dry boring

grasses that clever gentleman has contrived to find growing in the self-same meadows where I gather buttercups and daisies and fragrant creamy hawthorn! It appears there are great quantities of Common or Rough-stalked Meadow Grass (*Poa Trivialis*) and, would you believe it, miles and miles of *Iriticum Repens* (couch-grass to you and me, scutch to the local farmers) and one must not, one must never, overlook Sheep Fescue Grass (*Festuca Aminca*)! I spare you the rest—there are hundreds. I would prefer greatly to discourse on themes more entertaining (Heavens, he has infected me with his diction!).

Anything is more entertaining, even Papa's hopes for Heather Bells in the Dromalee Handicap. O'Flaherty who trains and rides him, passes his free time amusing me with tales of high and noble ancestry—it seems his family is descended from the ancient lords of somewhere called Iar-Connacht. (Mr Lockhart, Lord Baudry's agent, says they are all without exception descended in imagination from High Kings and warring giants!). Then there is O'Flaherty's sister Kathleen who cooks for us and whose English, under my tuition, has progressed from Chaucerian to Shakespearian. There is too, Peg Cassidy, much feared by the peasants, who has the evil eye and is reputed to make milk turn sour in its crock with a mere glance. They pay her to keep away from their cabins and in consequence she is very comfortably off indeed!

But the society, Emma! Supper this evening was a typical example: Mama yawning into her lace handkerchief (there is beautiful lace being made by the peasant women over in County Monaghan, not rustic at all; shall I send you some?). My eyes endeavoured to express sweet maidenly interest and the very minimum of encouragement. Mr Fielding droned on, looking up occasionally to flash me an ardently academic glance. Papa as always presided benevolently over us all. Eric has found his own level

and his own rather dreary pious friends (I hope they are
not closer than friends, but more about that in my next!)
so he is rarely here in the evenings. His very best friend,
unfortunately, is the worthy Mr F, who might be tolerable
if everybody did not expect me to marry him. Eric thinks
it would be a wonderful match for me. That is Papa's
opinion too—so much for the great noble's son he
promised me: the only nobles we meet are those mythical
ruined aristocrats, O'Neills, O'Donnells, O'Flahertys! Papa
says Nicholas Fielding is a serious (who doubts it?)
intelligent (hum!) young man of excellent family, with an
assured future. Yes, but *I* do not wish to be part of that
future. Oh if *only* Young Lochinvar would come riding
(or driving, or even walking) out of whichever point on
the compass he chooses! My Mother appears to be on my
side, because Nicholas bores her so, but with dear Mama
who can tell? She would like her only daughter to do
better for herself while seeming to hint, in her more
disillusioned moments, that this particular only daughter
may well end up doing nothing at all! So probably she
too will soon start forcing me on Mr Fielding. I am now
almost nineteen, a veritable old maid, I am not a beauty,
and there are so few young unattached men in the country.
Perhaps even you, Emma, from the heights of successful
marriage, will urge me to accept. Please do not. I had
rather sell myself into slavery as a governess! And indeed
it is not even certain that he is interested in me as a
possible wife. Sometimes I believe that what brings him
here is merely the certainty of finding an interested
audience—or at any rate a polite one—for his *Natural
History of Claghan*. There must be few people who would
listen as assiduously as we do, and of course we listen
only because we are so starved for civilised society. I
cannot, for instance, imagine poor Mr Fielding entertaining
the Hales for hours on end with Couch Crass and *Festuca*

Aminca! Those great lumps would be snorting and giggling and slapping their huge thighs for ridicule! Our Scots neighbours are impossible, Emma. Prosperous yes, and hard-working and pious, but oh dear so totally without fantasy in their lives. And the more elegant landowners either do not want to know us or else are absentee. So many of the neighbouring estates are in the hands of agents, some of whom are illiterate boors and the rest far more snobbish than their masters would be. Lockhart, our ghastly neighbour Lockhart! The peasants are more interesting by far in spite of their disordered imaginations— or perhaps because of them. While Mr Fielding was boring us with his manuscript this evening, a man went by in the avenue singing in Gaelic. I could not understand the words of his song but I assure you it was infinitely more inspiring than Young Nick's Latin grasses! On that frivolous and exotic note I bid you goodnight, dear cousin, and long to have more news of you and of marriage, and of your brilliant exciting life . . .

4 March 1842

Last night, in a fit of boredom, I wrote a most extraordinary letter to Emma! Superficial and mocking and whining; I do not think I shall send it. Why is it so difficult to write sincere letters? Oh, what I have written is true up to a point but there is more. There is much more that I can never write. How, for instance, could I give to someone who has never been here a feeling of this place? The wet hungry desolation of it, and yet the way I have in less than a year come to consider it as home? I wrote of the local society as though I were describing some polite Edinburgh suburb but here all that is totally unimportant. I have changed since I came to Ireland, I have learned to think, and yet I make such efforts to write as though I were still the clever silly schoolgirl of last year. Why did I pretend, in that slighting way, that I understand no Gaelic? "A man went by in the avenue singing in Gaelic." Why could I not have said, "Cormac O'Flaherty strolled home past our windows singing my favourite song about hopeless love, and how dry and meaningless everything else seemed in comparison." That would have been real and important. And if I wrote: "Emma, I am trying to learn the native language," that would be real and important too. Because reality here is a vast body of people (labelled for our convenience "tenants" and "servants") moving through our rooms, across our land, speaking an alien language, locked in an alien world whose key is hidden from us. Reality is my poor effort to find that key.

The educated ones speak English but it is not our English: in their mouths it turns into an ornate and oddly-woven cloak to cover their minds from us. So I learn Irish. My friends—yes, *friends* as Caroline and Emma used to be, as the Hales will never be—my friends the O'Flahertys are teaching me. Even without them I would still have learned it; I cannot bear to be shut out from anything! I notice that my parents and Eric, when the servants speak Gaelic, assume that they are laughing at us or concocting some mischief. I thought so too at first. This is, of course, ridiculous. These people have their own private lives and rarely give us a thought. At least, I do hope that Cormac and his sisters give *me* a thought from time to time. It is easy to forget that they are just like us—they speak an uncouth tongue, worship in an uncouth manner, eat disgusting food and dress for the most part in rags. That is what we think! Perhaps that is why I am ashamed to admit even to Emma that I have made friends among them? But Gaelic is not any more uncouth than French or Italian, and far less so than German. Their food and clothes are poor, yes, but I have been given roasted potatoes with salt and buttermilk many times when

I've visited their houses, and nothing could be more delicious! As for their religion, I'm convinced nothing *they* do could sound quite as loathsome as Florence Hale talking about washing her great fat self in the blood of the Redeemer!

I ought too to tell Emma about the landscape, which is so important. This long humped mountain rising to one side of us, cultivated to the very summit—poor stunted potato plants growing out of the very rock almost. How do they work this land? One watches them labouring away up there and they look exactly like flies crawling up a picture; climbers obliged endlessly to dig and sow and reap even as they climb! And after all this crushing labour they must live on a diet of potatoes, all else being sold to pay the rent. It seems so illogical, so meaningless to slave a lifetime just to pay rent on a patch of near-barren land; one could think them mad to waste themselves so on futility. Yet to stop would be certain death. And we, watching, accept the rents they pay and allow them to live like that! Perhaps it is their own fault. If they wept and cursed and threatened, and all descended on us together in a raging mass, we would surely do something? But they accept it all with such cravenness. A few of them form secret societies and commit scattered acts of violence (the violence that so frightened us last year!) but the majority simply accept all that is done to them. They laugh and joke and sing. They sing! And they dance. Weddings, baptisms, feast-days, they all gather in barns and they dance their extraordinary wild dances. All night long the men drink themselves into senselessness with raw home-made spirits. Then magically next morning one sees them toiling up the mountain again, greeting one another, laughing, calling a blessing: "*Beannacht Dé ar an obair!*" The men shout it from field to field; women call it to each other feeding potato-skins to lean pigs outside their cabins; young servant girls shout it to their friends spinning flax in doorways. If I had to live like that I should certainly not be inclined to believe that there was a kind God blessing me! And if these poor people were not so craven they would wonder why God takes so much more interest in the Hales and the Watsons and McLeods than he does in them.

He has granted good land and plenty of it to the English and Scots settlers. Their great kitchens have sides of bacon hanging from the rafters; their ample wives in white aprons work in cool dairies embellishing pats of yellow butter with pretty emblems, skimming rich clots of cream off teeming milk-crocks. What do the Irish make of this difference? And what do they make of us in our big house? Can they seriously imagine that the papist God is a merciful God who cares what becomes of them? Or are their prayers more in the nature of crossed fingers, magic spells, invocations muttered in the presence of evil to turn away a curse? How *do* their minds work? Cormac, being a man, is inclined to scoff at what he calls "this women's nonsense" but even he believes far more than he pretends to! And I cannot ask Kathleen or Fionnuala about their beliefs; they are so sensitive and would be sure to take offence. When I've mastered their language shall I be any nearer to knowing their souls? Will they trust me then?

How philosophical I am becoming. Or how eccentric! Is that what is happening to me? Am I turning into an oddity, like those crazy Englishwomen who tour the Continent in frightful clothes rescuing mules and things? It is not becoming to a young lady in my position to have such warm feelings towards the peasants! I ought to consider them quaint and picturesque, and wander about with a sketchbook making little watercolours of their thatched cottages. I ought to be genteelly frightened of them. I was, for the first few months. What changed me? Even Nicholas Fielding, though he tries to save their souls, views them with detachment as though they were just another inanimate feature of the landscape.

He makes dry notes about their odd customs and beliefs
and jollifications. He learned Gaelic not from the people as
I do, but in a college correctly from books of grammar. He
learned it as he would have learned Hindoostanee! And
why not Hindoostanee? Emma would say that the poor
Hindoos are as entitled to respect as we are. What *would*
Emma make of Ireland? We quarrelled all the time and yet
I miss her now more than anyone in Edinburgh. With
Emma I could have talked of these things. But when we met
every day I used to laugh at her outlandish opinions.
Chimney-sweeps and Negro slaves and fallen women in
workhouses! And maybe Emma, a rich married lady after
all, would laugh at me now. What it comes down to is that
the only person I can talk seriously with is Cormac O'Flaherty.
A peasant. Rather, a small farmer—they hate the word
peasant!—educated, yes, far better educated than I am, but
almost a servant. Paid to train Papa's horse. Paid to
accompany me on my outings. Yes, but then these people
are servants only because their armies were not as strong
as ours. One can't judge them by that. Cormac might have
been anything, given the opportunity. I am so mixed up in
my mind. I must write a truer letter to Emma. Perhaps she
will come in the summer and I shall begin to see all these
things in proportion again.

12 March

Outside it rains, it rains, it rains! The winter has been
unbearable. I can go out but seldom; that is why I feel so
dull. Since the New Year nothing but high wind and sleet,
and now this driving rain. Several of the flimsier cabins on
the side of the mountain were blown down and Papa has
allowed the occupants to sleep in a disused outhouse until
the weather allows them to be rebuilt. They are down there
now at the far end of the yard, between the cows and the
horses, and they are far more comfortable there than they

were when they had houses. No wonder if one becomes a little melancholy here! I wrote to Emma again today. A *real* letter.

17 March

It is the feast of St Patrick and McGregor is complaining bitterly that the younger servants are doing the smallest amount of work possible. Mama is furious because she hates to be bothered with domestic problems. There is a dance in Hales' barn and the O'Flahertys are all going. I gave Kathleen and Fionnuala (for she is old enough now to dance!) some material for dresses. I would dearly have loved to slip down there and watch but Kathleen was horrified when I mentioned it—she said it would be taken very amiss by the people, as though I had come to mock. I was very much wounded but, on reflection, it is understandable: most people of our class *do* mock. Still it is hard that I should be so excluded, who feel such sympathy for their way of living. And I do want to see whom Cormac dances with, so that I can tease him!

19 March

I surprised a conversation between Mama and Papa today: they are hoping that Eric will marry Elizabeth Hale! I have suspected for a long time that he had a fancy for one of the Hales. He spends evening after evening in their house and they have been here to dine several times and to spend boring boring evenings, Florence playing the piano and Elizabeth singing Irish and Scottish ballads. "My Love Is Like a Red Red Rose" is Eric's favourite. I wish mine were. *My* love is like. Like what? A mountain daisy? What nonsense! I am *not* in love. I shall not fall into the trap of imagining *that* again. But that Eric should consider marrying this dull girl. *I* could not marry anyone so conventional. How can a brother and sister be so different, so out of sympathy with each other, when they ought truly to be friends? I think it is the fault of Mama and Papa—they made such a favourite of Eric from the beginning and I was nothing. How could I help but dislike him? He was their handsome bright little son, so certain to succeed, so sure to fulfil their ambitions! So how can they welcome the idea of his marriage to one of the Hale girls? Would they not have wanted him to do better? And yet I do not know why I am surprised. The Hales are very rich and perfectly respectable: an ancestor fought at the Boyne—Ireland's answer to Norman blood. Old Mr Hale is the image of Grandfather McLeod, a strict and worthy Presbyterian with the same stingy way of talk. Eric is rather like that too. I would not care, let him marry whom he likes—only Elizabeth will be my sister-in-law and patronise me, and I shall have to talk about patchwork and jam and the Redeemer to her two great heifers of sisters, as Cormac calls them. And in a year or two I shall be a spinster aunt if I don't marry Nicholas Fielding first and I'd rather die than marry Nicholas Fielding and anyway he hasn't asked me. Nobody asks me. Nobody ever will.

30 March

It has stopped raining *at last!* The clouds advance in a growling mass as if they were determined to stop a wet-looking disc of moon from slipping out between them, but I think the moon is going to win! Tomorrow I may be able to walk as far as the turnpike, find new buds on the hawthorn, a lace of white blossom on the sloe bushes. Mama may allow me to ride over as far as Meads', with Cormac for chaperon. How delightful that will be; what a lot we shall have to talk about. It is weeks since we have had a talk; we meet of course in the stable yard when I go to feed sugar-lumps to Bonheur but it is not at all the same thing. I can see the stable yard from my window but he is not there. He went home a long time ago to that neat warm cottage and that gentle smiling mother who never scolds, who is so calm and tranquil and unworldly. How different from Mama! Where does he spend his free time? With whom? Is there a red red rose in his life as there is in Eric's? I expect he creates havoc in the hearts of the village-girls!

Down there in the yard the homeless people huddle for warmth in the outhouse under piles of straw. They have no fire; it is forbidden because of the danger of dry fodder catching alight. No doubt they miss their fragrant smoky turf, their skillets of thin gruel, their potatoes baked in the ashes. They are fed now on cold scraps distributed at the kitchen door. If the weather stays clear it will soon be possible to rebuild their shacks. Meantime they have no cause to complain: they are very lucky to have shelter of any kind. Thousands have not. Tens of thousands have not. Nine million people on this tiny island, the majority of them on the edge of starvation. It is almost unbearable to picture, all these people endlessly walking the roads and fields of Ireland, sleeping under hedges with never a chance to change their wet clothes. And they are not natural nomads. Most of them have had a home, a fireside, a roof to sleep under. They worked their little fields, grew potatoes and grain, fattened a pig to help with the rent—until one day came catastrophe. Failure of crops, loss of an animal. Or, quite simply, a landlord's whim. The whim of people like us. My parents have the terrifying power to smash a whole community of contented busy people as they would smash an anthill. The law allows them to do it. Encourages them to do it. Luckily my parents are kind and would never dream of doing anything so cruel. But if they did . . . Nice decent Christian people would understand and support Papa if, tomorrow morning, he set fire to the thatch of twenty cottages and sent their occupants out on the roads to beg for the rest of their lives! If they refused to go, he could call on Her Majesty's army to drive them out by force.

Logically indeed he ought to throw all these wasteful little
potato patches into one huge farm of wheat and cattle, keep
a small force of labourers and turn the rest off. Grain and
beef fetch excellent prices now on the English market. We
would become very rich if Papa did that and everyone
would applaud his good sense. What an odd country it is!

2 April

Such a lovely blowy spring day. Such a wonderful day! I
rode, not as far as the Meads' but only as far as the cottage
of Thomas O'Flaherty, the famous cabinet-maker and
Cormac's uncle. I set out for Meads'; Mama never objects to
my going there and my only fear was that Eric might want
to come too. Luckily he was too occupied, and I was sent
off with Mama's blessing in the care of Cormac—that loyal
worthy peasant, as Papa thinks of him! We had missed each
other's company this last while and had a great deal to talk
about. Half-way to Meads' it came on to rain suddenly and,
his uncle's cottage being nearby, we stepped in to shelter.
How neat it was, and so warm and full of books and pretty
things. Mr O'Flaherty is rather an awe-inspiring man, very
dry and solemn, but he made himself most pleasant to me.
We drank tea and talked of literature. He has read Sir Walter
Scott but was sadly ignorant of Jane Austen. I promised to
lend him some books. I think, though, that his manner was
over-respectful: he seemed too conscious that he was
conversing with "gentry." I have become accustomed to
Cormac's ease of address—*he* respects me because I am me
and not because I am Papa's daughter—and his uncle's
manner jarred on me. I hate it when people behave cravenly
towards us; we are no better than they!

4 April

Eric came home from the dispensary at noon brimming
over with village gossip—a young girl, Maire Brennan, was
abducted from her home last night by a crowd of young

men and her parents are loudly bewailing their misfortune.
We were all horrified, and talked of nothing else all afternoon.
Papa was in the act of putting together a party of able-
bodied tenants to search for the girl when Mr Lockhart
arrived, roaring with laughter at our foolishness. It seems
this is a quaint local custom: when a girl's parents are
opposed to her marriage or are making difficulties about the
dowry, she allows herself to be "stolen" from her home and
hidden away in the cottage of one of the man's friends. The
parents, fearful for the loss of her reputation, are obliged to
agree to the young couple's demands and, says Mr Lockhart,
in a week or two the whole village, outraged parents and
all, will be boisterously celebrating a wedding and deafening
us as usual with their jollity. Just another example of their
disordered imaginations, he says, for even the supposed
loss of reputation is purely fictitious, it being an open secret
that the girl is heavily guarded by a pack of her bridegroom's
female relations, for nobody in the world is more chaste
than these Irish peasants. The whole thing is simply a
device that allows a young girl to marry "beneath her"
without letting her family lose too much countenance. Their
minds really *are* far more subtle and complex than ours!

12 April

Heather Bells and Cormac won the Dromalee Handicap
Steeplechase! I watched from a place which looked down
on the last fence and the finishing line, and how thrilling it
was when I saw that there was no one else for a good half-
mile behind Cormac. I felt like a lady at a medieval
tournament watching her knight ride to victory. A knight
covered in mud, it must be said, from three months' rain on
the racecourse! Immediately, of course, Cormac became the
property of Papa and Mr Mead and all the knowledgeable
gentlemen who quite lose their senses when it is a question
of horse-racing.

The celebration afterwards was as boisterous as any village feast. Mr Fielding was thoroughly disapproving, especially when he saw that Cormac was brought into the drawing-room and given wine to drink. "Why don't they bring the horse too?" he was heard to mutter and Papa, flushed with victory and spirits, insisted that yes, yes, Heather Bells must be brought in to share the feasting! Mama soon put a stop to that idea and Mr Fielding left shortly, no doubt seeing no possibility of doing the Lord's work in that gathering. Mama and I and Eric and the Hales then went to the Race Ball over at Meads', which was very glittering, only I kept thinking of Cormac who naturally was not invited, but who stayed in Claghan Hall drinking and celebrating with Papa and a crowd of loud horsy men. Mr Mead would have liked to join them but was prevented by his position as host. Cormac did not look out of place at all in our drawing-room, which pleased me greatly. I had feared that he might be timid or awkward. Timid he surely was not when, on the way back to our house after the race, he was wildly embraced by a whole crowd of young village-women—one of whom, a tall yellow-haired young girl in an unfortunate bright green frock, flung her arms round his neck and kissed him loudly on the cheek! But then, he was well known as a jockey in Mr Henry Watterson's time, and must be accustomed to such adulation.

(Letter from Emma Watterson)

10 April 1842, London

Dearest Marianne,

How wonderful to hear from you again! But what a strange letter: is it Ireland that makes you so philosophical? It sounds an appalling place indeed—are you by any chance suffering from Melancholy? Because I cannot imagine the bright little cousin I knew getting into such a state over the woes of her servants! I am glad: I think it a good thing that you should be beginning to question the established order, and that you are making "friends" among the simple people. I have always felt that the uneducated can teach us a great deal that we, in our unwise sophistication, have chosen to ignore, and it is probable that a people so materially poor as your tenants have been able to preserve a simplicity of ideals, a spontaneity of manner that I for one would give much to attain! These O'Flahertys sound a very worthy sort of family and can only do you good.

But, Marianne dear, whence comes your information about the *particular* state of misery of the Irish labouring classes? I, who have travelled, can assure you that the condition is universal! You talk about the rosy-cheeked English cottagers as described in Jane Austen's novels. This is great nonsense—I am sure the lady novelists you read know nothing whatever about the way the poor live, and in fact Miss Austen rarely does mention them. You would do far better to read William Cobbett on the English peasants. I am about to parcel up a copy of *Rural Rides* to send to you, but in the meantime peruse and reflect on this citation from it:

"For my own part, I really am ashamed to ride a fat horse, to have a full belly, and to have a clean shirt upon my back, while I look at these wretched countrymen of mine; while I actually see them reeling with weakness; when I see their poor faces present me nothing but skin and bone, while they are toiling to get the wheat and the meat ready to be carried away to be devoured by the tax-eaters . . . We are reversing the maxim of the Scriptures: our laws almost say that those who work shall not eat, and that those that do not work shall have the food. I repeat that the baseness of the English landowners surpasses that of any other man that ever lived in the world . . . "

And of course Mr Cobbett was mistaken . . . the English

landowners are no baser than others. We have been staying in France with the Earl of Baudry, who is a friend of Jeremy's people and whose estate, I believe, marches alongside your papa's. He married, as you know, a French lady and owns a very pretty seventeenth-century château and estate. If only I could *show* you the abject misery in which his tenants live, because words are inadequate to convey even one-quarter of it. They own nothing, they belong body and soul to their landlord and are at the mercy of the brute of a *régisseur* who administers the estate. They live on coarse black bread and water which, believe me, is far less nourishing than potatoes! They are subject to the most incredible punishments—floggings, drenchings with icy water—for the most minor offences. We were horrified, Jeremy and I, and felt it our Christian duty to go to Lord Baudry and protest frankly about all this. He *laughed*: said that kind of thing was quite acceptable in France and that as long as he got his rents on time his agent was welcome to use what means he wishes! I imagine his Irish tenants are far better off; even if you do find Mr Lockhart a disagreeable neighbour, he does at least sound civilised. On travelling further in France we found that this misery is not at all exceptional—and when one thinks of the fuss that's made about their famous Revolution! So, though the poverty of the Irish must have come as a shock to you after your sheltered upbringing, don't make the mistake of thinking that English or European peasants are any happier. It has little to do with centuries of foreign oppression, with colonisation, or with religious persecution, but is simply a result of the pernicious class system that prevails in every so-called civilised country!

To descend from my pulpit—we are of course back in London now and have made *such* interesting friends! Could you not persuade your mama to let you come to us on a visit? All the people we know are clever or creative or witty, or quite simply want to change the world! You know *The Pickwick Papers*, of course? Well, *we* know the author! Imagine! He is a great radical and is absolutely passionate about the condition of poor slum children and workhouse people, but he is not at all boring about it. The hair-raising stories he tells! I should think his London slum children would be only too delighted to live as the Irish do—at least *they* have fresh air and beautiful surroundings, which must make it all rather more bearable.

You ask my opinion of this evangelist. Good heavens, Marianne, do not attempt to marry him! He sounds a great bore. One ought never to listen to one's parents in matters of this kind, and as for Eric—pay no attention to him! You know better than I what he is like. I expect he has already frightened half the Irish into church with his stern bedside manner. Let him stick to that and you choose for yourself whom you shall marry. You say there are no young men; I find this hard to believe. So many garrison towns in Ireland, surely teeming with personable and gallant young officers! Have not you met any yet? What *is* my aunt McLeod thinking of? And what are you thinking of, Marianne, that you cannot open your eyes to all the possibilities there must be in a country like Ireland? I hope you are not so plunged into your Gaelic studies and new-found revolutionary ideas that you are forgetting how to enjoy life!

Do write again soon and let me have a more cheerful account of your entertainments—because I am sure you do have many. I send great hugs to your parents and much love to you.

Your affectionate
Emma.

18 April
Oh I am so happy. This is a beautiful springtime, wild flowers and new leaves and rainbows. Naturally rainbows, because Ireland cannot resist raining whenever it gets a

chance. But the sun shines too.

I had the silliest letter from Emma today, advising me to look about for an English soldier to marry! At least, I think that is what she was advising. Perhaps she was only joking, because the rest of the letter is so exactly like the Emma I remember.

30 April

So little time to write in my journal now, and so little time to read books. How empty my life was last year when I filled so many pages with my complaints. Now I can put up very well with whole evenings of Hales and Fieldings and Lockharts, because the afternoons are so magical. How I bless the superstition of the people, because nobody except us ever dares to approach the fairy copse with its little humped trees and its bank of soft moss and its drifts of spring flowers. If the people had not such fear of fairies it would have been cut down years ago and potatoes grown there, but I think even starvation would not force anyone to touch it or even enter it. "We're sinning against everyone," Cormac said today, "God and the fairies and everyone. We'll be destroyed at the Last Judgement, girl!" And I believe he was only *half* joking; I think he really feels uneasy at times! *I'm* sinning against Mama's respectability and that can be destructive enough!

28 May

Eric is engaged to marry Eliza Hale! Had this happened even six months ago I should have been most annoyed. Now I know that I shall never be obliged to live under the same roof as her, so it makes no difference to me. They are to be married in August, on her twenty-second birthday. Emma and Jeremy will certainly come over for the wedding and that will suit my plans perfectly. I *know* I can count on their support, they are so completely against this wicked class system that keeps people apart. But August—what a time it is to wait!

15 June

Oh the funniest thing! I thought I should die laughing! Emma wrote to congratulate Eric on his engagement, and what a row it caused—our silly cousin, on being told that Eric was to marry an Irish girl, assumed that she must be Roman Catholic! Eric danced about positively stuttering with outrage: "What does she th-think I am? Does she really think I would lower myself to a p-peasant? It's a deliberate insult!" I attempted to hint that Emma, having recently travelled in France and Italy, might possibly consider Roman Catholics to be as marriageable as anyone, but he would have none of it: "I tell you it is an insult. It is exactly like her. Accusing me of marrying an Irish papist, it's like, like—like accusing me of marrying a Red Indian savage! She said it deliberately to insult me!"

His Elizabeth joined him in the highest dudgeon, her accent going flatter and more defiant than ever with rage:" "You just tahl your cousin, Arrak, that my ancestors got this land here from King Wulliam of Orange himself in person, and that we're as staunch Protestants as anyone in Ulster. You make sure and tahl her, Arrak!"

Really, they are just like twins. It is as though Mama's little god had created himself a bride in his own image. I foresee that I shall have weeks of good sport out of their combined pomposity. I need something to amuse me because I am becoming more and more nervous. C thinks there will be no difficulty at all when my parents are faced with the actual fact. He counts on Papa's friendship for him. Yes, but it is not Papa who counts, but Mama. I know her so well! She can be most arrogant and spiteful, and she can persuade Papa to do anything. Still, what real harm can they do us when we are together? And I *shall* have Emma to take my part, after all.

[The journal ends at this point.]

CHAPTER SIX

MAUREEN

"And what are you writing now?" asked Madame de Lapire-Vacherie, putting down her teacup and smiling a social smile.

"Oh, it's supposed to be a novel about Ireland," Maureen smiled back at her, "only I'm not sure I—"

"Ah, folklore. How sweet!"

Folklore. The French obsession with folklore. Their eternal need to convert other people's history into pretty folklore! Madame de Lapire-Vacherie once told Maureen that during the Long Kesh hunger-strike she'd paid well over a thousand francs for an authentic Aran sweater and worn it courageously, indoors and out, through those ten futile agonising deaths. "A gesture, Madame Watts, *vous comprenez*, one must do something." And that a few years earlier she'd dressed exclusively in alpaca ponchos and long embroidered skirts to express her solidarity with the South American *desaparecidos*. You couldn't really dislike her, Maureen thought, when she was sitting here in front of you, delightfully congealed in naïvety, sipping passion-fruit tea with all the discreet charm of the bourgeoisie, but you could and did have wild fantasies of making her live for a week in a sweet Bogside tenement, in a Claghan council house among all those simple spiritual people, in a shack up the Andes with picturesque guerrillas, armed to the teeth with authentic scalping-knives, creeping stealthily in her direction . . .

Madame de Lapire-Vacherie, to Maureen's initial disappointment and secret relief, was not a true aristocrat. Shortly after the Liberation, the pretty, convent-educated daughter of a rural *notaire*, she'd gone up to Paris, hung around for a while on the fringes of Sartre, Juliette Greco and the cellars of St Germain, before returning home with enough acquired sophistication to marry the middle-aged businessman who'd recently bought not only Lord Baudry's château but also the title of a defunct old family. Maureen gathered that neither he nor his chic young wife had ever been received by the neighbouring squires (any more than she and Trevor were being received, any more than the McLeods had been received), and that Madame had consequently taken to politics, as others take to religion and lovers, for consolation.

When Monsieur died, in April '68, Madame, childless and still beautiful, returned to Paris in excellent time to take part in the student revolt. Embarrassed by the ownership of a Breton château at such a time (and hard put to pay for its upkeep), she put it on the market. There it stayed for fifteen years until Maureen came upon the, by then rather desperate, agent's blurb in *The Irish Times* (. . . interesting seventeenth-century château . . . notorious Victorian rake and absentee landlord . . . eight acres of parkland . . . surprisingly reasonable . . .) and in a spirit of amused nostalgia talked Trevor into making an offer. With part of the seventy thousand pounds they paid for the place, Madame bought a row of labourers' cottages with some hectares of land where she reared goats and gave hospitality to political refugees from the more physically attractive ethnic groups, while Maureen from

Boharnamuc and her ex-Stepney husband rather self-consciously moved into Lord Baudry's château. A minor demographic upheaval, Trevor joked uneasily.

Madame was delighted to have a writer for a neighbour, though she was quick to point out that she herself, naturally, did not read romantic novels. She did not appear to read anything, except the more sentimentally left-wing magazines. From her conversation Maureen suspected that the world outside *l'Hexagone* was perceived by Madame de Lapire-Vacherie as an amorphous blob of suffering poor, ready when her eye lit upon it to transform itself into a collection of national dolls in fancy dress busy committing ethnic clichés for her delight. Thus, forty million Poles in traditional costume crossed themselves piously over a meagre ration of ham sausage and chewed endlessly on the glorious future of *Solidarnosc.* Thus, ponchoed Indians, worn out hurling themselves for days on end through weird Aztec dances, drank themselves footless on tequila and carried on cursing Cortez. And thus, Maureen feared, persecuted Ulster Catholics in moss-stitch and cable sat round the turf-fire of an evening keening away *ad nauseam* about the unending tragedy of their ancient race, breaking off only to sing a symbol-rich ballad or dance a wild impromptu jig of protest. Between that and Trevor's Paddy-jokes I'm well away, she thought, pondering the possible absurdity of trying to write a book about a place she'd cleared out of the first chance she got and hadn't set foot in for over twenty years. It would be all too easy to fall into folklore, let herself be waylaid by a simplistic article in the *Nouvel Observateur* or by an idiotically-remembered quotation from Peter Maguire's book: "Holy mother a God come quick, Cormac, the praitas is busy rottin' on their stalks!"

I'll have to keep in mind, she thought, that I'm writing for modern readers who most definitely do not want the stage-Irishry of tyrannical priests and dead men in bogholes. Yes, but if I'm going to be honest, she thought? *Could* you leave out the folklore and still be honest? The recent Irish fiction Maureen read might be about cool Trinity graduates discussing Chekhov over a feed of escargots with lean liberated blondes who knew all about birth-control, but the parish priest, the Pope and the Provos were still the stuff of her mother's weekly letter. Those lean liberated blondes did after all share an Ireland with frightened teenagers shamefully obliged to give birth at the back of a ditch in the snow, an Ireland where new-born babies were dumped into bogholes on top of the corpses of those martyred millions who died long ago precisely to keep their land holy and pure and sinless. The country of John McGahern's poised heroines certainly, the elite dinner-party world of Terence de Vere White, of John Broderick, of Julia O'Faolain, the country of Grafton Street chic, of drugs in Ballymun, of U2, of centrally-heated bungalows, video rentals in every village street—but also the country of Bobby Sands starving to death naked in a prison cell whose walls were smeared with the excrement of eight centuries' hate, the country of that poor girl shoving her unwanted child in a plastic bag, of beaten wives prescribed Valium instead of divorce, Librium instead of the Pill: *could* you, even in this day and age, ignore the folklore, Maureen wondered, while she poured out more tea, cut more cake, and watched Madame de Lapire-Vacherie devour amazing quantities of shortbread.

"The poor old thing was actually *hungry!*" she told Trevor that evening. "Do you think she's got through our seventy thousand quid already?"

"Probably financing half the world's terrorists, if I know the old bag," Trevor said gloomily. He lived in constant mild fear of being burgled or kidnapped by a gang of the depressed-looking foreigners they saw half-heartedly hoeing or herding goats in Madame's fields, and to Maureen's disapproval had recently applied for a permit to keep a revolver in the house, to defend himself if necessary. "It's *not* eccentric," he told her. "They all do it here. It's the big French thing, having a revolver permit. No fool, your froggie!")

I've escaped, Maureen thought, but wasn't I shaped by the folklore like all the rest? All those stories of a lovely Scots lady, those songs about Bold Cormac O'Flaherty and bold this and bold that, we all believed them. Maguire's book, and a hundred like it, was sold inside every chapel door in Ireland along with the lives of the saints: what's that, only folklore? With all the goodwill in the world, and in spite of the old tales, Maureen had never found it totally credible that any of the people she knew in Claghan should be connected with a beautiful aristocrat who sacrificed wealth and titles to follow a dashing rebel. It was, she recognised now, only too believable that both Catholic Kathleen and Protestant Eric should be descended from a very ordinary shopkeeping family who'd blundered innocently into Irish history. Kathleen, from whining romantic Marianne McLeod. And nice dull Eric, from the smug do-gooding brother. Nowhere, though, could she find any foretaste of Sarah, Kathleen's illegitimate daughter, who was Maureen and Trevor's godchild and became increasingly, as she changed from pretty spoilt child to lumpish adolescent to sullen discontented adult, their *bête noire*. The McLeod/O'Flaherty anecdote was over: a hundred and fifty years had watered down the families into banality. But then, banal they had always been. Ordinary people. No beautiful aristos. A fat little heiress with a red face!

Except that the Great Famine touched Marianne and destroyed her, whether she was great lady or shopkeeper's daughter. That was real. It touched Maureen's grandmother too and even, in a way, Maureen's own father—still alive in Boharnamuc—who had never *seen* his elder sisters, gone to America at thirteen or fourteen, before he was born, to send back dollars for Lord Baudry's rent.

A tragedy so complete and so far-reaching could not surely be regarded as folklore, Maureen was thinking while she smiled goodbye at Madame de Lapire-Vacherie. We did suffer, that's true enough. We were forced to live on potatoes, and they failed, and a good many of us died. It took generations for us to recover from it. Maybe we've never recovered. Maybe it explains Bobby Sands and the rest, explains our neuroses, our shame of birth, our easy acceptance of death? That's why I have to keep apologising for being objective. Martin McCormack thought it was disloyal of me to want to be objective. Given, he said, the continuing circumstances. Anyone in Claghan would say the same. Because we *did* suffer and that does, surely, set us apart. Justify us. Does it?

Could it?

CHAPTER SEVEN

MAUREEN AND KATHLEEN

Gardener's Chronicle and Horticultural Gazette

23 August 1845

A fearful malady has broken out among the potato crop. On all sides we hear of the destruction. In Belgium the fields are said to be completely desolated. There is hardly a sound sample in Covent Garden market . . .

13 September 1845

We stop the press with very great regret to announce that the potato murrain has unequivocally declared itself in Ireland. The crops about Dublin are suddenly perishing . . . Where will Ireland be in the event of a universal potato rot?

And where was Ireland? Where was Claghan? Where was that old story in Maureen's own history?

Well, she knew where it was, say, a hundred years later. Remembered, for example, where it was in the summer of

1957, when she was Marianne's age. Remembered where the famine was. Where Cormac and Marianne were. They were nowhere. They were nothing. A grey elderly intrusion into her golden daydreams. She remembered herself sitting at O'Flahertys' kitchen table, listening to records. Listening to Mario Lanza, her heart-throb, singing the "Serenade" from *The Student Prince.* Could this beauty last for ever, Lanza was singing, I would ask for nothing new. I would drift along forever, he sang, lost in a dream of you.

Yes, but lost, she was thinking. How could you be lost in O'Flahertys' kitchen with its smells of turf-smoke and cabbage and old women's liniment? Lost in a dream is it, with Kathleen sulking, with the harem of old grannies and aunties muttering away in the upper room, the Rosary or Claghan scandal who could tell? A dream—of who? Of you, my faceless future lover, my bridegroom who will bring me to a house where all's accustomed, ceremonious, and thank *you* Miss McGowan at the convent, out of your ignorant schoolteacher narrowness you at least gave me those few perfect lines. Yes but dream, she was thinking, dream with Patrick O'Flaherty sermonising and me, as a guest, bound by courtesy. Bound by quiet decent Murphy courtesy to listen: "Here now, Mary Brigid, would you take a wee look at this book, you that's supposed to have all the Murphy brains. You'd be fitter to appreciate it than this big heifer of a one that's."

Yes, yes, we *know*, she was thinking, we all know you came down in the world, Patrick. We all know your birthright was stolen by Cromwell or John Joe McCormack or some crooked solicitor. We all know that if the Wild Geese hadn't flown you'd be entertaining me with lavish wealth in Claghan Hall, but for once just for once would you let me pay a visit to your daughter without deafening me with your holy martyred ancestors? I come into Quarry Street, I walk the four flaming miles of an August Saturday for no other reason than to listen to records with Kathleen, I'm a *teenager,* did you never hear

116

tell of a teenager, Patrick, a girl my age doesn't want to hear an old beardy man telling her some daft yarn about rotten potatoes and emigrant ships and murder. Overhead the moon is beaming, Patrick, bright as blossom on the bough, and my head is full of caviare and champagne, O'Flaherty, and who *cares* if the spuds all rotted away back in old God's time? It was a hundred years ago, Patrick, so would you for Jesus' sake shut up, she was thinking, and let me listen to the serenade from *The Student Prince* and swoon and swoon and imagine I'm Ann Blythe and glamorous and rich and lovely and being clasped in the muscular arms of.

"A fat Italian opera singer!" Kathleen jeered. "He's such a tub of lard they couldn't even use him in the picture, had to dub his voice for Edmund Purdom's songs. Now there's a heart-throb and you're talking! Here, brainbox, would you take this friggin' history book before he pollutes us and for once in your life would you quit serenading yourself."

Kathleen was sulking, because Kathleen couldn't stand Mario Lanza, romance embarrassed the poor jeering cow. Kathleen was dying to listen to Bill Haley and his Comets and so Maureen, hating her but bound by courtesy, carefully lifted the precious disc off the turntable and balanced it on the span of her hand to avoid thumb-prints, and preciously slid it back inside the photoed sleeve: the treacle eyes, the lovely sexy mouth, the Brylcreemed waves . . .

"Looks a bit like Bogart, doesn't he? Only all bloated and *old*," Kathleen said. "Bogart's worse than old," Maureen retorted. "He's dead." Which wasn't much of a comeback, she knew, but it made Kathleen giggle and quit sulking. Poor Kathleen, she was thinking, typical big convent girl bursting with jeers and vulgarity, but kind and clever and even, I bet you, as the magazines say, "vulnerable" underneath.

Until she was fifteen Maureen had spent much of her time inventing sharper and sharper defences against Kathleen's jeers. She'd gone in terror of her shiny town claws. The day one of her defences tore Kathleen to shreds she realised with amazement that, Boharnamuc or not, *she* was the cleverer and the stronger and the better informed. Kathleen had realised it too and they became friends. Not great friends—but Maureen found her useful—a house to visit in the town, an alibi should she ever find the dream lover she'd been on the look-out for ever since she grew out of her grotesque childhood ugliness, and in the meantime a place to play her records.

That was the summer she managed to persuade her parents to let her leave the hateful convent and take a secretarial course at Claghan Tech. Kathleen's father had reacted violently to the suggestion that his daughter should do likewise. Maureen liked the phrase "reacted violently"; it drew a veil of decorum (she liked that phrase too) over whatever it was that Patrick O'Flaherty had actually done to Kathleen. Maureen's own parents were kind practical people and open to reason: she felt uneasy in the presence of the O'Flahertys who, though they treated *her* with perfect courtesy, seemed always to be hovering on the edge of, or recovering from the effects of, some embarrassing hysterical outburst that had to do (she couldn't think why) with the misty buzzing of flies over dunghills and Sacred Heart lamps stinking of smoky paraffin and bodies piled upon bodies in muddy bogholes—you're daft you're daft, she told herself, you're away in the head, Maureen Murphy, you'll end up in Armagh asylum imagining things so you will. But they were strange. A band of oul' madheads, her father always called them.

That Saturday: "Here now, Mary Brigid," old Pakky O'Flaherty said, "would you take a look at this if you want to learn all about the suffering and tribulations your own poor native land was forced to undergo by them huers of English. Wait now wait now girl till I find you a good bit. Here I have it—here listen now to this!" He opened the book somewhere in the middle and read: 'Shiploads of the best grain and beef were daily sailing out of Irish ports under armed guard'—armed

118

guard mind you, aw-haw the buggers—'*en route* to feed an England already teeming with wealth and plenty. Not a bit of wonder then that the young Cormac, watching his neighbours dying in agony under every roadside hedge . . . '"

"Oh Pop, give over and let her read it herself, would you!" (Kathleen always addressed them as Mom and Pop, and expressed fashionable contempt for them in public in an American accent, though it was widely known that in private they left welts on her for the slightest thing.)

Maureen, always slightly awestruck by old O'Flaherty's beard and dead fanatic eyes, sat meekly down at the blue oilcloth and tried to absorb Peadar MacEighire's forgotten hero . . . On the slopes of one of Erin's legend-rich mountains on a fine May morning of the last century, a clean-limbed bright-eyed young gossoon frolicked merrily amidst the (Jesus Christ such awful shite!). It all slid in yawningly and got lost among the pop songs and scraps of Yeats and Kavanagh and overhead the moon was beaming white as blossom on the bough . . . "It was Master Maguire out at the bridge wrote that book. A shocking great command of the language. He does have stories in *Ireland's Own*. Now doesn't that raise your mind a bit above your film stars and your picture love-romances?"

My film stars and my picture romances! Tread softly, you old blaggard, because you tread on my dreams. But she read it from cover to cover as she was bid . . . Cormac's innocent young eyes flashing dangerously as they lit on a pack of armed men tramping gleefully up the narrow mountain-pass towards the humble thatched cabin of poor Widow Hanlon, lowly descendant of ancient warrior chiefs . . . Kathleen behind her was gleefully hogging the gramophone now, gonna rock rock rock till broad daylight, gonna rock around the clock tonight, clicking her fingers and jiving in among the bits of furniture and old O'Flaherty was threatening her with the belt if she didn't quit shaking her behind like an effin' huer. Maureen used to die with shame when they screeched at each other and used language in front of her, never the slightest curse to be heard out of her own parents: "Well what can you expect night, noon and morn stuck 'ithin in Quarry Street as if you hadn't a home of your own and why can't you go and play your oul' records someplace decent like Nuala McCormack's?"

"Wasn't asked, Mammy, wasn't asked." She flattened her eyes into the book and attempted to close her ears. Nothing was heard but the song of a bird filling all the air with dreaming and the curse of the yeoman soldiers and the crackle of blazing thatch and the old widow wailing, and divil another penny's going to be squandered on your education miss if that's all they learn you shaking your dirty arse about like a gypsy begod, going round singing at fairs and football games with your fat kag full of porter like Maggy Barry that's how you'll finish up. Maureen was thinking, Maggy Barry, wouldn't mind finishing up like that myself, better than bloody teaching or typing. "Jealous Heart" snarled at you outside of McCormack's bar, magic banjo scattering down a shower of loose notes like drunkards' silver coins dropped careless twinkling on the grey old Claghan pavements where evicted farmers long ago stretched shrunken hands for alms under the innocent eyes of young Cormac O'Flaherty, ancestor God help us of this beardy old galoot here, and you have your poor mother's heart broke and my own slaving away wet and dry year in year out and what sort of thanks or gratitude, if my heart could still its beating only you can tell it how, young hero O'Flaherty every artery pulsing with new-sprung hate was watching his first eviction, gonna rock rock rock till broad daylight gonna ro-a-a-a-au . . . Oh Jesus! you bastard, you fuckin' mad bastard! Oh Jesus Christ! Mom Mom, come quick; th'oul' fella's having a fit; he's smashing the good new gramophone!

As Patrick O'Flaherty took off his belt to his daughter, Maureen was slipping quietly out and home, *A Forgotten Hero* still in her hand, her mind already dissolving into some warm comforting mist of sexy dreams of some faceless bodiless slim muscular gentle not-Lanza lover from your window give me greeting hear my eternal vow—when it came down to it she knew she would have run squealing from a stout Brylcreemed tenor—but not Bill Haley either or the fellas in the dance-hall and Yeats was dead and as far as she knew then Kavanagh was dead too. And all the heroes were dead, or else they went in for long-legged classy blondes like Nuala McCormack and wouldn't throw her the time of day. "The heroes have married the long-legged blondes." She manoeuvred it gently on her tongue like the host and knew, moment of truth arteries pulsing, that she had found her vocation and that she was going to use that sentence one day to convey the infinite pathos of life. Use it to buy herself a world where all would be accustomed and ceremonious, where innocence and beauty could safely be born, unblemished both by Quarry Street hysteria and by the pathetic zinc-roofed decency of her own townland.

She walked quickly out the road from the town, away from the singing and the squalor, home to her gentle pious parents and their gentle pious mediocrity, *The Student Prince* in one hand and *A Forgotten Hero* scringed up in the other.

Now, sitting in old Baudry's château, trying to iron out the scringe marks, she recalled that walk out from Claghan and how it hadn't once occurred to her to look over her shoulder at the shadows dancing on the legend-rich mountain where the innocent Cormac used to frolic. It meant nothing at all to her that Saturday that she was walking home through townlands where merciless evictions had taken place in the lifetime of those four old women in O'Flahertys' bedroom who deafly muttered prayers through the screeching and the music, along a road where starving people *did* walk in their miserable rags to the port where an emigrant ship *was* waiting.

And when she passed the gates of Claghan Hall, the McCormacks' big house, it didn't once enter her head that it was there Cormac O'Flaherty was supposed to have battered a pair of cruel Scottish landowners to death just before going on to die himself; on the way to America; of cholera—as *Time* would have put it, semi-colons and all.

By the time it did enter her head, Claghan Hall had twice been transformed beyond recognition: first into a neon-lit tourist hotel and then, when sectarian war made tourist hotels an irrelevance in Claghan, into a bombed-out ruin whose wide lawn was used as a convenient landing-ground for British army helicopters.

CHAPTER EIGHT

MAUREEN

So where *was* Ireland? Peadar MacEighire NT sounded as if he knew:

"The scoundrel is dead at any rate," announced Mr Robert Lockhart, "so we can rest easy in our beds from this out, Margaret!" His cold-hearted spinster sister, standing by the library window, asked him how he thought she could rest easy while these endless streams of ragged diseased people crawled past on the roadside, sometimes even managing to push open the front gate and fall dead between her carefully-tended flowerbeds! Decent people ought to be protected from such dreadful sights: were there not workhouses they could go to? It was a disgrace. What were the constables thinking of?

She and Robert gave willingly to Protestant relief funds. Lord Baudry, their employer, had authorised them to provide work for the able-bodied. She herself had established a soup-kitchen in the village—only to have the ungrateful papists refuse to recite a Grace before eating! What could one do for such wretches? "I would have preferred to see O'Flaherty brought to justice," she said coldly. "To die of hunger is no punishment. They are all dying of hunger nowadays; it is become the national pastime."

She shuddered as a skeleton-like child rooted among the laurels and flung himself upon a bare bone the dog had buried there: how could one feel any sympathy for creatures so close to animals? They might as well be a different species! She closed the curtains briskly and turned towards the warmth of the lamplit room. *She* could do nothing to stop the peasants dying, and it was certainly no part of her duty to watch them die. She rang the bell and ordered Brigid to bring tea . . .

Maureen closed *A Forgotten Hero* in distaste—the eternal cliché of starving Catholics, cold unfeeling Protestants—and wondered why she had kept the booklet all these years. She wandered into the next room where Trevor was watching the news on television. As if deliberately, a toothless shawled woman huddled in dramatic close-up against a windy rock, holding a dead baby. She appeared to be singing to it. A soft-centred French voice wheedled for donations, described the heart-rending efforts of yet another group of young volunteers in Ethiopia. She wondered how much of the money they collected would actually get there. She had her own well-authenticated charities and preferred not to support the incredibly enthusiastic, and surely inexperienced, bands of youngsters who were ready to drop everything at a moment's notice nowadays and fly off to the latest fashionable famine. (Or even non-famine: she recalled the ridiculous convoys of laden trucks Madame de Lapire-Vacherie had organised for Poland during the Solidarity panic.) Generosity was one thing but Maureen and Trevor preferred not to throw their hard-earned money out of the window just to give themselves a good conscience, as so many well-meaning people were doing nowadays. And if I'm not going to send money, she thought, (or even if I am), surely it's a rather unpleasant form of voyeurism to sit here in comfort watching that poor dying woman singing to the bloated face of her dead child? She quickly rose and switched off the television.

"So where *was* Ireland?" Trevor asked.

"Dead. In bits," Maureen said. "They died or they emigrated apparently, that was all. What do famine victims ever do? When Marianne was writing her journal the population of Ireland was nine million. Now there's what, about three and a half and when you think of the birth-rate . . . So they went to America, the ones that survived. As even *you* must have heard, Trevor!"

"Yes, but what about foreign aid? I mean other countries must have, well *you* know, sent them grain, powdered milk, that sort of . . . "

Poor Trevor, she could see, was full of Bob Geldof and *Médecins sans Frontières* and the pathetic close-ups on telly and his Christmas cheque to Oxfam and the Unicef greeting cards they always made a point of buying and the Live Aid concerts and records and Maureen's own Amnesty group where she tried to make friends among the local notabilities though Amnesty wasn't perhaps very relevant but still, he'd be thinking, it's the thought that . . . "I mean surely they weren't just left there to *starve?*"

It disgusted her suddenly that she was reading about, talking about, being moved by one distant famine when there were so many famines close to her, when by pressing a button she could sit here in the warm and watch them dying exactly as they'd died in Maguire's book. As the Lockharts and McLeods and Meads sat in the warm and looked out at them dying on the road. Concerned, very probably, wishing they could do more to help and yet . . . Not *too* concerned, not for example concerned enough to share all they had, welcome them *en masse* into their houses, commit extravagant acts of humanity. *They* lived in one world and the famine victims died in another. Gnawing on a dog's bone or singing lullabies to the rotting body of a dead child took away anything one might have in common with people, made them abstractions, easily switched off. And if the Wild Geese had not spread their wings on every tide, if the O'Flahertys had stayed lords of Iar-Connacht, would *their* tenants have been any better off? French peasants, after all, in a post-revolutionary land, living on bread and water and horsewhippings, English children slaving down the mines, typhus and cholera in every country in Europe at that time: we weren't the only ones. And now. Am *I* about to send for a pack of Ethiopians, pay their fares, give them the freedom of Lord Baudry's lovely château? Like shit I am, she thought.

"Look, Trev," she said, "I've got a wee game for you. Here's all the newspaper cuttings: well, you take them and sort them out and tell me which is Brand X, right? Which is *Claghan Chronicle* 1845 and which is today's *Times*, OK? Like for example: 'Here were corpses piled up at the side of their miserable cabins and no one left alive to bury them. Here were people not yet dead and accidentally buried alive. Here were coffins with false bottoms used many times over. Here were bodies lain shallowly in the earth, to be rooted up before long and eaten by pigs and dogs.' Or this one: 'You find them crowded on the great shelves of rock high on the mountain, whole families shivering in the dawn light beneath thin brown cotton shawls, as they plead with painful politeness for food and medical help. Some have found a few pieces of dead bush to make a shelter for their children while others look down hungrily on the few hundred sacks of grain piled in the desert, the only sign of EEC help.' Could let you have dozens like that, I've found myself collecting them recently, this old Cormac thing must be making me obsessive!"

"Yes, but what *I'd* like to know, it's those pigs, Maureen, the ones that dug up the corpses. I mean what about the pigs, ducky, if times were so hard? Why didn't Paddy eat the pig before the pig ate Paddy?"

"You're forgetting the landlords, Trevor. They still wanted their rents on time. Eviction meant slow death, you know."

"Well, so did starvation."

And so, naturally, did life.

How that slow death was drummed into us, she thought, how it was sanctified and consecrated, how it stunted and twisted us. How grotesquely our loves and dreams and ambitions were trimmed by it. I escaped though, she thought, *I'm* safe.

Yes, but safe for what? Safe to be able to say out loud that the Irish hadn't a monopoly? That they *haven't* a monopoly? That there's a hell of a lot worse than being unemployed on supplementary benefit in Quarry Street or up the Falls? I'd be stood up against a wall and shot if I said that in Claghan, that there's people, millions of them, who live picking through the rubbish tips in holy Catholic Mexico City, or fighting each other to get at a few grains of corn that fall off a lorry in Mozambique, or hoking through mass graves to find what's left of their children, or cringing in wee shop or suburban bungalow waiting for the next military coup. If I'm not careful, she thought, I'll drown in a thousand famines, a million inhumanities.

Better just ignore that side of it, she thought, better just write the love story I set out to do, a romantic tale of old heroes and heroines, even if they weren't all that heroic. Romeo and Juliet with the famine as background, that's what I'll aim for. I think . . .

CHAPTER NINE

Cormac O'Flaherty

Minutes of evidence taken before Select Committee
on Outrages 1852

Rev Joseph Molloy, called in, and Examined.

Chairman: Are you a priest of the Roman Catholic Church?
—Yes.

—Will you state to the Committee where you reside?

—The parish in my charge comprises the village of Claghan
and a rural district of about forty square miles around it. My
residence is in the village, adjacent to the chapel.

—How long have you resided in that parish?

—This is my thirtieth year in the parish, first as curate and,
for the last twelve years, as Parish Priest.

—Do you recollect the case of Mr Arthur Dobson, who was
murdered in your parish some years ago?

—I do.

—Will you state under what circumstances the outrage
occurred?

—It was in July, 1840. Mr Dobson was land agent for Mr Thomas Watterson, who owned considerable property in that region. Mr Dobson's dead body was found in a little-frequented lane known locally as Bog Road. He had been badly beaten and died from his injuries.

—Was any person arrested in connection with the crime?

—Two men were brought for trial shortly after but they were proved to have been elsewhere on the afternoon of the crime.

—Was Mr Watterson domiciled on his estate?

—No, he had residences in London and in the north of England. He never, to my certain knowledge, visited his Irish estate. He had been landlord only since 1838, succeeding to the property on the death of his brother.

—On succeeding to the estate, Mr Thomas Watterson appointed Mr Dobson to administer it for him. Do you know what were the duties expected of him?

—I believe he was ordered to make the property more profitable for its owner. He said his master gave him twelve months to collect all arrears of rent and to clear off the bad payers.

—Did he say this to you?

—He did. When I heard that he served eviction orders on one hundred families I felt it my duty to remonstrate with him on behalf of my parishioners.

—Were these evicted families habitual bad payers?

—There had been two very bad harvests in close succession and many of the tenants had fallen into arrears. I think in normal times the most of them paid up when they were asked to.

—Had there been any reduction made in the rent during the years of bad harvest?

—There had been no reduction. Mr Dobson's first act as agent was to raise the rents by, I believe, two to three shillings in the acre.

—And he served eviction orders on those who could not pay the increased rent?

—On those and on others who were unable to pay their arrears.

—Were those evicted able to find alternative accommodation and employment?

—There was no other accommodation and no other employment. They wandered from place to place living on charity if they could find it. Thirty or more of them were dead by the end of the winter.

—Some months after Mr Dobson's death, there was an unsuccessful attack on a man named Robert Baxter. Was he connected with the Watterson estate?

—Yes, he was Mr Dobson's driver.

—That is to say?

—His duty was to drive away the cattle and livestock of tenants whose rent had fallen into arrears, and in the case of evictions to clear tenants and their property out of the houses before the thatch was set alight.

—Did he carry out those duties on the occasion referred to: the eviction of one hundred families?

—He did.

—How was this Baxter generally regarded in the neighbourhood?

—He was disliked and feared by the tenants on that estate.

—So that very many people would have felt they had a sufficient motive to attack him?

—A good many people may have felt violent towards him.

—And yet no one was brought to trial as a consequence of that attack?

—No. Mr Baxter was attacked from behind and it seems that after striking one blow his attacker ran away. Mr Baxter lost consciousness for a time and was unable to give any useful information.

—It was not until eight years later that two men were found guilty and executed for the murder of Mr Dobson and for the subsequent murder of a landowner and his wife?

—That is so, Timothy Murphy and Sean Morris were arrested after the McLeod murders.

—Was it your opinion, or the general opinion in the district, that these men were guilty?

—My opinion was that they were guilty of the murder of Mr and Mrs McLeod and of Mrs McGregor the Scotch servant, but not guilty of the murder of Mr Dobson. To the very end they protested their innocence of that charge and laid the sole blame for Dobson's murder on Cormac O'Flaherty.

—Was O'Flaherty ever brought to trial?

—No. He and his wife died of cholera in 1847, on the ship *The Mary Jane* that was taking them to America.

—Were they emigrating to escape the consequences of the crimes?

—They were fleeing the potato famine. They had been reduced to an extraordinary level of poverty and were afraid that conditions would get worse.

—Was this after the McLeod couple were killed?

—Yes. The McLeod couple and their housekeeper were killed on the day before *The Mary Jane* sailed from Portnafinn harbour.

—How far is that from Claghan?

—It is just under eight Irish miles.

—Would it have been possible for O'Flaherty to have taken part in the murder and still have reached the port in time to sail?

—It would have been possible, but in my opinion highly improbable.

—Why is that?

—He was married to the McLeods' daughter. It would not, I think, have been in Cormac O'Flaherty's nature to commit such a dreadful act against his own wife's parents.

—Is that your own personal opinion, backed by no evidence?

—It is my opinion. I knew Cormac O'Flaherty all his life.

—Yet Morris and Murphy claimed that he was there and that indeed he was the ringleader; how do you account for that?

—I cannot account for it.

—Did you attend these two men in your capacity of clergyman?

—Yes, I attended them before their execution.

—Did you, during his lifetime, attend O'Flaherty in your capacity of clergyman?

—Yes, he was one of my parishioners.

—Your knowledge of his character and capabilities leads you to believe that he is innocent of the McLeod murder?

—That is my opinion.

—But not innocent of the murder of Dobson and the attack on Baxter?

—It is widely believed throughout the district that he was the author of those acts.

—What was the result, from the tenants' point of view, of the unhappy murder of Mr Dobson?

—I do not understand the question.

—Did the mass evictions continue under a new agent, for example?

—No new agent was appointed. Mr Thomas Watterson disposed of the estate shortly afterwards to a Scotch merchant, Mr George McLeod.

—The same who was subsequently murdered?

—The same.

—Did he reside at Claghan Hall?

—He did.

—Was he considered to be a harsh landlord?

—No. Not at first. It is my belief that he was a well-meaning Christian gentleman. When he first came to Claghan he spoke to me several times of his intention to lower the rents and make some improvement in the lives of his tenants.

—Did he, in fact, put those intentions into practice?

—No. That is to say, for a good while he was generous in alms-giving and behaved in a kindly manner towards his tenants, though he never lowered the rents or made any improvements. But his tenants felt that they were safe from eviction and from having their livestock seized. He bought the place in September of 1840, and for the next two years or so I think the people lived in some degree of contentment.

—How did the situation change after those two years?

—In the autumn of 1842 his daughter eloped with Cormac O'Flaherty and Mr McLeod then evicted the O'Flaherty family from their farm without notice.

—Was O'Flaherty one of his tenant farmers?

—His people were tenants. Cormac himself was employed in Mr McLeod's stable as trainer and rider. The family was well-off and respectable and Cormac had received a good education.

—But Mr McLeod did not consider the alliance a suitable one?

—He did not.

—On religious grounds?

—Yes, but also because he did not consider Cormac a good enough match for his daughter.

—What were O'Flaherty's relations with his employer up to the time of the runaway marriage?

—They were cordial. Mr McLeod thought very highly of him. I think you could say Mr McLeod and Cormac were on friendly terms.

—Might O'Flaherty then have hoped that Mr McLeod would in time overcome his objections to the marriage and accept him as a son-in-law?

—He did hope so, right up to the time of the eviction, which was carried out in a very cruel and humiliating manner.

—Did he tell you he was expecting a reconciliation?

—Yes.

—Did you at any time approach the McLeod parents to plead for the young couple?

—I did, at Cormac's request.

—What was their reaction?

—Mr McLeod said his daughter had lowered herself too far to be forgiven. He told me there was no question of a reconciliation and that neither he nor his wife any longer considered their daughter to be a member of the family.

—Was there in fact any subsequent reconciliation between the couple and Mrs O'Flaherty's parents?

—There was not. I believe they never had occasion to meet again.

—Were there children born of the marriage?

—There were two boys.

—Did they also die on the voyage?

—No. I have heard that they were brought safely to America in the care of their aunt, Cormac O'Flaherty's sister.

—Did the O'Flaherty couple remain in Claghan after the eviction?

—No, they removed to a farm some miles away.

—On another estate?

—It was a farm belonging to Mr James Mullen, a publican of Claghan village.

—Were they in good circumstances on this farm?

—They were in very poor circumstances. The land was of bad quality and the rent asked was generally considered to be exorbitant. I believe they were always hard put to pay it and relied on loans from Cormac's uncle. Then, after a quarrel with Mr Mullen, they were evicted and rented a poorer sort of cottage in the place known as Quarry Street, on the outskirts of Claghan. This was during the famine.

—Was O'Flaherty unable to find employment?

—He tried at first to find work in a stable but as the gentry naturally took Mr McLeod's part he was not successful. There is little other employment to be had.

—Is it your opinion that Mr Mullen, his new landlord, took advantage of the unfortunate situation?

—That is the general opinion in the neighbourhood.

—Was any act of violence perpetrated against the person or property of this Mr Mullen after the eviction?

—None.

—Were any threats uttered against him?

—Not to my knowledge.

—Was O'Flaherty ever heard to speak in a menacing fashion of Mr McLeod?

—I believe not. You see, Cormac was never a man to threaten or bluster. He was better educated than most and usually kept his feelings to himself.

—Was he more given to swift action?

—I have no opinion on that.

—He had been a jockey; would he not therefore have been accustomed to making swift decisions and acting on them?

—Yes, I suppose he would.

—Was the O'Flaherty eviction the only one on the McLeod estate?

—No. In the years of the potato failure many people were evicted for non-payment of rent.

—How many?

—To my certain knowledge 164 tenants were evicted. There were also many people who were not direct tenants but were in the habit of cultivating a small patch of potatoes on a share-cropping arrangement with a tenant. They lived in makeshift huts and their existence was at all times precarious.

—These people were all driven off the McLeod estate at a

time of general hardship?

—They were.

—Was this not considered to be extraordinary behaviour in a gentleman whom you yourself described as well-meaning and kind?

—Mr McLeod was known to have felt very bitter towards all his tenants after his daughter's marriage. At the same time, he was only doing what many other landlords were doing. I mean to say, several landlords took advantage of famine conditions to clear their land. They got rid of the small farms and turned large areas over to wheat and cattle, which was more profitable to them.

—In the case of the McLeod murders, as in the earlier Dobson affair, was the result of the crime a general amelioration in the living conditions of the tenants?

—There was that effect.

—Did the district as a whole gain from the unfortunate deaths of the landlord and his wife?

—It did.

—Had Mrs O'Flaherty survived the voyage to America, would she have gained materially from the death of her parents?

—No, she would not.

—She would not have inherited her share of the estate?

—At the time of the marriage, Mr McLeod stated that he had disinherited his daughter, and his testament proved this to have been the case.

—Were O'Flaherty and his wife aware of this?

—They were perfectly aware. They at no time expected to inherit a share of the estate.

—Who, in fact, inherited the property?

—The landlord's son, Dr Eric McLeod, was the sole heir.

—He is the present landlord?

—He is.

—Does he reside at Claghan Hall?

—He does.

—How is he regarded by his tenants?

—He is considered to be a fair landlord. He is well regarded by the people because during the famine years he was active in relief work and in giving medical care during the typhus epidemic that followed.

—He does not then continue to apply his late father's method of running the estate?

—He does not. Dr McLeod reinstated as many of the evicted families as he could trace. Many of course were already dead.

—Of starvation?

—Yes, and of famine fever.

—Did Mr McLeod also reinstate the surviving members of the O'Flaherty family?

—They are all dead or in America.

—In other districts which suffered agrarian violence in the 1840s—I am thinking particularly of the Fews Barony, Crossmaglen, and parts of County Louth—there has been a general re-evaluation of rents. Has this been the case in Claghan?

—Yes, it has. The rents were considerably reduced on the McLeod estate; sometimes they were cut by half, and the arrears were wiped off. I mean the arrears dating back to the time of the potato failure.

—So it is your opinion that the result of these three murders is that the tenants on the estate have gained greatly in the security of their tenure and the reduction of their rent?

—It is my opinion, and I think it is the general opinion round about.

The Ballad of Cormac O'Flaherty—Anon. *c.* 1850
(Recorded by Cuchulain McCool on Folkways Records, 1968)

From the pleasant bay of Portnafinn *The Mary Jane* set sail.
'Twas on a day of bitter cold, of lashing wind and hail.

Bold Cormac and his Marianne bowed down their heads
to weep
In woe to leave sweet Claghan town and venture on the
deep.

The landlord's brutal henchmen brave Cormac
had struck down
To venge one hundred families they drove
from Claghan town;
He struggled long 'gainst tyranny to break old England's
might;
His name is one of those that gleam through Erin's long
dark night!

But he loved a landlord's daughter, a lady proud and
fair.
She cast aside her jewels bright his poverty to share:
No wealthy lord I'll wed, said she, no tyrant stern and
cold.
I'll bid them all goodbye, said she, and follow Cormac
bold!

Her father was a cruel man, he turned them from his
door.
The lovers then were forced to flee and leave old Erin's
shore.
God's curse was on you, George McLeod, for the homes
you did destroy,
The hundreds you did force to roam and to Claghan bid
goodbye!

The ship had sailed a bare three weeks when fever
struck the hold;
It killed three dozen emigrants, among them Cormac
bold.

Fair Marianne had left her home and kindred for his
sake
And when she saw him lying dead her noble heart did
break!

Their two wee babes came safe and sound; the fever let
them be.
God stayed his hand and let survive the name O'Flaherty.
We bless the captain of that ship, a man named Hamish
Brown,
Who took those orphans in his care to friends in Boston
town!

Long life to those dear children, may they grow to man's
estate,
And look on Claghan town with love, on tyranny with
hate.
May their children's children keep in mind the place
from whence they came,
May they curse the breed of George McLeod and venge
brave Cormac's name!

Memoir by Thomas O'Flaherty
(Publ. Portnafinn Press 1855)

As it has pleased Almighty God to let me live far beyond the
natural span of years, I feel it incumbent upon me, out of
the merest gratitude to Him, to use my continuing clarity of
wits to testify in the cause of Truth against Falsehood. I refer
in particular to those events which disturbed the tranquillity
of our neighbourhood more than a decade ago and which,
I note with sadness, have lately been made the subject of
much boisterous patriotic sentiment.

As the events closely concerned a member of my family
and have, by that fact, brought upon me much personal

inconvenience, I must begin with a simple exposition of the chief events of my own life: events which through a lamentable vanity I long allowed to remain mysterious and a source of wild conjecture. I fear, alas, it may be this mystery, sheltering as it did the possibility of brave deeds, that inspired my unfortunate nephew to set out upon the course of violence that led to his downfall and to that of many others who were foolish enough to take example from his crimes.

I must therefore make it clear at the outset that there were no brave deeds: my life has ever been marked by the greatest caution and sobriety. My father was a prosperous grazier in the County Wexford who, in the severest days of Penal oppression, was enabled to save his lands from confiscation by cultivating the friendship and protection of influential Protestant farmers in the locality. I was schooled at a Classical Academy and, though my own youthful desires and talents inclined me more towards the life of a skilled craftsman, my father's wealth and ambition led him to send me abroad to study at a French university. Though at first resentful, I very soon became aware of the wisdom of his choice, realising that by a judicious application to learning I could fit myself for a position in respectable Irish society that would otherwise be closed to me by my race and religion. God or Destiny willed it otherwise and, when my course of studies was but half-completed, I was called home by the dreadful tidings that my poor mother had been accidentally killed by a Redcoat's stampeding horse; that my father, crazed by the tragedy and blaming it on the armed occupation of our country (though the unfortunate officer was himself killed in the incident) had thrown to the winds the discretion of a lifetime and led a group of small farmers and discontented labourers to join the rebel army then forming in the county under Bagenal Harvey; that my father had been speedily taken and hanged, and his lands and livestock confiscated to the Crown. I will not speak here of my bitter and heartbreaking sorrow, but will record only that I returned home with the greatest haste and secrecy and rescued the sole survivor of my beloved family, my young brother Matthew, who had been given refuge by a kindly neighbour; and that together we fled northwards (the whole South and West of Ireland being at the time steeped in murder and bloodshed).

My University career was necessarily at an end as nothing remained to us of our former wealth, and my only desire was to find some quiet place where we could live out our days tranquilly, far from violence and disorder. This mountainous region with its dispirited and kindly population humbled by poverty and the power of landlordism seemed a certain enough refuge, and we settled down to frugal existence in a squatter's shack, obliged for a time to live on the charity of our neighbours. This charity I repaid by teaching their children to read and write, and indeed I might have set myself up as a schoolmaster with little difficulty but that I was afraid this course might lead to careful enquiries being made into my antecedents, and in the long run I deemed it more prudent to fall back upon my only other talent: cabinet-making.

Thus I looked about for opportunities, living for a time like a pedlar, carrying samples of my handiwork around the houses of the gentry, gaining sometimes commands, more often rebuffs, until at last I had the good fortune to be befriended by the Honourable George Mead who commissioned me to make some small articles of furniture for his new house and, on being pleased with the result, set me up in a craftsman's cottage on his estate. Thenceforward my story was one of prosperity and the growing respect and friendship of intelligent men. I never spoke of my past but, years later, when I found that imaginative people were representing me as a hero of the Wexford rebellion I held my tongue out of vanity and did not disabuse them.

My brother Matthew grew up and was fortunate enough to obtain employment as a horseman. He married, sired children, and died tragically in the cholera epidemic of 1832. I was called upon to support his growing family which, being myself in relatively fortunate circumstances, I was very glad to do. Of my nieces I have nothing to relate: they led the modest commonplace lives of Catholic womanhood up to the time their brother brought misfortune upon them and upon my decent pious sister-in-law. Of that brother, my only nephew, I have much to say. From the first I regarded him as a bright ambitious lad and I hoped, despite a slight instability in his character, that he had good sense enough to realise that in books alone lies the key to advancement for members of our oppressed race. I wasted much of my time in attempting to form his mind and fit him for a scholastic career, only to be told in the end that his intention was to work as a jockey in his landlord's stable. My disappointment was great, and especially so when I learned that he had adopted the vices usually associated with that trade, namely drunkenness, wild gaming company and a loose disrespectful attitude towards the gentler sex. When his master, Mr Henry Watterson, died and the racehorses were sold, I hoped that Cormac, faced with a future as a mere tenant farmer, would turn again towards study as a means of escape, and to that end I declined to use my influence to obtain him a position in my own landlord's stable. Once again I was disappointed: my nephew still showed not the slightest inclination towards the life of the intellect. He had by then become accustomed to low public-house society and, in particular, to the society of the adulterous wife of that notorious tavern-keeper and usurer, James Mullen. So great was this evil woman's sway over his senses that he did not take the obvious course open to a jockey in want of employment and make his way to the Curragh region of the County Kildare where his talents would almost certainly have obtained him a position. It was, I think, in an attempt to glorify himself in her eyes that he joined a secret society devoted to the harassment of landlords and the destruction of their property.

It is now common knowledge that Mullen was deriving a comfortable income from selling his "protection" to agents, merchants, and even some of the smaller landlords after they had been reduced to a state of terror or near-bankruptcy by repeated attacks. I will not dispute the generally held notion that some good came out of these attacks and that, as a result of them, the tenant population lives at present with more comfort and dignity than before. It is a well-known fact that good does appear very often to come out of evil, and I have no doubt also that many of the young men who perpetrated acts of violence did so from the highest motives. I dispute only the notion that my nephew, Cormac O'Flaherty, was a hero or that he ever interested himself greatly in the misfortunes of his people. From the time he grew to manhood his behaviour had always seemed to be of the most heedless, and his conversation of the coarsest, thus giving the lie to descriptions of him in popular songs as poet, patriot, and romantic lover! Though he may well have carried out acts of violence against property, I believe he had little real physical courage and to my knowledge he was responsible for only one of the many murders imputed to him: that of Arthur Dobson, the land agent. It is my belief that he was so sickened by the crime as to fail miserably in his second attempt at bloodshed. I can certainly testify that on that Sunday evening in the winter of 1840 when Bobby Baxter was attacked, my nephew came to my cottage in a state of intense shock and nervous fatigue. He told me nothing but, on hearing news of the attack, I easily guessed what had occurred.

It is my opinion that he broke with the secret society shortly afterwards and settled down to the employment he was fortunate enough to obtain in the new landlord's stable.

He was well regarded there and I confess that I was at first naïvely pleased to think that my nephew was at last endeavouring to make a place for himself in the world, even though it was far from the place I would have chosen for him. Mr George McLeod, this new landlord, was a gentleman of the highest respectability, exactly the opposite in character and temperament to the late Mr Henry Watterson, and I expected that under his protection Cormac might yet grow to be a man of worth.

Picture my shock therefore when I ascertained—and ascertained from his own lips—the true baseness of my nephew's nature! He informed me that he intended to make a marriage of interest with Mr McLeod's daughter, that he had already charmed his way into her affections, that she was to his mind rather a foolish and credulous young lady and with so little idea of her own position that she would be prepared to marry him without a second's hesitation. I attempted to reason with him and to demonstrate the folly of his ambition, for it was unthinkable that the landlord would ever accord his only daughter's hand to a penniless horseman of Catholic farming stock. My nephew replied that he intended to make a runaway marriage, as is customary in this district when there is parental opposition to overcome. The practice is as follows: the young man "abducts" his chosen bride, with her own consent, and secretes her in the house of one of his friends or relations. He then bargains with the unhappy parents, bartering their daughter's good name against consent to the marriage and a substantial dowry. My nephew's intention in apprising me of his project was that *mine* should be the house in which the young lady was lodged while he impertinently haggled with his landlord! I naturally declined the honour and endeavoured to convince him that Mr George McLeod would surely not allow himself to be imposed upon as if he were a small farmer with ten acres and a houseful of daughters! The young lady was an heiress, I reminded him, and he replied impudently that he "would not have looked at her twice if she wasn't, and that the old folks would come round speedily enough when there was a grandchild in the cradle."

I then contrived a secret interview with Miss McLeod and spoke to her earnestly, counselling prudence. She refused to listen, said I knew nothing about young people, and indeed laughed at me as a timorous old man too fond of bending the knee to authority. "Mr Mead's tame Irishman" was the ridiculous title she gave me, and I realised that she was indeed as foolish and shameless as my nephew had described her, and hardly worth my effort to save her from ruin. On reflection, however, it occurred to me that Mr Mead might possibly attach some blame to me on account of my nephew's treasonable conduct towards his betters, and that I risked finding myself turned out upon the roads in my old age should he withdraw his patronage from me. I determined therefore to speak to Miss McLeod's parents before it was too late. Whilst I was still turning over in my mind various approaches that would not too much harm my nephew's position or my own, while yet ensuring the young lady's safety, the tragedy occurred. I learned that Cormac, with the help of his sister and two of his boon companions, was holding the landlord's daughter prisoner in a safe place and was attempting to bargain with the outraged parents. Attempting and failing, as I had warned him. Mr McLeod, in a great rage, publicly disinherited his daughter, whether she married or no. He announced that, having disgraced herself by eloping with a peasant, she might never, even repentant, hope to be received by her family again. While making it clear that he was aware of the voluntary nature of her "imprisonment" (it seems the unhappy girl had tried to enlist the support of a cousin in her escapade), he managed to hint that things might go very badly with Cormac if he refused to marry her when he found her to be dowerless; and indeed it has happened many times, even in this modern and enlightened age, that young men have been sentenced to transportation for similar offences. My nephew therefore was forced to bind himself for life to a penniless and far from beautiful foreign woman whom he did not love, and to become the laughing-stock of Claghan. My poor sister-in-law and her daughters were evicted from their home and at first expected that I would offer them a refuge in my cottage. My landlord naturally objected to this arrangement, saying that while no possible blame could attach to *me*, it might appear that he was condoning my nephew's conduct if he harboured the rest of the family on his estate.

Cormac and his wife rented a cottage and a plot of land from James Mullen, who had, as his prosperity increased, bought long leases on several such small-holdings on the Mead and Baudry estates and relet them at very high rents. Cormac's mother and sisters joined them there, and they all lived together in very reduced circumstances up to the time of the potato failure. It was then that Mullen, for his own reasons, evicted them and they returned to Claghan to rent a miserable shack in a settlement of such dwellings along the edge of the slate quarry.

It is certain that my nephew did not marry for love but his wife, it must be said, had some good qualities, being a sturdy cheerful young woman who made a praiseworthy effort to adapt to her new situation. Indeed the marriage might have been no more miserable than most had not Cormac foolishly kept up his immoral dealings with Mullen's wife. It was, I believe, on account of her that he refused to leave Claghan with his family and seek a better life elsewhere. Mrs Mullen gave birth to a child at around the same time that Marianne O'Flaherty's first son was born and, as soon as they were seen in public, these children became a source of scandal and gossip in the parish because of their close resemblance. I have heard that Marianne was made to suffer greatly at the sharp tongues of her neighbours, but James Mullen himself appeared for a long time to have no suspicion of the true state of affairs, which was curious as everyone else in Claghan referred to the boy as MacCormac, which is Gaelic for "Cormac's son." He is now a child of some ten or eleven years, exactly similar to my nephew at the same age. James Mullen has been dead these three years and more, and his widow has lately dropped her son's legal name and calls him openly "Master MacCormac" She is now, of course, an extremely rich woman and can afford to make a joke of scandal; her late husband having made a fortune by importing cheap Indian meal and selling it at high prices during the famine, and by his practice of foreclosing on mortgages during that time of general hardship. It is said that before his death James Mullen had become proprietor of more than two dozen houses in Claghan village as well as several outlying farms, but this report is no doubt exaggerated.

Before he died I believe Mullen ruined both my nephew's life and his character out of sheer vengeance. When Cormac in the end came to me in great distress to ask for his fare to America, he told me he was frightened of Mullen, who held sure proofs against him for Dobson's murder and who was threatening to use them to have him caught and hanged. He told me that if Mullen had not already carried his knowledge to the constables it was because he was using it to force Cormac into committing further crimes. I made no enquiries into the nature of these crimes, firstly because I have all my life preferred to shelter myself from even the awareness of bloodshed, and secondly so that I could not at any future time be forced to bear witness against my nephew.

I knew there was a ship sailing from Portnafinn harbour some time the following week and thought it advisable that Cormac should immediately secure passage for himself and all belonging to him. To that end, I turned over most of my savings to him, urging him to leave the district that same day and to take lodgings for the whole family in Portnafinn town while awaiting the day of sailing.

It is said that Cormac was seen back in Claghan on the day before the vessel sailed. If that is indeed so, it can only have been to take a final farewell of Mullen's wife. It is probable that they arranged to meet in some secret place. Knowing my nephew's character as I did, I have always argued strongly against the notion that he returned to the district to murder his wife's parents and that he would have been capable, after perpetrating such an act, of calmly washing off the blood and making his way to the ship where his innocent children were awaiting him. I know that had he participated in that crime—a particularly horrible one, I believe, in its details—he would certainly have been unfit to travel eight or nine miles immediately afterwards without attracting attention to himself by his disordered conduct. I myself witnessed the broken condition of his nerves some hours after the attack on Baxter. It is, of course, possible that in the seven years that had elapsed since Dobson's murder and the attack on Baxter, my nephew's mind had become hardened to killing, but it is my contention that all the accusations against him emanated from the jealous mind of a cuckold and that James Mullen, unaware that Cormac died shortly after leaving Ireland, hoped to have him pursued and brought to justice even in America. I cannot say if this would have happened had my nephew lived. I doubt it, America being a country that surely affords hiding-places aplenty; and it would have been well nigh impossible to trace one Irish immigrant among the many thousands who sought shelter there during those years.

My nephew's untimely death has unfortunately made him an object of veneration to the poor people of Claghan and these last few years have seen such a plethora of songs, doggerel verse, and tales of his supposedly epic deeds that my attempts to remind his former friends and neighbours of his true character go quite unheeded and have indeed earned me the unenviable reputation of renegade from my class! I, who attempted always to set his feet on the right path, and without whose generosity he would have been left to the mercy of the hangman, and his children to die of hunger! It is a fact that, in this unhappy country, a quiet reflective voice speaking truth is always drowned by the howls of the mob, and my misfortune is that even in the society of civilised gentlefolk who were beginning to accept me almost as an equal, I am now regarded with some suspicion as close kin and mentor to a notorious rebel leader!

It is my sincere hope therefore that these few pages will be successful in reducing this affair to its true proportions in the eyes of men of goodwill, and in disculpating me of any responsibility for the misguided deeds of my unfortunate nephew.

Thomas O'Flaherty, Claghan 1855

Maguire's book—the pure young girls, the clean-limbed clear-eyed patriot boys, the old men and women with pious enduring faces praying around the turf-fire across the centuries as Cromwell's bayonet lunged and gouged. Which it did of course, which it did. In its day. As they starved in their day. Yes, but starving peasants, she thought, what in the long run can I, comfortable in seventy thousand quids' worth of historic château, possibly know about starving Irish peasants? To begin with, *not* peasants. Small farmers. A quiet decent middle class of people, as my father calls us. Timid and conventional, without passion or revolt. That's what made it worse when disaster hit them.

Myself and my twelve brothers and sisters in our three-roomed zinc-roofed house on the edge of Claghan Bog. Not a shack or a cabin or a cottage: a house. Warm and happy: porridge and potatoes and good strong tea, Enid Blyton and the *Sacred Heart Messenger*. Old seventy-eights on the wind-up gramophone, bought second-hand in Smithfield market, the songs of Aunt Agnes's courtship, I was een Havana for a

night and you were close witheen my arms, Big Jim Malone
with his Brylcreem and his wee brush of a corporal's moustache:
Sure what trenches, there was no trenches in this war, Mrs
Murphy, winking away behind Mammy's back, the whiff of his
hair-oil rising off Agnes in bed at night inspiring tender dreams
of love. Come you back to Mandalay where the flying fishes
play, come you back you British soldier come you back to
Mandalay. You British soldier . . . His hooded body last year
left lying booby-trapped three days on a border road while the
blue flies buzzed and the helicopters hung in the air and a
thick mist of rumours hung over Claghan.

"Wee Sarah O'Flaherty's in with a shocking wild crowd
these days," Mammy wrote. "I hope for poor Lizzie's sake she's
not mixed up in anything bad, though God knows and the
way she was reared . . . " Gentle pious mediocrity, the hallmark
of the Murphys: we were always the innocent bystanders, we
always kept well out of everything. My great-grandfather,
strolling quiet and decent from his work, stumbled on Dobson's
corpse half-eaten by scawl-crows on the Bog Road and walked
back three miles to report it to the constables. Honest reliable
man. There was a Murphy hanged later on but it certainly
wasn't one of our crowd. South of the Border, she thought,
not de Valera's border or with Pearse in the Post Office but
down Mexico way that is where I fell in love when stars above
came out to play. We evolved after my grandmother's death,
we became corrupt. Never a mention of old Ireland or Cromwell
or the famine except when we turned on the Walton programme
on Radio Éireann, Leo Maguire sounding like a bishop, sounding
consecrated: Your heritage of *Irish* songs, the songs your *fathers*
loved! From the pleasant bay of Portnafinn *The Mary Jane* set
sail . . . Yankee parcels with cowboy shirts and jeans and
peanut brittle and the *New York Times* and boxes of macaroni,
the Yank O'Flahertys home on their holidays. Ah yes, she
thought, that was our only link with starving peasants: the
Yank O'Flahertys home one summer looking for colleens and

thatched white cottages, finding ugly concrete blocks and corrugated iron and cylinders of Calor gas in loudly-wallpapered kitchens, and ponytailed teenagers jiving to Bill Haley and Elvis in Claghan's answer to the Ballroom of Romance. Looking for the cottage from which their ancestors Cormac and Marianne and their two wee babes set out in 1847 for Portnafinn harbour and the coffin-ship. The cottage was in Quarry Street on the outskirts of Claghan town, one of a maze of mean Catholic streets hanging like a forgotten greasy cobweb between the town and the mountain. There was another, Protestant, cobweb in the other corner, spoking out from Lockhart Road. We hadn't a monopoly. Between the two slums, separating them, was a piece of waste ground bounded on two sides by the ruin of a high stone wall. This wall had been built in 1846 by starving natives, on the orders of Mr Lockhart, Lord Baudry's agent.

According to Maguire's book, Cormac O'Flaherty was one of the workers. They were paid seven pence a day, with which they bought Indian corn in Jem Mullen's depot. The corn, according to Maguire, cost three shillings a stone. They didn't at first know quite what to do with it. They had no way of grinding it—in a potato-eating country there were naturally no mills—so they boiled it whole and ate it. It wasn't sweetcorn, it wasn't Green Giant. It did appalling things to their stomach linings. Hundreds of children and old people died before Jem Mullen began importing ready-ground meal. Maureen, in disbelief, checked with the Ulster Folk Museum and found that Maguire's account was basically true though slightly exaggerated and, of course, coloured with prejudice. Baudry's agent, a just and God-fearing Presbyterian, had been acting out of benevolence rather than sadism. It was no part of the Victorian ethic to give the poor something for nothing, and Baudry's tenants were luckier than most. On the McLeod estate, its owners embittered by their daughter's disgrace, nothing whatever was done for the starving. But after all, Maureen thought, how much objective truth could Maguire have hoped to get by interrogating eighty-year-olds about events that happened in their parents' day? If objectivity was what he was after. She decided to leave Maguire's book out of her sources of reference, it clashed far too much with all the rest. Grand Scots lady, sensitive poetic young man, pious maidens, all too obviously a tale handed down from father to child and never questioned in adulthood. She looked at Maguire's book, its pages scringed up and slightly torn at the edges. She remembered her hand clenched round it walking out home from Claghan feeling— horror? disgust? Or only boredom at the slummy squalor of Quarry Street and Patrick O'Flaherty's ranting frustrations? Kathleen's father believed implicitly in the old legend, but then what else had he? His home mortgaged to publican and bookmaker, obliged to support an extended family in a rented slum—as Cormac had done before him. What remained only a past that grew more glorious and more martyred with every telling! She pictured Quarry Street as she had known it when Kathleen still lived there: the saints and heroes and Sacred Hearts hung over cheap modern wallpaper, the flowered lino, the net curtains, *Guerrilla Days in Ireland* sticking out from under *Woman's Own* and *School Friend*, Bill Haley and His Comets on the painted deal dresser. The exact image of her own home in Boharnamuc. Mario Lanza, her obsession with romance. Her bright hard determination to escape, because she sensed that there was no romance to be had in Claghan. And, according to Thomas O'Flaherty's memoir, it seemed there never *had* been any romance there either.

So what am I to do now, she wondered, am I to give up the whole idea of writing this book? You can't write a romantic novel without romance. She could have got over Marianne being neither beautiful nor aristocratic but she couldn't get over her not being loved. Not very well. Not if what she was writing was supposed to be a love story. And there was hardly much point having Cormac as a hero if he wasn't even heroic.

If he wasn't a rebel or a poet or a romantic lover, if he was just a poor galoot ready to grab at anything to hoist himself up in the world. Though he was very like myself, she thought, he had some notion of a life beyond the bogholes and the saints' wells, beyond the awful quiet decency that must have been Claghan even then. The prayers and the piously-endured hardship and the shoddy attempts at modernity—Victorian ornaments bought on credit from Jem Mullen—the low horizons and the snobbery of the mediocre and the meek acceptance of the poor, and the endless endless laying of wreaths upon the dead. Any dead would have done. He must have longed for the gutter or the stars; either would have seemed like an improvement. Only the poor sod buggered it up in the long run, the way he buggered up killing old Watterson's driver. He even made a balls-up of emigrating. But then he lived in a bad time for escaping. *I* was luckier: a child of the Welfare State and the Eleven-plus and the Heysham boat and full employment. *I* couldn't have escaped in 1840 either, and I probably couldn't have escaped now. Any more than, for example, Sarah O'Flaherty can escape, or any youngster for that matter up the Falls Road or in Liverpool or Brixton or Beirut or . . .

And if I wrote it like that, she wondered, if I wrote for once in my life a truthful novel with no heroes and no long-legged blondes? If I wrote about Marianne as a not very attractive gullible girl literally dying to escape from her dreadful parents and her dreary brother and the awful Hales and all they represented? And if I made Cormac just an ordinary bright country lad on the make? Upwardly mobile, only constantly getting kicked in the teeth by unemployment, social insecurity, his own basic inadequacy? Two communities living in a state of mutual ignorance and all that ever leads to of hate, injustice, violence, victimisation? It needn't even be in Claghan, I could set it anywhere, at any time in history. We hadn't a monopoly.

But I'll set it in Claghan because escaped or not it's the only place I really know: my grandmother's Claghan that hadn't changed in a hundred years when I was a small child following her round the hedges gathering food to supplement the rations, nettles and sorrels and mushrooms, under the contemptuous eyes of the McCormacks in Claghan Hall, as Murphys and O'Flahertys must have gathered food, conscious of McLeod eyes, Lockhart eyes, Mullen eyes. And of the kind prying eyes of Flowerdews and Fieldings sneaking round their cabins taking notes, shaming them with gospelly pity, trying to sell them an alien God, without the wit to realise that as far as the likes of my grandmother were concerned, old Cromwell had very efficiently shoved *that* God down the bogholes two centuries earlier.

Claghan had begun changing after the war, after my grandmother's death, but I from the intensity of my first five years can recall enough to see how it must have been in Cormac's time: the mean humped landscape of whin and reed and bog-cotton, the tiny hedged fields creeping up the mountain, the clusters of one-roomed stone huts in the shadow of Claghan Hall. The landlords and the moneylenders nourishing themselves on the not-quite-starving, meek old men and women nourishing their impotent bitterness on memories of old bloodshed— Calvary and Claghan and Vinegar Hill and Dolly's Brae all melting into each other in a past that surely had more meaning than the hungry anxious present. The inertia, the hopelessness of effort and yet the necessity of effort, tilling those humpy little fields year after year with nothing to show at the end of it but another few months' survival. The neurotic anguish of always living on the very edge of disaster; no heroics, only a thin pale sun of religion barely melting the ice of despair. And the scawl-crows on every bush, patiently awaiting the inevitable.

I could do it like that. Frost in a thin sun, November, Cormac waiting to pounce on Baxter, crows everywhere: symbols of a country on the verge of catastrophe. The absurdity of a young man lurking behind a graveyard wall on a winter evening when what he really wanted was to be inside in the warm making love to a beautiful woman. When all he *ever* wanted was caviare and champagne and cheering crowds and galloping horses and the moon and the song of a bird and the air full of dreaming and guitars and pretty girls and tender vows of love. Cormac, unemployed, frustrated, mixed up with a married woman in a country where love was the one big sin. Conned or blackmailed into joining the secret society? Or maybe no need for blackmail, maybe his own sense of guilt ("It was your own fault, son, and mine; the whole lot of us had a hand in driving those nails!") leading him to twist ordinary human passion into patriotism? Because, like myself, he'd have been nourished on old people's memories, he'd have had the dead men in Claghan Bog rammed down his throat from birth along with the hunted priests and the ferocious disfigured virgins and the martyrs and the Crucifixion: Cromwell's Protestant soldiers dicing for Our Lord's green white and orange coat. He might even have twisted Jem Mullen's wife into a symbol of Ireland, poor bitch forced or sold into a loveless union, egging him on to kill—because killing for her would have seemed that much cleaner than making love to her behind her husband's back in some outhouse.

A bit far-fetched, she thought, but roughly like that. That sort of thing. No glorification, no Peter Maguire stuff, no folk-heroes.

CHAPTER TEN

(LETTER FROM REV NICHOLAS
FIELDING TO REV RICHARD
FLOWERDEW, 1870)

I cannot resist troubling you with a line as I have recently returned from a most interesting visit to that wild portion of southern Ulster which we came to know so well—and attempted to chronicle faithfully in our different ways—so many eventful and tragic years ago. Much has changed. The village in which I laboured to bring the light of Christ to a benighted and superstitious peasantry is now a sprawling market town; many of the old respected families have gone, several estates have been broken up and the land sold off in small parcels to such tenants as can afford to purchase it; the former extreme misery of the people would appear to be to an extent mitigated—one's sight is no longer offended nor one's heartstrings torn by the spectacle of those thousands of huts in which the poor used to squat without hope. All that has changed. Most farmers now enjoy some security of tenure; they cultivate crops other than the potato; one rejoices to see small flocks of domestic animals and fowls around almost every cottage . . . The district appears to have achieved some slight form of stability in the quarter-century that has elapsed since I left to take up my ministry in England. The great disorder of the famine is by no means forgotten, nor will it ever be. I fear rather that it has entered into the folklore of the country, has been given epic dimensions—as catastrophes, victories, defeats, even the least little local risings always *are* given epic dimensions here!

And yet, even to the soberest mind, it was a terrible tragedy. But, if I may permit myself the utterance of such an extravagant thought: who can fathom the mysterious workings of Our Creator? It is a fact that the weakest elements of the populace were swallowed up during those five years and that those who remain are, by definition, survivors, able to make a positive contribution to their country . . . That is not to say that hardship has totally disappeared. Indeed no, there is still much poverty, much injustice, resulting in sporadic outbreaks of agrarian violence. Ribbonism and many other secret societies flourish, dedicated to the spread of terror among the landowning class. Rent-collectors have been attacked, the agents of absentee landlords go once more in fear of their lives, just as in those dreadful days when my dear friends, the McLeods, met with such a terrible and undeserved fate. Drunkenness, dancing and horse-racing are still rife, the lower orders are still as quarrelsome and gregarious as ever and almost as superstitious, though some of the barbaric old customs seem to have disappeared. I have never been one to condemn rustic merriment and innocent folklore but, as you know, Richard, in the past, weddings and funerals were conducted with a total absence of Christian dignity.

This, however, is no longer the case, due perhaps to the civilising contact with the outside world that results from widespread emigration. Most families have at least one member in America which, though economically a most desirable state of affairs, is considered a major tragedy by those who go, as well as by those who remain. On the eve of departure the emigrant is ritually "waked" by parents, relations and neighbours as though he or she were already dead. There is much extravagant weeping and praying and kissing—and indeed these departures *may* be regarded in the nature of a death, as few ever return home, even for a visit. In some families I have seen, out of twelve or thirteen children, only one remain in Ireland to inherit the farm, the rest embarking for America at the age of fourteen or fifteen. Far more sensible, you will agree, and far less likely to lead to famine than the old custom of sharing out a five-acre holding between ten or more young families! But these people are hopelessly emotional, and their nature leads them to convert even such betterment of fortune into a high tragic drama . . . .

The town, as I must call it, of Claghan now boasts several shops, twice as many public houses, and a surprisingly good hotel run by a handsome but decidedly whaleboned old character known variously as the Widda Mullen, the Widda O'Flaherty and the Widda McCormack. I have not yet been able to disentangle the complexities of her marital past! She is aided by her son, a great redheaded fellow, and by her rather browbeaten daughter-in-law, and there were some appallingly refined grandchildren home on holiday from boarding-school who were mercilessly put on show every time a new guest appeared. We were served the usual overcooked food, but the beds were clean and comfortable, and the establishment enjoys a reputation for the strictest sobriety and virtue. But why, you will ask, did I not stay at the Rectory? Well, the town is now divided very strictly in two, Protestants on the valley side towards the Belfast road, Romanists huddled round the slate quarry and tailing off towards the mountain. There is almost no friendly commerce between them, attitudes and resentments having hardened during the famine years and the subsequent agrarian violence, and, as I was interested in meeting people of all creeds and classes, I felt it incumbent upon me to sleep in as neutral a bed as possible!

The lower classes are more easy of discourse than they were a generation ago: the National Schools are well attended and all speak and read English. Nobody would be likely to snigger nowadays if I went around the meadows and hills collecting botanical specimens: indeed, on visiting the elementary school in the Protestant quarter my heart was warmed to discover that my own little work is used as a book of reference for natural history lessons! I saw, alas, no trace of my pamphlets; they, I fear, have fallen into oblivion and my words upon stony ground— evangelism has had but little success in this unhappy district!

You will be delighted, my dear Richard, to learn that while in Ireland I took the opportunity of travelling to the west of the country, and of visiting in particular the missionary settlement on Achill Island. I had the immense joy of being able to speak with the great Edward Nangle himself who, though increasingly infirm and living in semi-retirement, still takes a deep personal interest in his life's work. What an example to us all! And what a godly achievement to rescue an island of some 5000 souls from the grasp of Satan, to deliver so many poor people from superstition and darkness and raise up their hearts to the light of the Spirit. There indeed the disaster of the famine can be said to have had a positive aspect, affording as it did the opportunity for men of goodwill to nourish the souls of the suffering poor even as they nourished their bodies. Such a contrast to the region I had just left, where conversions have always been few, where the ignorant natives have stubbornly refused to trust in the cleansing power of the Blood of the Lord Jesus and remain sunk in popish idolatry, worship of graven images, and degenerate cannibalistic beliefs! Would that in my youth I had been blessed with the eloquence and inspired energy of the great Edward Nangle . . .

(Extract from *A Witness for Christ*, an account of the life and work of the Reverend Nicholas Fielding, martyred in India in 1875.)

(Letter from Charles McLeod to his nephew.)

Claghan Hall

3 September 1896

Dear William,

. . . upon reflection I do not feel that it would serve any useful purpose if I offered the journal for publication. It is a purely personal document, of interest only to the family, and though, as you remark, my aunt Marianne lived in an era rich in the sort of historic event recently made fashionable by Mr Yeats and his friends, it is unfortunate that she chose to ignore all but her own concerns and emotions and that indeed her journal should have stopped short a few years before the Great Famine. Not much Celtic Twilight about it, I am afraid! Your suggestion was a kind one but, given the limited interest of the document in question, I doubt if its publication would result in the alleviation of my financial difficulties.

I have, however, received a proposition which may well prove to be a godsend and which, in the light of your interest in the journal, has indeed a certain piquancy! I was approached last week by a young American named Matthew O'Flaherty who represented himself to be one of two surviving grandsons of my notorious aunt and her assassin of a husband! He has apparently come by a fortune in America and wishes to buy Claghan Hall, near-ruin though it is. I mentioned a sum far higher than the old barrack is worth and he agreed readily; we are to settle the legal details in a day or two. He resembles the typical brash American of popular prejudice but his wife, though showing little sign of *Mayflower* ancestry, has something of a ladylike manner and appearance—I rather fancy the fortune originated with *her*, rather than in the Black Hills of Dakota!

I made it perfectly clear to the young man that our relations must be strictly of a business nature and there can be no question of the McLeods claiming him as a long-lost cousin. For myself, I have no objection, but I am conscious of the damage that a Roman Catholic connection—and such a connection! —could do to you and George in your dealings with the Orange Lodge. Am I unduly sensitive in supposing you are already somewhat embarrassed by the presence of such a disreputable old rake as myself in your otherwise most upright family?

Well, whether or not it displeases my respectable relations, Claghan Hall is mine and I see no objection to selling it to this young couple who seem to have a most sentimental desire to settle there, though God knows why they should! I have long had a desire to settle my debts honourably and to end my days under bluer and more entertaining skies than those that loom over Claghan and, to be frank, young Matthew O'Flaherty comes as an answer to prayer. I thank you again, dear nephew, for your various well-meant suggestions as to the resolving of my financial difficulties. I will (very soon I hope) be writing to you from the Island of Capri and, should we not have occasion to meet again, be assured that I have every intention of leaving you Aunt Marianne's journal in my will!

Your affect. uncle
Charles

Which brought the story up to Maureen's own lifetime. She had often heard of the American Matt O'Flaherty who drank himself out of Claghan Hall the very year she was born, and whose granddaughter Kathleen was still one of her closest friends.

Matt O'Flaherty's brother Tommy stayed in Boston and built up a minor dynasty. At the turn of the century he married a Murphy emigrant and the two families kept in close touch throughout the decades. They were the Yank O'Flahertys who regaled Maureen's childhood with parcels of toys, clothes, *Popeye* comics and Babe Ruth bars, and whose occasional visits home during her adolescence compensated slightly for the disgrace of being born in a zinc-roofed cottage beside Claghan Bog. The relationship later became rather embarrassing, when Maureen's letters from her mother were full of how well the Yank O'Flahertys' sons were doing in Vietnam and, later still, as military advisers in small South American republics. Another member of the clan (all of whom were brought up to "curse the breed of George McLeod and venge brave Cormac's name") became an efficient Noraid fund-raiser, a prominent figure at St Patrick's Day parades in Boston and even, once—amid great publicity and several deaths—in Claghan itself.

They died on the voyage but why, Maureen wondered, did I imagine their story was over? You only had to lift a newspaper, or switch on the telly. Or indeed, ring home: "Oh God, Maureen, did you hear about the slaughter happened at the Yank O'Flaherty's Noraid meeting? Your brothers were out the whole evening ferrying victims to the hospital. Honest to God, Maureen, I near threw up when I saw the state of that car this morning. Floor, seats, everything all saturated. We'll never be able to get it clean again." All the perfumes of Arabia, she thought, Lady Macbeth in a carwash. *Nous sommes tous des terroristes irlandais*, as Madame de Lapire-Vacherie put it. Maureen's piously-bigoted parents, her beloved dead grandmother laying wreaths over bogholes, the Yank O'Flahertys keeping all too closely in mind the place from whence they came, pouncing and picking at death like scawl-crows. The nice well-off McLeods gently banning the bomb in a tree-lined Claghan suburb (while the little streets hurled themselves upon the little), careful all the same to march to the right tune. Maureen herself, as much as anyone, who'd wrapped herself in dreams and walked away: the rat/sinking ship syndrome? But then, as Trevor said: "If the whole batch of you cleared out, the poor bloody ship might have a chance of floating!"

Maureen had, at seventeen, briefly considered using the Yank O'Flahertys as a stepping-stone to romance, but had rejected the idea because, behind the America of dreams and Hollywood and New Orleans jazz, there lurked her grandmother's America of emigrant ship and steerage and cholera and Ellis Island and domestic service and lifelong Claghan-sickness, and *that* America, though only half-consciously perceived, frightened the life out of her. This is all you are, it told her, this is where you'll end up. You'll never escape, it told her, nobody escapes from Claghan.

CHAPTER ELEVEN

Daily Mail, 16 October 198-

Greenpeace Husband in Kidnap Drama

Police and army in Northern Ireland are carrying out a full-scale search for Protestant schoolmaster Eric McLeod whose car was found abandoned in a country lane ten miles from his home in Claghan early yesterday morning. Mr McLeod was last seen on Friday evening when he left Claghan to drive to Aldergrove airport, in order to join his wife in London. Mrs Myrna McLeod had flown to England that morning with a local anti-nuclear group to take part in a Greenpeace march on Downing St. It is believed that Mr McLeod may be the latest victim in a wave of IRA kidnappings across the province. Speaking on Ulster Television yesterday evening, a tearful Mrs McLeod stressed that her husband had no connection whatsoever with the security forces but that, on the contrary, he had always been a tireless worker for peace and understanding between the two communities, and she appealed to the men who are holding him captive to let an innocent human being go free. Both Mr and Mrs

McLeod are leading members of the Ulster Greenpeace group and have taken part in several anti-nuclear demonstrations on mainland Britain.

Maureen Murphy never read the popular English papers, though she did occasionally pick up *The Sunday Times* if she happened to be in Quimper on a Tuesday when it arrived. That autumn, however, she was so immersed in nineteenth-century Claghan that shopping trips and newspapers were given a miss, and she was totally ignorant of the final twist in the McLeod/O'Flaherty story when her friend Kathleen turned up on her doorstep early one afternoon in October, looking extremely odd and talking, talking, talking . . .

CHAPTER TWELVE

LIZZIE (1)

"Old Matt O'Flaherty took bad at Fairyhouse races and wasn't expected to live, he had the priest and doctor with him constant. It was the whole talk when I went home that Sunday, Mother and Auntie Bridgie and old Sarah Morris going over the family's pedigree for all they were worth and prophesying that there'd shortly be ructions between the sons and daughters over which of them was best fit to attend him in his last agony. He had a grand farm to leave and a big mansion of a house. The O'Flahertys came from America forty or fifty years before, bought up this great place and tried to pass for big-shots, but their children all turned out wrong. They had a son went on for the priesthood, then broke out wild and ran away to England the day before his ordination. Old O'Flaherty never mentioned his name again, he was a great disgrace. Some said he finished up a navvy on the railways but others said no, he was on the Liverpool docks and sometimes worked on boats that went as far as Hong Kong and Australia. Many a one had it on good authority that he stayed out there in some foreign country and was married to a black woman. It was believed he couldn't be right in the head, must have a slate loose, people said. Instead of accepting the honour of being let handle the precious body and blood of our Blessed Lord, young O'Flaherty had chosen to waste his life and his talents working as an ordinary labourer in some distant part of the British Empire.

"As you make your bed, Auntie Bridgie said, and there was never one of that breed came to anything. And Mother said: 'But sure if the lad hadn't a vocation . . . ' And then Big Jim Malone, who knew all the ins and outs of things because he went to England and Scotland every year to work at the harvest, said that to his certain knowledge the affair had little to do with vocation or the want of it. The crux of the matter, he said, was a wee servant girl in the college where young O'Flaherty was trained. And God only knows, said Big Jim, God only knows what distant parts of the British Empire yon unfortunate servant was exiled to when young O'Flaherty was finished with her. Not that I'm excusing her, he said, any girl that'd . . . But all the same, he said with a wee laugh, it must have been tough on a simple young gersha from the hills, I mean trying to tell a half-priest to get his hand off her drawers. Mother told him sharply enough to hold his tongue, there was an innocent girl present and would he keep his dirty talk for his cronies at the crossroads. And Big Jim got in a huff and said: 'Oh this child need have no worry about priests or half-priests, she's in no danger of coming across any of that breed in the Protestant house where her own mother hired her out to work.' Mother was livid. She said it was hard enough to find a place these days and would he kindly tell her where else there was an opening for a fourteen-year-old girl that wasn't too quick on the uptake? If he could find a good Catholic household looking for a servant she'd be only too delighted to take Lizzie away from Miss Wilson's this very day and put her into it. I was quaking, heart-scared Big Jim would come up with the name of some hard-jawed farmer's wife in need of a strong and willing girl. But he didn't. There wasn't much work about the country them times, not even across the border in the Free State since most of the big English families was left and their estates broken up, and I knew I was lucky to have such a good place with Miss Wilson that was the loveliest lady you could meet, even if she wasn't one of our own.

"Big Jim was a distant cousin of mine, an orphan. His father was shot accidentally by the Black and Tans and his mother died shortly after, giving birth to him. The parish priest gave a very patriotic sermon against the English and said Mrs Malone died of a broken heart, but everyone else knew it was hunger and hardship. They were always in a very bad way of doing and Jim's father was known up and down the country as a shocking fellow for the bottle. Father coaxed Mother to take the baby and bring it up, this was long before I was born, at a time when it seemed Mother was never going to have a child of her own. Father was still at home then, a barman in McCormack's and, from what we heard after, drinking most of the stock. Him and Jim's father were great cronies, that's why he took the child. When old McCormack gave Father his walking papers he went away to England. I was two years of age then and Big Jim was eight. Father sent money for a while; then he was lost track of. After a year or so word came home that he was quit attending mass altogether and that he was living up dirty with some Englishwoman. Everyone said Mother was far better off without him: she might have some peace and contentment now and be able to make a home for herself and the two children. Mother was a great hand at the sewing and even when Father was at home she always used to do a bit of dressmaking for the neighbours, not having a big dreel of youngsters to occupy her time. When it was known her man was gone for good, Father McGinty put in a word for her with the shopkeepers and professional people of the town. To start with, they gave her the odd garment to mend out of charity, but when they saw how dependable she was they never left her short of work. She didn't earn big money because the real swanks bought their clothes in Belfast but she made a steady living and with Father not there she had the house like a wee palace and even set flowers in boxes on the window-sills, which was a great innovation, I can tell you, for Quarry Street. But she lived in constant dread that Father would come home and fall into his old ways, wrecking the place and sponging off her. She knew she was in duty bound to take him back if he did, being joined to him in the holy sacrament of matrimony, as well as the house being in his name and all. Father McGinty urged her to make novenas and have Masses offered that he would give up the English woman before it was too late to save his soul from eternal damnation, and she prayed obediently because it was the priest asked her but I used always think she was in a torment in case God took a notion to answer her prayers.

"When I was ten or eleven I started having these awful dreams where the pair of them arrived on our doorstep and, without saying one word, Mother took me and Big Jim and all our belongings and made us wander up and down the streets all day with the whole town behind its curtains laughing. I had the same dream over and over again till I went to live in Miss Wilson's house. Miss Wilson said it was only natural for me to have these anxieties, since all I really knew about my father came from old women's gossip, and what a wicked thing it had been to inflict such knowledge on a small child. Had my mother no sense of her responsibilities to speak badly of my father in front of me? I told her that even if Mother kept quiet I'd have heard it anyhow. There was no privacy in our lives the way there was in rich people's lives like Miss Wilson's. Everybody knew where you came from and what you had for your dinner and they could dig up things that happened in your family from generations back. Bad things. Some way they never seemed to rake up anything good. The whole school knew about Father and his woman and some of the smart ones used to ask me: 'I forget, Lizzie, how many wee sisters and brothers have you now?' I was glad to be working in Miss Wilson's: it used to be always a worry to me that I'd leave school and go to work among people that'd never quit casting it up to me about Father. They laughed about Jim's father too but that was different; you could laugh along with them.

"And we did too. Me and Mother and even Big Jim himself—we laughed our length that whole summer. What happened was this: some patriotic crowd from the Free State was going round putting up memorials to heroes that died for Ireland in the troubles and someone gave them the name of Micksey Malone, Jim's father, that was murdered by the English. These big-shots from Dublin went round the town gathering information about Meehawl O'Something or other, as they christened him in Irish, and some of the smart boyos took it into their heads to make cods of them with a whole lot of nonsense about how Micksey was shot at dawn for organising a big resistance movement against the Black and Tans. Jim was sixteen or seventeen at the time and the Dubliners took him into McCormack's and filled him up with free porter and he said aye, to be sure, sir; me daddy was always a great Republican, winking away at the barman behind their backs. Them fellas had it all ready to put in a book and had a folk-song wrote and everything; and were making arrangements to have a Celtic cross put up on the spot where the hero fell. The whole town was killing itself laughing and they had me tormented at school though I was laughing as hard as any of them, seeing the strangers running around taking the measurements of the 'closet' with big important faces on them.

"In the long run Father McGinty put them wise and told them how Big Jim's father was a notorious drunkard and how the night in question he was staggering home from McCormack's as full as a lord and went to relieve himself behind a bush. It was known as the 'closet' this bush, because it was the only bit of shelter on the road, and a godsend to country people took short on their way home from the town. Unfortunately, when Micksey stepped in off the road there was a Tan sitting on his hunkers down behind the bush. Well, they may have been blaggards but I suppose they had the same insides as the rest of us, and Micksey lepped on the Tan, taking him for someone from another townland, a crony of his. 'Well, ye drunken huer ye, Harry Morgan!' Micksey roared in high glee. 'And who gave you leave to shite in our closet?' God knows what the Tan took Micksey for; he put a bullet in him anyhow. Old Jamesy Murphy the thatcher was after parting company with Micksey a few yards from the bush and he heard the whole ructions from his own lane but he didn't venture back to see. You wouldn't them times, any more than you would now. Them Tans had neither sense nor mercy, the sweepings of English jails let out on parole to slaughter the poor Irish and well paid for it too.

"Well, the Sunday after the Dubliners left, Father McGinty preached a sermon and said the town of Claghan had disgraced itself again. Not content, he said, with being a bunch of drunken wastrels that never, in eight hundred years of occupation by our Saxon foe, saw fit to produce one measly wee warrior for Grainne Wail, they had to turn round and make little of themselves in front of educated people from the city, and if that's all the way the young Catholic men of the town knew how to conduct themselves we might expect our fair Six Counties to writhe for another eight centuries beneath the British boot. He cited Newry and Crossmaglen and Mullabawn and all the other towns round about that sent men to fight alongside Pearse and de Valera, and then he asked what were our boys fit for, only sitting up in bars making pigs of themselves with porter. It was a lovely sermon and I remember every word of it to this day. He read out the names of the fellows who codded the patriots, and he read out Big

Jim in particular for having so little respect for the memory of his dead father that he was ready to make mock of him for a few pints of stout. Which led on to the evils wrought by drink, the broken homes and the wives and children beaten and deserted, making Ireland the laughing-stock of the world, and when he came to that bit the smarty-heels beside me gave me a nudge and said: 'The priest's talking about you, Lizzie!'

"Several things came out of that sermon. The first was that Master Maguire, lord a mercy on him, set up classes of Irish language and history in the school in the evenings. We were all supposed to go, but in the long run as usual it just turned into a meeting place for the swells; the likes of us would have felt out of place. For a while you'd hear the shopkeepers' and bank clerks' children going round gabbling to each other like foreigners. We all knew it was just showing off and wouldn't last too long, and I'm sure they talked English like everybody else when they were at home and had no audience.

"The next thing was that old Matt O'Flaherty went up and made a whole scandal in the parochial house, called the priest a bloody liar up to his face in front of the two curates and Tessie Finnegan the housekeeper. 'No heroes is it?' O'Flaherty roared. 'And what about my own granda that had to escape on a coffin-ship to America after killing landlords and British soldiers and tyrants of all descriptions the time of the famine? That married a great Scotch lady and converted her to the one true faith? That delivered the poor people of this very town from rack-rent and eviction? No harm to you, Father, but you're a stranger here in Claghan and it seems you're one of these that doesn't see any heroes at all unless they come from far away and long ago. Did you never hear tell of Bold Cormac O'Flaherty, the darling of Erin?'

"Tessie said it was ferocious, he must have had a good few in him to confront the priest like that. Though mind you he was a Yank. The upshot of it was that Master Maguire, the man that started the Irish classes, went round investigating and he wrote a CTS booklet about Matt O'Flaherty's granda. I have it there somewhere, Sarah, if I could put my hand on it. Maybe upstairs with your mother's books that she left behind. You might like to read it sometime. It shook a lot of people because the most of us never heard tell of any history happening around Claghan up till that, and there was a good few in the town didn't come too well out of it when their pedigrees was looked into. I'm not naming no names but there was a whole lot had to be hushed up and not printed for fear of insulting the high-ups.

"Well, the third thing that came out of that sermon was that Big Jim took the Pioneer pledge and never touched another drop. He spent his evenings with the other boyos at the crossroads giving oul' guff to the girls that passed by and dicing with pennies and halfpennies. He turned into a shocking bully and I only had to linger a bit on the street coming from school or give Mother a back-answer to feel the flat of Jim's hand across my jaw. And he's still like that I hear and even worse, a shocking man for making enemies they say; it's years and years since I spoke to the fellow. There's nothing worse nor a teetotaller; a fellow that can take a drop has some nature in him as long as he knows when to quit. That's a thing I'd never have dared to say in front of Mother or Jim, or your grandfather later on. They were all very down on drink. But from the time he took the pledge, Big Jim was as sour as a buck weasel and I was heart-glad to get away to Miss Wilson's."

CHAPTER THIRTEEN

LIZZIE (2)

I t scared her a bit, the speed they were going at, snaking in and out among the other traffic and tearing through all the lights, sirens blaring away. She imagined the people turning in their tracks to look, their mouths wide open, a few old country ones in black shawls stopping to bless themselves and mutter a prayer. Only, was there anybody still left these days wearing a shawl? It was a long time since she noticed. This last few years she hardly went out except to Mass and the odd night to bingo; Canon McGinty Park wasn't like Quarry Street, it was too far out to take a dander round the shops when you felt like it. She'd got into the habit lately of letting Sarah buy whatever was needed for the house. To tell the truth she wasn't too easy walking about in the town; she couldn't get used to the way Claghan was changed, she was frightened. Noise and death and confusion, neighbours' sons with their heads shaved, zipped into black leather, empty eyes staring hate from street corners, desolation of bombed-out buildings. And now Sarah. Sarah . . . No, there wouldn't be any shawls left, and there'd hardly be anyone left either to bless themselves at an ambulance passing. Or even a hearse, God save us and keep it away from us, Sarah, poor wee Sarah lying there broken, she couldn't take it in. It wasn't a thing you could think of . . .

The side aisle at Mass used to be thick with shawls, a sort of greenish-black and rotten with smoke. Turf-smoke. It would turn your stomach long ago if you came in late and the priest made you sit over there, under St Teresa's statue with all the old country ones. A laugh too, because you'd be looking straight across at the men's side aisle and that would be solid with baldy heads under St Anthony of Padua and him as baldy as any of them. Herself and Gerty Feeney that she was at school with, they used to make up romances, old Biddy on one side winking across at old Paddy on the other, sending messages in sign language under Father McGinty's nose. But they must be all dead long ago. Poor Gerty was dead of cancer this years over in England. You're well past sixty, Lizzie, she thought, it's you is the oul' one now. She was never in an ambulance since the time wee Gerard. But you were unconscious that time, she thought, you heard nothing. Imagined nothing. Shawls and baldy heads, the things a body does think of.

The very top part of her mind was embarrassed at attracting so much attention. A military procession no less: the ambulances escorted by police and British soldiers. What must the people be thinking? The rest of her mind, the serious real part, knew of course that this was not important. Knew, but that was all because it felt nothing. Was frozen, numb, anaesthetised. She was aware of the numbness, aware that she ought to be feeling, aware that this was the worst thing ever happened to her or ever would happen to her if you didn't count wee Gerard and she couldn't, to be honest, count wee Gerard because that was such a long time ago and she was so young. She prayed to be given the grace of feeling but her mind kept filling up with foolishness. The people's faces, what'd be said on telly, how well she forgot to put on her good shoes. She looked down at her feet sitting side by side in their blue plaid slippers with the red braid that Kathleen sent her last Christmas with a lovely warm dressing-gown to match, and it seemed the shockingest thing of all that she was blaring through the darkness with an armed guard and her in a pair of blue plaid slippers. Every bit as shocking as poor broken Sarah lying there on a stretcher. She thought of Mrs McLeod on the television yesterday saying her husband had no connection with the security forces and appealing to the wicked men who were holding him to let an innocent human being go free. "Securry furces," she'd seemed to be saying. A Protestant voice, Agnes Murphy said. And the headlines in the paper: "Greenpeace Husband in Kidnap Drama." It was sitting there yesterday with Agnes Murphy, watching young Mrs McLeod crying on the television, that the thought came to her about Sarah, that she knew where Sarah must be this last few days, what Sarah and that lunatic of a fellow must be doing, only she couldn't really believe it, because it was too much like something you'd see on the telly. But she stayed awake the whole night long worrying, and she thought: if I hadn't told her anything about it, if I'd left her in ignorance, she was happy enough the way she was, the creature . . . And she thought: Quarry Street, and she thought: if you had the courage last night, Lizzie, to mention it to Agnes Murphy and the two of you go down there, to Quarry Street . . .

" . . . breathing, she still has a good strong pulse all the same, Mrs O'Flaherty. Please God . . . " A nice nurse. A Catholic. But the man at wee Sarah's feet—what was he? A guard? A male nurse? — looked blankly past her and said nothing at all.

"In the long run it was Mrs McLeod the bank manager's wife that found work for me. She was a young Protestant lady and bought her clothes in Robinson and Cleaver's in Belfast but Mother did some mending for her and she mentioned that a friend of hers was looking for a nice reliable girl. A Miss Wilson that was principal of a little village school across the border. Mother said aye ma'am and don't think I'm not obliged to you but Lizzie's only fourteen and I couldn't let her go away to any place where her faith might be in jeopardy. The bankman's wife said Mother need have no fear because Miss Wilson was a very good-living lady and would give me ample time to attend my religious duties, she was accustomed to having young Roman Catholic maids and was on excellent terms with all the local clergy. Mother still wasn't too contented but it was the only place that offered and I was coming up to school-leaving age and not near bright enough for a shop. So she agreed that it would do for a turn and please God before long something more suitable might turn up.

"Miss Wilson came to the house to inspect me and she was a plump wee lady about Mother's age driving a pony and trap. She said, laughing, that she wouldn't be a hard mistress to me. In fact, she said, the parents of her pupils were always reproaching her for being too soft-hearted. She taught Protestant children of around my age. There was a lot of Protestant families in that county who stuck it out and didn't leave when the Free State government came. Well, where would we have gone, she asked with another laugh; it's our homeland too, isn't it? Mother said maybe so but the likes of us doesn't take much heed in them class of things, ma'am, and what sort of work would Lizzie be expected to do? Miss Wilson said oh just the plain cooking and housework but I wouldn't have to do it alone; she kept her own room and study tidy; the main thing, she said, was to have someone there for company at night and to help out when needed. Every second Saturday I could sleep at home and have my Sunday free. It was arranged that she would come for me in the trap on my

fourteenth birthday. She said as it was my very first place
she'd have a little cake ready for my tea, with candles. I said
to Mother when she left that it sounded a nice easy place and
wasn't Miss Wilson friendly? Mother said aye a great talker,
only wait till you're there a month or two before you judge.
And if she tries to get round you or even as much as opens
a Bible in your presence you're to come straight home, walking
if need be, do you hear me now? I said but she solemnly
promised to let me out to my duties and isn't it nice of her
anyway to think of a cake? Mother said you poor eejit there'll
be no cake, that's just a rich people's joke; they love to take
a hand at the likes of us and when you're working for swells
as long as me, daughter, you'll learn to take them with a grain
of salt.

"But there *was* a cake and fourteen wee white candles on
it, and she told me I had to blow them out and make a wish.
I wished into myself that she wouldn't be as hard on me as
Mother seemed to think, and then I regretted not wishing for
something more worthwhile. It was the first time I ever saw
a birthday cake.

"I hadn't to work nearly as hard for her as for Mother. It
seemed funny to be getting paid for it, I mean just for doing
the wee turns that I'd have had to do anyway at home. I had
to tidy round the house and have her dinner ready when she
came in at noontime and her tea when school was over. She
often sat down and ate with me in the kitchen, but when she
invited the other teachers or the minister or the McLeods over
from Claghan to take their supper with her she did the
cooking herself and I had to serve it, dressed in black with
a white apron. That was the only time she used to speak
sharp to me, mistress to maid. Most of the time it was like
being at school, with a nice easy teacher! Would you credit,
she used to make me sit down and read books when my
work was finished, or else talk to her about my family and
our neighbours in the town. The first few times I was quaking.

I was convinced she'd give me some bad books to read, to pervert me from my faith. But they were only long story-books about high-up children that went to boarding-schools and done foolish things like searching for buried treasure and never seemed to go to the dances or Mass or even to their own church. She told me it was important to read these books, she said it was an essential part of being a child.

"Only I wasn't a child. In a year or so I'd be going to the dances and looking out for some nice boy to get married to and rear a family with. That's why I always regretted not being smart enough to serve my time in a shop. Shopgirls always had the best chance of hooking the nice-looking boys and of getting fellows that were in steady work. Mother always said it was as well not to be too fussy about looks; the first thing to watch out for, she said, was the Pioneer pin. Any lad that had that badge in his lapel was guaranteed to be good to his wife and make a decent home for his family. If he wasn't a teetotaller you should watch out for yourself, you might well be walking into some hell on earth and wasn't she the right one to know? I didn't pay her too much heed because I knew there was a lot of men round about that liked their pint and never did no harm to anyone; they weren't all like Father or Micksey Malone. That sort of carry-on was a thing of the past when people were wilder and not as educated. What worried me most was that I'd be left sitting when I went to the dances, that I wouldn't get a look-in at all with all the smart girls there were in the town. Maybe if I kept well in with Miss Wilson she might give me her old dresses and Mother could take them in to fit me, no nonsense them times about special clothes for teenagers. Although Miss Wilson was old and a bit stout she had some lovely clothes.

"But I read the books to humour her because she was so good to me and I told her all the funny things that happened in Claghan. She knew them all already from Mrs McLeod but she said she liked hearing things from different angles. She said you wouldn't credit the difference it made. She told me how a few years before when there was all the ructions about Michael Malone's memorial, she and all her friends, whatever their colour, had been shocked and horrified at such a display of thick-witted ignorance. It had seemed a senseless drunken joke played on well-meaning if misguided people. But when I explained the ins and outs of it to her she said she saw how annoying it must be for the likes of us to have outsiders walking in whenever they saw fit and cross-questioning us in the cheekiest way as if we were just there for their entertainment. Because at that time all sorts of big-bugs were in the habit of coming to Quarry Street and round about, writing in notebooks and taking pictures and trying to get us to talk Irish and sing old-fashioned rubbish for them, though by then only a handful of real old people spoke Irish without having to learn it, a very low-down class of people they were. I mean they were nothing to brag about and you wouldn't have expected high-ups to be so interested in them. Yanks and everything used to come. But it was hard on the young fellows of the town that were in the habit of going over to England every year and earning good money and that thought themselves the height of fashion with their foxtrots and hair-oil and *Bing Time* on the wireless and all the latest slang talk, and then to be treated like savages out of the jungle and ordered to dance jigs for foreigners. You could understand them, I mean, but people like the priests and doctors and schoolteachers just thought they were thick. Ignorant gulpins, Father McGinty used to call them off the altar."

CHAPTER FOURTEEN

LIZZIE (3)

They let her sit on a wee stool in the corridor outside the double doors and she sat there quietly for hours, fingers linked tight on top of her square brown handbag. Now and again someone would come through the doors and she'd half-lift herself to her feet nervously, her mouth opening to ask, but the person would rush past her as if she was a piece of furniture and she'd subside tiredly on to the stool again. The reality of it was beginning to come through now in fits, a stab and a throb like the worst toothache: she couldn't take hold of it and suffer it and try to make sense of it the way she used to do long ago with labour pains, this came on her unawares, knifing swiftly through her fatigue, leaving her helpless.

Someone touched her on the shoulder, coaxed her to rise. "We're taking her to the intensive care unit, Mrs O'Flaherty. No, I'm afraid you can't, not just yet. She hasn't regained consciousness, you see. Well, we can't really tell you yet how successful . . . Yes, I know you're worried about your daughter, naturally. Oh, she's your grand-daughter? I see. And the parents, are they . . . Oh yes, well it's only an hour's flight, isn't it, she'll probably get a plane straight away at this time of the year. Yes the shuttle service is great, isn't it, and so cheap. I hope you'll both be able to see her then. But you do realise, Mrs O'Flaherty, the circumstances are rather . . . "

Yes, she realised. The circumstances. Not an ordinary patient this. She was surprised they let her come at all, let her stay like this, waiting. Young Father Callan must have put in a word, and Doctor McCormack, that was it, they were there at the time calming her, bustling her into the ambulance. Maybe she was meant to be treated, sedated or something, maybe no one realised. Hospital routine turned inside out. Armed occupation. Though the doctors and nurses must be getting used to it after near twenty years. Claghan hospital must have seen some shocking sights this last while. The time McCormack's hotel got bombed. Jamesy Murphy came in like a butcher to use her bathroom after helping the rescue team, poor May would have had a fit it he landed home to her in that state, so they rigged him out in some old clothes of Pakky's that were still hanging in a wardrobe and threw his own in the bin . . . And the day seven working men were shot down one after another coming out of Lewis's shoe factory . . . And Big Jim himself, lord a mercy on him, left lying with a bag over his head at the side of a road. Jim Malone had no need of the hospital. And Sarah now. Wee Sally . . .

The first thing as soon as she got up this morning she went down to Quarry Street thinking, "I'm daft. It has nothing to do with Sarah, how could it have anything to do with Sarah? She's out the whole weekend making a huer of herself with that lunatic of a fellow, that's why she didn't come home. It's not the first time. I'm making an eejit of myself. Away mad to Dublin or some place on that motorbike, that's all it is." But thinking: if she's there she'll maybe listen to me. Knowing well she was there. But when she came to the top of Quarry Street she saw it was full of soldiers and they wouldn't let her past.

There were two policemen guarding the ward. They'd want to question poor wee Sarah. There were waiting to question her as soon as she came round. *If* she came round. God help us, she thought, it's them will have the right to see her first. It's them she belongs to now. The kind nursing officer (they were all surprisingly kind and gentle with her though in the circumstances. After all some of them must be on the other side, must be Protestants?) took her by the elbow and supported her to a carpeted waiting area. Armchairs, green plants, a tweed-curtained bay of window: would you like a wee cup of tea, Mrs O'Flaherty? No, it's no trouble, no trouble at all now . . . And to ring your daughter again maybe? But when she rang Kathleen there was still no answer, and when the tea came she found she couldn't make the effort to drink it. As the time went by, it sat untouched on the glass-topped coffee-table, growing a dirty yellowish skin on top, and no one came to remove the cup, or came near her at all.

"I was wary for a while about telling Miss Wilson the sort of things that mightn't do us credit in the eyes of a non-Catholic. It came to me that she was every bit as nosy herself as any of the busybodies that came to question us, but after a time I realised that she was just a very lonesome woman and trying to make friends with me.

"Although she went here and there and asked people to the house she had no family of her own and that's an awful lonely thing for anyone. She had a photo on the piano of the fellow she was supposed to get married to only he got killed in the war. She said there was a lot of Protestant girls in her position up and down the country, because the young men of her generation all went away to fight for the English against the Kaiser. I said not only the Protestants because

there was a family on our street that was nicknamed the
Kaiser Bills because the father always made a show of himself
when he was drunk, crying like a youngster and making up
wild yarns about the slaughter in the trenches. And there was
even an oul' fellow called the Bayonets Bogan that went out
long ago to fight the Boers of Africa. Miss Wilson said the
yarns about the trenches were very probably true; it had been
a most incredible massacre, and she said maybe it was just
as well she never got married because if she'd had sons
they'd be just of an age now to go off and fight this dreadful
Hitler. But you could see she regretted being single and she'd
have grabbed the chance of getting married even then if
anyone had asked her.

"I honestly think she didn't realise she was well past the
age to hook a man and she used to run after the Protestant
minister something shocking. She was famous for it in the
village. The doctor's maid told me that some people thought
the Protestant teacher was a bit touched but, odd and all as
she was, I never thought that about her. Mind you, I thought
her ways were strange. She was very particular about wee
things like doilies. She'd half-kill you and call you a peasant
if you put biscuits or anything down on the bare plate. And
then the garden. She was mad daft about that garden. A blue
garden. She wouldn't have the smallest flower in it that wasn't
blue. All shades and colours of blue, and she'd go wild with
delight when she came on a new breed of flower that colour.
You could understand if she'd been a Catholic, blue being
Our Lady's colour and all, but no it was just sheer childishness.
Them class of people always had the full of their stomachs
and no real problems to worry about so their minds got took
up with all sorts of wee foolishness. Mind you, it looked
lovely that garden. Odd but lovely. And then this thing of
making her servant girl read children's story-books. The other
maids round about used to laugh their length when I told
them that. But in spite of her wee oddities she was just a nice

ordinary woman and I was fond of her. And sorry for her, too, believe it or not.

"So, that Sunday I mentioned, I was glad to have a bit of gossip to carry back to her, about Matt O'Flaherty having a stroke at the races and how his sons and daughters would soon be home killing each other over who'd get the place. I didn't know any of them only to see old Matt himself in the town of a fair-day, shaking his walking-stick and acting the gentleman. The family was all left home before I was born but they were a legend for miles around. How old Matt built himself up from nothing in the States to buy back what he used to call his ancestral home and pushed his children into good positions in banks and offices and how one after another they turned out wrong and went away to work in England as if they were ordinary people's children and reared on stirabout. Bad blood coming out, they used to say in Quarry Street, mentioning how years and years ago one of the same O'Flaherty clan got into some awful trouble for killing his father-in-law. I never heard no word of him being a hero till Master Maguire wrote that book. And then the youngest son of all turning his back on the priesthood on the very eve of his ordination. But Matt O'Flaherty never seemed to be crushed. No matter how many misfortunes came, he got more and more of a gentleman, running to the races like a priest or doctor and treating the high-ups to whiskey in McCormack's bar. Miss Wilson said the high-ups apparently didn't treat him back, because no one *she* knew in Claghan had ever heard of him, but wasn't it tragic about the poor boy who had to emigrate over a piece of youthful folly? I said he was no boy, he must be coming up on forty by now, and you hadn't to feel sorry for him because wasn't it the awfullest thing to be given the honour of going on for the priesthood and then renege on it at the last moment over some girl? There was no higher calling, I told her, and even if he found it hard itself he ought to have respected it.

"Miss Wilson laughed and said it was extraordinary to hear a child of my age talking so obsessively about religion and doctrine, one minute I was all light and ordinary and the next there I was up on a pulpit. She said she simply couldn't picture her pupils or her friends' daughters getting so excited over some middle-aged stranger who'd decided he wasn't fitted for the ministry. I said, and what do Protestant girls get excited over, miss? She said, oh their frocks and their hair and boyfriends and dances, things like that. Normal things. I said *I* think of them sort of things too but Father McGinty told us we must always keep our one true faith in the forefront of our minds and be ready to defend it, because the poor Catholic church needed all the support it could get, seeing it was pressed down and persecuted in every corner of the globe. Miss Wilson gave a dry sort of a laugh and said: 'But that's sheer nonsense, Elizabeth! It is common knowledge that the Roman Catholic church is the most powerful organisation in the world. And the wealthiest.' I thought that was the stupidest thing I ever heard. You only had to look at the difference in Catholics and Protestants, sure you only had to look at the difference in Miss Wilson and me. I thought maybe it was true she was a bit touched to believe a thing like that, and then I remembered Father McGinty saying that no matter how nice and how friendly they let on to be they were always watching their chance to get the dirty gibe in about your religion. I thought it wasn't a bit of wonder that Big Jim and Mother were always chivvying me to tell straight away if she tried to pervert me, and that when I went to confession in the village the priest never stopped questioning me about whether or not my mistress let me out freely to my duties.

"I finished my supper in silence, washed the cups and plates and went straight up to bed. She always had a good supper waiting for me when I came back after my day off and she'd sit at the kitchen table and drink a cup of cocoa and listen to all my news from the town. I had a second-hand bicycle by then that I was paying her for bit by bit out of my wages, and it was great because I didn't have to depend on Big Jim or a chance lift. But it was a hard old road from Claghan and she'd never let me do a hand's turn when I landed back of a Sunday night, the tea wet for me and everything. She was a kind woman, I'll say that for her, and that's why it was such a shock to hear her talking in that bigoted way about the Catholic religion, because I never would have thought she was so black. It just went to show that you couldn't trust even the nicest of them. It was a double shock to me because from the first day I went to work there I had a dream that I would be the one to influence her mind and bring her by words and good example to the one true faith. Thanks be to God I never mentioned it to anyone, but if it had happened it would have been a great victory for Our Blessed Lord and Lady. But lying in my bed that Sunday night I realised what an eejit I was even to be thinking of such a thing. She was as black as any of them underneath it all, with no respect for anybody's beliefs only her own. Before I went to sleep I resolved that in the future I wouldn't be as flah-flum with the chat and the friendliness."

CHAPTER FIFTEEN

LIZZIE (4)

B ut when was the last cup of tea she drank? When had she last eaten? Yesterday morning—no, it was only *this* morning, she thought. It was barely twenty-four hours after all since she sat watching the news with Agnes Murphy—this morning for the first time in her life she was stopped at the entrance to Quarry Street and asked her business as if she was a foreigner. I'm taking the short-cut to the chapel, she had the wit to say. Well I'm afraid you'll have to go round the long way, missus, the soldier said dry enough, this here street is closed for the present. At the bottom end, in Lockhart Road, she came on a little group of people huddled together with their eyes glued to the top of Quarry Street, though you couldn't see much at that distance. She recognised a few families, neighbours from long ago, who hadn't been rehoused in the new estate. They could tell her nothing, had been told nothing themselves, only knew that the police and army had come and evacuated them in the early hours of the morning, that there was something going on in the block of condemned houses. A siege of some sort, they thought. Or a bomb to be defused. Or maybe that kidnapped Protestant even, that McLeod man, maybe they took him to Quarry Street.

"To the old famine museum," someone laughed. "And what better place? Wasn't it him started it, wasn't it him went round collecting the money yon time? Preserving our heritage!"

"I'd say that's where they're surrounding all right," someone else said. "Sure it's maybe even in your own old house, Lizzie, isn't that where you used to live, one of them houses with the plaques on them?"

And she knew then that she'd guessed right, about Sarah, about Sarah and her mad-head of a fellow, but that it was far too late for guessing anything. "Just as long as it doesn't fall in on them," a woman joked, and the old people remembered poor Sarah Morris, lord a mercy on her, who was crippled when her house fell down on top of her, years and years ago.

Lizzie had stood around with the others for an hour or so, helplessly, watching Quarry Street—where there was indeed very little to watch, only soldiers with their guns ready and a man with a loudspeaker. Whatever was happening was at the other end of the street, Lizzie's end, but people were being turned away from there and not allowed to watch. After a while the police came and ordered them out of Lockhart Road as well. She'd offered shelter to any of the evacuees who needed it but no one did, they all had their friends or relations to go to. Then she'd walked back alone to her house in Canon McGinty Park, and waited and thought until she felt she could wait and think no more.

"As things turned out I hadn't long to be cool with her because on the Tuesday at dinnertime Big Jim arrived at the house on his bicycle. I was certain sure Mother was sick or dead and I could feel myself turning as white as that wall there. Miss Wilson got into a flurry too, she must have been thinking the same thing, and she said: 'Sit there child, sit where you are. I'll go.' And she ran to the back door and asked him in a whisper what was wrong. He said, very curt and embarrassed: 'This girl's wanted at home, ma'am, straight away, there's a position found for her.' Miss Wilson laughed at him: 'But Malone, what are you talking about? Is this some joke? Have you been drinking? Elizabeth *has* a position. I am perfectly satisfied with her work and conduct.'

"'Aye, ma'am, sure I know that well, but the parish priest's after finding her a position with a good Catholic family and he gave me strict orders that I'm to take her back home with me straight away. Their own maid left sudden and they're in jeopardy, with sickness in the family and everything. They want her to start this evening, the priest said.'

"'But that's ridiculous, Malone! Elizabeth is perfectly suited here, and even if she wasn't she could hardly expect to leave without giving me warning.'

"I asked who was the Catholic family and Jim told me Matt O'Flaherty's servant girl refused to take on with the extra work of attending an invalid and walked out without notice. 'Well, priest or no priest, you won't get me to work in O'Flahertys'!" I said. "Amn't I far better off as I am?'

"'Troth and you'll do as you're bid, girl, or you'll feel the flat of my hand across your jaw. Old Mrs O'Flaherty's desperate, she went and appealed to the priest to find her someone quick and he guaranteed himself you'd come. Your mother says you're to leave here with me and that's all about it.'

"'But it's illegal!" Miss Wilson said in a sort of squeak. "Don't you realise, Malone, that I can take the lot of you to court and ruin you for breach of contract. You'll be paying me damages for the rest of your life over this!'

"Jim didn't know Miss Wilson as well as I did and he was scared enough. He thought she was a hard-headed Presbyterian lady like some of the farmers' wives he used to work for up beyond the Black Banks that'd be capable of mustering whole armies of solicitors and judges to destroy the likes of us. I was wishing to God she would but I knew that, non-Catholic or not, she'd be helpless against Father McGinty. One guldher out of that gentleman and she'd be frightened and flustered in no time. She was a woman that couldn't cope with raised voices at all, the whole village knew she couldn't even keep proper order in a class of schoolchildren, the bigger ones played rings round her.

"And that was what happened. Big Jim went home and told that Miss Wilson was preparing to go to court over me, and the next thing we knew Father McGinty drove up to the front door in his big Humber. He came ranting and raving into Miss Wilson's pretty wee house—honest to God I thought he'd break every ornament and gewgaw in the place—and he went for me like a bull at a gate. He had me by the ear before I got time to duck: did I not know I was in danger of excommunication, eh? A child of my age that persisted in putting her immortal soul in deathly danger, closing her ears like a heathen to the entreaties of her family, stubbornly continuing to live in surroundings where the very foundations of her faith were daily put in jeopardy, did I not know that, eh? What had the Catechism to say about wilfully seeking out the occasion of sin? And about giving scandal? Was I already that lost to all decency that I didn't realise the example I was setting? Maybe leading younger than myself astray, choosing publicly to wallow in the temptations of an alien household, eh?'

"'No slur on Miss Wilson,' he said, calming down a bit and bowing to her where she stood plastered up against the far wall with her eyes standing in her head from outrage. 'From all accounts she's a decent lady that lives according to her own lights. Aye, but they're not our lights, are they, girl?' he roared, working himself up again. 'And can you not see the disgrace it is to refuse employment with a Catholic family when it's offered to you? Wouldn't the greatest heathen out on the mission fields have more heed in her immortal soul than you have? Troth and there's many a poor Irish girl slaving away in pagan England this very minute that'd go down on her knees and thank me for offering her this chance that you're so wantonly casting aside!'

"I thought of the maid that walked out of O'Flaherty's and that she must have been in desperate straits altogether to put herself in the way of such condemnation, but I knew already that it was all over and that I'd be taking her place. It wasn't just the ranting and roaring and knowing that all decent people would be against me if I stayed. After Sunday night's performance I realised in my heart that Father McGinty was right. How long would it have been before my faith was shaken by Miss Wilson's gibes? And how long before she got tired of letting me run out for the odd hour to confession and benediction and the novena? Say what you like and she may have been the kindest woman I ever met, but when all's said and done they were two totally different ways of living, and it could only do the greatest harm to try and mix them. I said to myself that I'd be far better off among my own, no matter what class of people they were or how hard they worked me."

CHAPTER SIXTEEN

SARAH AND MALACHY

"Bored in Claghan? No, I wouldn't say I'm bored. Actually I'm bored just about everywhere else except here. It's hard to explain, Malachy, but ever since Mum first brought me over here I've never felt really *right* back in London. Never felt London's real, the way Claghan's real and all. I've never had a place before, see, where I seemed to exist. You're probably going to think I'm bananas or something but it's only here in Claghan that I know for sure that there's a person called Sarah O'Flaherty and that she's *me* and that anyone gives a shit what happens to her."

"But you can't go on forever like that, Sal. Unpaid companion to some old woman! It's weird, like. Do you not think it's a bit sick? At your age? I mean, I'm not complaining, Christ, anything that keeps you coming back to Claghan! But you couldn't exactly call it *living* could you, Sal?"

"I *could* call it living—that's just exactly what it is, luv."

"Living with your old grandmother? In a council house in Claghan? In Canon McGinty Park of all places! No one could call that living."

"Listen, my old grandmother, as you call her, actually thinks I'm human. I mean she's glad I exist. I know it sounds yucky but she needs me and all. Even if it's just to do the shopping. The poor thing's scared stiff to walk into Claghan, she thinks a bomb's going to go off in every shop, she thinks she's going to get mugged. She's scared to sit in the house, she thinks some gang of junkies in black leather is going to burst in and rape her and scorch the soles of her feet to get at her savings. It happened to someone she knew. Out in the country. Or she read about it. So she lives in the past, it's the only place the old dear's comfortable these days. Only she needs someone around her, and I'm all there is. If I wasn't there she'd be just another pathetic old woman propped up in front of the telly, depending on the neighbours. But I'm her audience. I'm the proof she still exists. And *she* makes *me* exist. She sees me. She talks to me. She's the first person ever did."

"Oh come on, Sal, *I* see you! Christ, I see no one else, do I?"

"I said she was the first person, not the only one. Sure, you see me. Sure, you're important. You're another reason I'm happy to hang around Claghan. Only I don't want to marry you or anything, and the last thing I want is to go back over to London with you if that's what you're intending. I've *had* London."

"But your mother—"

"I keep telling you. I fucked up Mum's life. Mum's a mess, even I can see that. If it hadn't been for old Maureen and Trev she'd probably have taken an overdose years ago. Did you ever read that poem about the albatross? Well, that's me. In person. The last thing she'd want is me back in London. She's living with some guy. Unless he's left her by now. Or she's left him. They never live up to her expectations. No one does. *I* sure don't, baby! Actually I can't think why she didn't just dump me on Gran years ago, when I was born. I mean it happens all the time doesn't it, girls dumping babies on their parents? Gran would have been delighted. She and my grandfather would have brought me up . . . They'd have been fantastic for me. I'd have had a family. I'd have grown up in Claghan like you. I'd have gone to school with you, imagine! And Mass and everything. I'd have been nice. I'm sure I'd have grown up to be a really nice person, Malachy. Not all screwed up and snarling!"

"I wouldn't have fancied you at all if you'd been nice! All sweet smiles and rosary beads, wouldn't have looked at you. It's the exotic I go for, didn't you know? Like you're a half-savage, same as me. Coupla misfits, that's why we're good together. No but, what does the old cow talk to you about? Her arthritis or what?""Oh, things. Her life. Sits there for hours telling me her life story. You should hear her, Malachy, she can remember every single thing that ever happened to her. I keep telling her she ought to write a book instead of leaving it to pseuds' corner types like Maureen Murphy that get it all out of the library. You should hear some of the things happened in Claghan. Straight out of the dark ages some of it, medieval history. Really traumatising. I mean, you can see why the poor old thing can't cope with modern life. And hey, rich boy, you can stop making nasty digs about Canon McGinty Park! She told me about your family and all, want to hear? Well, did you know your old grandad or great-grandad fought in some war and everyone called him the Kaiser Bill Larkin? Honest. He was sort of the town joke, they lived in this absolute tip in Quarry Street, how do you like that? She says your dad changed his name to Caiserbuill Ó Lorcáin when he went up in the world, because it sounded posher. That's what she *said*."

"Your granny's out of her tiny mind, Sal. None of our crowd was ever in the British army, where did she get that from? Typical Claghan, I can see how it'd happen all right— Caiserbuill Ó Lorcáin, Kaiser Bill Larkin, must have been a gift to the local comedians! But for frig's sake, Sal, don't go spreading yarns like that around, my father would do his nut over it. Could even be *dangerous*, do you realise, if some weirdo got hold of it! Do you *realise*? Good Christ, Grandad a British tommy! That old woman of yours must be crazy!"

CHAPTER SEVENTEEN

LIZZIE (5)

"Well, that first day in O'Flahertys' I thought I walked into a madhouse. The old man in the bed roaring for attendance, the poor wife screeching, wait now wait now Matthew, I'm doing my best; the sons and daughters not doing a hand's turn only sitting there in the parlour with cigarettes in their gobs, jandering and jawing at each other and calling for tea and coffee, the servant boys coming in and out of the fields to be fed, trailing muck and dirt over the red tiles of the kitchen. From eight o'clock in the morning till nine or ten at night sometimes I never quit dancing attendance on the crowd of them. Big feeds of bacon and cabbage and porter and tea and then, just when I'd be in the greatest hobble teeming a pot of spuds or something, the old invalid would let a guldher out of him that he needed the vessel and me knowing well that if I didn't run brave and sharp he'd let go regardless over bed and bedclothes. Not a blessed day went by but I had some dirty mess to clean up after him. Every night I used to cry my eyes out riding back the three miles to the town and swear that as soon as I got a few shillings together I'd run away altogether and get on the boat for England. Surely to God if I turned up on my father's doorstep he wouldn't be barefaced enough to chase me away? I knew in my heart I'd never do it. Sure I wouldn't even know the man if I met him along the road! But the thought that I had that outlet was all that kept me going from one day till the next.

"Mother was that sorry for me. She said if she'd known she'd have left me in Miss Wilson's where I was contented and well thought of, only Big Jim and the priest between them had her head moithered to put me into O'Flahertys', when the chance offered, and she only tried to do her best for all hands. But sure anyway, she said, the old man can't last long and things are bound to settle and quieten a bit when there's only the ordinary housework to see about.

"She was wrong. The old man lasted a brave while and there was great changes for the whole lot of us before he died.

"When I was there ten days or so the spoiled priest arrived. He walked out from the station, no one expecting him, and was landed in the kitchen before the family knew a hait about it. I got the shock of my life when I saw this queer-looking vagabond walking in. He was clean and tidy enough with a good tweed suit, only hadn't he this pointy wee beard on him and, like a fool, I took him for one of the travelling men used to go round them times fixing clocks and watches. The master was sick, I told him, and the mistress in the yard giving orders if he wanted to speak to her.

"'I'm Patrick,' he said, 'the youngest son. Just call me Prodigal. How's the oul' fella keeping?'

"All flustered, I told him he could go to the sickroom and see for himself; there wasn't much change, I told him, he was holding his own.

"'His own what, girl?' he said with a laugh. 'Well, in that case there's no hurry, is there? I'm in no danger of missing the holy last words. Would there be a drop of tay on the go maybe? I'm parched from th'oul' train.'

"He talked like the people round about but it sounded put on; all the sisters and brothers were great swells and talked very nebby. There was no kettle on the boil so I told him I'd open a bottle of porter but no, no, he said, he'd rather wait for the sup of tea—it was years since he touched the other. Another sour old teetotaller, I thought, like Big Jim. I made him the tea and told him who I was and how I came there. 'So poor Elly walked out,' he said, sounding very sad about it. 'She was with us this thirty years or more. I'd say the oul' fella's a devil when he's sick; he's fierce enough when he has his health.'

"I wondered of a sudden was Elly maybe the servant girl that he got into trouble and then I started remembering the stories I heard about him and I turned bright red. Lucky enough he didn't twig what I was thinking. 'Are they bad to you, then?' he asked. I couldn't very well say they were a pack of blaggards so I passed it off, oh I'm not right settled in yet, I'm not used to the work so . . .

"'What age are you?'

"'Fifteen.'

"'Jabus! Only fifteen. You'd be far better off in England. There's plenty of work over there now for girls, in factories. Making ammunition and everything. A hell of a lot better than being a hired girl in this kip. Did you never think of going over to England?'

"I explained that my mother was dead set against England and then he seemed to remember something and said: 'Oh bejabus aye! Oh be the holies!' and I knew that he knew about my father. I was waiting for him to make a jeer of me or to be inquisitive like all the rest but he didn't say anything more.

"'Well, I suppose I'd better face the firing squad,' he said when he finished the tea, 'Keep your fingers crossed for me, Liz!' There was a whole lot of shouting and roaring when he went to the old man's room and I ran out to the henhouse and made a great performance out of collecting eggs in case there was murder done. But the meeting must have passed off the best in the world because from that evening on the beardy man seemed to be the ruler of the roost, giving orders right left and centre.

"I was let home early from then on, and Patrick O'Flaherty said there was no need for a hired girl to attend his sick father, *he'd* do all the lifting and laying that was needed. He said he worked for a while in a mental hospital while he was on his travels and was well used to looking after invalids. The mother and sisters were hopping mad when he said that. They tried to make him shut up, afraid no doubt that I'd go broadcasting round the town that one of the O'Flahertys used to work in an English lunatic asylum. And, God forgive me, I did tell Gerty Feeney and she spread it round and in no time at all, it was twisted the way everything gets twisted in Claghan, shocking tongues they have, and in the finish up everyone believed Pakky O'Flaherty spent fifteen years in an asylum when he was supposed to be in England, and it used to be cast up to him a dread later on. And to the whole lot of us, your mother and all.

"There was a great commotion in the chapel the next Sunday over the new arrival. Hardly any men had beards in them times, only a few old fellows, and there was a lot of jeering and pointing. Gerty Feeney said she wouldn't work in a house that lodged yon thing if you paid her. She asked me wasn't I scared witless? I was a bit to tell you the truth, and I tried never to be alone with him, remembering all the stories about how he tumbled maids rings round him in the very seminary itself, but it was great all the same to have the old invalid taken off my hands. The beardy man was the only one in the whole crowd that had a bit of consideration either for his father or for anyone else. The others were all talk: 'How's Dada today? . . . Now Lizzie, I hope you're not neglecting poor Dada?' But when the old man needed feeding or cleaning poor Dada was forgotten and the pack of them disappeared into the parlour and left me to it.

"I missed Miss Wilson a dread, and our wee talks and jokes and the way she used to tell me not to kill myself working but to sit down for half an hour and read a story-book. I never saw one of the O'Flahertys reading a book, gentry and all as they were, and as for talking, they'd as soon think of talking to a cow or a pig as to me. The servant boys were no company either; awkward big lumps of fourteen or fifteen that turned beetroot if you as much as bid them the time of day, convinced by Father McGinty that every girl was a shameless hussy that'd make a grab at their chastity as quick as look at them. When I went home at night I was too tired to talk and Mother was never great crack anyhow. Soon after I started in O'Flahertys', Big Jim went away to England to work in a factory seeing that Mother didn't need him at home now because I was there at night. Mother always claimed to be afraid to stay alone in the house in case Father turned up suddenly, though God knows what good either me or Big Jim would have been to her if he did. My friend Gerty Feeney went to England too. They were going wild looking for Irish people to work the factories seeing how all their own labour was conscripted into the army. I never felt as lonesome in my life as I did them months waiting for old O'Flaherty to die.

"In the long run I rode out to the village one Sunday to see Miss Wilson, with the excuse of paying her what I owed on the bicycle. Mother was at me to post it and save myself the run and me so wore out, but I was that much in need of some friend to talk to that I'd gladly have rode fifty mile instead of twenty. As soon as I arrived at the door I saw it wasn't going to be the same at all. A new servant let me in, and her and Miss Wilson seemed to be getting on like a house on fire. I never felt more of an outsider. Miss Wilson hoped I was well and happy in my new place and I said I was. I didn't know how to start explaining how things really stood, with the other one in and out making the tea and her ears flapping. I said I was sorry about all the ructions and hoped she was well suited in her new maid. She said yes, Susannah was an excellent girl, a former pupil at her school, and for the future she intended to engage only Protestant servants: that way, she said, one doesn't risk unpleasant surprises. No harm to you, Elizabeth, she said, after all you are not responsible either for your foster-brother or your parish priest. The trouble is, she said, that they feel only too responsible for you. There was a definite coolness and I didn't stay long. When I was leaving she relented and told me I was free to call on her if ever I had any troubles or difficulties. I said I would and was near blinded with tears all the way home, knowing well that if I'd told her the truth about O'Flahertys' she'd have been as warm as ever to me. Only where would have been the point in telling her? I'd have only been making little of myself in front of the Susannah one, and Miss Wilson couldn't have lifted one finger to change things anyway.

"Old O'Flaherty hung on like a warrior. He had a bit of a speech defect and was half-paralysed but for all that he showed no signs of dying. Father McGinty was in and out to see him; they seemed to be very great. Young Mr McCormack from the hotel came now and again too, and the solicitor and the vet and one or two of his racing friends. There was a great roaring and raging at times.

"I kept waiting to see Mr McLeod the bank manager and his wife landing on the doorstep and I was planning that I'd run out and hide in the henhouse if ever I saw their car on the avenue because I'd have been ashamed of my life to meet them there after the nice friendly way they used to greet me at Miss Wilson's. But they never came, and then I remembered Miss Wilson saying her friends had never even heard of

O'Flaherty. I suppose even among swells the Protestants kept to themselves and wouldn't mix.

"I had to serve food and drink to all these people that came to the house, as well as the family and the labourers. There was an old countrywoman came in for the scrubbing and the washing, but she was no company. She was a poor woman that was never too right in the head. Looney Lennon we used to shout after her when she came in to the town to buy her few groceries.

"When I was there a few months the sons and daughters started leaving. They said there was no point in staying on and they couldn't stand it any longer, stuck there in the middle of the fields like vegetables. Vegetating, that's what one of the daughters called it, and she for one was going back over to the bright lights. To the black-out, her sister said, and isn't that even better kiff! And she laughed till the eldest brother lit on her for being a vulgarian. The eldest O'Flaherty son was very gloomy. He said the dada will bury us all out of sheer contrariness and he had his own business to go back and look about. It was his wife's business. She was a Scotchwoman, though a Catholic it seems, and owned a couple of grocers' shops in Glasgow.

"In the long run all that was left was Pakky. I had quit thinking of him as the spoiled priest long since. I heard him saying one day when they were having a row that the old man had a lot to answer for pushing him on for the priesthood against his will. He said from when he was no size he had that drummed into him, that he was to be the priest of the family. Every gentleman's family has a priest in it, he said with a sort of jeer. And the others said well what about us, shoved into banks and solicitors' offices, do you think we had any choice either? And Pakky said it's not the same thing, not the same thing at all. And the brother said: 'No, you're damn right it's not! The rest of us were fit to escape without dragging ourselves and some innocent young boy in the mud first!'

They used to tear strips out of each other in front of me, as if I was no more than a bit of furniture, casting up things that happened thirty or more years before when they were children. Honest to God, I thought they were all away in the head, because when you're fifteen it seems centuries and centuries since you were a child and all you want to do is forget about it. It's only when you get older that your childhood comes right up close to you again.

"There was never no word at all about Pakky being mixed up with a servant girl. Big Jim for all his smartness got the story wrong. It seems there was some scandal about a young kitchen porter worked in the college, I never understood the ins and outs. It seems Pakky lured him away to fight for de Valera in the troubles but before they got very far the boy's family made a whole scandal out of it, and Matt O'Flaherty was waiting for them when they landed in Claghan to get money or whatever they wanted, and he beat hell out of Pakky with his walking-stick and sent him back to the college. Poor Pakky was only an innocent wee lad of eighteen himself at the time and he dropped college and de Valera and the whole lot, and off with him to England, where he stayed working at this and that till old Matt got the stroke. I put the story together from bits and pieces I heard and maybe I got some of it wrong. You wouldn't know what to believe and I suppose everyone, brothers and sisters and all, had their own version of it. All I know for sure is that your grandfather never had no vocation to the priesthood and he was only in the college that one wee year altogether. It was just people's lies that he left on his ordination day. They never care what they say around Claghan or how the truth gets twisted.

"When they were all left it settled into ordinary drudgery without the screeching and rows. It was great only having the three of them to cook for, though the old woman was very particular and made sure she got her money's worth out of me.

"Then I got a letter from Gerty Feeney saying she was having a whale of a time in London and why wouldn't I come over—there was plenty of work to be had and no shortage of high life, gorgeous fellows home on leave and everything. If I'd make some definite plans to go over she'd have a job waiting for me when I landed. For a while it seemed a lovely thing to plan for and I thought of nothing else morning noon and night. I was bent on finding some way of bringing Mother round to my way of thinking.

"But it had to stay a dream. Before I got even mentioning it to Mother there came two more bits of news from England that kiboshed my plans completely. The first was that Father was killed in an air-raid. The house where he was lodging with this woman and children got a direct hit. There was no question at all of sending his remains home for burial. Mother broke down and cried for days. I suppose she must have been remembering the early days when they were happy and loved each other. They must have loved each other some time, to get married. When I said that to Auntie Brigid she turned on me as if I wasn't right in the head: 'Sure to be sure didn't they love each other, there wasn't a finer pair in the country! Wasn't it only the curse-a-God drink and gallivanting put ructions between them. Aye, and between many another pair. McCormack up there in his big hotel may be proud of himself, the homes he ruined with drink and debt.'

"So I suppose underneath it all Mother always had some hope that Father would mend his ways and come back to her. She must have hated that woman in London. I never thought much about it up till then, the London one never seemed real to me before, I mean she was just a mortal sin, a sort of statue with paint and powder and perfume like the bad women in CTS booklets. But when Auntie Brigid said that, I began to see her as a real woman that took Mother's place and I saw how Mother must have been hopping mad with jealousy all the time.

"In the house one evening she said: 'Wasn't he the loveliest man going in the whole country?' And Auntie Brigid said: 'Aye, indeed, if he'd kept a bit of control over himself.' And old Sarah Morris said: 'Lizzie here takes after him, she's filling out to be a fine girl. We won't find now,' she said, 'till she's giving us the Big Day. But let her mind herself and look out for a Pioneer. That wee pin in the lapel is the only boyo.'

"It was the first time anyone said I was a fine-looking girl. There was big tall looking-glasses in O'Flahertys' and I often used to study myself when I was making the beds and think maybe I wasn't too bad. And lately I'd think if I was in London and had nice clothes I'd meet some lovely boy that'd take me walking through the parks like in Gerty's letters. The beautiful London parks that she was always writing about with the bands of a Sunday playing music and the soldiers on leave and trees and shrubs and nice places to walk. And some good-looking boy in maybe an airforce uniform holding my hand and saying he loved me, the airforce uniforms were by far the nicest Gerty said, but how he had to put his king and country first and go away and risk his life trying to beat Hitler. And I used to think the old ones were daft with their nonsense about Pioneer pins because if I really loved him I'd wait anyhow whether he was a drunkard or a Protestant or a Chinaman even . . . Only Father's death put a sure stop to London.

"Before we were right over the shock of that we got a second piece of news that was a stunner altogether. Big Jim came home to comfort Mother and give what information he could about the bombing, and before he left he announced that he was joining the British army and was going over to bate hell out of Jerry. It was a terrible thing. The whole street was up against him, at least all the old people were. Father McGinty came to read the riot act, saying had Jim totally forgotten the respect he owed to the memory of his dead Father that he was conspiring to go off and join forces with his murderers? Had he gone clean out of his mind? 'Because if so, Malone, I'd far rather see one of my parishioners locked up in Armagh asylum than bringing disgrace on his family and native land by taking King George's dirty shilling!' Big Jim was long enough in England not to be cowed by the priest, and he answered manly enough that as far as he could see he owed little or nothing to the memory of Micksey Malone, but that he owed a hell of a lot more to the memory of a man that took him in and reared him when he had no one and that, by God, he intended to revenge himself on that man's killers. Which surprised us all because poor Mother was the one that done the rearing and Big Jim was always one of the bitterest to condemn Father in his lifetime. I suppose he was just in the mood for fight and Hitler happened to be handy.

"Mother was convinced that he'd be slaughtered first go-off but he got through the war all right and was made a corporal. When he came home he had a wee brush of a moustache and talked very Cockney for a while. They learned him a trade in the army and he got a job in Meegan's Garage and later on went into business on his own. But sure you know all that, child, it's your big uncle Jim I'm talking about. Malone's Taxis. He went up in the world a lot since then, the same Jim. Another fellow from Quarry Street joined up at the same time but he deserted and landed home shortly after, begging to be hid, and some patriotic crowd got him safe across the border. Big Jim was a lot criticised for not deserting along with his comrade, but in the long run it simmered down and I don't believe there's one in the town now would even remember he was ever a British soldier.

"Mother failed greatly after Jim joined the army. She thought of nothing only watching letters from him and waiting for the telegram that would tell her he was killed in action. She was far fonder of Jim than of me, even though I was her own child. I think now it was because by the time I was born things were getting bad between her and Father, while Jim belonged to the years they were happy, but at the time I used to feel very left out and jealous. From the time Jim left she took very little interest in what I was going through at O'Flahertys'. It was poor wee Jim and do you think he's getting any sort of feeding at all, and the Kaiser was telling me last night it's slaughter in them trenches, the filth and the muck, up to your very thighs sometimes he was saying, and stepping unknownt on the faces of your dead comrades, God bless us and save us gersha, my poor wee Jim!

"She had no heed at all in me beyond warning me never to touch a drink and to stay pure and good and not let them big-shots get too familiar with me. This was because Pakky O'Flaherty left me home a few nights when it was raining. She was right to warn me. Only it would have been better if she had enough interest in me to take me away from there altogether, or to let me go over to England to Gerty. Or if she'd never took me away from Miss Wilson's in the first place. Because I was overworked and lonesome and only too glad for someone to take an interest in me, even if it was only the beardy man and him an old fellow of thirty-six years of age. I thought of the place too, I won't deny it, that lovely big house and farm and how it was certain sure to be left to Patrick, the great way he was getting along with the father.

"Oh I thought of that all right, God forgive me, and many a one round about had a bad name for me, especially when things turned out the way they did in the finish up. But it wasn't just greed. Pakky was kind and considerate to me and I wasn't used to that since I left Miss Wilson's. You have to think of the way I grew up, without a father and hired out the minute I was fourteen. It was the same for everyone them times but och it was hard. You couldn't blame me for taking what was offered. 'Deed there's many took worse! That house of O'Flahertys', McCormacks' you'd know it as, that got bombed, well it seemed to me a big palace of a place. You never seen inside Quarry Street. Poor Mother done her best but it was wee and dark and damp, and me that was used to Miss Wilson's lovely doll's house of a place and then O'Flahertys'. There's no one living in the Quarry Street house this long time. It's condemned and so is the houses on both sides of it. I hear it's ready to fall in, roof and all, and even the soldiers keeps well away from it and doesn't use it for shelter, handy and all as it'd be. It was some sort of a museum for a while, I hear.

"But that's neither here nor there, gersha. What happened in the heel of the hunt was that when I was sixteen years of age I was married to your grandfather and expecting a child. And I was living in O'Flahertys' and doing the exact same work that I done for the last year. Only from that time out I was doing it for free gratis and with no pay."

When Matt O'Flaherty died in 1942, shortly after his second stroke, Mr McCormack the hotelier and Father McGinty the parish priest shared out his property between them. Nobody contested their right of seizure, the IOUs were there for all to see. Any solicitor could testify that O'Flaherty had been gambling and entertaining on borrowed money for years before his death. The sons and daughters, after vainly trying to rally some support among the high-ups their father had ruined himself trying to impress, retreated (with the exception of their young brother Patrick) to England and were never seen in the district again. The two girls were said to have married GIs and gone to America and indeed many years later a couple of young men with foreign names, dressed in beads and embroidered robes, got off the Belfast bus in the town centre and asked directions to Claghan Hall, the old O'Flaherty farm. They told Big Jim Malone, the taxi-driver, that they had come all the way from San Francisco to search for their Irish peasant roots, and expressed an intention of buying the old homestead and settling down to a life of honest toil and quiet unquestioning spirituality—such a life indeed as their ancestors had very probably enjoyed there. Malone said he'd drive them out to look at the place surely, but there would hardly be any question of them buying it because it belonged to John Joe McCormack this years and years and was a real goldmine. A big popular tourist hotel with riding-stables, medieval banquets and everything. He said their best bet, if they had dollars to spend, was to drop in on Peadar Ó Lorcáin the solicitor. Peadar'd see them right.

But the Yanks, disappointed at the absence of thatched roofs or else aghast at the price of property in Claghan's boom years, contented themselves in the long run with squatting in a derelict zinc-roofed shack on Quarry Street, where they prepared to sit out the remainder of the Vietnam war in safety. They attracted a considerable following among the local youths and girls who nightly gathered in the three small damp rooms to be debauched with talk of peace and love and non-violence. Troth and the boys of this town would do better, quavered dying old Canon McGinty, to learn to stand up and defend themselves when some Protestant get of an Orangeman insults and persecutes them in the name of King Billy. The old respectable inhabitants of Claghan muttered about drugs and recalled how, for all the wild talk and folk-songs, not one of that O'Flaherty breed ever brought credit either on their family or their native land.

The house the hippies occupied was the one their Uncle Pakky moved into in 1942 with his recently-widowed mother, his seventeen-year-old wife and their baby daughter, and in which he lived uncomfortably enough until he was allotted accommodation in the new council estate shortly before his death in the summer of 1968.

CHAPTER EIGHTEEN

LIZZIE AND SARAH (1)

"We were happy enough all the same, we pulled along grand the first three or four years. Your mother was the loveliest child and then when Gerard was born your granda was as proud as anything. Nothing was too good for his wee son. Maybe Kathleen did feel left out of things—it's hard to tell. It wasn't that we thought any the less of her after Gerard came but a gasson's a gasson when all's said and done. Why? Well, it's hard to explain. You see, your poor grandfather had a shocking pride in the family name, in the very name of O'Flaherty, and so had old Matt. I think they honestly believed they were God's chosen people that crowd. And the ones over in America is every bit as bad. There's one of them very high up in that Noraid crowd, he gives speeches and everything—a first cousin of Pakky's he'd be. He be's over here from time to time, I do see it in the papers. He never bothers his head coming to see me. So of course your grandfather was beside himself at having a son to carry on the name. A daughter's different, they get married and . . . Aye, I know your poor mother didn't and, God help her, she'll hardly now but still. Anyway, would you hold your tongue, Sally, you're putting me through what I was trying to say.

"I was talking about them first few years in Quarry Street. It was a shocking blow about the place and the money, and I thought Pakky would go out of his mind. He had fits of hysterics worse than his mother even: the pair of them cried their eyes out when we knew it was all gone for good and I cried along with them. But we got over it in the long run. We had to. And it was lucky enough we had Mother's wee house to go to because poor Pakky had no job nor nothing. He didn't save a penny the whole time he was in England. He was with the Vincentian Fathers till he was seventeen and then that year in the seminary, but it wasn't a bit of use to him when he started looking for suitable work. There wasn't many office jobs going, and what there was didn't come the way of Catholics. Oh they never said anything out loud: they called him for interviews, Lewis's Shoes and Lockhart's Furniture and all, and they were as nice as you like, the wee cup of tea and the biscuit. But then it was what school did you go to? Do you support soccer or Gaelic, cricket or hurling? Sorry but your qualifications are not quite what we hoped for, and then a week later they'd take on some wee skitter of a Prod that never passed an examination in his life but had a daddy in the Orange Lodge.

"Over and over it happened. Mind you, Pakky might have had more of a chance if he was younger or had a steady job all the time he was in London . . . We were years and years in Quarry Street before he got anything at all except casual labour. It was the Kaiser Bill's son, Petey, put in a word for him in the long run with the creamery manager and got him that driving job he was sacked from just before he died. Aye, Petey Larkin, your boyfriend's daddy. There was no word about Lorcan O'Caiserbuill them times. That all came later when he was made a solicitor and mixed up with Gael-Linn and the anti-partition movement and went up to some place in Belfast and changed his name by deed-poll. He was the Kaiser Bill's son when we knew him, at the University and pushing himself in with all the big-shots, getting asked to parties in the creamery manager's house and all. Things changed a terror the time of the war. Up until then the people stayed quiet in their own wee corner, it must have been the wireless put them all to hell and then the television later on. Look at yourself, Sarah, stuck in McCormack's Singing Lounge night after night with the Kaiser's grandson that got himself expelled from every school in the country for drugs and God knows what, and I don't know what other trash you're mixed up with, but I do know this, you'd have been run out of it in my day. They'd have stoned you, gersha!

"Not sight nor light of the inside of a public house did any decent girl ever get when I was young. Or even when your mother was young. Aye and no solicitor's son, good-for-nothing and all as he is, would have let himself be seen in public with the likes of you either them times. And 'deed and maybe it's not all that much changed, no fear of him taking you home to his big house and showing you to his family, oh no! He's making a fool of you, Sally, that's all he's doing, trying to use you for some bad purpose of his own. What am I going to do with you at all, Sarah dear? If it was for that you came home from England! I thought it was to keep me company, Sally. God forbid that you turn out like your mother and make a show of me over again. Or that you get in with some bad crowd. There's some awful bad people round Claghan these days, it's not like long ago, no heed in nothing only murder and destruction. I hope to Almighty God you won't let yourself be led into . . . "

"Oh Gran! Come out of the middle ages! Malachy's the nicest fellow, there's hundreds like him these days, you don't want to go by the way he dresses! He wants to marry me and all. Honest Gran! He'd do anything for me. I only have to ask, he'd put his hand in the fire! We talk, that's all we do, listen to the music. They get some great groups up there you know. Tell you what, Gran, I'll take you some night to McCormack's. Come on, Gran, make up for the decent days of your youth, eh?"

CHAPTER NINETEEN

LIZZIE (6)

The bay window stared across a high narrow back yard full of dustbins to the Maternity block. A cube of lighted rooms, busy beehive, every bed with its cot alongside it. A young woman, pretty in a blue frilled nightdress, picked up a baby, smiled, talked, cuddled it against her neck in delight. Looked across its wee head at the lighted waiting area, caught Lizzie's eye on her, stopped smiling. Old cow spying on us, is that what she's thinking? Miserable old cow, who do you think you're gaping at? Young people was far harder now than they used to be, stare through you as if you had no right . . .

And what right have I to look over there, she thought, life's over there. The two ends of human life staring at each other across a yard full of garbage. No connection, no way of crossing back over there. Not even a right to look. She huddled herself down farther in the plastic armchair, slid her eyes away from the courtyard, looked humbly in another direction. Lights were winking down in the dark town, the long black hump of the mountain stretched behind. She studied the rubber plant in its tub; the stemmed ashtray sent up a stink of wet cinders and old apple-cores; she looked away up the corridor. Everyone seemed to have forgotten she was there, surely she had no right to be there, what time was it anyway, visiting must be over? She'd lost track of time. The police stood in twos, like nuns, guarding the lift, guarding the ward.

"All that for you, Sarah, you'd laugh if you knew. Or you'd come out with one of them shocking words you used to say, you always had a desperate mouth on you. And your mother before you. And Pakky. A shocking blustery sort of a crowd. To think I finished up like that, when all I ever used to dream about was a quiet wee life with a good-looking fellow beside me and a houseful of nice furniture and ornaments, like Miss Wilson's—and then to end up in a crowd of O'Flahertys! Cursing and swearing, and that they wouldn't care what you done for them or what you said. You were no value to any of them, Lizzie! Talking to the wall I was, all these months, these years since she started coming over to Claghan, I might as well have been talking to myself for all the heed that one took of my advice . . . "

She'd heard it on *The World at One*, just a mention: Police and army are surrounding a derelict house in a largely Roman Catholic area of Claghan where it is believed that . . . She sat at the kitchen table trying one station after another but there was nothing else so she made herself a pot of tea and sat there thinking about old times. At four o'clock she was just going to try the *News Headlines* again when she heard the big rumbling and tearing, and then the sirens going and she grabbed her coat and handbag and walked quickly off the estate and round the back lanes towards Quarry Street. Lockhart Road was crowded and there was a barricade blocking the entrance to Quarry Street. She pushed and elbowed her way through the crowd that had collected, and she heard someone saying: "They're digging for bodies."

Were the RUC men shameless enough to be stuck above

in the intensive care unit itself? Were they standing beside the bed, staring with their blank eyes at tubes and drips and bottles of plasma hanging upside down like the drinks in McCormack's that time Sally treated her. A year ago? Or two? "Come on then, Gran! Senior Citizens Lib! I'll buy you a Pernod."

"Senior Citizens, my eye! I'm just over sixty, you young whipster you!"

Were the nurses and doctors lounging against the desk laughing, flirting, handing round sweets? And sure, why wouldn't they be? They were young and it was only a job like another. Or were they impressed? Intimidated by the armed guards? Butterfingers stumbling over the temperature chart, blushing at being spied on? Afraid to bend over the poor broken bit of a girl in the bed in case some young get of a policeman was studying their backsides?

She thought, will I ever be let see her? Thought: am I in any way responsible for what happened? Could I have stopped her? Talked reason to her? Maybe if I hadn't been living in the past so much I could have talked reason to her. But sure when would that girl have listened to reason! Maybe if I'd never told her who she was, who she belonged to. It was wrong of me to tell her when I knew the sort she was. I might have knew she'd take it bad, she took everything to heart that one, it was wrong of me to tell her but what could I say when she egged me on? Will Kathleen blame me? Will she come in here shouting, blistering me with accusations the way she used to? Kathleen must be on the plane now, she thought, she'll have got the messages I left. A couple of hours now and she'll be here. Will there be any change by then? Will they let us up to see her? Isn't it funny, she thought, that in the heel of the hunt there's only the two of us left to bother about her? But the poor Kaiser Bills, she thought, they haven't even that much hope. And that unfortunate wee Mrs McLeod and his children. And his mother. It was her got me the job in Miss Wilson's, she must be well over seventy now.

"But I'll never forget, Sally, the longest day I live, I'll never get over that awful day we had the party for Big Jim Malone. The war was over months and months and Haw-Haw was hung and the bomb dropped on the Japs and everything. There was VE-day and the schools were all shut and the youngsters careering up and down Quarry Street annoying the people and shouting Jerry's dead! Jerry's dead! And then months after that Big Jim was let home from the army. Mother was beside herself, she never thought she'd see him again— lying dead in some trench or other, son, and no one to bury you. And he laughed his length at her foolishness: there was no trenches in this war, woman, you're away behind the times as usual. Talking very English and showing off. You're no good at all, I said to Pakky, it's a wonder you never learned to talk like that and you fifteen years beyond! Oh bejabus, Liz, he said, I had better things to learn in England than elocution, making a grab at me. We were above in our room but I shoved him away, I was expecting again at the time. That was the last time your grandfather ever tried to lay a hand on me.

"But as I was saying, nothing would do Mother only to have a big party and ask the whole street in. Everyone chipped in with their rations of tea and sugar and butter so we were able to have a good spread. It was of a Saturday at teatime and half Quarry Street was in our wee kitchen. I was kept busy handing round sandwiches and Mother and old Mrs Flaherty were slashing tea into cups for all they were worth. There was no stint on cakes and dainties because poor Mother couldn't get over Jim being delivered back to her alive and well. He was leaning up tall against the window-frame with a wee brush of a moustache, I can see him yet: sure what trenches? That's only old yarns of Kaiser Bill Larkin. Where *is* the Kaiser, he said then. Did you not ask him to the party?

And Mother: Oh the Kaiser's away out of Quarry Street this long time, oh bedad, son, you may quit laughing at the Kaiser now! The brother died out in America and left them a big lump of money and they bought a grand house at the other end of the town. And do you mind Petey, the long lingel of a fellow that won some scholarship? Well, he's at university this three years and more, going on to be some class of a lawman. And they all started codding Jim about being a stranger now in his own town—away learning a good trade at King George's expense and troth and if we had to have any sense we'd have went with you.

"There was a few criticising behindbacks all the same, I heard them when I took round the sandwiches: how it was an awful thing to fight for the King of England even so, and how everyone knew the English was every bit as big a huers as Jerry, look at India and Palestine this minute, not even counting poor Ireland. And someone said: after the Tans shooting his own father, shot him through the head like a beast and him stocious. And then there was a laugh: Jasus boys will yous ever forget when yon heroes came to put up the statue to oul' Micksey? Aye and Jim never touched the drop from that day to this, a very dry class of a warrior! And Jamesy Murphy was grumbling away: wouldn't you think he could have come up with something stronger than tay all the same for oul' Hitler's wake? I thought it was awful to make fun of Jim like that and them in his house being fed and all, but I didn't say anything for fear of starting a row.

"Pakky was sitting at the table with wee Gerard on his knee and all the old women were making much of the child and saying he was the spit of his daddy and feeding him sweet cake and lemonade. Your mother was standing near them with a slice of carvy-seed cake in her hand and a long miserable face on her because no one was paying any heed to her. She was nearly five years of age and far too big to be sat on knees but she was the shockingest child for jealousy,

if you didn't watch her she'd leave poor wee Gerard black
and blue with nips and pinches. But I knew she hated carvy
seeds and was too shy to say, and I was just going over to
give her a slice of fruit cake when Pakky noticed her there:
what are *you* gaping at with the long oul' jaw on you? Honest
to God a man can't drink a mug of tea in this kip without
being pestered by a clatter of snotty children! And he put
Gerard down on the floor very suddenly and Kathleen all
smiles made a dive for his knee seeing it vacant but he
pushed her away and said: 'Take your wee brother away out
and play in the hallway, and mind you don't let him near that
road. I swear to God I'll flay you alive if I catch either of you
outside, do you hear me now?' And everyone round the table
started to laugh, that's the way, Pakky, let them see who's the
boss, and the two children pushed their way out between all
the legs and the crack started up again.

"Big Jim was busy telling us about some great adventure
he had over in France and the whole room was quiet listening
when we heard this motorcar tearing down the street at a
shocking speed and then there was awful screeches and
squeals and an almighty noise of brakes being pulled on
sudden and Pakky was the first out of the room and everyone
after him and I fainted beside the table and just before I
blacked out completely it seemed to me that the war was
over and finished a second time because I could hear them
all screeching and shouting: 'Gerry's dead! Gerry's dead!'"

"That old guy with the Pioneer pin, Malone's Taxis, see the
way he's eyeing you up, Sal! Want me to go over and break
his jaw for him?"

"Don't be a twit, Malachy. That's not lust, that's the wrath
of God. He's my uncle isn't he, sort of. My big uncle Jim,
Gran says. I can't stand the bastard actually. You know he
tore a strip out of me the first time he saw me in here? Cast
up about . . . You know, about Mum and all. About me being

illegitimate. Said I'd have to watch it. In my position, he said real nasty, a girl in my position better not be seen around the pubs boozing. Get my gran a bad name, he said, and if I want to act the tart why don't I just go back to London and have done with it. Told me if *he* had any say in the matter it's into a home I'd have gone as soon as I was pupped. I mean straight out of the middle ages! What is he, one of these lay preachers or what?"

"He's the town mouth. Never stops slabbering about one thing or another. Today's youth. Mindless violence. He can go on for hours, knows all the answers, knows what everyone's up to. Eyes everywhere. It's not as if he drank, even: 'Pineapple juice for me, boys!' pointing to the pin all pious. That guy's heading for trouble you know. I mean some day he's going to open that big gob of his once too often and get done for it. Your uncle?"

"Well. Not exactly uncle. Gran's adoptive brother or something, but she can't stand him either. I mean they never see each other at all nowadays. Apparently he was always like that, dead aggressive and all, and his mum, his foster-mum, she spoiled him something rotten. Gran reckons that's why he joined the army in the war, just so he could bully the Germans."

"Malone was in the army? The *British* army? I never knew that. Nobody ever mentions that."

"That's what Gran says, that nobody remembers. He never talks about it and who *would* remember except a few old codgers down Quarry Street and why should they bother? I mean it's not as if it was something important, is it?"

"Important! Are you joking? Old Malone a Brit! This I've got to make public, this I've got to spread around, Sal! Hey, Sean, Kieran! Come over here a minute boys, know the latest? Go on, tell them, Sal. Jesus, that's the best news yet! You're *sure* of it, Sal? *Go* on, tell them!"

CHAPTER TWENTY

LIZZIE AND SARAH (2)

"I lost the wee baby I was expecting and when I got out of the hospital it was all over, the two funerals and everything. It seems the driver went straight through the windscreen the effort he made to try and save poor wee Gerard. It was a couple of demobbed soldiers from the Protestant end taking a short-cut home from a soccer match, stocious they were and going far too fast. That night when the word spread round, a crowd of neighbours, young fellows, went over to the town centre and started smashing windows in all the Protestant shops, but they gave up when they heard the man was dead.

"Your grandfather never got over that blow. He changed completely from one day to the next. 'There'll be no more children in this house,' was all he said to me when I came home from the hospital, and from that out he slept in the one bed and me and Kathleen in the other.

"There was no sign of Kathleen in the house when I came home and then Sarah Morris came in with her by the hand. The poor wee thing was quaking, and she cringed away from me, afraid of her life I was going to beat her too. There was long red marks standing up all over her back from where Pakky flogged her. It seems he went clean mad, even smashed up the lovely big doll Big Jim had brought home to her. He swore she pushed Gerard out on the road deliberately out of pure jealousy. They had to drag him away, two or three neighbours, or he'd have been hung for her. Sarah Morris took her and looked after her all the time I was sick. It was months before her father could bear to as much as look at her. Your heart would break for him, Sally. I know he was maybe a wee bit too harsh with her but if she'd done as she was bid . . . Oh he forgave her in the long run and always done his best to be a good father and sacrificed himself to give her an education but she was that headstrong that . . . "

"And my mum? Did *she* ever forgive *him*?"

"Forgive him? What are you talking about, Sarah? Sure what had she to forgive him for? She was only a wee child when it happened and she forgot in no time at all. She never once mentioned she ever had a brother and we never mentioned Gerard to her. Children forget easy. And he was the best of fathers to her in spite of all. He worked hard all the hours there was, to pay for her schooling in the convent, and got no return for it—not one word of gratitude out of her till the day he died. She broke his heart a second time, so she did. That's what killed him you know, when he found out how she disgraced her name."

"I bet she never forgave him. I bet she still doesn't, it could explain a lot about Mum! And I bet *you* never forgave your dad either. Bet that's why you married an old guy, Gran, looking for the dad that walked out on you. It's called psychology, Gran, never heard of psychology? Nobody ever forgives their fathers. *I* don't, for a start. Whoever the bastard is I'd like to nail him to some cross where he couldn't get away, where he'd have to hang there in agony listening to me, and I'd rub his rotten nose in what he did to me and my mum. She could have got married and we could have had a decent life and everything only she never got over him. She thought there was no one like him and—"

"Quit shouting, Sally, and stop talking foolishness. Your mother didn't get married because no one would take her, that's why. Second-hand goods. What fellow with a sense of decency would take on with another man's child?"

"You're living in the past, Gran, you're back in the middle ages, who *cares* nowadays? There's plenty of men would have . . . But *what* other man's child, Gran? Go on, tell me. *You* know who my father is. Go on tell me! Tell me, Gran!"

"Did Kathleen never tell you?"

"I know it's someone here in the town, that's all. That's all she ever let slip. That's why she won't come back to live here. I keep looking at men all the time. Every time I go out someplace. When I met Malachy I was scared stiff I might turn out to be his *sister* or something! That's why I kept asking you and asking Mum but neither of you would ever say. Only then I did meet Mr Ó Lorcáin and he's far too old. But I have a *right* to know, Gran! Go on, Gran, Mum said my dad and she were students together, is that right?"

"Troth and they weren't studying together! We made paupers of ourselves sending her to a good Catholic training college so that she wouldn't fall in with bad company and then she had to disgrace herself with some Prod picked her up at a dance. I bet she never told you he was one of the other sort, did she? Mr Snooty McLeod, the bank manager's son. I got that much out of her. She was in love, she said, she was heartbroken when it ended. Oh a very romantic lady, your mother! But as I said to her, the romance was all on the one side. He can't have thought a great deal of her because he was married to that Save-the-planet woman, a big white wedding full of big-bugs plastered all over the *Claghan Chronicle*, months before you were born even. Just making a cod of Kathleen, that's all he was doing. In love aye!"

"But he didn't know about me. Maybe if he'd known

about me. She said she never got in touch with anyone after she went to London. She said she didn't want to mess things up any more than they were messed already. I bet if he'd known I existed. Gran, does everyone in Claghan know about it? Do the Ó'Lorcáins and all know?"

"Nobody knows, only me. And if she didn't tell him, it was because she knew she wouldn't get any change out of him. He never had no notion of marrying a wee Taig from the back streets—that sort never does, laughing at her behind her back. Just passing the time with her, that's all he was doing, and then when he took a notion to settle down, away with him to the minister along with one of his own breed. How could any fellow have respect for a girl that'd let herself down like that? Take what they can get and then laugh at you, any girl that's eejit enough . . . You may tell me that times is changed but there's still a God above in Heaven. He ruined her life for her anyhow. And he ruined yours too, whatever you may think. Look at you, carted about like a parcel from one slum to another since the day you were born. Oh I know all about it all right, I know the way she was living, God forgive her. And still is. And you with no proper schooling, living up on the dole and you well over twenty years of age, in and out of one useless job after another since you were sixteen. Back and forward like a yoyo between here and London making a show of yourself with one of the Kaiser Bill's crowd, another wild good-for-nothing! And when you see how his real children was reared in that big house up the Belfast Road, the best of everything, the eldest that's not a year younger than yourself doing an honours degree at some big English university. Her picture will be in the paper. 'Deed and *you'll* never be in no paper, Sally! God above, when I think of the sacrifices we made for Kathleen and that she could have had a good career for herself and stayed in Claghan and married anyone she liked, she was the loveliest-looking girl, a doctor or anything she could have had. And when you think of that country gawk of a Mary Brigid Murphy one that's the next thing to a millionaire from what you tell me . . . She could have had anyone, she could have bought back Claghan Hall for us, she could even have married into it if she had to play her cards right and poor Pakky would have been alive to this very day so he would . . . "

"Malachy, do you know who it is, Mal? I just found out who it is. Gran just told me. It's that ban-the-bomber, Mal, would you believe it! Him with the wife that was on Ulster Television last week rabbiting on about something called Greenpeace. Eric McLeod's my *dad*, Malachy!"

CHAPTER TWENTY-ONE

LIZZIE AND SARAH (3)

She must have dozed off sometime in the night, slept. How long for? The police guard was gone now, the lights seemed dimmer. It was a silence of some time after midnight, a silence she used to know years and years ago when a child had the toothache or a sick stomach, a silence when you were the only ones in the whole world awake. Only herself awake and Kathleen wasn't arrived yet. The nurses hadn't come near her this long time, the cup of cold tea was still there. Only she saw that it was a different cup, one of her own cups, and she remembered Agnes Murphy coming for her with a taxi and taking her home and making her tea and sitting with her for a while and saying she'd be back first thing in the morning. What was happening in the hospital now, in that ward where the light stayed lit the whole night long, where some nurse's eye was always open? God in thine infinite mercy grant that . . . But maybe Kathleen couldn't get a flight. Or maybe she didn't get the phone messages. Out gallivanting someplace and never even got the messages I left. At her age! Does she still go out gallivanting? I don't know one thing about her, Lizzie thought, not the first thing about what she might be doing at this minute. Has she any friends at all now since that pair moved over to their big house in France? She must miss them. Maybe Kathleen has no friends, she thought, maybe she has no sort of a life when all's said and done. I never knew the first thing about her, not since she was a wee small child, never knew what she might be doing or thinking. But poor wee Sarah, to go and do that. To let herself be led into doing a thing like that. I should never have said, and me knowing the oddness of her, I should never have told her. Should have let the past be the past.

"So you didn't like living with Mary Brigid Murphy and the man? She was always a whipster that one, nothing in her head only film stars and fashion. Mind you, your mother was every bit as bad, only Maureen as she christened herself was as tough as an old boot besides. *She* wouldn't have let any man cod her, she knew what side her bread was buttered all right. Her and her love stories! You should write a book about Claghan, I said to her that last time she came home. There was always plenty of history round here, I bet you if Georgette Heyer came from Claghan . . . 'Oh no, Lizzie,' she cut me off, all nebby, 'there's no romance in that Oirishy-Irish lark! Or money either. Ireland's ashamed of its history these days. What the Irish want to read about now is tycoons with mid-Atlantic accents eating snails on expense accounts with international models.'"

"Christ! Typical Maureen. Well anyway, poor Bobby Sands soon killed off that notion of Ireland, didn't he, Gran?"

"That's nothing to do with the likes of us, Sally. I never had no interest in politics and violence and I'm not going to start now. God forbid that I'd condemn the poor wee gasson and all he must have went through, but I hope I'm not going to hear any oul' talk from you about patriotism and oppression. There's enough at it God knows and let me tell you now I don't like the cut of that crowd you're going about with since you came home this last time. Not one bit. The old Kaiser Bill that used to be a laughing-stock round Quarry Street, stocious from morning till night, crying his eyes out over dead men in trenches. Great company for you!"

"You're two generations out of date, Gran! And I just mentioned Bobby Sands's *name*. He's a hero: everyone, Christ even the English, Gran, the young kids. You ought to have heard them at my school way back when he . . . I mean I only mentioned him as a reference is all, today's climate etcetera. Doesn't mean I personally am about to blow up Claghan barracks or anything. So go on about old Maureen then!"

"No but it was the nebby way she answered me and when you think how she was reared, out there on that bit of a bog. If Pakky's Yankee cousins hadn't kept them supplied with parcels they'd have starved many a time. Mind you, I don't know what your mother would have done without her in London. She was a godsend to you both. She put a roof over your head many a time, whatever we may think of her. That's what she was over for, that time I mentioned, to tell us about you. Came over especially because Kathleen couldn't face it herself. You were three or four years of age by then and us wondering why Kathleen never came back to see us after she went to London. Always some big excuse, and the explaining I had to do to the neighbours. And then the Murphy one arrived on the doorstep with a mini-skirt on her and white plastic boots. Oh as nice as pie with long rigmaroles and a pile of photos she took of you to try and sweeten us. It killed Pakky, you know, that's what killed him. But he was reasonable enough, ready to take her back and everything. Let her come home here, he said, and she'll find the door open for her and we'll forgive her and there won't be one word said about it. Let her put that child in a home, he said, and she'll be welcomed back here where she belongs."

"He wanted to put me in a home? In an orphanage? When

I was three or four years of *age?* My *grandfather?"*

"It was twenty years ago, Sally. People wasn't as lenient. There wasn't all this immorality there is now with the television and everything. People knew the difference between right and wrong, you wouldn't credit. Canon McGinty, lord a mercy on him, was alive at the time and he said the same thing: let her put that child in an orphanage, he said, and come back here where she'll have a chance to lead a decent Christian life."

"It was barbaric, Gran, barbaric! The fucking middle ages! To put *me* in a *home*, Gran!"

"So what did your mother do, Sal? She didn't agree, did she?"

"Well *obviously* she didn't agree seeing I'm here, you twit! But, Malachy, the humiliation! Those awful old people, that ghastly priest, I sat there and listened to her telling me and she wasn't a bit shocked at any of it. I mean she thought it was quite normal, Mal. She'd have done it herself. I mean she'd have been far happier if my mum had had an abortion or had me put away or something. As long as she didn't have to know. And me wishing Mum had dumped me on them when I was born! God they'd have made short work of me, that old pair. I'd have been scrubbing floors in some convent orphanage before I even learned to walk! I just don't exist for my gran either, Malachy. I'm nothing really to her. I mean she's known me for years, we've sat and talked for months on end every summer since I was about fourteen. I never talked to Mum like that. I never talked to anyone. All my shitty little adolescent dreams. Oh Christ Jesus! I figured she cared what became of me and I'm nothing, I was nothing all the time. She'd have let me grow up in a home and thought nothing of it. She wouldn't have missed me. She'd have had no regrets. I'd have been some shitty little mess in Mum's past that no one ever spoke about. I'm going to kill that guy, Malachy! I swear I'm going to do him. I'm going to fucking do the bastard for this."

"Poor Kathleen was always just in the halfpenny place with the Murphy one. The time Mary Brigid won the scholarship there was no standing them. 'We're sending her to St Monica's,' the mother told me, 'along with the McCormack girls. They say it's the best school in the north of Ireland for exam results.' And her standing there with holes in her shoes. 'Mrs McCormack told Agnes she'd pass on Veronica's old uniforms to us because she's buying all new for Nuala. She said we weren't to worry about anything in that line, she'd see us right. Agnes is well thought of there.' Agnes Murphy, her that lives across the road there, was maid in McCormacks' for years, as if that was anything to brag about! They were supposed to have the cure for the whooping cough, Maureen's parents, two of the same name married to each other. Old pishrogues, it shows the class of people they were, you that's always giving out about the middle ages!

"'Oh bejaburs and we're sending our lassie there too,' Pakky told her. It was the first I heard of it because poor Kathleen didn't pass the scholarship and we intended just to send her on the bus to the Poor Clares. 'Are you gone mad or what?' I asked him when the Murphy one left. 'Where do you think the boarding fees are going to come out of?' And he said: 'If all the labouring trash in the country can send their daughters to boarding-school with the high-ups I'll not have it said that the O'Flahertys was left behind, us that if we had our rights would be higher up than any of them.'

"So I went out to work here and there in people's houses, cleaning and laundry work so that your mother would have as fair a start in life as the next and grow up, with God's help, to put her family back in the house that was rightly theirs."

"You must have been crazy, Gran. I swear the whole pack of you was crazy with that old name of yours. From that old Matt you were talking about, on down. What did you *need*

231

Claghan Hall back for, what was so great about it? Did you ever see it lately, ever get a good look at it? It's a ruin, just an old heap of stones; it's not a *house* any more—it's been all bombed to bits. Would have been bombed just the same if the O'Flahertys were still in it. What would you have *done* with the place if you'd had it? It was just an illusion, Gran, it wasn't worth slaving for . . . And my mum, what did my mum think of being pushed around like that? What did *she* think of your sacrifices?"

CHAPTER TWENTY-TWO

"PUDDLES OF THE PAST" BY
MAUREEN MURPHY

(Short story sent to *New Irish Writing*, December 1968)

M iss McGowan yawned into her big freckled fist and
drawled as no doubt, Kathleen thought, she'd been
drawling every September for the last ninety years or so:
"Now would every girl put *David Copperfield* away neatly
inside her desk. Without banging any lids, mind! That's right.
And now would you all take your fountain pens and write
your names as neatly as you can on the inside page of your
Merchant of . . . Ennis."

Kathleen couldn't help turning to wink at the girl on her
left, it sounded that comical choking its way out through a
yawn: Merchant aw-aw-awv Ennis, the oul' one could hardly
keep herself awake. She must have been up half the night.
Hardly out dancing at her age. But the wink was stifled when
she remembered that the girl on her left was Nuala McCormack
and that she had strict orders from her father not to as much
as let on the McCormack ones existed. Land-grabbers, her
father called them, gombeen men and the curse of the country.
And from the way the Nuala one turned away her head
Kathleen suspected that the McCormack girls had exactly the
same instructions concerning her. She felt her face flooding

red and concentrated very hard on writing Kathleen O'Flaherty, Form A1, St Monica's Grammar School, September 1953, on the flyleaf of her new book.

She didn't feel one bit homesick even though most of the other new ones had snivelled half the night in the dormitory, and the wee fat Murphy girl from Boharnamuc that won the scholarship was even eejit enough to go to sleep with a tomato sandwich clutched in her hand and woke up with it plastered into the pillow and got a wild telling-off from the nun with the long fangs who came round ringing the bell to waken them. "Recite the seven deadly sins for me, Miss Greedy," the nun said in a thin slithery voice, and the Murphy one started off in a sort of sleepy gallop: "Pride-covetousness-lust-anger-gluttony," and then Fangs stopped her: "That's you. A dirty glutton. It seems we're to have a glutton in St Monica's this year," and the Murphy one burst out crying and said: "It was because me Mammy made them, miss. I got lonesome in the night and that's all I had, miss, that Mammy made with her own two hands." And everyone in the dormitory roared laughing, even the ones that passed the whole night crying themselves and Fangs made her voice colder and slimier: "There's no need to add the sin of lying to that of gluttony," and she took wee bawky Murphy away in her pyjamas to apologise to the Sacred Heart statue and made her print "I Am a Glutton. I Am a Liar" on a bit of cardboard and she was going to have to wear it on her back for a week. To Mass and everywhere she'd have to wear it. I'd have *died*, Kathleen thought. I wouldn't have done it, I'd have spat on the bitch. But the Murphy one went away meekly with Fangs and came into the refectory late with "I Am a Glutton. I Am a Liar" pinned on the back of her gymslip. She was sitting just over from Kathleen in the middle row of desks crying in to herself by the look of her and the girl behind her was drawing something on the cardboard with her fountain pen and Murphy was killed wriggling her shoulders trying to stop her without

McGowan seeing.

"Now girls," Miss McGowan said, "you have been given a whole lot of nice new English books and I hope you're going to take great care of them and put them to excellent use during your time at St Monica's. Now! We have, let's see, we have more than half the period left and you'll be relieved to hear I don't intend to waste it giving you a pep talk! I'm sure you've had enough of those already this morning! But since this *is* supposed to be a literature period I'd like to discover just how much you learned about literature in your junior schools. Now who's going to stand up and say a nice poem for me? It needn't be anything grand, you know, just some little recitation you learned from your last teacher."

The McCormack one shot up her hand. When she stood up her blonde hair danced on her long stem of a neck and her voice was high and piping. Kathleen was suddenly very small and very alone. She'd have given all she had to have someone from Quarry Street, even her worst enemy, beside her to whisper: "Jasus, would you listen to nebby!" and make it all right and homely.

"My name is Nuala McCormack. I am twelve years old. 'The Hosting of the Sidhe' by William Butler Yeats.'

There was an emptiness inside Kathleen's head. Her whole body shook at the very idea of standing up there in front of twenty strange girls and making a show of herself. She could see her hands trembling and flattened them down on the clean wood of the desk to make them stop. The desk lid was firm and smooth, not a name or a bad word carved on it, and with a warmth coming up through its coolness. She looked at the classroom walls, so clean and cream-coloured, with nothing stuck on them. In St Ronan's PES there had been pictures cut from magazines, missionaries holding black babies and that. There had been a calendar with a bird and a flower for every month of the year: "Make Every Day a National Savings Day," and another one with tractors and seagulls on it: "Till the Soil on MS Oil." Several holy pictures too, and an alphabet chart for the infants: "A for the apple so rosy and red; B for the baby asleep in its bed," right down to "Z for the zebra we see in the zoo." Mrs Mooney used to explain that a zoo was a big field, like a football field, only with cages for the wild animals. They had them in Dublin and Belfast. For the big ones in St Ronan's there was a special blackboard in the corner where Mrs Mooney wrote ten spellings every day and a new poem every Monday morning to be learned off before Friday or it was six slaps for you. Kathleen would have no trouble at all finding a poem to recite if she was asked, she knew hundreds . . .

There was a crucifix on the wall above Miss McGowan's head, and a painting on each side of it. The one nearest Kathleen showed a princess or something having her portrait painted and she was the spit of Nuala McCormack—long whitish hair and a spoilt wee face and a sticking-out skirt you could near sit on, like a table. The princess was painted all shimmering and clear and the ones round her were dark and less important, you could see she fancied herself like anything. Kathleen looked away past Nuala and McGowan and the princess to where the far wall was almost one big sheet of glass. Lough Neagh lay like dull silver in the distance and there was silver on the gulls' wings as they wheeled and twisted round a crowd of workmen digging. Foundations for a new chapel they were digging. She knew because on the foot of the prospectus, Mother Imelda had scribbled a request for donations. "Oh bejaburs they're losing no time!" her father had said. "Them ladies are a great hand at fleecing the people!" But he sent a pound anyway so that Kathleen could start off on the right foot and not let the O'Flahertys down. When the chapel was built it would hide the pine woods and the lovely lake. All you could see from the window would be it.

Verses of poems sparkled and danced in front of her. It might be nice to stand up if she was asked. If the teacher asked her. Miss McGowan would coax her: come on now Kathleen, we're all dying to hear you, and then she'd stand up and recite "Cargoes" or "The Burial of Sir John Moore" very sad and slow with all the stresses in the right place. But the teacher would have to ask her . . .

"The host is rushing 'twixt night and day,
And where is there hope or deed as fair?
Caoilte tossing his burning hair,
And Niamh calling *Away, come away.*"

"Well that was beautiful, Nuala. Now wasn't it, girls? A lovely Irish poem. They may say what they like about their Wordsworths and their Tennysons and their Shakespeares but when all's said and done it was our own Irish authors made English literature great and we must never forget that, now must we, girls? Yeats, O'Connor, Lady Gregory, Æ. And of course Tom Moore and his lovely melodies. You said that really beautifully, Nuala, I can see you love poetry, don't you?"

"I took private elocution in the summer holidays, Miss McGowan. From a real actress. She used to be in the Abbey Theatre."

She must mean the mystery woman everyone was talking about that stayed awhile in McCormack's hotel. Maybe she wasn't able to pay her bill and old McCormack made her give the children lessons till he got the value out of her. Kathleen's father often said old McCormack would skin fleas and auction their hides, and all belonging to him the same. He didn't *look* mean, didn't look like Scrooge or anything but big and jovial and going a bit baldy. Three jovial huntsmen upon St David's Day, that's what he looked like. He went to Mass in a bumfreezer coat and his wife in Persian lamb with Nuala, Veronica and Martin between them like steps of stairs all dressed the same in grey overcoats with black velvet collars. They all sat in the front seat of the men's aisle. They were the only women or girls there—the Canon would have taken a stick to any ordinary girl sat up among the men—but for them it wasn't shameless or an occasion for sin because they were big-shots, too big shots even to sit with the doctors and teachers on the front gallery. When Kathleen was small she used to stick her tongue out at them every chance she got and whisper: "Mucky Feet! Mucky Feet!" because that's what you always said to the ones in from the country. Country ones only wore their shoes of a Sunday and went to school barefoot. Only the McCormacks never let on they heard her so there was no fun in it, and anyhow when she got bigger she realised they weren't like real country gawks and that even if they had ten pair of feet each they'd still be able to buy shoes to cover them.

Kathleen thought Miss McGowan looked a bit disappointed when she heard about the elocution lessons. Maybe she was hoping to earn a bit on the side herself giving lessons and hated the thought of competition?

Nuala McCormack sat down spreading her skirt daintily, moving her long neck and her shimmering hair to see who was going to dare stand up after her. She's as big a snob as she looks at Mass, Kathleen thought, that's the one I'll have to watch. She's sure to cast up Quarry Street and how my granda drank and gambled our home away. Her father said they'd all cast it up to her if they got the chance, about how the place was lost. Aye and about the dirty old renegade over in England too, he said, and her mother and her two grannies cried and said Aw now Pakky, Pakky, can you not let the dead rest in their graves? But he got wild and said this girl has a right to know about the badness of people's tongues and not go out into the world like a poor innocent. They'll all laugh at her, he said, and try and drag her down in the mud if she lets them. "Make sure you don't give them the chance," he said. "Let you always be on the watch out, girl, and let you never trust anyone or let anyone know what you're thinking. And always make sure you get your own kick in first!" It was a worry on top of everything else. On top of this new strange school and wondering would she be able to keep up with the lessons and having to try and make new friends. "Because we're rising you up above Quarry Street," her father said, "and above all the ignorant glunthakamays round about. And we're counting on you to put us back on our feet and let the countryside see the O'Flahertys is the equal of anyone." It would be awful if she couldn't keep up with the lessons, and the sacrifices her poor parents were having to make to pay the fees. Auntie Brigid said she had a sacred duty to her poor Mammy and Daddy to go through all her examinations with flying colours and be a credit to her family and her name. Kathleen didn't dare tell any of them that she was frightened or that she would have been far happier just going on the bus to the Poor Clares like one or two other girls, or even to Claghan Tech when she was fifteen to learn a trade. It wasn't her place to decide.

A few girls stumbled giggling through babyish poems like "The Swing" and "The Land of Counterpane." Nice ordinary wee girls with plaits and check ribbons and freckled faces. Kathleen thought it might be easy enough to make friends with them and the thought disappointed her, because deep in her secret mind she had been hoping to find a friend something like Nuala McCormack. A princess-friend.

"Well that was very nice, everybody, and now just before the bell goes is there one more girl to entertain us? Ah yes, who's that hand waving over by the middle there?"

Scraped-back short hair and a beetroot face, as awkward as all-get-out with the poster stuck on her, Mucky-feet Murphy from Bohamamuc that was in the *Claghan Chronicle* for winning the scholarship. She was some sort of a distant cousin but Kathleen had no intention of letting on. She came into Quarry Street sometimes with her mammy and sat blushing and tongue-tied in the corner, afraid of her life to go out and play with Kathleen in the street. "Moy-name-is Merry-Brudget-

Mourphy-'Shancoduff.'" She began slowly and then, probably panicking at the sound of Kathleen's stifled giggle, she rattled off at the top of her voice an unfamiliar poem without rhyme or reason to it: "'Shancoduff.' Moy blah kills ave never seen the son roisin eternally they luk nawarth towards Armagh." Miss McGowan kept a straight face but Kathleen could see she was worried, not quite sure the girl wasn't exaggerating the rough accent to make a cod of her. Not sure whether she ought to laugh or not, but restrained all the same because poor Merry-Brudget was so serious and so unfortunate-looking. She was short and fat like a wee tub and her gym-frock was tripping her. Her oul' ma thinks she'll grow into it, Kathleen thought, but *I* know she won't. Trying to make up a nickname that would stick, a joke good enough to deflect unto Murphy any ridicule that might otherwise come her own way. Get your kick in first.

"Moy blaak ills that are happy when dawin whoitens Glazdhrimen chapel."

"Thank you, Mary Brigid. Is it a poem of your own? Did you make it up?"

The twenty girls exploded over their desks, all except Nuala McCormack. They snorted and exploded, wondering how anyone could be thick enough to stand up and recite some rubbish she composed herself. Kathleen thought with flat dismay: they'll expect me to make friends with that; that's what I'm going to be stuck with the whole six years. Just because she's from Claghan she's going to latch unto me like some slimy wee leech . . .

Murphy hadn't even the wit to sit down and hide herself. She stood there redder than ever, like the horrible crimson lake in the paintbox, like Rumpelstiltskin with his foot stuck in the floor, and the tears tripping her. "No miss it was wrote by a famous poet called Patherick Kavanagh, miss, and he's from Annaskeen where me mammy's people lives, miss, and me Aunty Agnes showed him to me in the holidays, so she did miss!"

Miss McGowan smiled with immense understanding and kindness: "Ah, a *local* poet! And I'm sure he writes very nice verse indeed, it's just that we didn't know of him. And where do you hail from yourself, Mary Brigid?"

Kathleen called out before she could stop herself: "Glazdhrimen chapel, miss!" Nuala McCormack giggled, surprisingly, and piped: "Shancoduff!" It ran through the room: "Annaskeen!" "County Armagh!" "Nawarthurn Oirelan!" "The British Oils!" "The Wurreld!" "The You Knee Verse!"

"Girls stop it! Stop it at once! Stop laughing this instant or I will send for Mother Imelda. There's no need to cry, child. We are not all gifted verse-speakers. We haven't all had private elocution teachers. I'm sure you have many other qualities. Tell me, did you win a scholarship to come here?"

"Yes, miss." Beaming, the poor eejit, as if it was something to be proud of.

"Well you see! You must have plenty of brains to do that. Many of these foolish gigglers who are making exhibitions of themselves would have been incapable of passing the eleven-plus so you have every cause to congratulate yourself, Mary B, and I hope you will do very well here. Indeed I'm *sure* you will. Now children, there's the bell for lunchtime. Line up quietly please, boarders to the right for the refectory, daygirls to the left for your own canteen. Not another word now. Good morning, girls."

"Good morning, Miss McGowan, and thank you."

When Kathleen left her desk to join the line she saw, victoriously, that Nuala McCormack was keeping a place for her and that Shancoduff was weeping quietly alone at the back as if she knew already that that's where her place was, standing alone with a poster on her back for the rest of her life.

Well, I've escaped that anyhow, Kathleen thought, slipping in with a giggle beside Nuala McCormack. It's going to be all right from now on, she thought.

> (*Some supple writing here, but on the whole too glib and*
> *anecdotal for N.I.W. So sorry!*
> *David Marcus*)

To Maureen's surprise, Trevor got up on his fair-play English pulpit when he read the story: "You don't care who you use, do you Maur? Like a vulture, like a bloody vulture. Sitting there listening to her going on about her hang-ups, *encouraging* her for Christ's sake! I mean she came here to us when she was in trouble because she thought you were her best friend, right? And we've both sat here in this room evening after evening and let her go on about all these hang-ups she had about her parents and Claghan and about that rotten boarding-school and all. I mean you're supposed to be her friend, Maureen, sympathetic and all that, the big cheering-up act, and what do *you* do? You go and write it all down and make a story of it. Try to feather your bloody nest with it. I mean it's sick, isn't it, it's really sick. You better watch it Maureen, you're turning into a right little vulture!"

"Ducky, your Cockney slip is showing! Surely it's magpies feather their nests, not vultures?"

"You could have changed the names at *least*, I mean, that's the least you could—"

"Why? You seem to forget I have debts to pay, Trevor. I'm the one was the victim, don't forget. It wasn't her or Nuala or stupid old McGowan. *I'm* the one was standing up there that day getting laughed at! I mean they'd have destroyed me that crowd, if I'd let them. If I hadn't had the wit to get out in time. I mean there'd have been no point writing that story if I was going to go changing names, or changing the name of the school. I *owe* that friggin' crowd a few insults, do you not think?"

"Well you won't be paying your debts in the *Irish Press* by the looks of it. Just as well that guy Marcus won't have you, those Sisters of Cruelty would have sued us for all we've got if they're as bad as you say. Old *Kathleen* might have sued us for libel! Just as well he didn't print it!"

"Yeah. Don't really think serious literature's quite my thing, do you? I'd better stick to *Her World* and my love stories. More money in it anyhow. You know, Trev, some day I want to roll up to that convent in a mink and a Mercedes and donate a cheque of tuppence halfpenny to their rotten old chapel. Just to see their faces!"

"Why not? But are you *sure* you got out in time, love? Are you *sure* they didn't destroy you?"

CHAPTER TWENTY-THREE

ERIC

Scene: *The sitting-room of 'The Laurels', Claghan.*
Time: *A Saturday afternoon in 1956.*

Cast: Robert McLeod, bank manager; Flora, his wife; Eric and Deborah, their teenage children; Mrs Dorothy Jackson, Flora's mother.

Mr McLeod: We can't *not* ask them, Flora. I see McCormack nearly every day; we take a glass together; we're the best of friends. Do you not think it would look odd if we never invited them to the house? The man has feelings, you know!

Mrs McLeod: Bob dear, *I* see old Mrs Sullivan every day. I mean I've even been known to sit down and have a cup of tea with her for goodness' sake, but I suppose you wouldn't suggest I ask the char to dinner?

Mrs Jackson: Who *are* these McCormacks, children? I don't seem to know the . . .

Mrs McLeod: Nobody, Mother, that's the whole point! Some Roman Catholics who own a lot of property. *He's* on the council with Bob so of course my big-hearted husband here thinks we ought to give them the run of the house.

Mr McLeod: Run of the house, Flora! One dinner-party!

Mrs Jackson: Flora's perfectly right, Bob. Maybe I'm old-fashioned but I think it would be a terrible idea. Heaven knows I'm not narrow-minded but. And then we have to look at it from their point of view as well, dear. I'm sure this Mr McCormack is a very able businessman but think of his poor wife! Do you not think she'd feel very out of place at a dinner-party here? Who would you invite to meet them? And what on earth could you talk about?

Eric: Oh gawd, Gran! You and Sir Basil Brooke!

Mrs McLeod: Apologise to your grandmother *at once*, Eric! Well no, it's not exactly like that, Mother. Actually I do see Mrs McCormack from time to time, at the play-reading group; she's not bad at all. And so elegant! The loveliest Jaeger outfits!

Mrs Jackson: Jaeger! *I* can't afford to wear Jaeger! Good heavens I'm broad-minded but.

Mrs McLeod: And they've got two really pretty daughters and a son who's doing medicine at Queen's. There's nothing *vulgar* about them, Mother. I was only joking when I mentioned poor Mrs Sullivan. I'm just a silly muggins really, I suppose! I mean in this day and age . . . But I do worry about people's reactions, I mean what ever would Clifford Lewis think of us for a start? You know what he's like about . . . I mean there's not one single Roman Catholic employed in Lewis's Shoes even, so we could hardly ask *him* to sit down and eat his dinner next to one! And then there's Deb and Eric to consider . . . Oh dear, it's all so difficult!

Deborah: Us? Consider us *how*, Mummy?

Eric: Mum doesn't want us to have low friends.

Deborah: She's scared stiff you'll marry one of the really pretty daughters.

Eric: Scared you'll end up in a convent.

Deborah: Barefoot, chilblains and sleeping in a coffin.

Eric: Human sacrifice for old man McGinty.

Deborah: A sad old maid telling my beads and kissing the Pope's toe.

Eric: Or worse, so I'm told!

Mrs McLeod: Eric! I don't mind a joke but there *are* limits, in front of your grandmother.

Deborah: Actually you don't have to worry about Eric, Mummy. Imagine old Marx here even *looking* at a rich plutocrat's daughter! I mean it's not as if the Taigs were poor blacks slaving away in the cotton fields.

Mrs McLeod: RC is what we say, dear. "Taig" sounds so . . .

Eric: Hey, *I've* got an idea. Say Dad, if you're really bent on building bridges why don't you dig up an O'Flaherty and ask *it* to dinner instead of McCormack? Keep things in the family, like?

Deborah: Oh yes, please please, Daddy! I do so want an O'Flaherty, my favourite sexy dream! A Flaardy, a Flaardy, *I* want a Flaardy! Lovely lovely Flaardy it is my favourite thing!

Eric: Ee-uck! Deb's been reading old Marianne's true confessions again.

Mrs Jackson: She's been reading Nancy Mitford by the sound of her.

Deborah: Oh Gran, what big ears you've got. Can't get away with anything in this house! Tell us, Gran, *are* there any O'Flahertys left in the town?

Mrs Jackson: Heavens, how should I know? I doubt it though; surely the whole point was that they all perished in a famine?

Eric: Oh poor old Flaardys! With the Blackfoot lying low. With the Pawnee lying lo-o-ow. All right, Gran, identify that one!

Mrs Jackson: Well, but I'm afraid I'm not an authority on

jazz songs, dear.

Eric: Jazz songs! Only *the* most exciting American poet and she thinks—

Mrs McLeod: Stop showing off, Eric. Actually there is, or was, an O'Flaherty family nearby. I'm *sure* you remember them, Mother; pushy sort of people. Americans. I'll never forget when they stole poor Emily Wilson's servant girl that I'd gone to the trouble of finding for her. I've never been so embarrassed in my life! Poor Emily was shattered by it all. You know the old dear gets into a twitter, and apparently her house was overrun by great hordes of priests and heavy fathers accusing her of perverting the girl!

Deborah: Mum! How exciting! You never *told* us Miss Wilson was a lesbian.

Mrs McLeod: From her *faith*, Deborah, as you know quite well. And darling, I'd rather you didn't mention things like that, in front of Granny.

Mrs Jackson: Oh don't mind *me*, Flora. I know how modern and enlightened Bob is supposed to be, so it was bound to wash off on the children. Actually yes, of course I knew of that family. Didn't they buy the old McLeod place, Bob, from your great-uncle Charles and then drank themselves out of it? But they must be gone fifteen or twenty years ago surely?

Mrs McLeod: Yes, it was during the war there was all that trouble with poor Emily's maid. I expect they've all died out or emigrated again by now.

Mrs Jackson: Emigrated perhaps, dear, but those people *never* die out! There's more and more of them in the province all the time; in a generation or so they'll have the majority if we're not careful. Quite frightening really. And a lot of them really high up in the professions too, I hear. You'll see one of them standing for Prime Minister next, mark my words! Give them an inch . . .

Eric: Good old Gran, no surrender! Bring on the gunboats!

So, Mum, are *you* going to be all modern and enlightened and let this pair of lovely Roman temptresses invade our 'umble 'ome?

Mrs McLeod: Don't be whimsical, Eric. And there's never been the slightest question of inviting those girls here, it's the *parents* we're talking about. It's all very well joking but you *are* at an impressionable age both of you. I've just been thinking, Bob, why don't we just have them in for a drink sometime; they *do* drink, I suppose, I mean they're not teetotallers or anything? Oh silly me, how could they be! You know, Mother, *they're* the ones bought Claghan Hall after the O'Flahertys. Do you see now who I mean? They have that big hotel and public house near the station? Can't you place them?

Mrs Jackson: I prefer not to try. Good heavens, Flora, people like that! I'm broad-minded but—

CHAPTER TWENTY-FOUR

NUALA

The portrait was life-size. Larger than life for most people, but Maud Gonne had been a big woman. A six-footer, Nuala's aunt Moira had told her. Aunt Moira, when she was still a young girl living in Clonskea, had quite often travelled in to the city centre on the same bus as Maud Gonne McBride, who was then a very old white-haired lady but still remarkably beautiful and noble-looking. Even the cheeky young bus-conductors, Aunt Moira said, had been completely lost in admiration of her. In the Municipal Gallery portrait she was young, a young girl with magnificent golden hair holding a pet monkey on her arm. Maud Gonne had never been conventional; she had never accepted the normal life of a beautiful rich girl. She had never accepted, either, to be merely the object of Yeats's passionate love.

Nuala McCormack, at fifteen and a half, had not yet been the object of anyone's passionate love, at least not that she knew of, but she was well aware by now of her own worth and fully expected that in a year or so all the fellows in Claghan would be queuing up to make dates with her the way they queued now for Veronica who, everyone said, was

249

not a patch on her young sister. This would not be enough for Nuala, as it seemed to be enough for Veronica. Sitting up among the horse-brasses in the Bit and Saddle coffee shop chatting to the best-looking senior boys from St Brendan's College was all very well but Nuala knew from her reading that beautiful women have the choice of doing far more exciting things with their lives than just letting themselves be loved. Ugly women or even ordinary nice-looking ones did not have those choices. Maud Gonne, during some famine in the last century, had ridden around County Donegal on a white horse with her golden hair streaming in the wind, urging on the starving people to disobey their priests and storm their landlords' granaries for food. They had obeyed her without question because she was tall and beautiful. If she hadn't been beautiful they'd have said she was half-cracked. They'd just have laughed at her and died of hunger. Maud Gonne had known that beauty was better than any weapon, and Nuala knew it, and all the other lovely women who were paraded through picture galleries and poetry books knew it too: Countess Markievicz, Eva Gore-Booth . . .

Nuala knew the Dublin galleries by heart from visiting them with Aunt Moira on shopping trips to the city. Aunt Moira always made a point of spending some time looking at pictures or browsing in second-hand bookshops along the quays in between shopping in the big stores and going off with her friends to eat cream cakes in Bewleys. "Tempering our feminine futility," she called it, "as well as carrying out your dear mother's wishes." Mrs McCormack sent Nuala and Veronica to Dublin for a part of every holidays as an antidote, she said, to awful Claghan. The antidote consisted of shopping, theatres, concerts and galleries, with odd suburban parties (not so different after all from Claghan parties) where doctors and solicitors flirted harmlessly with one another's wives under the paternal smiles of tame priests (invited, Aunt Moira always said, to keep the proceedings respectable). Though the priests often flirted too, coyly and disgustingly, standing slightly too close to one, with whiskey-smelling faces. It oughtn't to be disgusting, Nuala thought, because you knew all the time that they weren't actually going to *do* anything, you were quite safe. Not like with some of the men who tried to grab you on the bathroom corridor. But then, maybe that's exactly why it *was* disgusting, because you knew they couldn't do anything, not as much as put a hand on your knee, without having to tell it to some other priest and do penance as if you were something dirty they'd have to wash off. As if it would soil them to go near you. Give Canon McGinty his due, he mightn't be the most polished man in Ireland but at least he had that much dignity.

Veronica enjoyed the shopping and the dreary old parties, she even enjoyed flirting with the priests. In a few years she and all the other professional wives would be like twins. Nuala preferred just walking about in Dublin; she enjoyed the feeling that she was very probably being fleetingly admired by any number of famous poets and artists and novelists. She didn't want to meet any of them: she would have hated above all things to be introduced to Sean O'Casey or Brendan Behan or George Campbell at one of Aunt Moira's parties and discover that they no more resembled their vocations than the suburban priests did theirs. What was precious to her was the awareness that in that small area that was central Dublin she shared pavements and air and shop doorways and the tops of buses with some of the greatest people alive. And dead. Yeats used to stride along between these grey eighteenth-century houses, nodding his head to the 1916 heroes as they passed him with vivid faces, lost in their dreams of conspiracy. In earlier days there had been Robert Emmet and Wolfe Tone and Lord Edward Fitzgerald; there had been Anne Devlin and Sarah Curran, a whole long procession of consecrated men and women passing and repassing along these crowded streets, their minds and faces illuminated with that terrible beauty.

Four years ago, when Nuala was eleven, a beautiful woman came to Claghan, an actress and writer who'd actually known Yeats. She'd come to Claghan to see Nuala's father who, she claimed, was descended illegitimately from the rebel patriot, Cormac O'Flaherty. She was writing a book about Irish heroes and her aim was, she said, to discover what human realities were hidden behind the sacred old myths. "Too much hagiography in this country. I'm intent on the warts as well as the dimples!" There's a book about him already, Nuala's father told the woman, it's by a local man who had all the facts at his fingertips, but *we're* not in it, that's for sure! You're making a mistake, he said, there's none of that sort of warts about *our* lot! Trying to joke her off. But she insisted on staying in Claghan and came up with some witnesses, old people who swore that the connection was there all right. It'll make a fascinating book, she told Nuala. She'd taken a fancy to Nuala, taught her to recite Yeats's poems and, on her birthday, gave her a copy of Maud Gonne's book, *A Servant of the Queen*. The queen was Ireland. Nuala had been delighted to learn that she was, from now on, something else besides a rich businessman's daughter: she was, however obscurely and however her father denied it, part of the glorious bleeding drama that was Irish history.

That was how the woman put it: a glorious bleeding drama, and Nuala could see what she meant—for eight long centuries the Irish people had suffered every torture and every massacre rather than go on their knees and be slaves. "Slaves of the *English*," the woman had corrected, rather bitterly. "We've never minded being slaves of the priests and slaves of the gombeen men!" She was bitter and less friendly even to Nuala at the end of her stay, because Nuala's father and Canon McGinty had put a stop to the book. There was no need, the priest said, to drag up old sins and scandals: that sort of filth, he said, is not the sort of history the Irish people want to read. And Nuala's father said he had a position to

keep up in the town and, hero or no hero, that was a dirty
scandalous episode if it ever happened, and anyway it's over
now, he said, and I'd rather it wasn't shoved up in front of
the noses of my neighbours and customers—thank you very
much ma'am! And the woman left, disappointed and angry,
when the old people she'd arranged to interview refused to
talk to her, saying they hadn't realised she intended to write
a dirty book making little of the town hero. "This is an
ignorant priest-ridden slum of a country," she said, "afraid to
look the facts of life in the face. I could write a hundred
pages describing in the goriest detail how he butchered a
landlord and they'd be yelling for more, but one mention of
love . . . The whole thing's a dirty joke to them." But Nuala
carried like a treasure ever since the knowledge that *she* was
directly descended from Cormac O'Flaherty, the man who
had fought and died to deliver Claghan from the tyranny of
English landlordism.

What she was seeking in front of Maud Gonne's picture
now was moral support. Inspiration. A wink of complicity.
The courage she was going to need to cross into O'Connell
Street, push open the door of the *United Irishman* office and
ask the men inside where she could go to join the IRA. If *they*
didn't tell her, she'd have to fall back on the redfaced fellow
from Claghan who was on the run in Dublin after blowing
up a customs hut and who'd tried to make a date with
Veronica in the Metropole Ballroom. She would prefer not to
have to fall back on him: Veronica and the girls at school said
that if you rang up a fellow on any pretext he would instantly
assume that you fancied him and that you were just an easy
pick-up. It seemed a bit far-fetched to Nuala that an uncouth
ex-barman from her daddy's hotel would assume she was
prepared to risk her life in an illegal organisation just as an
excuse to get a bit of a court with him. But presumably
Veronica and the older girls knew more about these things
than she did and, really, when you thought of the actual

vanity of most men, the way they assumed you were ready to stand still and let them grope you outside Aunt Moira's drawing-room door just because they wanted to, redfaced and fifty and balding as they were really, when you thought of that, the less you had to depend on them the better . . .

"The IRA headquarters? You wouldn't be wanting them, miss! No, what you'll likely be looking for is *Cumann na mBan*. The women's branch. You'll find them in *Sráid Seán Uí Threasaigh*, about half-way down on the left; you can't miss it. *Beannacht Dé leat!*"

That meant Sean Treacy Street. One of the sixteen dead men who'd come from counter or desk to strike their blow for. She'd never noticed a street of that name in Dublin and when she asked for directions, neither had any of the locals. It took her over half an hour to find it. Well of course! The shame of it: thirty years since Independence and the people of Dublin were content to go on using the old Imperialist names, didn't even *bother* to use the Gaelic, didn't even notice it was there. The apathy. *My* generation's going to be different, she thought; *we're* going to make things move all right.

The headquarters were disappointing. An ordinary little office where you pushed open the door and walked in. Two women knitting behind desks. Shabby gloss paint. A typewriter. Filing cabinet. It's camouflage, she explained reasonably to some childish part of her that had been expecting masks and rifles and passwords and armed sentries. That's all, just camouflage.

One woman was scrawny and greeted her in a Belfast accent, the other was plump and southern. Nuala instinctively spoke to the northern one. "My name is Nuala McCormack. I've come to enrol in the women's section of the organisation." She hoped she was looking resolute and determined and adult, and wished they would look more interested in her. Or at least have the manners to ask her to sit down. "What age are you, wee girl, may I ask?"

"I'm eighteen. I'm a student at Queen's."

"And what do you want to join *Cumann na mBan* for?"

"I want to free Ireland from British rule. To *help* free Ireland. My great-great-grandfather was a hero who fought against landlordism. So I think it's important that I should do something useful with my life, don't *you*? Not just get married, I mean, and . . . " The scrawny woman continued knitting, with a ball of khaki wool and several steel needles. Socks. Her lips moved in a silent counting for a minute, then she looked up and said: "Aye well, would you mind going over and talking to my friend over there? Only I'm just starting to turn this heel and . . . "

Nuala looked at her open-mouthed and then told herself calmly that it must be some sort of a test. Fitness to obey orders without question. Like in the British army the young recruits in Armagh barracks were made scrub the yard with toothbrushes, her father said. She turned to the plump smiling southerner and said firmly: "I want to take part in the IRA campaign along the border. I know how to shoot: Daddy and my brother Martin go duck-shooting every year and I've been taught to use a gun. I've been told I'm clear-headed and intelligent and . . . "

"Tell us, who sent you here, darlin'?"

"Nobody. I asked at the *United Irishman* office and they gave me your address."

"And have you no contacts at all in the organisation?"

"You mean do I know anyone in the IRA? Well, yes, I do know one fellow, a man from home who's been on the run in Dublin for a few months. They near caught him in Crossmaglen, the police. He blew up the Culloville customs post and so he had to swim down the Fane practically to Claghan. My daddy got him across the border."

"Aw I see, he's your wee boyfriend, is he? That'd be why you're wanting to join?"

"He certainly is not my boyfriend!" Nuala snapped. "He just happened to work for my daddy. I mean is there any *reason* why a girl can't make up her own mind to join the IRA? Without having to be inspired by a boyfriend? I mean I'm as fit as any fellow to shoot B-Specials or put a bomb in a wooden hut. Fitter. I mean, that fellow I've just mentioned, he's about as thick as a plank of wood and I bet you nobody ever asked *him* if it was someone else put him up to joining! I mean I'm not just some wee brainless girlfriend!"

"No to be sure you're not, darlin'. But there's no shootin' in this campaign you know, and anyhow you wouldn't be let out on active service. None of the women goes out on active service. It's just the men does the blowin' up and all."

"So what would I be doing?"

"Well the same as us here, a wee bit of typing, addressing a few envelopes, or if you're up in Belfast it might be different. Was it Queen's you said you were at? Aye, well you might have to take your turn of duty in a safe house. Looking after the fellas like. Having the tea ready and sandwiches and all, for when they come in. Or if you can knit, there's always a big call for socks and ganseys for when they're out on active service in the winter . . . Wee things like that, you know . . . "

Maud Gonne knitting socks. Countess Markievicz frying up the eggs and sausages, waiting for the fellas to come home . . . "Who decides this?" she asked. "*Who* decides that women volunteers are just to be domestic servants for the men? It's totally unjust. *I* certainly have no intention of being a skivvy to a pack of fellows." The scrawny one put down her knitting. "Aye, well maybe when you get to be chief of staff, wee girl, you could do something about it. Now tell us the truth, go on, what age are you?"

"All right," Nuala said, "so I'm not eighteen. I'm fifteen. What difference does it make? About eighty per cent of the population is out earning its living at fifteen."

"Aye but *you're* not, are you? *You're* out earning no living.

You only have to listen to you. You're a boarder in some wee convent, aren't you?"

The plump one was friendlier: "Och don't mind her, darlin'! And you could always join *Cumann na Leanbh* if you liked. That's for the wee ones. It's sort of like them Girl Guides the Protestants have. And then in a year or so, when you're sixteen, you could start selling the *United Irishman*; it's banned in the North. You could sell a few copies round your wee schoolmates, couldn't you? And Easter Lily badges and all?"

"She's not interested in that sort of thing," the scrawny one said. "*She* wants to be out among the men, you only have to look at the cut of her! No, you go on away, wee girl, and discuss it with that boyfriend of yours. Him that's on the run. And come back and see us when you're grew up!"

Bitch, bitch, ugly frustrated skeleton bitch, Nuala muttered, going back up Talbot Street. Boyfriend, nothing in her head only boyfriend, that skinny old cow wouldn't know what a boyfriend is. Who'd look at her? Knitting socks and selling papers, it was just like the Legion of Mary. The pair of them were two typical old Legion women, socks for lepers or socks for IRA men, that's all they were fit for. Six counties of Ireland are still a colony of the British Empire, the Catholics in Claghan have to lock themselves in their houses every Twelfth of July while the Unionists march through the streets hammering on their big drums, threatening to massacre us, and that scrawny old bone of a thing is sitting on her skinny bum knitting socks. Was that why she hated me, Nuala wondered. Because she did hate me—you could see she had it in for me from the minute I opened the door. Is it because she's ugly and old and bony and stuck there for life in that awful office? Was it because maybe long ago *she* wanted to be Maud Gonne or Cormac O'Flaherty or Patrick Pearse and all they let her be in the finish up was a dried-up old maid knitting socks behind a desk for other women's boyfriends?

I'll be back all right, she thought. Next year or the year

after I'll be back and I'll be grown up and they won't be able to stop me joining. And I won't let them do it to *me*. They'll make no skivvy of *me*. Nobody's going to be let kill the warrior that's been inside of me since I was born. Since a century *before* I was born. *I'm* not going to end up knitting socks for the boys. Or blowing up customs huts either, she thought, seeing for an instant the utterly laughable picture of the red sweaty barman swimming like some obscene fish down the river from Crossmaglen to Claghan. Like Toad of Toad Hall, RUC men running comically along the bank waving their batons. Taking him for a smuggler, most likely. Who'd take him for a hero?

Who'd take any of that crowd for heroes, she thought, recognising for the first time the absurdity of the present IRA border campaign: cutting telegraph wires and blowing up wooden huts and selling badges. Cormac O'Flaherty selling Easter Lily badges!

It'll be different in the future, she thought. *My* generation will make it different. *I'll* make it different all right! Those bitches in that office won't know what hit them.

She looked at her watch and it was time to meet Aunt Moira and Veronica for lunch.

CHAPTER TWENTY-FIVE

A CLASSROOM IN ST MONICA'S GRAMMAR SCHOOL, 1956

Nuala McCormack: Is it true, Murphy, that your mother's expecting again? How many's that?

Maureen Murphy: Nine. There's four boys and four girls already. I'm dying to know what it'll be this time!

1st Girl: Goodness, you *must* live in a big house! Do you have to share bedrooms or do you have bunk beds or what?

Maureen: Well, it's not really that big; it's—

Kathleen O'Flaherty: Jesus, girls, don't be so innocent! Do you want to hear about Murphys'? I was sent out to their house one day for a message. It's stuck in the middle of a bog. House did I say? You see that wee workman's hut over there? Well, Shancoduff here and the mammy and the daddy and the whole eight of them are all squeezed into a dump that size if you want to know! Isn't that true, Nuala? And isn't Shanco's aunty your skivvy? Doesn't she have to wash your dirty knickers and everything? Huge house, aye!

Nuala: Honestly, Kathleen O'Flaherty, you are going a bit far. Agnes Murphy *isn't* a skivvy and she doesn't actually have to do any washing. She's a nice dependable person and a terrific cook and we all think the world of her.

1st Girl: Gosh, but is that really true, Murphy, that your aunt is—

2nd Girl: My aunty's married to an architect.

3rd Girl: I have three aunties and they're all teachers and my aunt Siobhán is engaged to a doctor. Are *all* your family maids and things, Shanco?

1st Girl: I wonder what it must be like being a maid? Does she listen at doors and read all the letters and tell you all the dark secrets of the McCormacks, Maureen? Mother says that's what our char's best at!

Maureen: Listen, Kathleen O'Flaherty, you thick bitch, you think you're great being an only child, don't you? As if the whole country didn't know why! Your oul' mammy was a skivvy herself and she got herself up the spout and hooked your da because she thought he was rich and she got the buck of her life when McCormacks grabbed the place and everything. The whole town of Claghan's still killing itself laughing over it if you'd clean out your ears and listen! And they say your oul' fella's not right in the head and he doesn't even *like* women and it half-killed him to produce *you* and he could never face doing the job again. Everybody knows. So you can shut up about my family, so you can, and look at your own for a bit!

And then the teacher came in and everyone was silent, only risking an odd embarrassed side glance at Kathleen O'Flaherty who sat there seeing nothing, wondering what Murphy meant and why even Nuala McCormack, her very best friend after all, had turned beetroot and looked away. Remembering and puzzling over mysterious old phrases and warnings from home: "They'll cast it up to you, girl. They'll make a laughing-stock of you if you let them! . . . the time I worked in the lunatic asylum over in . . . "

"Hush, Pakky, there's no need to broadcast that sort . . . "
What was Claghan laughing at? What did the whole town
know? Why was it awful being an only child? What couldn't
her father . . . ? And then vaguely something. An idea. A
memory came to her. The taste of . . . of cake? A houseful
of big people talking, laughing away up above her head.
Carvy-seed cake and loud talk. Old Sarah Morris. A forest of
big people's legs to push yourself through crying. Hating.
Rejected. The people laughing: that's the way, Pakky, let
them see who's . . . Holding a small hand sticky with cake.
There were two of us, she remembered, there were *two* of us
pushing our way out through all the legs. There used to be
two of us . . . What happened to . . . ?

"Miss, Miss McGowan! Kathleen O'Flaherty's crying, miss! Miss,
quick, Kathleen O'Flaherty's sick! She's vomiting, miss, quick!"

CHAPTER TWENTY-SIX

LIZZIE (7)

The first few years she was grand. She'd come home for her holidays and she'd chatter away telling us all the wee things she learned, Latin and Science and everything. Pakky went through it all in his day so he was well fit to advise her about this and that, but the half of the time she might be talking Greek for all I understood! And then when she got on a bit I used to look at her wee companions in Quarry Street that was left school and away to England to work or signing on the dole and running to dances and all, and I thought it was a bit unnatural to see our Kathleen just like a child still. She seemed very soft and backward compared to them. And she had no friends. Pakky wouldn't let her play with the ones in the street and who else was there? The big-shots didn't want her, convent or no convent. There was a few Protestant families, ordinary working people, round in Lockhart Road that their children passed the scholarship and went to Claghan Grammar, and Kathleen fell in with a couple of them in the bookshop one holidays and nothing would do her but to join some history club they had for investigating old stories about Claghan long ago, and of course we had to put a stop to that. Canon McGinty would have destroyed us if we had to let her go ahead inveigling Protestants into the house.

I used to see the Murphys at Mass and I said to the mother one time that maybe she could let Mary Brigid in some day in the holidays to play with Kathleen or go to the pictures, but Kathleen turned on me like a tinker and said what do you think I am? Play with yon thing, Christ, and the cut of her! I won't deny she was an unfortunate-looking child compared to Kathleen though you wouldn't think it later on. She changed a terror, lost stones and started plastering herself with lipstick before she was right fifteen. Mrs Murphy wasn't too keen on letting Mary Brigid in to Quarry Street either. She said the child had her own companions round home and there was no point in her trudging miles to the town for a playmate. Don't they see maybe enough of each other at school, she told me. And then anyway Kathleen told me that the Murphy one carried nits back to the convent one term, so it was just as well. We never had none of that, thanks be to God, though there used to be fierce epidemics them times, though the way the Murphys lived, a whole big dreel of them on top of each other, it was no wonder they caught every bit of vermin going. Anyhow, Kathleen used to spend her holidays stuck above in the room reading books and comics. She done well enough at school considering that she never passed the scholarship nor nothing, and we always planned for her to be a schoolteacher.

She was happy enough till she was fifteen or so and then one holidays she came home and she'd hardly look the side we were on, started giving back-answers and acting the lady. Pakky used to flail her with the belt but it didn't do her one bit of good. I used to tell her if she was out earning like a normal girl she'd have less of the old carry-on, and many a time she turned on me real wicked: well go on then, she'd say, hire me out to be a servant girl if you want to, *I* don't care! Honest to God, I don't know what got into her. Then she started spending whole days moping round the shops, she'd hardly come home to eat. She said one day it was like a bloody asylum, all the old women. My poor Auntie Brigid was crippled with arthritis by then so we took her to live with us, and then old Sarah Morris that was always so good to us was left without a home one winter in a terrible storm—them houses in Quarry Street was always rotten—it's a wonder no one was ever killed. Anyhow, her ladyship Kathleen started complaining about not having a room of her own no less, and not even being able to do her wet without an audience. Old Sarah Morris was the only one in the house could say a word to her without having the face ate off her, she was always very friendly with poor Sarah, lord a mercy on her, that's who she called you after. But her father and me, honest to God you'd think we were her worst enemies, I mean it just wasn't natural the sudden way she took against us. And she never changed back either, not till after her daddy died and she started taking you over to Claghan for your holidays.

It was round that time, when they were sixteen or so, that the Murphy one started coming to the house. They must have made friends someway, and it was nothing only Top Twenty and Radio Luxembourg and film stars and the latest fashions, and Kathleen got it into her head that we should let her leave the convent and do shorthand and typing at the Tech like the Murphy one. All they could think of was being secretaries and getting glamorous jobs, as they said, in London and buying clothes and make-up, not another word about the teaching at all. Pakky soon put a stop to that. If you think we sweated ourselves sending you to that convent for you to finish up crossing the water to be a typist, he said, sure you could have done that straight out of Quarry Street school! It's up to you now, he said, to build up the family and let us lift up our heads again in Claghan the way we have a right to. But she only laughed at him and said it was *her* life and she'd do what she liked with it. Well Pakky wasn't having that and he took the belt to her over and over again till she saw reason. There was still a lot of fight in her all the same and I used to have to listen to awful scenes and ructions between them. I suppose he was a bit harsh with her but it was for her own good and in the long run it worked and she started to see sense and paid no more heed to the Murphy one. *She* started riding in to Claghan Tech on her bicycle as if she was never near the convent, and she took up with some very odd crowd, Protestants the most of them, and you'd see the gang of them round the town making a scandal of themselves with their tight trousers and their hair hanging round them, and then she went away to London to be a typist and got married in no time at all and started writing them books of hers.

But your mother went back like a lamb to the convent and passed her exams and went up to Belfast to St Mary's Training College to learn to be a schoolteacher the way we had it planned for her.

CHAPTER TWENTY-SEVEN

ERIC MCLEOD

He was spread out over the sofa listening to a Billie Holiday record when Dave arrived all eager to thrash out ideas for a motion for Monday's debate. "Just a minute. I'll turn this thing down in a minute," Eric said, but making no move to get up. "No, don't turn it down," Dave said. "This here's one great track coming up." He sang along with the record, deliberately flattening his voice and his accent in a way that, in Eric's opinion, killed the whole thing dead. "Black baddies swingin' in the Suthe'n breeze," Dave sang, "strange froo-oo-oot hengin' frahm the paaplar trees."

Had it been Bryan Watson or Ian Lewis, Eric would have told him to for fuck's sake shut up, it was Billie Holiday *he* wanted to hear, but with Dave you had to be careful. Dave took offence easily; often felt he was being slighted or condescended to when he wasn't; was aware of course (as Eric too was aware) that the McLeods and especially old Granny Jackson thought him an odd sort of friend for Eric, seeing how his dad worked in Lewis's Shoes and all, seeing how the family (and it was a large one: six kids) lived in a poky corner house on Lockhart Road with a huge and tasteless mural of King Billy on the gable wall. Practically a slum, Mrs McLeod said. As if it *mattered.* As if where he lived diminished Dave in any way. As if people were somehow more human if they had a garden and parquet floors and used fish knives for Christ's sake to eat their fish with. "They *are*," Deborah said. "Of *course* civilised people are more human. I thought that was the whole point of your famous socialism, that everyone should finish up using fish knives? Anyway, your friend Dave's not exactly the most couth of boys, is he? And his feet pong."

It was true. Dave did smell a bit, and again, if it had been Bryan or Ian you could have said straight out: "Get away, you pig, you stink!" but there was no way you could say that to Dave without wounding him deeply. There was no bathroom in Lockhart Road.

Eric found it quite incredible that all the people he knew, nice decent *kind* people who went to church and were gentle with animals, did not seem to be aware of the injustice of it. That they couldn't *see* there was anything illogical in Dave's parents working so hard and being given so little while Eric's own parents and relations worked so much less and were allowed to keep themselves clean and warm and comfortable at all times. He found it even more incredible that Dave's sort of people (though not Dave himself, naturally) should see nothing illogical in this arrangement either and seemed quite cheerful and happy with what they were given and marched on the Twelfth and voted Unionist and thought the Ulster Labour Party (such as it was!) was some sort of a popish plot. He was even more shocked when he discovered that *they* looked down at in their turn, and labelled as "layabouts" and "lazy Micks," people who had no work at all and lived in even less comfortable places than Lockhart Road. Things were perhaps simpler in the America of Billie Holiday and Pete Seeger? On one side you had the smug middle-class majority, and on the other the oppressed blacks and Puerto Ricans and migrant workers, who were all perfectly well aware they were oppressed and didn't attempt to pretend they had anything at all in common with their oppressors.

"Why don't we propose this motion," he said, "'that Ulster badly needs a communist revolution?'"

"Because we'd get the boot, that's why," Dave said. "You know what old Hamilton's like!"

"But Dave, the old Ham Roll's about as broad-minded a head as you'd get anywhere! The way he has us reading *Lucky Jim* and *Room at the Top* and all? Questioning the established order, those are his very words, Dave!"

"Yeah, questioning it in England. You never heard him questioning the established order over here, did you? I bet you old Ham'd be shitting his pants if the Red Hand of Ulster showed any signs of actually turning red. I mean, if what you *want* is to be expelled why don't you just propose something like: 'Taigs are Ulster's Oppressed Blacks' and *really* give him ammunition?"

"Yeah, I wouldn't mind but I've got no real arguments, have I? I mean, the only Roman Catholics I know much about are the McCormacks and they practically own the town."

"That's only them. Most of the Taigs down my way own nothing. Quarry Street and that, unemployment rate sixty per cent at the latest count! And what about Mrs Sullivan? And Maureen Murphy's family? By the way, I left Maureen home from the club last night. Did you know?"

"Yeah, I saw you leaving together. Get anywhere?"

"A few chaste kisses. I tried a finger under her bra up against a turf-clamp, rustic idyll and all that, and she told me it was a mortal sin."

"Theological chastity belt, yeah they're great on that. I didn't know you fancied her?"

"I don't, really. Not all that much. I'm still mad about Debbie. Could you not do something, Eric, like tell Deb I exist or something?"

"Yeah, OK, I'll do that, I'll tell Deb you exist. Would *you* say Maureen was Ulster's answer to an oppressed black?"

"I dunno about that, but I tell you I was good and ready to hang the pious bitch on the nearest poplar tree last night! About six frigging miles and nothing to show for it!"

Eric wondered if Dave *ever* had anything to show for it, or if he was just bragging half the time? He hadn't gone all the way with a girl himself yet and couldn't really believe that Dave had. Though Dave probably had better chances. He probably met the kind of girls who didn't mind doing it. Some of the girls down Lockhart Road looked right scrubbers, but again you couldn't *say* that to Dave; it would be like criticising his social background. And then too, Eric wondered if it wasn't a sort of treachery, a loss of socialist integrity, to be having thoughts like that because presumably the girls down Lockhart Road were as much victims of capitalist injustice as, say, unskilled labourers or Claghan's chronically unemployed or migrant cannery workers in California. Their awful thick make-up and brash clothes weren't necessarily a badge of availability. Debbie and that crowd could afford to buy *Vogue* and *Queen* and learn to look nice, the factory girls in Lockhart Road couldn't. *Why* couldn't they, though? After all, Deb didn't get all that much pocket money and neither did Maureen Murphy who was always going on about how poor her family was, and when you thought of it, it probably cost the Lockhart Road girls a fortune to tart themselves up the way they did with muck from Woolworths. So maybe they actually chose to look like that? Maybe it *was* a badge of availability? In which case might it not be a good idea to ask Dave to try and fix him up with one of them? Except that a scrubber was not exactly what Eric required. What do I require exactly, he wondered? Oh he knew the answer to that one all right: what he required was a deep satisfying earthy relationship with a big sexy woman like Simone Signoret or Ella Fitzgerald or

Peggy Lee. Only try finding *that* in Claghan!

Ian Lewis had gone all the way at fifteen; no wanking off in an old sock for *him*, he said. But then the Lewises had two quite young maids who lived in and were ever ready to oblige. Well, according to Ian. Eric imagined himself trying it on with old Sullivan . . . Though she must be fairly hot stuff too: a kid every ten months or so. Dave said his dad said they were forced to do it non-stop, the married Taigs. If they didn't, Old Man McGinty would excommunicate them; it was their duty to outbreed the Protestants whether they enjoyed doing it or not. Which, Eric reckoned, was nonsense and just the sort of thick ignorant prejudice you could expect from Lockhart Road. Except that Eric's gran, who barely knew Lockhart Road existed, said much the same thing. And so did Mr Lewis, Ian's father. There probably *was* a grain of truth in it somewhere: after all, it would be in the Roman Catholic interest, wouldn't it, to have a majority of votes in elections and then try for a united Ireland, whatever good they thought that would do them . . . It seemed extraordinary, and even slightly obscene, that Maureen's parents voted on the same side as that fat capitalist pig, Mr McCormack, just because they happened to attend the same church. And that Dave's dad and the dads of all the Lockhart Road scrubbers went out campaigning for Mr Lewis who paid them as little as he could get off with. And you only had to take a look at the inside of Lewis's factory. Ian had showed him round last year and how, he had wondered, could people have any sort of human dignity being forced to spend all their working lives in a place like that? Afterwards he'd asked Dave was his dad not in a union and did the union not demand better working conditions? And Dave said all his dad's union cared about was keeping Romans off the workforce, and as old Lewis had exactly the same idea they all got on like a house on fire—no strikes or anything.

Eric sometimes wondered if he and Dave were the only

two sane human beings in Northern Ireland. Bryan Watson did share some of their ideas but in a very abstract way. You could tell that Bryan thought it was on the same level as wearing tight jeans and chasing girls—a gimmick you would grow out of when you became a doctor or barrister or architect and had to choose sides and settle down. Bryan didn't believe anything would ever change in Ulster or South Africa or anywhere else—and why should it?—but meantime he boycotted Cape oranges and Rothman cigarettes, and didn't mind coming with the crowd to paint rude slogans on Ian's dad's factory wall. Bryan's sister Myrna did believe you could change things if there were enough of you but she was only a kid, not even sixteen, and still wore her hair in two plaits; you'd never think actually she was only a few months younger than Debbie. Myrna believed in revolutions but she probably got most of her ideas out of Yeats's poetry. Always hanging round after Maureen Murphy as if she was waiting for her suddenly to cast aside her ordinary clothes and turn into Cathleen Ní Houlihan or something. Some hope! Debbie and Judith said Maureen wasn't a socialist at all but a social climber. You couldn't hold it against her though, because she was so open and single-minded about it—like Joe Lampton. Eric thought if there was ever a revolution it would be his duty to put Maureen up against a wall and shoot her first thing. Working-class people should have some solidarity with one another and not just keep trying to grab what they could get. The trouble was, nobody bothered to educate working-class children to see social change as the only answer. They were trained to be competitive and get ahead and join the middle classes, that was the whole purpose of the eleven-plus exam, wasn't it?

Most of the teachers Eric knew were poor crushed people with nothing in their heads beyond pay cheques and pensions or else they were rotten with silly bourgeois ideas they swallowed whole out of the *Manchester Guardian* or *The*

Observer. He knew by experience how narrow-minded and selfish middle-class values were, and he intended to encourage, or even *force*, his own students to question and reject them. The problem was that there was going to be one hell of a row when he told his parents he wanted to go to teacher training college with Dave. *They* thought he was going to do law, at Queen's. So far he hadn't done anything to disillusion them because Dad could be a bastard if you caught him in the wrong mood. He thought it would be far simpler to belong to a family like Dave's who looked on teaching as a great step up the social ladder. Or like Maureen's, for whom teaching was the only hope of getting out of the bog if you wanted to stay in Northern Ireland. When he thought of it like that, he supposed Roman Catholics *must* be a bit oppressed. They didn't seem to have quite as many choices as ordinary people. After all, Dave's parents couldn't afford to let him study law or medicine, but if he hadn't wanted to teach he could have had quite a good career in the Civil Service or Local Government or the police or industry or broadcasting. Maureen and her brothers couldn't. Though some of that might be the way RCs deliberately kept themselves outside the system, their bishops excommunicating parents who sent their children to state schools and all. Why couldn't the Murphys have sent Maureen to Claghan Grammar for free instead of paying a fortune in boarding fees at that convent where the standard was so much lower? Well, maybe she would have come in for a few insults being a Taig and all, but from what she said they treated her like dirt at the convent anyhow, that's why she left. So what had been the point of all the segregation? It wasn't as if they'd taught her any Irish history or geography; it wasn't on the programme for Senior certificate,. She'd had exactly the same syllabus as he and Dave had, totally unrealistic. Eric thought it was lunatic to be living on an island called Ireland and to spend thirteen years at school with teachers and inspectors and examining bodies all pretending like mad that you were living on quite a different island, called England. Straight out of *Alice in Wonderland.* He and Dave, and presumably Maureen too, knew all about Pitt and Gladstone and Disraeli and the Pennines and the Thames valley and Dickens and John Osborne and Stonehenge and Dick Turpin, and not the minutest thing about the history and geography and culture of the country they were actually living in. He hadn't the faintest clue where he could go to look up any information about Ulster, not Orange propaganda but ordinary objective information.

When he wrote that essay for the Rotary Club competition, on The Victorian Age, it had been all about sides of mutton and piano-legs swathed in frills and hypocrisy and children at factory benches and women down the mines and music-hall and Dickensian Christmasses and . . . It had won first prize. But the country he lived in had no mines, and the Victorian Age had been one long succession of famines and land wars and revolts. He knew that because of the old Marianne McLeod journal his father kept in a glass case in the study, but when he wrote the essay it hadn't even occurred to him that it was relevant. Only England and English history had seemed real and relevant.

When he and Debbie were about twelve they had been fascinated by the journal and the exotic suffering peasants, and they had tried hard to cast poor Mrs Sullivan as some re-incarnation of Kathleen O'Flaherty, the McLeod cook. It hadn't worked. Mrs Sullivan didn't know what they were talking about. She had never heard about famines around Claghan, she thought they were making fun of her because she was a Catholic, and threatened to give in her notice. Mrs Sullivan had no sense of her own past in the way that, say, an old black mammy would be weighed down with the knowledge

of chains and cotton fields and the overseer's lash. Mrs Sullivan
had only petty prejudices and a fear of being made little of.
Maureen Murphy had no sense of her own past either . . .

And yet there must be Roman Catholics who had: all those
men who blew up transformers and customs posts must have.
Must surely hate England and not just see London as some
sort of Mecca the way Maureen did? He wished he could
meet some of them. He felt far closer emotionally to the rich
exuberant Celtic mentality that he knew must exist somewhere
out there than he did to the dreary lace-curtain refinement of
middle-class Protestantism. Or of working-class Protestantism.
One of Dave's uncles was a B-Special and swore all Taigs
were bloody murderers underneath, just waiting their chance
to let slip the civilised mask. After all, he said, wasn't the Free
State Prime Minister a known assassin who'd only escaped
being shot in 1916 because he had an American passport?
Eric didn't believe the Roman Catholics would ever want to
make another 1916-style rising. He wasn't sure whether or not
he regretted this. Any revolution at all would surely be better
than the shabby Ulster respectability into which every new
exciting idea sank without trace nowadays.

"What side would you be on, Dave, if the IRA really went
to town again?"

"You mean putting aside our traditional loyalties ha-ha big
laugh! But it's not likely to arise, is it? Granted a customs shed
here and there but have you noticed: they make damn sure
they don't kill anyone! Political massacre's a thing of the past.
They know as well as we do that the revolution of the
future's economic, not romantic. Old O'Leary's in his grave as
yer man said, comrade!"

"Yeah. Freedom's a poetic word, and who needs poetry
in the nineteen-fifties?"

"Speaking of which," Dave said, "Maureen wants to bring
some mate of hers to the Christmas do at the jazz club.

Smashing brunette, she says, thirty-eight, twenty-two, thirty-eight! Name of Kathleen O'Flaherty. She wouldn't be one of your notorious ancestors, would she? Come back to life panting after her ration of McLeod flesh and all?"

CHAPTER TWENTY-EIGHT

MAUREEN

"What I dig about you, Maur, you're a posh girl, I mean you can see you were dragged up nice and went to grammar school and all—that sticks out a mile, but like I can talk to you I mean. I mean you don't scare the pants off me like some of these snooty King's Road bitches."

Posh girl. So she spoke nicely and she washed behind her ears but so what? Christ, posh girl! It seemed to be pinned on her nowadays like a label on her back. Like "I am a glutton" on that first ghastly day at St Monica's, "I am a posh girl." I'm a lot else besides, she thought, and none of them ever seems to notice. It seemed to be all they ever thought of, fellows in London, getting off with posh girls. Not that she had anything against London. Not that she'd go back to Claghan if you bribed her but at least if someone took you out in Claghan you could let your hair down and relax and sort of be yourself. There seemed to be no way of relaxing when you were taken out in London. They weren't taking *you* out, they were taking out some ready-made image they had of the kind of girl they felt they deserved. She felt slightly homesick for Claghan Jazz Club and Myrna and Debbie and

Eric, and even Dave with his pimples and his sweaty socks. Even *Kathleen*.

Straight in front of her, behind Trevor's back, was a life-sized mural of Henry the Eighth lolling on a huge divan showing all he'd got and more, surrounded by his smiling wives. Presumably wives: she counted them and there were six all right. She thought of saying: "That sticks out a mile too!" but held it back in case he disapproved of obscenity in his girlfriends. You never knew with English men, no matter how switched-on or with-it they were. Relic of their puritan heritage, she supposed, though God knows . . .

The restaurant was called The Contented Cod, was very expensive and served tarted-up fish and chips. Maureen had assumed that being taken out by the boss would mean the Savoy Grill at the very least but Trevor said no, these gimmicky fish places were the in thing; the Savoy, he said, was just for hicks who'd won a few quid on the pools.

The scampi, she thought, would have been all right except for the fishy taste in the middle. She hadn't yet got over the idea of fish as a Friday penance and amused herself with the idea that scampi would be nicer made with cubes of pork (or cat or rat, Trevor retorted when she said) as in Chinese restaurants. Prawn cocktail followed by scampi. It was a bit much all the same, what was he going to dream up for dessert: shrimp doughnuts with whipped cream? *Her World* said that on the first important dinner date it was best to let the man do all the choosing: it flattered his ego and showed you respected him. And, she thought, it also let him keep inside the limits of how much he was prepared to spend on you. Your own ego was supposed to be sufficiently flattered by being asked out for a meal in the first place. Especially by the boss who, everybody knew, fancied her like anything, who'd been chatting her up for months before he actually took the plunge and whose well-known vanity wouldn't have let him take it if he hadn't known for certain that she'd just split up with her previous fellow and was available.

Anyway, even if she *had* insisted on choosing the food herself, there wasn't anything on the menu that wasn't made of either fish or seafood. Except the wine. And even that was a bit fishy, the way Trevor kept on trying to bottle it into her. She hoped he wasn't going to be naïve enough to try anything on. She hoped he was going to stay the flip go-getting Trevor of the boutique. That thing about him being scared of King's Road bitches sounded just a bit too phoney and pathetic. Just a bit too much like the preliminary to a gooey love-me-tender pass.

She supposed there were places a man could get away with being pathetic and tender but this wasn't one of them. There were no candles or soft music or bowing waiters in dinner-jackets as there had always been in the places Kieran Hoare took her to. Places where you got an aperitif in the lounge first and then ate Escalope Milanese and cassata and drank thick sweet liqueurs with your tiny cup of espresso and held hands and listened to him going on and on about the hospital, as *Her World* and your own gratitude at being chosen out of all the girls in London told you you ought to . . . The food here was dumped on the table by beefy types in vaguely sixteenth-century costumes who fished notebook and pencil out of their cod-pieces when they came to take the order. Suggestive actions Canon McGinty would have called *that* sort of conduct, but then Canon McGinty was far away in the past and would have disapproved of everything in London just because it *was* London. Pagan England. She glanced at her watch and realised that her parents were, at that very minute, saying the Prayer for Emigrants for her, after the family Rosary. She saw them for an instant, kneeling on the cement floor of the kitchen, their backs to the open fire with the supper kettle burbling on its crane, surrounded by her six brothers and sisters who still lived at home, and all that seemed very far away too. She most certainly did not feel like an emigrant.

She supposed The Contented Cod was funny, she supposed a lot of people would find it quite amusing. Trevor seemed to find it quite amusing. She told herself she was old-fashioned, that romance was just a dormitory dream, an out-of-date song by a dead singer, overhead the moon is beaming white as blossom on the bough and all that sort of nonsense. She recalled how last year she'd very nearly cried on the bus to work when she'd happened to look over someone's shoulder and saw in the *Express* that Mario Lanza was dead. She hadn't actually cried because there had been Kieran then and *real* romance, to make up for it. He seemed far deader now.

Over in the corner a man in a top hat was thumping away at the piano and you had to roar to be heard. Trevor had roared that about her being a posh girl and, a while before, she'd roared: "*You* choose. I said, *you* choose what I'm going to eat!" Not maybe exactly what the article in *Her World* had meant, they probably had more of a submissive whisper in mind, but then let's face it women's mag techniques hadn't got her very far with Kieran, had they? Not in the finish up.

Top Hat was roaring too, swinging his bull head and thumping and bellowing: "My ole man said follow the van/ And don't dilly-dally on the way!" It was an improvement on the one about the marrow: she hadn't known whether to laugh at that one or not. All the people in groups at the big tables had been laughing and making rude gestures and joining in the chorus: "I've got the biggest biggest biggest . . . *marrow* in the world!" (sounding, she thought, *exactly* like people who'd won a few quid on the pools), but the couples on their own had looked vaguely embarrassed and tried not to catch each other's eye. Victorian music-hall, she thought. What on earth has that got to do with Henry the Eighth? She wondered which of the Mafia-looking types chewing cigars around the cash desk had got his centuries mixed up? "But I dillied and I dallied, I shillied and I shallied . . . "

"They should have called it The Contented Sole-cism!" she

bellowed across the table and Trevor, when she'd explained what "solecism" meant, roared with laughter at the pun and forgot about his attack of pathos, as she'd intended him to, while they invented various kinds of fishy names for places. "Contented Herring!" she shouted. "For a jewellers. Get it?" and he topped it with Contented Whale, for a whips-'n-leather brothel. *Not* so prudish after all. "You'd have to be an aitch-dropper for that one though," Maureen said, which unfortunately brought them straight back to her supposed poshness.

You invent a synthetic accent, she thought, to stop ignoramuses laughing at you, and you starve for six months to buy a designer suit in the sales, and then these poor sods of men start expecting blue blood to gush out every time they give you a lovebite. Which mightn't matter if they didn't turn on you like tinkers when they found they'd made a mistake. This time last year: ecstasy! "Dear Mammy, I'm going steady with the most gorgeous fellow, just wait till you meet him! It's the Real Thing, you can start any time choosing your Mother-of-the-Bride outfit!" And then the lead-up to the home visit, and: "What the hell do you mean, a five-acre farm? Are you pulling my leg or what? A five-acre *farm?* I thought you were a posh girl! You let me think you were a posh girl. Jesus, Maureen, I can't let myself in for, I mean it was a waste of time me coming to London if I'm going to finish up with, I mean Christ I could have done better for myself staying at home in Kilrush!" Kieran Hoare. Fisherman's son from County Clare. Dead ambitious. Came to London and worked his way through medical school. Needed a wife who wouldn't be a daily reminder of his gnarled oul' Mammy stirring the skillet. Going out now, she'd heard, with a surgeon's daughter. He'll marry that one all right, she snarled to herself. Convince himself he's in love, holding hands in trattorias, the style to which one hopes to become accustomed. Hypocrite, bloody hypocrite! Hoare by name and Hoare by nature! No, just a poor galoot running from mediocrity, the way I ran from Claghan. Yes, but begod it's not going to be let happen again. It's not friggin'-well going to happen this time.

She rolled up the enormous menu, decorated with headless women in fancy dress, and trumpeted across the table: "Hey you over there, Trevor Watts! Fancy doing the Whaling Whall for a bit? I'm feeling all homesick like. I'll swap you my barefoot Claghan childhood for your kindergarten romps with the Kray twins, right?" Maybe he'll walk out and leave me sitting with the bill, she thought, but at least it'll stop him having any fantasies about me. "Are you sitting comfortably?" she called. "Then I'll begin."

"Och shure and begorrah," he said in a funny accent when she'd finished, "shure Oi knew all the toime you weren't posh," digging his dessert spoon like a spade into the Olde Englishe Apple Pie, "I mean to say, how *could* you be posh? Being a Paddy and all that, I mean. I mean, let's be honest; you don't see many blue-blooded Pads about, do you? But you fit in, Maur, I'll say that for you, you do fit in. You look the part. I wouldn't swap you for Jackie Kennedy! No, but seriously Maureen, I'm dead nuts about you, been trying to work up to this for months actually . . . You know that flat I just bought, smashing mews flat, bloke I know from the art school's doing it up and all, all mod cons and I do mean Mod . . . Well what I mean is: it's yours, Maureen, if you fancy it. I mean, suppose we shacked up for a while; see how we get along. What do you say, Maur? Fancy the idea at all?"

Beloved from your window give me greeting, she thought, swallowing a mouthful of Spotted Dick, hear my eternal vow! Tears, could he not see the tears flopping plopping slopping invisibly into the Olde Englishe Custard? A tall slim blond muscular witty cultivated not-Lanza strong heroic every adjective a tear dropping plopping making whirlpools in the bright yellow custard . . . Trevor Watts: stocky perky bumptious vain (his peaky East End face witness to ten thousand chip suppers, bread-'n-marge breakfasts), left school at fourteen after eight years of homework hastily scribbled at a corner of an oilclothed table in a squalling kitchen. How well she knew it, still needing words explained to him, knife like a pencil, fork like a spade, mashing his cardboard pastry into his synthetic custard, watching her with wary anxious scared eyes, ready to turn the whole thing into a flip defensive joke if she didn't . . . But Trevor with most of the shares in three boutiques already, Trevor intent on making a million before he was thirty: "This street, baby; it looks nothing now, but give us two or three years and I swear Carnaby Street's going to be the centre of the earth. And I've got myself in on the ground floor, you can't deny that!"

You couldn't deny it. He was the sort would get on. She didn't actually believe he'd ever make a million, but he *would* get on. And he's teachable, she thought, and he's anxious to learn, as they used to put on my report cards. And you can have a bit of a giggle with him. And he's with-it, or at least he tries hard to be. Kieran wasn't with-it. Kieran was smashing to look at and he had lovely manners but, let's face it, he would have made a Godawful husband. Dead conventional, Sacred Heart Sodality and all the rest, a litter of kids every nine months. So what are you waiting for? *What* poet? *What* hero? Look in the glass, Maureen, she thought, you happen to fit in for the time being but you're no great beauty . . .

There was no glass to look in, only the big bright mural in front of her, everyone having a whale of a time, Top Hat bouncing over the keyboard: "Ah'll do the cookin', honey; Ah'll pay the rent!" What you need, she told herself, is a background. You're twenty-one; you're not a teenager any more. It's time you were looking for a background. No more nine-to-five, no more worries, someone to pay the rent, loads of cash—you can read poetry all day long if you like. *Write* the bloody stuff if you fancy. Get dressed up and go out to places like this every night: parties, nightclubs. Let on you're enjoying it; it's dead easy. You probably *will* enjoy it after a bit. "Wontcha come home, Bill Bailey, tell me wontch a *please* come home?" Trevor, all anxious brown eyes looking across the table, not bad at all, customers always chatting him up, Sloane Square debs and that. You can sleep with anything if you put your mind to it. Might be quite nice actually to . . . Beloved from your window. Oh Christ, Lanza, would you belt up, would you? You're dead, old son! Yes but. What's in it for me, she thought, shacked up? Shacked up for how long? A month, six months, a year? Teach him to walk, teach him to talk, like the country gawk that went to Dundalk, teach him to eat with a knife and fork and then: sorry babe d'you mind moving out? Only there's this fantastic King's Road bitch you see . . . Yeah.

"Problem is, Trev," she called through the menu-trumpet, "did you never hear how peculiar the Oirish are? I still write to me mammy every week, still go to confession and all that jazz! I mean I fancy you like mad—who wouldn't? Only I couldn't ever, couldn't possibly ever, shack up without, *you* know . . . the old *orange*-blossom! The family tears! Old Canon McGinty's blessing! I mean it's a shame, I mean I know it's daft and all but that's what I'm, I mean I know I'm . . . " Top Hat thumped and pounded: "Ain't that a shame! I know I'm to blame! I know I done you wrong!"

It's like having a bet on the National, she thought: you shove your five bob across the counter and then you sit tight and cross your fingers and pray that your big outsider will come up, knowing all the time that it won't exactly ruin you if it doesn't. Trevor was getting into his stride now, taking all the fences one after another: old-fashioned, typical convent, what are you saving it for, Brigid from the bogs, thought we got on so well, Christ I thought you fancied me, frigid or what? It's nineteen sixty-*one* for God's sake! Crazy about you, Maur. I mean most birds would jump at the, everyone these days, thousands of couples, mean I'm not just after a one-night stand or, it's just *like* being married . . . Maureen said nothing, she smiled across at him and studied the mural in detail. The six women had identical faces: Anne Boleyn or Anne of Cleves, it was all one. So why all the drama, she wondered, why all the beheadings?

The waiter leaned back against an Olde Englishe Sideboard, summing up their faces. "You'd like the bill, squire?" he roared, groping for his notebook. Maureen began tearing up her betting slip, and reached back to unhook her posh evening coat off the Olde Englishe Hallstand. But Trevor cleared Beecher's. "'Ere, Maur, what's your hurry?" he yelled. "We're not *going* yet. And you, squire yourself, mate," he said to the waiter, "you just squire off and bring us a bottle of bubbly, right? The best you've got, we're getting married. OK? Chop-chop! Prestissimo!" He looked at the wine-list and shoved it across the table with a theatrically face-saving groan: "Christ, Maur, have a look at their prices. See what they sting you for a bottle of champagne in this joint? Bleedin' Contented Shark they ought to call it!"

Maureen was altering, erasing, substituting, converting the scene and the decor and the singer and the song and the food and the waiter and, above all, the hero and the proposal, into ten guineas' worth of romantic short story that would be published in *Her World* four months later and that she would read, in Hamburg of all places, on her honeymoon, before going out with her switched-on husband to listen to yet another pop group singing with Liverpool accents in a converted cellar.

They had a quiet smart wedding in London. A friend of Trevor's lent his Richmond house for the reception. There was an orchard but the blossoms had already fallen so they stuck paper flowers in the apple trees instead and had an Edwardian-style picnic on the grass, with catering-firm footmen (looking exactly like Claghan teddy-boys,

Maureen's mother said) handing round the food and winding up the period gramophone.

Maureen's family would have preferred to do the thing decently with a hired banqueting room in McCormack's hotel, and her brothers had to be taken aside beforehand and warned off any such traditional customs as tying tin cans and chamber-pots to the back of the car, or sewing up the legs of Trevor's pyjamas. They drank a lot to make up for it, and flirted heavily with Kathleen O'Flaherty as being the least formidable of the females present. Kathleen, who was looking very glamorous and very happy, smiled in a dreamy way and let them chat. She'd arrived in London the day before, told Maureen she thought weddings and wedding presents the height of bourgeois decadence, and had then spent the afternoon in Oxford Street buying a Dali Crucifixion in a gilt frame and an expensive French cookery book inscribed "To the happy pair."

Maureen and Trevor decided that a house slightly out of London would give more stability to their marriage than a mews flat with all its connotations of casual affairs and bachelor orgies. The old cottage they eventually found, just off Richmond Green, was elegant and easy to run. The perfect place, they agreed, to give fun parties and bring up a small, also fun, family.

But they never did manage to have children and the nursery wing of the house was empty two years later when Kathleen arrived out of the blue looking for comfort and accommodation. It was still empty when (Kathleen's daughter Sarah by then grown up) Maureen and Trevor moved to a French château to escape, they told their friends, the squalor of poor old Britain in the Eighties.

CHAPTER TWENTY-NINE

KATHLEEN (1)

"We were just lying there afterwards waiting for it to be time to get up, not waiting too impatiently, and we were stroking each other's hair and shoulders the way we did, not saying anything. It all having been said more or less silently and very ecstatically in the last hour or so. Not to mention the hour or so before we went to sleep. So I was in no hurry to get up, only thinking vaguely that a coffee would be nice. Black coffee and Cadbury's Wholemeal. I always made a point of buying nice biscuits when he came up for the weekend, and later on I intended to curry a chicken with rice and raisins and all, the way Ahmed's wife taught me. I made a big thing of our Sundays, exotic foreign cookery. Makes a change from the old roast and two veg, I used to say to him, pretending that I as well as he grew up in stout middle-class circles where they religiously ate roast beef of a Sunday. It really sickened me, the thought of ever having to tell him otherwise but he'd be obliged to know sooner or later and, even though he never quit going on about social structures tumbling and equality and all the rest of it, I just could not picture Eric McLeod and me getting off the bus in the town centre and drifting romantically hand in hand through the web of greasy back streets to our house and Pakky and Lizzie and the two grannies and old Sarah Morris and oh God! Oh God I would really die! Because usually if we travelled down on the same bus—and we generally tried not to—what happened was we said: 'Right. See you!' and I trailed home to Quarry Street and he went off in the opposite direction, loping along like James Dean in his jeans and duffle coat, back to his posh home on the outskirts.

"I didn't believe he had a clue how I lived, not the slightest idea. I mean, he knew in *theory* there were thousands of really poor people in Claghan, men that had been out of work for years and women all worn out by about thirty and young fellows on street corners who never would have jobs. Prods too he told me—don't think it's only your sort, Kath, he used to say—only I assumed he thought I came from a better class of Catholic, having been at the convent with you and Nuala and all. I used to think he imagined our house to be just like The Laurels, nicely furnished with a garden and gravel drive, only smaller and with holy pictures on the wall because I was a Taig and my father wasn't a bank manager. Maybe he didn't. Maybe Paul was right and he knew all the time and it didn't bother him. I've often wondered since about that. But at the time it used to worry me sick that he'd have to know sometime. I mean I couldn't keep him a secret forever from the family.

"Oh well, I was thinking that Sunday, I can worry about that later. For the present it was Sunday morning on Fitzroy Avenue and I was saturated with Eric, mad about Eric, devoted body and soul to Eric, and if the worst came to the worst and I couldn't face showing him my parents we could just get on the Heysham boat and sail away for ever and ever and he'd never have to sit in our awful old kitchen listening to my father raving away about British tyranny and about a pack of bloody old ancestors out of the ark. We could get married in

England the way you and Trevor did and he'd never even have to meet them.

"And then Eric, still stroking away at my shoulders, said: 'Kathleen, I have something to say to you.' In a voice that didn't go with the stroking at all, that had no connection at all with anything we'd been doing for the last hour or so, and my hand stopped there in his hair, my frightened telepathic hand froze, didn't come away or anything, just lay there like a dead thing in the cold straight blondness of his hair and I said, lying there rigidly beside him: 'Is it good or bad?'

"'That,' he said, 'depends on your point of view, Kathleen.'

"It's like one of those daft dialogues, I thought, where the girl's working up to tell the fellow she's pregnant and he knows damn well but he's praying to God there'll be an earthquake before she gets a chance to say it. The roles are reversed, I thought, it's the female lead should get the line: 'I have something to tell you.' Only if *I'd* been pregnant there'd have been no need for working up or breaking the ice or anything, I'd just have burst out: 'Eric, guess what! Guess what, we're going to have a baby, Eric!' with a face on me like a Christmas tree, and we'd start writing to the bishop for a dispensation and I'd drag him up to Clonard monastery for instructions and. And lying there, with my fingers in his cold clean head of hair I was afraid to hear what he had to say to me. 'Look, hang on a bit, luv,' I said, 'I'm dying to take a leak.' And I stepped into my candlewick and mules and down to the toilet. I wasn't dying for a leak but I took one anyhow and then I wandered into the bleak, green and cream bathroom to kill time. Six o'clock on a Sunday morning. I'd go back upstairs and we'd make love again and then I'd get up and make us a coffee and by then we'd be engaged. Because wasn't that what he was going to tell me? The house in Quarry Street would be miraculously enlarged and renovated, my father would shave his beard off, they'd get a sudden Yankee legacy, and we'd have a big white wedding at home in the summer holidays. If they didn't break my neck for me before that for consorting with a Prod behindbacks.

"Early and all as it was, I found Ignatius in the bathroom with the geyser full on and a steaming hot towel clamped up against his jaw. Ignatius was prone to toothache and abscesses and wouldn't believe a word you told him about Novocaine injections and general anaesthetics. He said it was probably just like in Uganda where they shoved a pair of pliers in your mouth, stuck a knee in your stomach, and tugged. That's what he *said*: I knew he was exaggerating, trying to make it sound all picturesque and non-British, but we did Uganda in Social Studies at college and I knew it was supposed to be the most progressive and civilised of the colonies. Ignatius was no thickie himself. He was studying law on a government grant and was going home shortly to participate in the benefits of independence. His country would have a real chance to become great and prosperous now that the British were gone. The previous night when we'd gone to his room after the pub to watch *That Was the Week* he got very homesick, even though he was only drinking orange, and he never quit going on about this lovely green fertile homeland of his, and how as soon as he was qualified he was going back there to go into politics and help build Uganda up to be a great nation. And now here he was dying with the toothache and afraid of his life to do anything useful about it. A bit of a comedown, I thought. 'You want to take a wee nip of whiskey,' I told him, 'I have some upstairs; will I run up and?'

"'It is forbidden!' he snapped. 'You know damned well that it is forbidden by my religion!' Loathing me because I was not in pain. Since independence he made a whole big thing out of his African roots, though I knew he'd been baptised and all by the Medical Missionaries, that was who gave him his education, and he'd been brought up as a Catholic. I might even have sent money to him years before— I might even have bought him. We used to buy black babies at school; well, of course, you did too, didn't you? Funny, I always keep forgetting you're Irish these days, Maureen! I often used to think: imagine if I bought Ignatius long ago when we were both kids and look at him now! If it was Ibrahim or Ahmed or Paul I could have said that to them and had a bit of a giggle over it, but Ignatius was far too touchy. One thing, I certainly *didn't* buy Ibrahim or Paul. Their parents were rich and could pay for their schooling so they were let grow up in whatever religion they liked. Ib was a real practising Muslim, Ramadan and everything, and Paul went nowhere. Except maybe where his current girlfriend went.

"The Drogheda nuns out in Uganda had brought Ignatius up as a little gentleman and, toothache or not, he felt obliged to make polite conversation. 'And why are you down here, Kathleen, drinking cold water from a plastic cup at six o'clock in the morning? Miss Elton's tooth mug, I believe. It is Sunday, Kathleen, you ought to be sleeping peacefully beside your lover.' In his stripy mission-school pyjamas, standing in his bare feet on the greasy rubber tiles of a Belfast tenement bathroom, Ignatius dying of toothache felt he had to converse flirtatiously in his correspondence-course Oxford accent. And Eric up there on the next floor waiting to tell me something. Waiting for me to slip in lovingly under the blankets like a lamb and listen to what he had to say. And how did I know with such terrified certainty what it was? If Ignatius had been well I would have asked his advice, followed him to his overheated bedsit where the three of us watched David Frost of a Saturday, begged for a coffee, pleaded with him to for godsake go up and knife Eric before he got a chance to tell me. But I stood there drinking glass after glass of rusty bathroom water trying to drown the truth, nattering away about Oil of Cloves, Miss Elton always has that sort of thing, Ig, will I go down and? And he said no no Kathleen, it is Sunday, do not waste your Sunday old girl, go to Eric. And I couldn't go, wasn't it daft?

"He might have been about to suggest an engagement. It's what you'd expect after two years isn't it. It's what you'd expect after the hundreds of perfect lovemakings, it's what all my friends would expect. Except maybe Nuala McCormack. Maybe Nuala would know what he was lying up there waiting to tell me. Nuala warned me. Nuala was an insulting bitch. Because she was doing a degree in psychology she thought she could just tear her friends to bits, tell them what nobody else could get away with. I hated Nuala, I didn't trust her one inch. Standing there in that bathroom I hated Nuala, though I hadn't seen her for months and there was no reason even to think about her. 'Listen Ignatius, will I get you that—'

"'Go *away!*' he suddenly roared. 'Go away you smug chattering bitch and leave me with my pain!' So I went.

"'I was ages,' I said. 'Poor Ignatius is suffering again, I had to hold his hand for him. Fire away,' I said, sliding my fingers through his hair again without much hope.

"'I like you Kathleen,' he said, 'I'm very fond of you and our nights they're, I mean you're great and everything but I'm not, I mean I hope you're not in love with me or anything. I wouldn't want you to get—'

"'Go way outa that with you!' I laughed. Light light laughter I hoped like in the pictures, real wee Gaumont comedy I was, smoothing his lovely blond hair, go on sink your nails sink your nails, girl, rip scalp and all off the bastard, smoothing gently his lovely cold Protestant hair: 'Eric son, are you mad? Me in love with you? And all my plans, what about Israel and Cuba and all the places I'm saving up to go to? You didn't think I was lying here pining for the scrap of diamond, did you? Tell me honestly now, do you think I'm one of these who spend all their free time strolling through Robb's basement pricing electric cookers and all? Och, don't tell me you're that daft, Eric!' And with relief he was randy again and I in love, in love. 'Sure it was just a bit of a giggle, Eric, we always knew where we stood, didn't we? I mean, I don't know about you but it's always seemed to me the perfect set-up. We're stuck here in Belfast for the time being so we may's well enjoy it. No strings attached.' Oh his lovely cool hair and his shoulders and the long smooth bones of his back and his nice long legs imprisoning me. And really, in spite of knowing, it was as good as any other time. Except for knowing it was the last time.

"I made us a coffee on the gas ring and put on Billie Holiday. Yesterdays, days of love and joy and youth. I hoped he wouldn't read any great significance into my choice but of course he didn't, he was far too full of himself. 'I've been seeing this girl,' he said, 'this last while. Used to be a friend of that mate of yours, actually, friend of old Maureen. Well anyhow, I've known her all my life but it's only these last few months . . . Myrna she's called, that's her name. Myrna Watson. Maybe you've met her? Maybe you saw her sometime with Maureen?' The way he slid out her name. Kissing every dirty letter of it. The way I said Eric. The way they all laughed at me for saying Eric. Sequestered days, days of innocence and truth. A nice Protestant name. A nice respectable Protestant girl. 'God, you must be worn out, screwing the both of us!' He was shocked: 'I don't *sleep* with Myrna!'

"Well, that was something. Nuala always maintained that a girl who's slept with a fellow always has that much over a girl who hasn't. We drank our coffee and he talked about Myrna, couldn't stop talking about her, and I listened and I thought well it's only a few weeks till the end of his teaching practice and he'll be safely back in Belfast and it'll all blow over. He didn't seem to do very much with this Myrna except listen to records and go to the local jazz club. A right dump it was, dead respectable, bank-clerks and Protestant schoolteachers and kids from Claghan Grammar. Oh, and from the Tech, of *course!* You went to that club for a while, didn't you. It was you brought me, that Christmas I met Eric. Right lot of pseuds, weren't they?"

"Yes, but what I don't understand," Maureen said, "I was still hanging round Claghan for months after that but I never even knew you were going out with him. Myrna was always mad about him, you know, but we thought he never bothered with girls, just sat at home reading Karl Marx or something. You must have kept it pretty dark!"

"I didn't go out with him, not then. He was dead shy with me that time. I met him again in Belfast, oh about two years later, at a party in Nuala's flat, that's when . . ."

"So he went on telling me about this Myrna. She ran the Guides, imagine, went to church and all, but she played the guitar and she liked modern jazz and blues singers. Well, so did I, so did I. Eric had taught me to like jazz as he'd taught me to be a socialist and read the *New Statesman* and *Private Eye* and say JFK was a clod and be all in favour of Cuba and African independence and living in kibbutzim. So what was Myrna? Some snooty cow from down home who ran to fucking church every Sunday. But I was crying and crying inside of me, and the coffee was choking me.

"Wee Lily from downstairs rapped and put her head round the door looking for shillings for the gas. She had to climb three flights not because she liked me but because she was scared of Ahmed and Ignatius and Ibrahim ('Well, I *know* they wouldn't lepp on me but'), and because Miss Elton was an elderly Protestant lady and she was a bit scared of Prods too. I said come on, on in and have a coffee because we were decent by then with our jeans on and everything, and I said I'd go down to the kitchen and make some toast. We all shared this big barn of a kitchen and it ponged of curry and fried bananas and boiled tripe, with Miss Elton's scrambled eggs trying to manoeuvre a wee corner in the middle of them. Lily and Eric were flirting away as usual when I came back. Lily was never all coy and sort of submissive with him the way she'd have been with a Catholic fellow because she didn't really see him as a man at all—well I mean not as a potential marriage prospect. She was conditioned just to see him as a Prod, and of course she'd never have considered having anything serious to do with a Prod. Eric thought she was a scream: typical Catholic virgin, he always said, saving it all up for the wedding night. And Myrna, I thought now, watching him teasing her, what's Myrna saving it up for?

"'When are you two going to apply for a dispensation anyway and give us a Big Day?' wee Lily asked, her eyes slithering around furtively, what was the bitch looking for, splashes on the wallpaper? I knew she was always full of maidenly embarrassment in our presence. Well, I used to be like that myself, never knew where to look when I was alone in a room with a couple I knew went the whole way. As if I wasn't embarrassed too, my God, struck dumb by such a question at such a time. 'Oh Kathleen doesn't want to get married,' Eric said. 'She's in no hurry. Kathleen's far too ambitious to settle for anything as dull as marriage!' And all my stupid hopes rose up again and I was beaming. Sweet Christ, I thought, maybe that's what's biting him. Maybe he thinks I'm hard and ambitious, maybe that's it, maybe what he wants is something feminine and sweet and. Well I can be sweet, I can go in for marriage if that's what he wants, I can do anything. This afternoon he won't know me I'll be that sweet, serving up his chicken, like more coffee, darling? I'll tell him straight out I'm crazy about him, I don't care if he laughs at me or shoves me away or anything, God, if I want, I can settle this Myrna one with my hands tied. Something always held me back before from mentioning love. I could never say it, even in the beginning when *he* never stopped saying how much he loved *me*, I could never actually get the word out. And I could never make the first move either, to kiss him or even take his hand at a bus-stop or anything. I mean I'd be standing there beside him counting up how many hours we had together, revelling in how many hours we had before I had to go to college or school next morning, but I couldn't bring myself to move that half-inch closer and be touching him: it always had to be him. I was scared of something. I don't know why. Maybe that's all was wrong, I thought. This afternoon, I thought, I'll be different.

"When Lily left I said: 'Will I run out and get *The Observer*, luv?' and he turned red. 'No, I meant to tell you,' he said. 'I have to be back down home for lunch. I'm sorry, there's this function . . . the church . . . my parents . . . '

"'Fair enough,' I said, 'you're going straight away then?'

"'Yeah, there's a bus at ten. I meant to tell you. I forgot.'

"'OK then.'

"'I'm not sure when I'll be up in Belfast again. Maybe not before next term. I'll ring you.'

"'You don't have to. I'm not always in myself these days.'

"'Ah now Kathleen, don't take it bad. Nothing's changed, is it? I know you have things bought for the lunch and all but.'

"'It's not that, Eric. I just mean I'm a bit tied up too. There's this fella. You didn't give me a chance to say.'

"'God, that's great, Kathleen! You've got someone? Look, we'll keep in touch, stay friends, right? Let's all get together some time next term . . . Only listen here, Kath, now I'm only saying this for your own good, don't fly off the handle or anything . . . I mean I *like* Ignatius and Ib and all that crowd, don't get me wrong, I'm no racist! God you know *me*! Only you could get a bad name for yourself easily, Kath, if you're seen going around too much with. I mean I hope it's not, that this new fella's not one of the . . . Well anyway, Fitzroy Avenue's not the most savoury place to live is it, for a girl? I mean, couldn't you find yourself a nice room up the Lisburn Road or somewhere?'

"'I'll think about it, Eric. Bye, luv!'

"'Oh and do you think you could let me have my Billie

Holidays and the rest? Only I promised . . . I promised Dave I'd.'

"'Fine. Sure, Eric.' And two years of lovely yesterdays ended with a Presbyterian church function."

"Do you not think we ought to let Maureen know about this?" James Murphy worried. "She was always very great with the O'Flahertys. Sure she as good as reared that poor wee girl. And with them McLeods too."

"Let her know *how*?" the mother said. "With this old postal strike and now the phones out of action today and everything. Honest to God, the country's going from bad to worse! Are we never going to see an end of it? After all the peace movements and the Pope coming over that time preaching love and reconciliation and everybody turning out in their millions to see him, wouldn't you have thought the people would begin to see sense? He'd have been as well staying where he was, God bless him, for all the heed he got here. Both sides seems to be going to hell altogether this last while with their kidnappings and bombings, and now this. Poor Lizzie, it's her I'm sorry for. Between inquests and post-mortems and all these so-called patriots trying to pull her in ten different directions at once, the Yank O'Flaherty worse nor any of them, that she won't even be let have the wake and funeral in peace! That's the third big blow for Lizzie now inside a lock of years, if you count Big Jim Malone that was reared along with her. And that slut of a Kathleen one, for that's all she ever was, not even to come home when her own daughter. Has she no nature in her at all? Lizzie was telling me she phoned her and phoned her the night it happened and left messages with her neighbours and not even so much as a. It's poor Lizzie I'm sorry for, that wee woman never had no class of a life."

"We could send Maureen a telegram. Maybe it'd take her home for a few days at least?"

"Divil the home! If she was coming wouldn't she have

come before now? Sure won't it have been in all the foreign papers and on the wireless. They get the BBC great over there. That lassie's always far better informed about the Irish news than we are ourselves. Far better."

CHAPTER THIRTY

KATHLEEN (2)

"There was still the chicken and the rice and the curry sauce. The last thing I wanted was to ask wee Lily to share it with me. Wee Lily had the same effect on me as that school up the Falls where I was teaching. There was something in her always trying to drag me down into some ghetto and show me where my place was. I could just hear: 'I told you, Kathleen, I told you ages ago, what else can you expect? I *told* you there was no future in going with a non-Catholic!' And she'd lend me one of her C&A crimplenes to go up to the dance in Andersonstown with her. To take me out of myself and start acting like other people again. Find myself a nice Catholic teacher to marry. A wee virgin mouse from Trench House with a good blue suit and a nice line in harmless gropes.

"Wee Lily shamed me whenever I saw her. I'll never forget the time Eric's cousin, you know, Judith Hale, got me this Saturday job in the Stepaside café. Well, wee Lily applied for a holiday job there and when she came to be interviewed Judith and me and this other girl from Stran were just standing round nattering round the manager's desk. 'You're a student are you,' the manager said. 'Queen's?'

"'No, I'm at a teacher training college.'

"'Which one?' the manager asked.

"'Stranmillis,' wee Lily said. 'I'm fourth year English at Stran.'

"'Well, that's funny,' this other girl said, 'because so am I and I never laid eyes on you before!' And Lily turned beetroot and confessed she was at St Mary's. God, *I'd* have run out and flung myself in the Lagan before I admitted I told such a cringing sort of a lie. I mean, you'd have to be real thick. She honestly believed they wouldn't take her on as a summer waitress if she let on she was at a Catholic college! I don't know, maybe they wouldn't have. Maybe I only got taken on because I was going with Eric. I don't really know, though, because I mean they were always very good about giving me fish on a Friday, I mean I don't really think they gave a damn what church their staff attended. But honestly, people like Lily really drag Catholics in the muck, they just *ask* to be persecuted. I couldn't look Judith in the face for ages in case she thought I was like that too. She depressed me, wee Lily, and I knew that Sunday that I'd rather go on hunger-strike than have lunch with her.

"I rapped on Miss Elton's door and she said yes of course she could let me have some Oil of Cloves, oh poor Ignatius, she said, not again! That unfortunate wee lad, why won't he go to the dentist? Ignatius's room would knock you down, the oil-heater blasting fumes, and he was groaning away there on the divan. I gave him the Oil of Cloves and he said: 'Kathleen, oh Kathleen, I shouted at you!' and I said: 'I know, Ignatius, how you felt. It's all right, *I'm* suffering now too.' And he said: 'Don't be polite, Kathleen, go to Eric, he is waiting. It isn't fair that he should have to wait while you minister to me.' And I ran out of the room before I started sobbing. He was in no state to eat lunch anyway. Poor wee Ignatius, do you think he got caught up in anything, Maureen? Do you think he really did go back and get mixed up in politics? He'd have been on the wrong side, that's for sure . . . "

"There were no right sides," Maureen said, "as far as I know. In Uganda or anywhere else. If he got mixed up in politics he knew what to expect. When you grab a shitty stick you get shit on you, right? As the man said."

"He couldn't have stood it you know. Dismembered bodies and rivers full of blood, and when you think he couldn't even face going to the dentist . . . Maybe he never went back. Maybe he just settled in England like a lot. Maybe he's even lecturing away at this very minute in some English redbrick. With a mouthful of gold fillings. Do you think he might be, Maureen?"

"Hardly at this very minute," Maureen said, "hardly at ten o'clock on a Sunday night."

"I went back upstairs and stood at my window and looked at Fitzroy Avenue. It was spring but how could you tell, there was nothing but houses and a bit of grey sky. All you could recognise there was winter. That last winter was fantastic—the worst for centuries they said—snowdrifts yon height and no food in the shops. For weeks Eric couldn't get up to Belfast. All the roads were blocked. That's when Myrna must have hooked him, stuck there in Claghan on three months' teaching practice with nothing to do only listen to Bessie Smith and the huer of a minister. *I* had the city and Ignatius and Paul and wee Lily and Nuala. We used to snowball up and down the avenue. But snowbound or not I couldn't have fancied anyone. I couldn't have fallen for anyone. Not even for Paul. Everyone fell for *him*. It wasn't like real life, those snowy weeks. It was more like being up in a plane with everything behind you and everything in front of you. It was innocent as all-get-out, the city white and smothered and no traffic and the schools shut. We lived in one another's rooms by candlelight, eating peanut-butter sandwiches round the oil-heaters and talking about when we were children. We thought we *were* children again playing there in the snow. I lived inside the warm womb of Eric's love, knowing that he was being kept safe for me in the womb of another peaceful smothered town. He rang me a few times but mostly the phone lines were down. When the others talked about Nigeria and Kenya and Uganda I talked about Eric; he was my home and my people, the only homeland I cared about. I never talked to anyone about Quarry Street and my parents. I didn't really miss Eric those weeks, he was there with me. When the electricity was working I played Billie Holiday and Charlie Mingus. I was happy. I was never happier. It was a most enchanted time. The last enchanted time. But you know, Maureen, that was the winter, that was the very *month* Sylvia Plath couldn't take any more and put her head in the oven. And in one of the dirty brick streets near my school a woman beat her tenth kid nearly to death out of sheer cold and hunger and frustration. And up the Shankill another woman took a knife to her unemployed husband because he went out and drank all the dole money. And out in that island Eric and I were so mad about, a farm-labourer was starting twenty years' hard labour just then for doing a Little Boy Blue and letting the cows into the cane-fields. But I was happy. For a start I was free of thirty-five brats in a slum school, I was safe for a while from that. I could never tell Eric how I detested those children. Their snotty noses and smelly pants and their skinny white freckled faces and their chopped-off sandy hair walking with nits. And the homes they came out of. Those dirty red prisons of streets one after another for miles and miles, identical, without as much as a flower or a tree, even the odd geranium on a window-sill was dried up and hopeless in no time. It was called Mimosa Street where the school was. Mimosa Street! And there were nine other identical streets called after the nine muses. And a hundred others after glorious victories of the British Empire. All identical dirty red brick.

"They were too close to me, those kids. This is all you are, I could see their eyes telling me. You're no better nor us, miss! I'd turn up there of a morning sure of myself and ready for anything and there'd be a dreel of them round the school door, pulling me down. Kids and toddlers and prams, and mothers with bare purple legs, pipe-cleaners in the dried-up perms and the eternal Woodbine trailing out of the corner of the mouth and these sarcastic street eyes seeing right through my suede jacket, seeing that my bra and knickers came out of Woolworths the same as their own. Oh they'd be dead friendly: 'Leather into him, Miss O'Flaherty, he's a holy terror! Don't be afeart now to leave welts on them, miss, no good being too soft with weans!' And I used to want to spit Froebel into their hungry depressed faces, child psychology and. I used to want to take them down the pub for a drink, buy them a Chinese meal, tell them for Christ's sake to get out of it, get on the boat, get anywhere. As if it was Quarry Street. As if they were me. I thought they were me. I thought terrible things were going to happen to them. I was right. And I used to say to Eric, all hypocritical: 'Poor little sods all the same, what an environment to grow up in!' As if I was some, some caring outsider. As if I hadn't a clue what it was like growing up in a home like that. A street like that.

"And Eric thought it was great they were all miserable and hopeless because it only brought the revolution that much closer. 'You just wait, Kath, in ten years or so these kids will be dead-end school-leavers, right? With no jobs and no future. You think *they'll* just put up with it and run to Mass and the Orange Hall and listen meekly to priests and ministers and politicians the way their poor daft dads did? Not a chance, the world's changing, dig? By about, I'd say by about 1973 your lot and the lot up the Shankill—because believe me, Kath, the lot up the Shankill are as deep in the shit as anywhere—the kids from both sides will pour into the streets and join forces. *They* won't let themselves be manipulated, they'll get together at last and oh boy! That'll be worth seeing, they'll pull down the whole fucking establishment. Orange lodges, Catholic hierarchy, the lot. It's jobs that'll matter to them and housing, and Christ, by about, I'd say by about 1980 at the latest Ulster will be a completely socialist state. Everywhere will be, Britain and America and all. It's the only future, Kath, don't you see? Or else it'll be mushroom clouds for everyone, and the world's not *that* stupid!'

"God, Maureen, do you see what I wasted my life on? Do you see now what I was in love with? I thought he was some big hero! These last years, seeing it all, seeing all that's happening, I started hating him. In the long run I hated him. For being stupid. For not knowing one small thing about the country he was living in. People like him ought to *know*. I wonder how many of my past pupils are in Long Kesh, Maureen? Do you think maybe I taught poor Bobby Sands? Do you think maybe *he* went to Mimosa Street school? Imagine wanting to die for Ireland when the only bit of Ireland they were ever let see was the top of Divis mountain sticking up behind the dirty back streets!"

"Maybe that's precisely why," Maureen said. "Maybe they wanted to be let see the rest of it. Maybe they caught on eventually that neither you nor Eric, for all your big talk, was ever going to take them by the hand and show them any more than they could already see from Mimosa Street."

"And *you*, Shanco, what about *you*? Writing lies about Cormac O'Flaherty, about things happened over a hundred years ago. What good do you think that's going to do anyone in the North?"

"Ducky, I don't owe a thing to the Catholics of Northern Ireland. Let them solve their own problems the way I had to solve mine. I escaped long ago, remember?"

"So you keep saying. No, but don't think I swallowed all Eric said. I didn't, not really. I could have told him. I could have said not a chance boyo, not a hope! But it would have meant explaining what I came out of myself and I couldn't do that. I thought that for Eric I had to be like himself, clean and middling, with mahogany furniture and stamp albums and Meccano sets and big roasts of a Sunday. I had to have all that behind me to reject. You know? What was I scared of? Well, if I took off the mask, if I once took it off I'd have stopped being me. I'd just have been another hope for the future, another slum woman with purple legs and a dangling Woodbine. I was afraid.

"And anyhow it wouldn't have done a bit of good *me* telling Eric he was wrong and that this famous solidarity among the workers he was always rabbiting on about just didn't exist. Just couldn't exist. I mean, if I'd told him what I knew about the hatreds and bigotry and all the remembered insults—if I'd told him one-quarter of what went on inside my father's head—he'd only have given me a lecture about scapegoats and defence mechanisms and how all that would disappear when the two communities united for a workers' victory. If I'd told him Pakky O'Flaherty didn't *see* himself as a worker but as a potential boss, done out of his just rights centuries ago by foreign tyranny, he wouldn't have believed me. He'd have said all that was out-of-date folklore with no relevance to the nineteen-sixties. Oh not that he was exactly behindhand with the folklore himself, old Eric. You know this diary they sent you, this load of old tripe you're stuck in? Well, he used to *quote* from it! He knew bits of it by heart! This landlord's daughter learning Irish and sort of communing with the peasants. *He* reckoned it was a message of hope for the future. He conveniently forgot, or maybe no one ever told him, what actually happened to the poor bitch and all belonging to her once she'd *learned* the bloody language. And what happened to those peasants she communed with.

But my father didn't forget. Nobody in Quarry Street or Lockhart Road or up the Falls or the Shankill or Sandy Row could ever be coaxed into forgetting that! Jobs or houses or whatever they were promised. And if they showed any signs of forgetting it there'd always be some priest or minister or gombeen man on the make, only too ready to remind them. No but if I'd explained all that, he'd just have said I was in no position to judge objectively from where I was. Only the educated middle class, you see—people who'd been educated for centuries— *they* were the only ones could judge objectively: the rest of us are just a shower of thick galoots fighting over which church to attend. A bunch of friggin' ayatollahs, they think. And he kept on judging objectively, Maureen, right up to the end. I bet he and that Myrna one were sitting in their nice booklined house up the Belfast Road still judging objectively. If I'd told Eric back then, if I'd told him the truth, I'd have just become part of the inarticulate masses for him. Even revolutionaries don't marry the inarticulate masses do they, they marry nice girls like themselves. Myrna must have been like himself, same background. Safe and ordinary to come home to of an evening. And objective."

"So do you think that's what happened in the end?" Maureen asked. "That he eventually noticed the Woolworths lace on your drawers?"

"Yeah maybe," Kathleen said. "Can I have a refill, please?"

"Sure, go ahead." And Trevor measured the bottle with his eyes and said nothing at all.

"Yes but I stood there that Sunday looking out at Fitzroy Avenue. It used to be a red-light district, you know, before my time, but then that year it was all students. Not the goody-goody student teachers who lived in what was called approved digs up the Falls Road and danced in St Teresa's Hall where they were sure to be picked up only by their own kind. And not the sophisticated ones like Nuala who gave quite daring parties in University Avenue. No, Fitzroy was more of a no-man's-land where all the tribes mixed, where the black and brown and green and orange got a bit fuzzy round the edges from trying to pretend they were all just shades of red. The demarcation line was a bit fuzzy too actually. I mean wee Lily downstairs really belonged up the Falls, and then Eric and I often went to parties like the one where the Minister of Something's daughter was found dancing in her skin when the lights came on again. There was Miss Elton too, the essence of respectability. She wrote stories for magazines and did verse-speaking with the Belfast Poetry Circle. You came across her name in *Woman's Own* about once in a blue moon, she can't have been very successful or she'd have moved on years before. Bought a château in France or something *n'est-ce-pas*, Shanco? And there was a legend too about another respectable elderly lady who staunchly sat it out through the decline of the street, through the whorings and dopings and the drunken sailors and the Saturday night knifings, only to be finally driven away by an alien religious rite. Typical Belfast that, oh typical. It seems at the end of Ramadan one year Ibrahim decided to throw a party and he went down to the market and bought two chickens. Live ones. He was new in Ireland—it was his first year at Queen's— so in all simplicity he took the two birds outside to the only open space there was, the wee square where the dustbins were kept, and he started slaughtering them according to Muslim ritual. The old lady in the downstairs flat looked out the kitchen window and near had a stroke. She staggered to the phone and called the police: 'Come quick! There's some pervert of a medical student tortyering animals in my back yard!' It seems there was this tremendous squawking and cackling and flapping of wings, and a Black Maria oozing RUC men armed to the teeth with batons and revolvers, and poor Ib standing there all innocent and bewildered in tribal robes and covered in feathers: 'But officer, there is no shop here where I can buy poultry that has been cleanly slaughtered.

I am a Muslim, you see.' And the constable: 'Ah don't care if you're a Roman Catholic, ye still have no right to vivisack livestock on a dacent widda's property!' The next week the downstairs flat was empty and wee Lily and her cousin moved in. It was Ib told me himself and from then on he stuck to Vesta curry like the rest of us . . .

"I could usually amuse myself for hours thinking of the history of that house but the fact remained that I had an empty Sunday ahead of me, every single thing in that city shut down except the churches. A whole vacant Sunday without Eric. Sunday after Sunday from then on with nothing to do only write up my lesson notes and make visual aids and pick out poems that might fit in with the life-style of the wee so-and-sos in Mimosa Street. When I was a kid at nursery school they told you to go down to Kew at lilac time and no nonsense about it. Big bourgeois treat, we all loved it, took you out of Quarry Street for a while anyhow. But by 1963 teachers were supposed to be more ethnically aware—kids that lived in the slums had to be told that slum life was beautiful and significant. Or at any rate that it rhymed. I used to really puke hunting through all these switched-on anthologies for things that were supposed to be on the wee brats' wavelengths. Things like: "Me dad's on the dole, Me ma's up the pole, Me sister's out screwing a Ted." They all seemed to be written in Manchester accents, poems like that. Which wasn't very relevant either. Not that I could see. Not relevant for the kids up Mimosa Street with the family Rosary and lace Communion veils and First Confession up at Clonard monastery. But the inspectors seemed to like them, the education lecturers seemed to like them. Because when the education people tried to peer up through all those layers of colour supplements they were buried under they weren't seeing Mimosa Street, Falls Road, Belfast. They were seeing a typical British working-class neighbourhood as described by Hunter Davies or some other with-it features editor, where all the kids' dads looked like Andy Capp and voted Labour. And where all the kids would grow up to safe boring jobs and plenty of them, and safe boring council flats with all mod cons, so why not, they were thinking, give them a slice of nice safe boring literary revolt *à la* Alan Sillitoe so they won't forget their ethnic realities. Only the ethnic realities of Mimosa Street! Or of Quarry Street . . . Do you think I'm drunk, Maureen? Well I'm not drunk. I'm *going* to be drunk but I'm not drunk yet. That's what teaching was like, then. That's what fuckin' Belfast was like.

"Yes, well, I stood there stunned I suppose and empty, and thinking that the chicken below in the meat-safe was already started on the inevitable process that would soon have the shared kitchen humming like the inside of a coffin because I didn't intend ever to set eyes on that bird again, let alone take it out and cook it like some—some forsaken spinster. In the end I decided that the only person in that awful city that I could bear to see, the only person who could maybe give me some grain of hope to grab on to, was my friend Paul Achebe. So I put on my red Courtelle sack dress with the mandarin collar and back-combed my hair up high and put plenty of Max Factor on my eyelids, and in the hallstand mirror I thought I looked cool and sophisticated and not at all like some poor victim who'd just been given the push, and I walked across Botanic Avenue and up past Queen's to the Malone Road.

"It was getting close to Easter but the wind would walk through you, and in Paul's flat the paraffin heater was blasting away just like in Ignatius's bedsitter. But Paul was not like Ignatius. He was the most beautiful man I knew, as beautiful as Nureyev, fantastic bones and all, and just as much out of my reach. Even if I hadn't been in love with Eric. Even if I'd met him before Eric I'd never have dared try my chances with Paul. I knew I wasn't his type. But we were friends and I went as near talking to Paul as I did to anyone. With most

people I just sort of joked. You know. Or said what I thought
they expected of me, which usually wasn't much. But even
I knew that wouldn't do for Paul, he wanted you to say real
things.

"When he opened the door we kissed and cuddled a bit
the way we always did, like kids playing around, and then
he said all surprised: 'But I thought Eric was in town?' I was
about to tell him all when there was a knock at the door and
this very tall fair girl with a plain beautiful face and a plain
grey suede coat came in. Paul introduced us, Carolyn
Something-Something, and she said: 'I just dropped in with
that book on Company Law, Paul, and to remind you that
Mummy's counting on you for this afternoon. Apparently old
Judge Burroughs is dying to meet you.' Then they went out
and the door was still half-open when she gave a little giggle:
'Is that one of your women?' In a light amused voice but with
a shudder behind it, like at cockroaches. Paul shut the door
quickly and shut her up and she went away.

"'Why did she say that, Paul?'

"'Well, because she is in love with me, of course.'

"'But what did she mean, one of your women? Why not
girlfriend? *Women* sounds so . . . '

"'Women is so. I'm afraid Carolyn took you for one of
those little *femmes du peuple* with whom nice young Belfast
boys beguile their *samedi soirs*. While keeping their better
selves pure for Sunday tea with the Carolyns.'

"'And the Myrnas.'

"'What?'

"'Nothing. But why would anyone take me for a tart? Did
she take me for a tart, Paul?'

"'Oh, just an amateur, probably. A pick-up from the Plaza
ballroom. Not to worry.'

"'But *why?*'

"'Because you are plump and bosomy and because, as I've

told you a hundred times, you wear far too much make-up. Because your dress is too cheap and too bright. Because your hair is, as the natives say, standing up on you like a whin bush.'

"'What's wrong with my dress? It's the latest fashion. I bought that dress there in Wallis's and it cost me six guineas, so it did.'

"'Precisely. And then of course your name is too obviously Roman Catholic.'

"'So what? What do you mean, Paul? Do you mean Catholic girls are all supposed to be scrubbers or what? Do you think we're dirt or something, Paul, do you think we're all scrubbers?'

"'Your name and your appearance together place you for people like Carolyn, that's *all.* Don't get emotional! Does it matter? Where's your sense of humour, Kathleen? Don't you see how pathetic it is? You can't expect a Malone Road magistrate's daughter to be aware that a Taig from Quarry Street functions in much the same way as she does herself, for love not gin, as it were! Don't you find it amusing, such narrow-mindedness?'

"'Well I do not. I think you're sordid, Paul.'

"'I'm not sordid. I see clearly, that's all.'

"'You're not even Irish.'

"'So. I see even more clearly. You ought to be laughing. There's a whole sociology in that poor girl's attitude. There's more: there's a whole national tragedy. No, on second thoughts, Kathleen, maybe you ought to be crying.'

"'What for? She's just an ignorant stuck-up cow, that's all. I wouldn't put it past you to end up marrying a bitch like her!'

"'Yes.'

"'*Her?*'

"'No, of course not! I shall marry a Nigerian girl, naturally. With an impeccable pedigree and pots of money and a fantastic figure! But black. Why are you crying, Kathleen? *You* are not in love with me too, at least I know that!'

"'Eric's left me. He's going to marry some Protestant bitch called Myrna. She goes to *church*, Paul!'

"'I see. So it has finally happened.'

"'How do you mean it has finally happened? Were you expecting him to give me the boot? Did he say anything to you? Did he go behindbacks talking about me? Did he tell you he was fed up with me, Paul?'

"'I have not seen Eric for months but I was expecting this. I would have liked to warn you long ago, Kathleen, but you would not have listened. You would have simply stopped speaking to me. How could he have stayed with you? You were too cold with him, too egoistic. You didn't behave like a lover. You didn't know how to give him love. You were ashamed of love, all you Irish girls are. You are all puritans, you feel dirtied, you are obsessed by sin. Catholic sin, Protestant sin. Do you imagine English girls are like that, or Americans, or Continentals? You are not enlightened, you people! And then, Kathleen, you were always busy hiding yourself, creating a pretty role. You gave Eric nothing of yourself.'

"'I gave him everything!'

"'Ah! There it is. That is what I meant about Catholic girls just now. You are told it is the ugliest sin: God's mother will blush, Hell will open, your parents will break their poor old hearts—so you think it is everything. You meet a man who requires to be loved and amused and excited and inspired, so you lie down on your back and you open your legs and for you this is the great sacrifice. You say: "I gave him all." You think there is no more to give.'

"'But we did things together, we went to parties, to meetings, to . . . '

"'You went because Eric brought you. It was part of your Irish Catholic submissiveness to go where he suggested. But he offered you a certain enlightenment, an awareness, and what did you offer in return? *You* had as much to give as he, after all! You came from a different world. You had a whole exotic culture to give him, a whole rich way of living. A history. And I watched you, Kathleen, I watched you being ashamed of yourself and ashamed of your parents and ashamed of your race. You hid yourself away, afraid of being jeered at, afraid of being persecuted. You saw persecution everywhere. I watched you try to protect yourself with camouflage, aping this narrow little middle-class Protestant world that *he* wanted to escape from. You were trying to turn yourself into a copy of him. Or of the sort of girl you thought he'd meet at a church social in Claghan!'

"'Well, that's what he chose in the long run, isn't it, so I wasn't too far wrong.'

"'But he needn't have, Kathleen. As they say in all the worst movies you could have done anything with that guy if you'd had something to offer him. The two of you together could have created something great. And you offered him emptiness. *Are* you empty, Kathleen? Surely *you* don't move through life as vacantly as your friend Lily, waiting to be filled up with a wedding-ring? Are you such a cliché, Kathleen?'

"I was mortified. All the way up to his place I'd been expecting sympathy. I was really counting on Paul to cheer me up and say that of *course* Eric loved me, that he never quit talking about me and that he'd be back to me on his knees when he got over this cow down home. What's the use of having friends if they just turn round and attack you whenever you go to them for comfort. Nuala was just the same. She said the same thing, you know. She said to me once I was going to lose Eric if I didn't change my ways. 'No man will ever love you,' she said, 'because you don't know how to give love.' I told her to quit spouting bits out of her psychology books, but now for the first time I started wondering.

"Sitting there on the carpet while Paul went to make

coffee, I thought about it. I *knew* I couldn't be that empty and artificial. If I was, Eric would never have bothered about me in the first place. Or Paul either. If I was that empty I'd have stayed up the Falls Road, in nice Catholic digs, running to Catholic dance-halls, going home every weekend, repeating all the old clichés like some parrot in a cage. It took some sort of wit to turn my back on all that. I knew what I was *against*, all right, I knew what I *didn't* believe in. The trouble was, I didn't right know yet what I was *for*, so I suppose that made me an easy target for any kicks there were going. Do you not think, Maureen?"

"That's all over and done with," Maureen said. "You've crossed plenty of bridges since then." And Trevor looked at his watch again, and said nothing at all.

"Well, Paul came in with the coffee, a percolator on a tray, and china cups and chocolate biscuits. I said to him: 'You must have been discussing me with Nuala McCormack, all those things you were saying.' He said, 'I never discuss anything with Nuala if I can avoid it. Why, what's she been saying to you?' I didn't like to tell him and he said: 'Oh, don't be coy! We all know Nuala. If it makes you feel better do you know what she said to me? She told me the reason I live in a luxury flat on the Malone Road is to compensate for being black. As if *I*, Paul Achebe, in a bush village like Belfast . . . Anyway, you see how ridiculous! So what did she tell *you?*'

"'She said nobody will ever love me.'

"'Does that matter? When you love yourself so much?'

"'I hate myself! I hate myself! If you knew how I detest myself, Paul!'

"'Ah? Honesty at last. And why do you hate yourself, my beautiful Kathleen?' But I couldn't lower myself to tell him. 'Oh just. I suppose I just hate my job. I hate teaching.'

"'Why did you choose it then?'

"'My father made me. Do you know what he.' But I stopped, because imagine telling the son of a foreign diplomat that my father stood over me with a leather belt in our smelly damp kitchen in Quarry Street, with Auntie Brigid and old Sarah Morris watching, and literally *beat* me into teacher training college? Like some, some melodrama out of the Deep South. Poor white trash and all that. It wasn't a thing you could tell, standing there all sophisticated in stiletto heels and a lacquered beehive on the wall-to-wall carpet of a Malone Road flat. I had *some* sense of proportion. 'So you drifted into that too. Why don't you simply drift out of it again?'

"'I have to stick it two years or they won't give me a diploma.'

"'Why do you want a diploma if you don't like the job? Why not go now? Drop everything, make a choice for once in your life. It's the ideal time. Stop just letting things happen to you, Kathleen. Wash off that make-up, comb out your silly beehive. So dated, if you but knew! *Belfast! Mon Dieu*, even the Hausa women have stopped wearing it by now! No, seriously, Kathleen, you could look as classy as poor Carolyn if you only put your mind to it. And get out of Belfast. You keep on talking about London, and about travelling, so *go.*'

"'Yes, but how will I live if I haven't my diploma?'

"'Well, wash dishes for godsake, paint pictures, drive a bloody bus, how do *I* know? Just go. Go tomorrow. I'll drive you to the airport, I'll lend you the money. Why not?'

"Why not? Only. 'If I stay on in Belfast I'll have a chance. I'll keep seeing him, Paul. I'll see him the whole summer term. He said we'd stay friends.'

"'And he'll go back to Claghan at weekends, how lovely for him! But not so lovely for you, Kathleen. You'll be helping keep Myrna's virginity safe for the wedding-night, won't you? And then I suppose he'll come up to town for the odd stolen hour after he's married. How romantic. When she has the curse. Or when she's in labour. Like those old married men you were telling me about who try to pick you up in Maxim's ballroom.'

"It was completely obscene to hear Paul say things like that to me in his dry detached voice and I went away, back to my room in Fitzroy Avenue. He was going to lunch anyway, with his landlady's family, and then going to Carolyn's for tea. Afterwards, he told me, to Evensong. A bit hopelessly I thought maybe I'd drop in on wee Lily after all, but she'd gone to twelve o'clock Mass. The whole damn city, black and white, green and orange, seemed to be constantly hurling itself into churches that day just to get away from me.

"I finished the packet of Cadbury's Wholemeal and scraped out the bottom of the peanut butter jar, deliberately hurting myself with the skreek of knife against glass, scraping and scraping to see how long I could stand it. I switched on the record player to listen to 'Yesterdays' and then I remembered he'd taken it. And of course he'd taken Leadbelly and Miles Davis and even Frank Sinatra. I could have fancied 'Blues in the Night.' I realised I didn't own any decent records at all—they'd all been his. All I'd got left were a couple of musicals from the dark ignoramus days before I met him. *South Pacific* and *Oklahoma*. I'd seen the films when I used to live in digs up the Falls Road and I liked them so much I bought the records. When I met Eric and moved to the university end of the city I'd stopped listening to them. They'd seemed cheap and nasty and disgustingly linked with Quarry Street and the whole narrow-minded life I was giving up. But that Sunday lunch-time, it seemed to me they might be warm and homely and that they might maybe give me more consolation than anyone I'd tried so far. I put *South Pacific* on the turntable, expecting to hear the innocent white Yankee chirpiness of Mitzi Gaynor. Or that black woman singing 'Bali Hai.' I used to love 'Bali Hai' long ago and I was suddenly longing to hear it again. 'Bali Hai will whisper in the wind of the sea, I am

your special lover, come to me . . . come to me . . . ' I mean,
I knew it was trash but. But all that came off the disc was
this horrible lepping and hiccuping, and then I remembered
how one evening when I was a bit tight I dragged the point
of a compass several times across each record to mark my
emancipation from the Falls Road. But also to kill in advance
any temptation to make Lizzie and Pakky a present of two
nearly new LPs. I sometimes had these overwhelming
remorseful temptations to give them presents: money, affection,
part of my time—whole summer weekends I was often
impelled to devote to them instead of hitching with Eric to
Donegal, whole pay cheques to repay them the sacrifices I
never wanted them to make—and had to go to extremes of
destruction to stop myself. Eric's relations with his family
were not such a deep muddy pool of hate and remorse and
guilt and grudged dependent love. Neither were Paul's nor
Nuala's nor Ibrahim's, though I suspect wee Lily and Ignatius
might have suffered as I did. Was it just some sordid question
of economics, of overcrowding and ignorance? I couldn't see
Carolyn, fresh and scented in her Malone Road bedroom with
gymkhana trophies on the wall, feeling such disgust for the
womb she came out of and for the scrawny ugliness that
planted her there. I remember wondering would Eric's socialist
revolution cure all that too.

"He'd left his *New Statesman* behind and I looked vaguely
through the Rooms to Let. I knew Chelsea and Hampstead
were the only places to live if I went to London. 'Spacious
room in professor's flat. Overlooking Heath. Some baby-sitting.'
'Girl to share creative couple's shabby riverside house and
keep us up to the mark.' I imagined Nuala saying: 'Whips?'
to that one and it put me off. And wouldn't I, through poverty
or discouragement or an inferiority complex, just finish up in
Kilburn or Harlesden or Cricklewood, the ugly disenchanted
addresses on all Quarry Street's letters?

"But the idea was there. I could go to London. I could go tomorrow on the Heysham boat. Just not turn up in Mimosa Street tomorrow morning or ever again. Stay in the YWCA, look around. Find a nice flat and lure him over for the weekends. Ronnie Scott's. Richmond Jazz Festival. He'd go to London for Ronnie Scott's and CND marches but he'd stay for me. With me. In a sunny riverside flat overlooking the Heath. And, though I wasn't aware of it yet, some baby-sitting. Because all unknown to me there was this wee spermatozoon swimming at top speed towards this unfortunate egg. Great handshakes and what's your name and how do you do and won't you come in and make yourself at home this time? Creative couple getting together like old friends in my ignorant insides. But I didn't know that yet. I thought of Eric and me doing *New Statesman*like things up and down the King's Road and in the Tate and round old Marx's grave.

"And suddenly I was euphoric, seeing our love take off from the tenements and the brick slums and the churches and ministers and priests, from the whole dismal sense of cheap sin that hung over Belfast of a Sunday. Take off from the unacknowledged fear of a visit from my parents, of their sudden bursting in upon my nakedness with leather belts and tears, with rage and jeers and shame and mourning and broken hearts and prayers for my redemption. I must have always unconsciously been expecting that. Expecting the door to open, expecting to see them there staggering under the weight of Catholic Truth pamphlets and *Sacred Heart Messengers*, ready to crush me under a coffin-load of ancestors' bones. The saints and the scholars, the poor starved martyrs and the bloody heroes. Sitting there in a shack in Quarry Street wallowing in old glories, cursing away at dead enemies while the world went rushing past them. And I thought of Eric's parents whom we'd met by accident one evening leaving the Arts Theatre, who'd frozen me with the kindness of their smiles. She's one of his women, had they been thinking, little Kathleen from the slums of Claghan—shopgirl, typist, waitress? Boys will be boys, had they been thinking, and wild oats are there for the sowing?

But in London I could be a phoenix. And I was happy."

CHAPTER THIRTY-ONE

KATHLEEN (3)

"She's gone up to bed?" Trevor asked.

"Yes."

Maureen was an expert at looking busy: ashtrays emptied, bottles away in the cupboard, dirty dishes stacked nicely ready for old Madame Merot in the morning, glasses over here, spilt orange quickly mopped off the tiles, someone could break a. Keeping unpleasantness at bay till later. Till next day, next hour, next minute. It came. "Made herself at home in our drinks cupboard, hasn't she? How long is she staying, did she say?"

"No, she didn't, actually. Just said 'Hi Maureen' and dumped an Aer Lingus bag in the hall."

"Well, what's she here for? What does she want?"

"To reminisce, by the looks of it. Reveal all, twenty years later. Sounds like Dumas, doesn't it? Heavens, I'm as tight as she is! I hadn't known it went on so long actually, her and Eric. Hadn't known it was so serious. I mean I always assumed it was more or less a one-night stand, that's what I always thought. It never occurred to me old Eric would have . . . And there it was, a whole big romance. Imagine her keeping it so dark, Trevor. I mean she did live with us off and on for years, and all that time after Sarah was born and never a word. Never one word apart from telling me Eric was the father. Not that I encouraged her, I suppose, I mean I suppose I was thinking more of poor Myrna, I was so shocked and all so I suppose I wasn't too . . . But why now, I mean why all the startling revelations at this stage?"

"Who cares? I can't stand it, Maureen, I can't take it. All those boring little tales from the past. She's back living in the past. Christ, she hasn't bloomin' quit for three days! Just sort of wallowing in that old affair and all those nignog boyfriends of hers. It's sick, Maureen, that's what it is. I'm sorry for her, sure, she seems to have been hard hit but, Jesus, it's *over*. It was well over twenty years ago, she can't *still* be pining, nobody can pine that long. Why doesn't she snap out of it, get married or something, get on to Dateline. There must be dozens of creeps who would . . . Why doesn't she, at *least*, why doesn't she take her mind off herself long enough to do something about that layabout daughter of hers? Where *is* the lovely Sarah? Couldn't she manage to scrounge her air fare off the DHSS this time?"

"I don't know. Actually, she never mentioned Sally. I expect she stayed behind in Bogland with Granny." (Now why did I say Bogland, she wondered, why still make these cringing little concessions to appease Trevor's English racism? *I* didn't bomb Harrods, *I* didn't blow a leg off his best friend's daughter, so what do *I* have to feel apologetic about?) "She seems to be settled in Claghan for good nowadays. Last I heard she had a steady boyfriend, punk or football hooligan or something. No, of course they don't *have* football hooligans at home, do they? Anyway, Mammy was saying the pair of them have identical shades of bright purple hair!"

"Well, you better send old Kathleen back to her and bloody quick too, I can't take much more of it. Tie a label round her neck: This Side Up, and plant her at the nearest airport, why don't you?"

"We can't just turf her out, Trevor, we did say she was welcome to come and stay with us whenever she liked. I mean we *are* her best friends, I've known her since I was about three. God, she used to be fun even! You used to like her far more than I did. Remember some of the times we had, in Richmond?"

"She's gone off a bit though, hasn't she? I mean, face up to it, Maureen, I reckon old Kathleen's been going steadily downhill for years. Right old soak she's turned into. I wouldn't mind, even with the price of gin . . . But it's the reminiscences! God, that's not my idea of how to spend a relaxed weekend!"

"Oh well, I'll drop her a gentle hint tomorrow. It'll have to be gentle, though. I mean we've got a."

"Oh, all right, all right. I *know* we can't just give her the boot, only . . . "

Kathleen, awake in the immense echoing guest-room, heard their footsteps on the stone stairs as they came up, and knew they'd stayed behind to discuss her. The atmosphere was not what it once had been. Of course, it might have been simply the grander surroundings. She missed the doll's house cosiness of the house at Richmond. Or it might have been because they were all middle-aged now. Trevor seemed to be ageing into a grumpy respectability, and even Maureen . . . Or perhaps it was quite simply because she drank too much of their gin? People were sensitive about such things. She had not, this time, thought of bringing a bottle, or chocolates, or some pretty thing from Laura Ashley. An offering to buy their love. She had not thought of anything except getting there.

When she came in that evening to the house where she lived, there were three messages in three different handwritings propped up on the hall mantelpiece: Your mother rang. Mrs O'Flaherty phoned, you're to ring her back at this number. You're to contact Claghan hospital immediately, about your daughter. And she guessed at once what it was, because she'd been watching the news on telly in the pub and they'd mentioned . . . But she didn't dare ring the hospital. Not then. She'd thrown a few things into an airline bag and started making her way blindly out to Heathrow. The last planes to Belfast or Dublin had gone by the time she arrived. She sat in the buffet all night, drinking coffee, and at six o'clock in the morning she rang the hospital. "I'm her mother," she said to the night nurse, fearing that she wouldn't be believed, because she felt too young and helpless to be anyone's mother. And she wasn't believed, apparently, because the nurse sent for a sister and the sister said Sarah's mother had been contacted urgently and had just arrived at the hospital. "Just a few minutes ago, poor thing." She knew from the woman's voice that Sarah must be dead, and she forced herself to ask more questions and to identify herself, and she was told everything. It was public knowledge anyhow.

When the booking-desks opened, she walked over to buy a ticket for the Belfast shuttle. On the way she passed a notice flashing the times of flights to Paris and suddenly Claghan seemed a place of complete cold emptiness. She bought a ticket to Paris instead. On the five-hour train journey to Brittany her mind too was cold and empty. She had run straight to her friends for comfort, as empty and as empty-handed as she'd been the very first time she ran to them. Except that the very first time there had been Sarah. And the very first time it had seemed a bit of a joke to be turning for help to Shancoduff, of all people. In the years since then it had come to be the most natural thing in the world to go for sanctuary to Maureen and Trevor. But she'd counted on them already knowing. Even in France, buried in an old ruin in the depths of the country, she'd assumed they'd have heard of it. But they hadn't.

It shocked her immensely that Eric and Sarah and Claghan and herself were not, after all, of international importance. It shocked her to find Trevor, dressed up in a military-looking uniform, shooting pheasant in the woods along with the local doctor and vet. It shocked her to find Maureen sitting on the drawing-room carpet surrounded by Marianne McLeod's diary and books about nineteenth-century murders, while the grounds and out-buildings of the château echoed with small explosions of harmless gunfire. "Claghan!" Maureen laughed. "I'm up to my eyes in dear old Claghan. Brought me any anecdotes about your gorgeously bloodthirsty ancestors, have you?" While the real Claghan was once more empty of everything but horror. "Look at that, Kathleen!" Trevor said, holding up a brace of dangling dead pheasants. "This is the life and yer talkin'!" he'd added in one of his funny accents. She hadn't known how to respond. She no longer had any idea why she'd come there or what she'd been expecting from them.

If she'd burst in and told them, just blurted out her story, if she'd done that they'd have straightaway offered the lovely comforting things: the open arms, the clasping to their hearts, booze poured down her without a thought of the cost. But she hadn't. Faced with Trevor in camouflage uniform brandishing his make-believe parody of murder, with Maureen happily surrounded by the past, the only possible reaction had been to make-believe herself.

Seeing they didn't know, seeing she couldn't tell them, she tried to pretend for a while that they were living again in the years when Sarah was small and they were her world. When they talked for half the night in the pretty old house off Richmond Green, drinks circulating without stint after one of Maureen's exotic meals, the jokes and the anecdotes and the way they used to roar at her stories about Belfast.

She had tried, these last few days, to be amusing in her recollections, to entertain them too as she bandaged and blanketed and warmed herself in that dead time. But they hadn't responded. They had only just tolerated her and, sensing this, she'd drunk more and more and become more and more garrulous, and Trevor hardly spoke and Maureen made cutting little remarks that were meant to be funny (or funny little remarks that were meant to be cutting?), and she couldn't stop drinking and couldn't stop talking. While the one thing that was to be said grew more unutterable, faced with their hostile indifference.

She would never say it now. She knew that they were not now the people who could give her comfort. If comfort was what she needed? Surely she, with say thirty-five or forty empty years ahead of her, would need more than just comfort to live them?

She decided that she would stay another day, behave normally and buy them presents in the village, exclaim over the latest renovations to the château as no doubt they were expecting her to do, then she would go back home to London without telling them anything. Without asking for anything. She felt incapable of knowing what it was she'd need to live those empty years, but perceived already that whatever it was she'd have to find it for herself, because she was unlikely ever to be offered it.

Paul wouldn't hear of her taking the Heysham boat. "Like an emigrant!" he said. "You'll turn up at Euston all bleary and dishevelled and the Legion of Mary girls will grab you by the arm and drag you off to some hostel in a ghetto. It's what they do: I've seen them at it, pouncing on gormless young Biddies from the bogs. Not that you're a Biddie, Kath, but haven't I an excellent command of the native idiom? They're there to keep you from ending up in Algiers or Buenos Aires. Or, worse still, in a mixed marriage. And the beardy boys from the Connolly Association will grab your other arm and press-gang you to Camden Town to print commie leaflets. You will be torn neatly in two between them. Or are you already torn neatly in two? Is your poor oppressed daddy praying for a Workers' Republic?" She wanted to say: it's Eric who wants a Workers' Republic, just for a chance to mention his name, but she was afraid of Paul's contempt. "Anything but," she said, "it's ghettoes all the way for Pakky!"

So he drove her to the airport and gave her an address to go to. Some friends of his who would help her find a job and see that she had some sort of interesting social life. "Above all," he warned her, "don't dump yourself on that Maureen girl you mentioned, or on anyone else from Claghan. Stop letting that town run your life for you. Cut loose, Kathleen, and grow up!"

When he'd gone and she was in the plane she realised that she couldn't turn up in a stranger's house like some waif looking for shelter. What would they think of her? Paul's friends. People like Carolyn. As soon as she arrived at the air terminal she bought an *Evening Standard*, and by teatime she had a job and a room. The job was in a café on Queensway, the Guernica: a sixty-hour week, half a crown an hour and tips. The owner said she could easily make twenty pounds a week tax free if she worked evenings. It was a nice job, serving paella to Spanish exiles and Greek gamblers and Bayswater call-girls. The room was off Westbourne Grove.

The first thing she did was buy a record player on HP and a stack of Billie Holidays and Bessie Smiths, and when she wasn't working she sat in her room playing them. It was just like her room in Fitzroy Avenue really. She lived as though Eric might drop in at any minute. She kept writing to him and she kept not posting the letters. They never sounded quite right when she read them over and anyway, she thought, let him see I've just disappeared without a trace when he goes looking for me, and then when I do write he'll be all the more interested.

She was so taken up with all this and with making plans for him coming to London in the summer that it was weeks and weeks before she even noticed she was pregnant. And then when she did notice, it was a thing so real and so immediate that she realised she'd been living up till that time in a dream world, and that there'd never been any hope of him coming to London and that even if she told him about the baby he'd just be disgusted and tell her he couldn't care less, because nothing mattered to him now, only Myrna. She couldn't face being told that straight out so she decided to say nothing about it. She didn't even get in touch with Paul to tell him where she was.

CHAPTER THIRTY-TWO

KATHLEEN (4)

They gave him a lift as far as Marble Arch: "Now, if you have nothing else planned for the night, Harry, you know you're very welcome to come on ahead along with us." He smiled something, shook a vague hand in at them, no no see you later, thanks for the offer but. They knew damn well he had nothing planned. What would he have planned in a strange city? Were likely at this minute joking in their wee flat accents about his wife's hand reaching heavily across the Irish Sea to keep him in check. Or joking about him going off alone to read a dirty magazine in his digs: that pair wouldn't have missed *Playboy* rolled up inside the *Evening Standard*—eyes like hawks. And why am I hiding it anyhow, he wondered. I'm not at home in Claghan, am I? I'm not likely to run into Margaret or Flora McLeod or someone, round the next corner. I'm in London, the centre of the world. The big bad city. I'm not a schoolboy. I'm a member of Parliament this three months or more. I should be running to, thought I'd be running to, big sophisticated parties every night; thought I'd get invited here and there to people's houses. You'd think it would be different, wouldn't you think now it'd be different? It *would* be different if I lived here, if my constituency wasn't on another bloody island from the one I'm on, if I hadn't to commute over home at the weekends. If I was longer in politics, maybe if I had my way made . . .

Aye, but the other two are in it this years and years, safe Unionist seats from way back, and *they're* not exactly being asked down to Cliveden for weekends either. We're not all that much wanted over here, he thought walking up the Bayswater Road on the Park side, eyeing the substantial houses across the way. Great book that *Forsyte Saga* plenty of beef in it. Mutton rather. Timothy, wasn't it Timothy lived on the Bayswater Road? Houses like that, big sides of mutton, your carriage and four. Or was it cars already by then, wasn't there something, didn't Soames one time pick up some girl in his Rolls? Security. They knew where they were, those old boyos. Sometimes lately he felt his own prosperous security slipping a little, trembling a little under his feet. The young generation. Judith now, the best of an education, working in some coffee-bar, in and out to slum houses up the Shankill Road. Voluntary work! She could catch anything. Do they still get lice these days? We were all hoping she'd go in for the law. Voluntary work with the poor. The poor how-are-ye! They don't know they're living these days, not like back in the Thirties. Housing estates and free medicine: they never had it so good. That's one great man for you, Macmillan, the way he carries himself. The real aristocrat's head, that. Say what you like but it takes England to put a bit of. To put polish on you. We're only in the halfpenny place when it comes to.

He put a brake on his countryman's stride, hummed a tune under his breath and trailed his rolled magazine easily along the park railings. Was his face just that much too red? Were his trousers not maybe a wee bit too ample? Were the office- girls nudging one another at bus-stops when he passed? It was the same every time he came over to the mainland: he felt diminished, like an alien bloody immigrant. They made him feel. Big Harry Hale, well-to-do farmer, man-about-Claghan, elected representative of his people, was reduced to a provincial, to a Paddy, walking alone up the Bayswater Road under the sniggers of suburban typists at bus-stops. Walking back to his digs to pore over a few excited pages of females in their buff. A lonely man in a furnished room. A service-flat off Queensway, they called it, but that's all it bloody well amounted to when you came down to it: single digs for a man on his own. He regretted for a minute not having gone on the town with the other two but, when he considered it, that would almost certainly have been worse. He had no idea at all what his colleagues got up to when the House wasn't sitting, but suspected a discreetly sordid tourism. Pathetic. A pack of ageing Ulster Protestants, men of dignity and substance at home, reduced to living it down in Soho, synthetic sequinned tarts winking away at young gets of barmen behind their backs while the pound notes ran out of wallets like a dose of salts. I want none of that class of filth, he thought. Though for all he knew they were just going off to have a respectable meal in the Savoy Grill, entertaining some constituent over on a business trip. Meeting Cyril Lord or someone. I want none of that either. For all he knew they were only having high tea in a Temperance hotel, Jack Campbell looked that sort of a keoboy all right. A bleak teetotal face, though you couldn't always go by. Good solid man, though. Fine big place near where is it? Lurgan, Portadown? Never asked me had I a mouth on me that time. Him and the other fellow's very great. Big men at home, wee men over here. That could be a Claghan pun, do they go near the women at all when they're over? English women are as odd as. We're only Paddies to them, they can't tell the difference, Loyalists or the other crowd, it's all one to them. Some of the other side's not too bad, fellows on the council, McCormack there . . . Have a bit of a yarn, handy man with a glass, no nonsense there about my drink my drink is water bright from the crystal stream. That lad, what was his name, out on the tear that time up in Dublin, that agricultural thing, the fellow that wouldn't take his seat in parliament after? They never take their seats, cod of a game, why else do they stand for election? Nice handy way of being martyrs, I suppose, no blood needed. Fat lot of use to their constituents though. A philosophy: never until Ulster is free will we clap our chaste backsides on a British back-bench! That'd be it. Cods. Might get the buck of their lives if Ulster ever did join up with the Free State lot—de Valera might take one quick look at that crowd and send them straight back to the bogs. Where were yous in 1916? Under the bloody bed, *mein Führer*, like ninety-nine point nine of the population. Off with his head! How do you say that in Gaelic? A returned Yank, reared in Cuba, Spanish name and all. An Irish mammy that's where he got it from, must go down in the female line like the Jews. And they want to join up with that! Don't know what's good for them. Be back up home inside of five minutes begging for their free milk and National Assistance so they would. What am I saying, *back*? They'd never have gone: it's us poor sods would have gone, chased out with brimstone, fire and sword; the Pope strolling down Donegall Place with a nun on each arm, the Royal Avenue Hotel black with priests drinking themselves footless. That might be a sight worth seeing, all the same! No, but there's people believes that. I'd say most of the oul' dolls that goes to Reverend Clyde's meeting-house believe that. What am I talking about, I wouldn't put it past half of my constituents to believe that! Let them go on believing it, is what I say. And who knows? Who knows what could happen yet? Years and years ago Claghan ran red with Protestant blood, that's an historical fact. There was massacre done and that's not so very long ago either. Historically speaking. A few generations is all. The same breed. Wouldn't do to trust them an inch, the quietest of them . . .

Smell of trees in London. A different smell from home,

smell of dust and sap and petrol fumes all mixed up, that must be it. And the stale perfume of Bayswater tarts. Notorious this road. There's talk of a strangler prowls round at night, Jack the Ripper sort. Has it in for them. Some kink about bad women. They say it comes from the mother, if their own mother was a bit, wasn't too particular . . . Or is it if they had too much respect for? Filthy old hole when you think of it, the things goes on in these parks here. We're a cleaner race altogether . . . I wonder is. Profumo. Wonder how much of it's true? They clam up quick enough when you try to bring the crack round to . . . All these public-school bastards all the bloody same, shoulder to shoulder. All for one and one for all, catch them letting the likes of us in on. Paddies. That's all we are. Paddies . . . That fancy bit with the hair over there, loitering or just strolling is she, is she one or not? Too early to try and anyway. If she wasn't one she might screech. *News of the World.* Margaret's face. Poor wee Judith. The hired boys sniggering when I go round the farm. All human life. I'm not like some, though. I take on both sides equal, first come first served. There's neighbours wouldn't hire a Roman Catholic to dig a drain. Me, I'd hire them if their references is all right and they're fit for the job. Never found them any lazier nor our own. I wouldn't go electioneering down Quarry Street, though! No point in it anyhow . . .

What's this band of? Oil paintings for sale. Fresh off the brush. Nudes hanging on the park railings, if you could call them nudes, arse where their elbows ought to be. "No, no, thanks very much, some other time now. I left my wallet at the." Now do I look the sort of cod would buy an oil painting off some beardy at the side of the road? Artists aye! Fit to draw the dole is about the height of it . . . Queensway. Central Line. Will I ever get used to the tube? Claustrophobia they call it. Afraid to go down into the. As the tree falls. Now what put that into my head? Spike Milligan lives across there, facing the Gardens. Irish they say, or the parents anyhow. I

wonder does he. Hardly bothers his head, good lie-in of a
Sunday morning like the rest of the English. *I* am English.
British. If the Hales had had to settle in Africa long ago that
wouldn't have made me a nigger, would it? Try and tell that
to some Tory tart at a party. The Unionist vote, oh aye,
sweeten you up, good dog Paddy! Wag your tail now when
you're bid. Thank you ever so, and then off to their orgies
with top models and Lady This and Lady That. Lady Muck
from Clabber Hill. I wouldn't want any of that. No. Look at
that Roman church over there, Star of the Sea, not much
dignity about that. Used to be a cinema they say. Still doesn't
look much like a. Spanish chambermaids praying up in the
gods, usherette comes round with a tray of wafers before the
big picture . . . Is it worth my while crossing over to the
Kenco? Decent coffee, waitresses with legs. No, full of office
boys at this hour, gobbling Danish pastries before they toddle
home to Mum and Dad in the suburbs. Judith had a book of
that fellow Milligan's. Funny enough. A socialist, though. Funny
all these brainy sorts. Wee Eric, there was no standing him
at all these past few years, you'd have swore he was all set
for Moscow. Flora was worried sick. Seems to be settling
down lately though. Nice wee girl, Myrna, she'll have a lump
of money from the granda. And what about all the wee
scrubby Labour lads up from the mines! Welsh accents.
Yorkshire. What do *they* do of an evening? Hardly living it up
with the Duchess of Argyll any more than myself. Home to
fish and chips I suppose and HP sauce. No, that's *Private Eye*
sort of talk, the most of them lives up in Hampstead, big posh
mansion flats. To be near Marx's tomb, no doubt. Yon party
we went to, Anthea something. Great pair of tits she had and
not slow to show them. Told me she was a communist, paid-
up member of the party and everything. I thought I'd never
get out quick enough! A whole big act with bitches like that.
Why don't you go and live in Russia, I asked her, fur coats
and caviare and everything, if you're that fond of them? No,

but it could ruin you all the same, carry-on like that, never know who they're mixed up with. What I'll do is I'll eat a bit here on Queensway, not go back to the digs at all. There's clubs, bohemian sorts of places where you can . . . Not professionals. What is it? The Blue Danube. They were saying you buy a sketchbook and pencil at the door and there's all these models posing in their skin. An art class sort of . . . Just have to scribble a few lines for shame's sake. A coffee-bar, nothing dirty, not like a . . . Not like strip clubs. Artistic. A bite to eat first all the same, few pints maybe, chance my luck there later. They serve food but. Wouldn't much fancy chewing on a steak with some damn woman's rump stuck up under my nose . . .

He stopped before a glass-fronted café: Guernica. Greek, sounded like Greek and with the Olympik Casino across the way . . . The sort of place they gave you a good feed. They usually had an English menu. He fancied an escalope and chips with a couple of fried eggs on top and maybe a slice of chocolate gateau for afters. Neither Margaret nor Judith would as much as look at veal, the way they treated calves or some such nonsense. You'd think the pair of them was reared up the Malone Road, and as for chocolate cake, Margaret wouldn't have chocolate cake in the house, afraid he'd grow a belly. Lean meat and fruit salad. Still, for once in a while . . .

Behind one of these trailing screens of green plants they all seemed to go in for, he could see a dark-haired waitress setting tables. Not bad at all, bright blue eyelids, great pair of, twenty-one or two, no teenager, looked as if she knew what it was for all right. A small place, ten or twelve tables. Red carpet. Juke box. Just the one waitress. Nothing Guernica about that one, ten chances to one she was Irish. Oh aye, Irish all right, something about the expression, you couldn't miss. False modesty. Good-looking though. Paella 6/- it said on the menu, Chile con carne 7/6. Precious little else. Danish pastry. Espresso. Those small glass cups with the half of it sloshed in the saucer. And she'd want to talk to him: they always did in these places when you were the first customer and they twigged you were Irish. "Are you long over? How's the digs?" Emigrant ship talk. All exiles together. They had a way of reducing you. No, he'd look for some place decent, with a solid menu and a bit of service. He could afford it as well as the next man. And when all was said and done, he hadn't got himself elected to the House of Commons to spend his evenings eating foreign muck and talking to some Bridget in a cheap café. No. There was a good steak house on Westbourne Grove, pricy enough but they had a licence. A rump steak and salad after all, maybe. Safer. With maybe a wee glass of red wine. Then the Blue Danube . . .

Now who's this he reminded her of? A big lump of a redfaced man, with one eye studying the menu outside and the other, furtive, trying to get a good gawk in at her through the potted plants. When was it, sometime round Christmas or after? A big man with a blonde by the arm ducking furtively into the Royal Avenue Hotel, same sideways eye, quick-glancing shame. Eric laughing: "Did you see my uncle Harry, the old hypocrite! Did you see him? Pillar of the community, going to stand in the by-election, Christ if they only *knew*, in Claghan!" And she: "Why don't you blackmail him, Eric, make us a wee fortune!" That's who the big man reminded her of, Eric's uncle. Judith Hale's daddy. A Claghan face. Catch yourself on, she thought, give it a break for godsake. In every London face these days she found herself peering for echoes of Claghan. Of Belfast. Of Eric. If you go on like that, she thought, you'll end up having to see a doctor.

A doctor, a *doctor*! Oh she was going to have to see a doctor all right. What on earth was she going to do? What *did* people do? Part of her was stupidly exultant, ecstatic. She couldn't resist cradling herself in her arms when she was alone, cradling the child. Wanting to wave her womb like a banner, Eric's child. I'm having Eric's child! Part of her was terrified. Part of her was dying with shame: I'm pregnant. I'm in trouble. I've been caught. I want to kill it. Jesus I'll have to kill it. I'll ring Maureen, she thought. Maureen is *bound* to know people, she's the sort that would. Maureen will help me to get rid of it, she'll know where to go. But she didn't want to get rid of it. What else had she left? She went into a daydream of Eric coming over for Christmas, of the two of them bending gently over a crib, and banged the knives brutally down on the tables to stop herself. Daydreams were over. But old Shanco will know what to do, she thought, and felt comforted. Maureen would take her briskly in hand and make decisions. She herself wouldn't have to decide anything, Maureen could decide it, she would not be responsible. She glanced towards the window again but the man was gone. He *was* the image, she thought, and the thought too gave her comfort, like a good omen. The spittin' image. A real Claghan face, in the middle of London.

CHAPTER THIRTY-THREE

LETTERS FROM HOME

Boharnamuc,
Claghan,
24 November 1963

My dear Maureen,

. . . but honest to God I can't get over what you told me. It's your own decision, of course, and you can be sure I won't breathe a word of it to Pakky and Lizzie but it's an awful responsibility you're taking on, giving shelter and encouragement to that shameless lassie. If anything went wrong, Maureen, you'd be destroyed. Them O'Flahertys would kill you, you know well what they're like. As you say, you couldn't very well leave her on her own in London at a time like this but I don't honestly know why she had to turn to you of all people in her disgrace, mixing you up in the mess she made of her life, after the way she used to make little of you and of all of us when you were in that convent. Lizzie seemed very upset when I was talking to her shortly after she skedaddled to London but of course she never suspected anything like this. I don't know how she'll take it if she ever finds out, and Pakky will go mad altogether. Kathleen would have been far better off and you'd have been better off too, Maureen, if you had managed to coax her into a home for unmarried mothers where the nuns would have seen about getting the child adopted by a good Catholic family. I hope you'll talk her into coming home to her parents once it's born and everything settled. Lizzie and Pakky can't understand at all why she let them down like that, walking out of a good job and everything. It was a shocking blow to them after all they done for her. Her trouble will likely be over by Christmas from what you tell me and the best thing for all hands would be if she came back to her parents and no one in Claghan need ever know a word about it. What has Trevor to say about all this? For God's sake, Maureen, don't make trouble in your own home over a girl like that. Pack her back to Claghan the minute she leaves that hospital.

Wasn't it awful about the poor President, honest to God, I don't know what the world's coming to at all. The Yank O'Flahertys will likely be sending us the American papers with pictures of the funeral and all. It seems no time since they sent us the inauguration, that lovely woman, God help her, and the poor children.

Well, Maureen, I'll say goodbye for the present and like a good girl look after yourself and don't let yourself be walked over by one of them O'Flahertys. I hope all goes well for her in spite of everything and I won't say a word to Lizzie. Love from all at home,

Mammy.

Boharnamuc
28 May 1965

My dear Maureen,

Now I hope you're not going to take this letter as bad as you took it the last time I tried to give you a bit of good advice. What's the use of living to over forty years

337

of age if I can't even tell my own daughter what's right and wrong? I know times is changed and maybe myself and your daddy are old-fashioned and intolerant as you say, but when you have the good luck to belong to the One True Faith and be taught the difference between right and wrong there's things you haven't any business to condone. I still maintain you're doing wrong in giving a home to that woman and her child and letting her live like a lady free gratis instead of turning her out to fend for herself and reminding her that she has a duty to her poor parents and that her place is at home with them. If you sent her packing she'd come to her senses quick enough once the easy life was finished. If she's that fond of children she had only to stay at home where she belonged and find herself a good Catholic husband and have a family decently. And she still could do that. Nobody need know about her mistake. She needn't fear *I'd* go slabbering it round the town . . .

10 July 1965

My dear Maureen,

. . . and I'm glad we're friends again anyhow. It was my Catholic duty to say what I said and it's up to you now. We're looking forward to seeing you home for Jamesy's wedding. May is a lovely girl, her mother says she's a great wee cook and housekeeper. I wasn't fit to say that about you but Trevor doesn't seem to mind! Isn't it great the way English men are able to do their share of the cooking and all, I wish you'd send him over here to train the Irish—servants they want, not wives at all! Jamesy and May will be living very close. Just behind McCormacks' their bungalow is, a lovely view over to the mountain. I'll be handy for baby-sitting, please God! No sign of an English grandchild on the way yet?

I'm looking forward to reading this next book of yours. I liked the other one and I never miss your wee stories in the magazines. Did I ever think long ago that I'd have the leisure to put my feet up and read love stories? You all grew up very quick. The younger ones are doing well at school. Teresa and Peggy had no luck finding jobs, there's nothing round here. I pray they won't have to emigrate. Dominic has great talk of going on for the priesthood, but of course he's young yet. It would be a great honour for us if he did.

I nearly forgot to tell you I heard from the Yank O'Flahertys last week. They have their two eldest out in Vietnam, may God protect them and send them home safe. I be thinking aren't we lucky to be in Ireland. We may not be as prosperous as them but at least we need have no fear of war or violence, all that's a thing of the past and indeed didn't the people suffer enough long ago? The pair of them are in the Marine Helicopter Squadron, the daddy seems very proud of them but poor Joanne is just praying they were safe home to her. She was saying it's a disgrace all the same to see the crowds of beardy layabouts out protesting about the war and very hurtful too for any family that has sons away fighting the communists. She said there was twenty thousand students and beatniks and hooligans of all descriptions marching on the White House last Easter. Too good of times they have. If they were out earning a living they'd have less time to make little of decent young lads that's fighting to make the world free.

Well, I'll finish off now, Maureen, and give our regards to Trevor. Don't be taking what I said about Kathleen in the wrong spirit, I'm only trying to do my duty as a mother and as a Catholic. Love from all,

Mammy.

13 March 1966

My dear Maureen,

Thank you very much for the book. I sat up till two o'clock one morning finishing it. Your daddy is half-way through it at present, though he's complaining that it's more of a woman's book. As you know, all he likes is Agatha Christie and the Saint. He's soldiering on bravely with yours, but he wants to know could you not write a good murder mystery for him! I won't tell you what Jamesy and Dominic said about it, but May and the girls liked it too. I'm very proud that a daughter of mine has her name on the front of two books, I wonder where you take it from? There was just one thing that didn't please me in this one and that was that girl Miranda getting married to a divorced man. I know it's only a story but when you have a talent you should use it wisely and not give scandal and bad example with it and maybe lead young people away from a pure and modest way of living. Especially you that's in England among non-Catholics, being Irish it's your duty to influence people for good and let them see the Irish can stand staunch to their faith the way they always done in spite of the Penal Laws and Cromwell and everything. Don't think now I'm criticising you, I know that in England divorce is thought nothing of but to tell you the truth, Maureen, I was a wee bit ashamed May's mother and old Mrs Maguire reading it, them that's always running to daily Mass and devotions and all. I mean it would be nicer if the people in your books were Catholics. Most of the books I get out of Claghan library when they're by Irish writers you can always know, there's never any such thing as immoral conduct in them except for one I got out a couple of months ago by a woman called O'Brien. Honest to God, Maureen, it sickened me altogether. I know a lot of dirty things goes on in this world but there's no need to write them down. I hope to God you'll never turn your hand to that sort of filth and bad language.

Anyway, this is only a short note, I'm looking forward to going over at Easter. I'm glad that Kathleen one is moved out to a place of her own or I wouldn't have come. I wouldn't have known how to face her the way she let her poor parents down. She's very lucky to be let teach in London, she'd never have got into a school over here, not with an illegitimate child on her hands.

I'm enclosing a couple of bunches of shamrock as usual for St Patrick's Day, now don't be sharing them out with that targer of a one.

Love from Mammy.

"She writes a good letter, me old ma-in-law! I can see where the talent comes from. But she wants to turn you into Graham Greene by the sound of her."

"Indeed she does not! Mammy's Catholicism is nothing at all like that. No scruples or soul-searching about that lady! God no, she'd sling Graham Greene in the fire as quick as she'd sling Edna O'Brien!"

"Actually," Kathleen said, "I do believe he's banned in the south of Ireland."

"What would your mum say, Maur, if you ever wrote a realistic book? Telling life as it is, like?"

"I wouldn't. I couldn't. I don't think I could ever write anything that sort of questioned their values. It would break their hearts. I could never go home again."

"Did you never see the Canon, Trevor, peering over her shoulder while she's at the typewriter? And the dacent Irish mammy peering over the other one? That divorcé must have slipped in while they were blinking."

"London's corrupting you, love, you'll be putting in the Big Bad Word next and she'll have old McGinty over to say Masses for you."

"To exorcise her more likely!"

"You're forgetting, ducks, that my publisher's every bit as prudish. Claghan hasn't a monopoly, you know. *And* look at *Her World* and the average British reader. Persil white! So you can quit knocking my mother if you don't mind, Trevor. And you too, Kathleen!"

Boharnamuc

19 September 1966

My dear Maureen,

. . . Well, all my visitors are left. Kath, Dominic and Brendan are away back to school. Dom gave up the notion of the priesthood, unfortunately, and is talking of applying for a university scholarship. May is expecting. I went in to the doctor's with her yesterday and who did I see in the waiting-room only Veronica McCormack. She's married to an architect in Portnafinn but was home spending a few days with the parents. There's great talk of them turning the house into another hotel, a real luxury job this time, so I suppose they'll have the son-in-law doing the plans for nothing! Veronica never asked about you at all but she was civiller than she used to be—marriage must have taken her down off her high horses. I *did* hear that he's very bad to her, big-shot and all as he is. I suppose she was in on the same errand as May but I didn't like to ask. She was telling me Nuala is away to America for two years' voluntary service work, I could nearly swear she said among Red Indians, could that be possible do you think? Maybe she was only joking. Your daddy says a bit of a scalping would do that one no harm!

The new housing estate is near finished. It'll be a blessing for a lot of people. Thank God *we* have no need of it, especially now with all our renovations and central heating, we don't know we're living. I heard tell the O'Flahertys are going to be rehoused, that half Quarry

Street is to be knocked down, but I didn't see them this long time. Has Kathleen any word of it or does she write to them any way regularly? I hear tell Pakky's not too well, he does have fits of depression and wild rages. They were saying he had some incident last Sunday, it seems he went up to Mr McCormack after Mass and threatened if he didn't hand Claghan Hall back he'd burn it down round them. Doctor O'Donnell had to take him over to the surgery and give him something for his nerves. They were always a crowd of mad-heads at the best of times. Well, that's all for the present. Love to you both.

Mammy

20 January 1967

My dear Maureen,

At last I'm getting round to answering your very welcome letter. I hope you're keeping well and that the book is going all right. It was great to see you at Christmas. I hope Trevor didn't think we're all mad, tell him it's only at big feasts and festivals we carry on like that! You were saying you see great changes in Claghan every time you come home, I suppose it *is* more modern and of course there's a lot of new buildings and then the big new housing estate and all. There's shocking bitterness about that in the town, it seems there's childless Protestant couples being given houses while Catholics with big families are away down on the bottom of the list. Mr McCormack and Dr O'Donnell are having great battles about it on the council but of course being the only two Catholics they don't get much of a hearing, so it seems they intend to approach Mr Hale, the Unionist MP, to ask questions about it in the London parliament. Mr McCormack maintains there's no use even mentioning it to the Stormont crowd because Catholics are never given any heed there anyhow . . .

12 February 1967

My dear Maureen,

. . . and there's such awful ill-feeling between the two sides since that young Meegan lad got knifed a few weeks ago, Lord have mercy on his soul. Though I don't suppose you heard about it? You know Mary Meegan that was at school with you, well it was her younger brother, only eighteen. He was going with a Johnson girl, a Protestant from somewhere off Lockhart Road, and he left her home this night from the pictures, the end of January it was, and he never came home all night and the parents were in an awful state. They phoned the police and he was found early the next morning on that waste ground at the side of Lewis's factory. He was in flitters, God bless us and save us, the poor mother nearly went out of her mind. No one was got for it yet, they say her brothers had it in for him. A lot of young fellows swore they heard him being threatened and told to go courting his own kind but the two Johnson lads were away at a dance in Portnafinn that night so nobody knows who's responsible.

There's a lot of ructions this last year or so between the two sides but this is the first time it went that far. I hope the shock of it makes both crowds come to their senses and stop their violence. It's a worry when you have young ones running to the dances, if they stuck to St Ronan's Hall itself but they're away mad round the country to Pop concerts and folk festivals and God knows what all, Teresa and Peggy as bad as any of them. They say a lot of this ructions is started deliberately by that mad-head of a minister, you mind the wee man that used to preach of a fair-day and promise the people all classes of damnation? Clyde his name is, we used to have a good laugh at him. Well, there's nobody laughing this last while, he's getting very wicked about the Catholics and he seems to be well in with a crowd of big-shots, getting reported in the

Chronicle every time he makes one of his dirty speeches about the Pope, wouldn't you think they'd have the sense not to print it, only making trouble among the people. But sure I suppose all they care about is selling their paper. I hear it's the same everywhere this last while.

The Yank O'Flahertys was saying Boston is a holy terror. They're nearly afraid to go outside their house at all in the evenings for fear of the blacks. It seems they're protesting and marching up and down the streets whatever they're looking for, I suppose they want to have the same privileges as ordinary Americans, and they think nothing of moving into houses next door to decent white people and putting up posters claiming civil rights and the devil knows what-all! Joanne was saying it makes the place look like a slum and destroys the value of the property. It's a shame when they both work so hard and were doing so well and bought that lovely big house in a nice prosperous neighbourhood. She sent me a photo, it's like a wee palace, but she says if this goes on it'll be worth nothing at all in a few years, and it's the same with the schools, blacks moving in all the time, and her with three children still in junior school. Their eldest lad got some sort of a decoration for bravery out in Vietnam, and they're very proud of him. I hope he comes through it safe. The younger one's home and back at college but Cormac is making his career in the army.

I'm looking forward to reading that interview they're going to do. You're getting a real big-shot now altogether, we'll see you on the television yet! Your daddy watches it all the time now, he hardly bothers with the books at all lately, *Coronation Street* and *Doctor Kildare* and everything and of course he gets all the cowboy pictures he wants without stirring out of his chair.

I'm not saying a word about that Kathleen one being back with you. You know best what you're doing, but I hope you're charging her a good whack of a rent. I'm not surprised that landlady gave her her walking papers. I knew well she wouldn't have it easy with a child. I saw poor Lizzie and she's very failed. She nearly cried saying Kathleen hardly writes at all and with Pakky not being so well. I don't like all these lies but seeing she's determined to keep that child could she not take a run over without mentioning it for the time being? It would do them the world of good to see her.

And what about yourself, is there no sign at all? I hope and pray you're keeping staunch to the church's teaching and not doing anything unnatural, you know what I mean. I know you're ambitious but there's no need to let it lead you into mortal sin. And it'd be a more normal life for you if you had a family to look after . . .

I'll finish off now with love to yourself and Trevor from all at home,

Mammy.

CHAPTER THIRTY-FOUR

LETTERS FROM HOME

CLAGHAN CHRONICLE 31 MARCH
AN INQUEST WAS HELD YESTERDAY ON MR ROBERT ANDERSON,
19, OF RIVER LANE, CLAGHAN, WHO WAS FOUND DYING OF
MULTIPLE STAB WOUNDS IN AN ALLEY OFF QUARRY STREET
EARLY ON SUNDAY MORNING, AND WHO SUCCUMBED TO HIS
INJURIES SHORTLY AFTER ADMISSION TO CLAGHAN GENERAL
HOSPITAL.

The coroner was told that Mr Anderson had attended a
dance in St Ronan's Hall on Saturday evening in the company
of his fiancée, Miss Brigid McElwee, of Quarry St, and had
become involved in a mêlée with local youths who, according
to witnesses, had jostled him and told him he had no business
in a Catholic dance-hall. Strong language had been used and
one unidentified person had shouted: "Remember Sean
Meegan!"

Mr Patrick McCreesh, manager of the dance-hall, stated in
evidence that Mr Anderson and his fiancée immediately left
the dance and things quietened down. This was around half
past ten. He had not recognised any of the youths involved
in the incident. It had lasted only a minute or two and no
violence had been used. In his opinion it had been boisterous

high spirits and had no connection with the subsequent crime. None of the youths involved had drink taken. He never allowed anyone to enter the hall in an inebriated condition.

Miss McElwee stated that Mr Anderson escorted her to her home and accompanied her inside where they watched television in the kitchen for half an hour with her parents. Afterwards her mother made tea and they chatted until about midnight. No reference had been made to the incident in the hall and it was the first time Mr Anderson had ever encountered ill-feeling although he had been coming to Quarry Street for several months. At about ten past twelve she left him to the door and they had not noticed anyone waiting for him in the street.

Miss McElwee's father stated that neither he nor any of his family had objected to his daughter's engagement to a person of another faith. Mr Anderson in his opinion had been a decent hard-working man and had been perfectly agreeable that all children of the marriage would be baptised and brought up as Catholics.

Witnesses stated that Mr Anderson could have had no part in the murder last January of the Roman Catholic youth, Sean Meegan: he had been on a six-week training course in Belfast at the time and did not return to Claghan at the weekends. He was well known in the district and had no known enemies.

The coroner brought in a verdict of wilful murder by a person or persons unknown.

The police investigation into both killings is continuing.

Church Leaders Speak Out

Religious leaders on both sides of the community strongly condemned the senseless murders of two young men, Sean Meegan and Robert Anderson.

Rev George Carpenter, Church of Ireland, said that he

was shocked and horrified at the killings. For generations, he said, Protestants and Catholics had coexisted peacefully side by side in Claghan even at times when there was religious and political tension elsewhere in the province. It was a great tragedy that the violent tendency of the modern world, brought into our homes via the cinema and television screens, should have to manifest itself here in terms of sectarian hatred.

The Roman Catholic leader, Canon James McGinty, condemned the killings and expressed sympathy with the parents and relatives of both families as well as with Mr Anderson's fiancée. But, he added, it was a pity young Catholic boys and girls found it necessary to seek marriage partners outside of their own faith, thus exacerbating the tensions that existed and had always existed between the two communities.

He reminded the people of Claghan that much of the terrible nineteenth-century violence that had rent the district asunder originated in a mixed marriage between members of two local families, and that such alliances were to be deplored today just as much as a hundred years ago. He added that the recent murders were the outward expression of wrongs and injustices that had for generations been festering away beneath the surface, poisoning the relationship between the upper and lower ends of the town.

He forecast that if a move was not speedily made to rectify the glaring political and social inequalities that were obvious to anyone of good faith, there would in the near future be an escalation in the unrest and violence between the two communities.

The Reverend Abraham Clyde called a public meeting to raise funds for the dead man's widowed mother who was in very poor circumstances with several younger children to bring up. Addressing the meeting, in Lockhart Road Presbyterian Hall, he said he deplored the tendency among

modern young people to forget the aims and ideals their
forefathers shed their blood for. It had been brought to his
notice many times by distressed parents that their sons and
daughters were in the habit of frequenting Roman dance-
halls where, under a pretence of entertainment, Popish
proselytisers were waging a campaign to destroy the very
foundations of the Protestant faith and the Protestant way of
life.

It was a well-known fact that the promoters of St Ronan's
dance-hall, under the secret leadership of one of the bitterest
foes of the Protestant people, were investing large sums of
money to attract popular singers and showbands, knowing
that this was the best means in a selfish pleasure-ridden age
like the present of drawing innocent young people into their
web and setting their feet on the primrose path to perdition.

He said there had been an alarming number of mixed
marriages recently, decent young boys and girls mesmerised
into having their natural instincts inflamed by the Scarlet
Whore until they were ready and willing to betray the blood
of their martyred ancestors and even sign away their unborn
children into the slavery of the Church of Rome. He himself
had witnessed, at an open-air concert, the shameful spectacle
of decent Protestant youths and girls joining in the singing
of a notorious popular song that glorified the memory of a
local murderer responsible, not so many generations ago, for
the massacre of one of Claghan's most honourable families,
a song that advocated continuing hate and vengeance against
the Protestant population.

He forecast a time, and that not too far in the future, when
all right-thinking people would be once again obliged to lay
their hands on the sword to defend their faith and their way
of life against the Babylonian monster that was growing daily
more powerful and more menacing.

The sum of £282-5-0 was collected, and presented with
expressions of sincere sympathy to Mrs Martha Anderson.

CHAPTER THIRTY-FIVE

From *Her World* June 1968

"I'm afraid we're cat people," Maureen Murphy said, welcoming me into her delightful period house near Richmond Green, "so do be careful where you sit—kittens under every cushion!"

Maureen, in private life Mrs Trevor Watts (her husband is a director of the Trewatt chain of fashion boutiques), looks totally unlike the traditional chintzy image of a cat-lover. She answered the door herself in a trendy Pucci tunic over mauve velvet slacks, and led me into a drawing-room which is a startlingly successful blend of the classic and the ultra-modern. "Like Richmond itself," Maureen exclaimed, "or indeed like England at the present time."

The immense Chesterfield sofa is covered in a William Morris fabric, the pattern repeated in yards and yards of floor-length curtains. The dominant tones throughout are deep mauve and old rose, with an unexpected flash of sharp turquoise to give the room its young vivid character.

There were indeed cats everywhere. Maureen took me into her streamlined aubergine-and-lime French kitchen where a huge tabby stared balefully at us from the top of the fridge. "That's Eeyore," Maureen explained, "and how very grumpy he is too!" On the far wall a rather more modern cat—made of wire, milk-bottle tops, and black acrylic paint—stuck a wicked-looking paw two feet out of its frame. Painting or sculpture? "It's called a shaped canvas," Maureen told me. "Amanda Wedge from Liverpool. Very talented."

We carried immense Casa Pupo mugs of coffee back into the drawing-room where Maureen sank into a deep armchair with Baby Roo, a tiny white Persian kitten, on her lap, and happily answered questions about herself and her work. "There's book number five," she said, pointing to an untidy heap of paper on the hearthrug. "It just needs typing up." Maureen has her work typed professionally nowadays but makes no secret of the fact that she herself started life as a five-pound-a-week typist. "I arrived fresh and green from Ireland nine years ago and I was stuck for six months in a very boring typing-pool before being lucky enough to land a job as Trevor's secretary. And, eventually, wife!"

She wrote her first story at sixteen. "My best friend at that time was a very pretty girl who lived in a slummy street with terribly neurotic parents. I *hated* going to her house. It was quite frightening actually, and I used to imagine what life would be like for a girl with her looks if she lived in beautiful surroundings among calm cultivated people. Of course, the result was a totally different person, a typical romantic heroine. So one evening, after a particularly traumatic visit to her house, I made up a story about Kathleen and, believe it or not, sold it to *Her World*."

"And you've been writing for us and for our sister paper *Two's Company* ever since. With four very successful novel-writing interludes."

"Yes. The novels just grew out of the short stories. Same characters, same type of background, only longer!"

"Why did you find it necessary to change your friend's

background? Don't you think that nowadays romantic heroines *might* possibly come out of a slum?"

"No, I don't. I'm realistic about this because I come from a fairly modest rural background myself and one simply doesn't have the space or the privacy to develop qualities like charm, elegance . . . Inner beauty, if you like."

"Well, *you've* certainly managed to develop a very elegant style of living!"

"Only because I got married young to a man who became rather rich. This is all bought: my clothes, my scent, my furniture. Even Baby Roo. Even the leisure to write books. I mean, most of the girls at home, if they come to London they just drift into a sort of dreary Irish ghetto. Or even provincial English girls too, I mean, there's not many factory girls taking part in Swinging London! They just very quickly become boring housewives with perms and ghastly square clothes."

"That's not a very fashionable viewpoint these days, Maureen!"

"You mean because of this meritocracy thing? I don't think that's really what we're talking about. I mean most of the people who're doing amusing things did start off with certain advantages—Mick Jagger, Patrick Lichfield, John Oaksey . . . And well, take say a top jockey like Terry Biddlecombe or Chris Collins, both of whom we know quite well actually, well, they do tend to go out with debs, don't they, rather than typists?"

"Edna O'Brien is rural Irish like you, and so are her heroines . . . "

"Edna O'Brien grew up in a manor-house. Broke, but a manor-house. *I* grew up in a three-roomed cottage with a zinc roof and cement floor. There were fifteen of us in it!"

"So you had the classic unhappy childhood?"

"Far from it! We were incredibly happy, very united. It was like living in a nest, all warm and crammed in together.

No, what I mean is, it would have been impossible for any of us to have grown up as a romantic hero or heroine type. There was literally no *space* for fantasy in our lives, living like that you have to be very stereotyped or else you end up trampling all over everyone else's territory!"

"Did you ever feel deprived compared to other children?"

"I never noticed, I thought everyone lived like us till I went to boarding-school on a scholarship! Nuns have this big thing about rich pretty little girls and they made me very miserable because I was poor, wore second-hand clothes and was an ugly duckling into the bargain! Everybody's father seemed to be a building-contractor or a doctor or a wealthy coal-merchant and they wore themselves out trying to show me where my place was and shove me down into it head first! That's what's made me so bolshie, it was so awful I gave up my scholarship and left at fifteen."

"What a pity!"

"Oh, not really. I've come to terms with it—as witness, I'm able to talk about it out loud! Especially as, if I'd stayed on, I'd have ended up as a respectable little schoolmarm in Claghan. Maugham's verger, you know!"

"Do you intend one day to use your childhood experience in a novel? Getting back to Edna O'Brien again!"

"Not directly. But there *is* a book I'm dying to write, actually. It's a legend I used to be told when I was a child, about a local rebel and a beautiful lady. It's got everything: heroism, romantic love, tyrannical parents, tragedy. I'm going to write about that one day when I have time to sort of dig up all the background material. But I can't see me doing an Edna-O'Brien-type book—my parents would never let me darken their door again!"

"Do Irish people read your books?"

"I'm probably the only Irish writer who isn't banned in the Irish Republic! But I don't in fact have big sales in Ireland. Perhaps they're more cynical about love there? And in fact

I don't see myself as an Irish writer, or indeed as an Irish person. I'm from *Northern* Ireland, you see, and that's very much part of the UK. I think nowadays we *all* consider ourselves as British as anyone else. I mean, most of my friends do see me as English."

At that point a small blonde girl came in, swept Baby Roo off Maureen's lap, and climbed on herself. "I didn't know you had a daughter!" I said, amazed.

"Oh, this is Kathleen O'Flaherty's child," Maureen explained, "you know, the pretty Irish friend I mentioned. Kathleen lives with us now and helps in the house. Little Sarah gets dreadfully spoiled, I'm afraid. I'm sort of an au pair girl in reverse! It's fab really. Like having a family without all the grotty bits like nappy-changing."

"I'd never have expected a romantic novelist to have such domestic tastes," I commented. "Cats and babies! But to get back to Ireland: there *have* been demonstrations lately . . . "

"Oh, that's just part of the general unrest, don't you think? I mean, everyone's demonstrating these days! I should imagine it's more Che and Mao than Bold Cormac O'Flaherty!"

"Bold who?"

"The romantic rebel I was telling you about. What I mean is, I can't see even the Irish getting up another rising, 1916 and all that! It's not really a Sixties thing, is it? And certainly the part I came from, the British part, is very twentieth-century. Not a thatched cottage in sight!"

"Well, let's hope you're right, Maureen. And let's hope too that you soon get time to research your romantic rebel hero. He sounds fascinating!"

CHAPTER THIRTY-SIX

PROTEST MARCH

They'd marched on the American Embassy again and stood rather awkwardly outside in the rain, holding their banners. A boy with a wispy beard handed Kathleen a flower and they exchanged first names. Did Eric look like that nowadays with a blond beard and his hair even longer than five years ago? Every protest march she went on, she scanned the marchers' faces looking for him: he might surely one day, one weekend, fly over to London to join a demo? Or were they marching in Belfast now? In Claghan? Did Eric care about Vietnam? Well of course he must, the whole civilised world cared about Vietnam. Even empty bourgeois types like Maureen and Trevor and their phoney friends were at least aware the problem existed. Aware enough to look pained and say "Curr-ri-i-ist!" when Maureen got yet another letter about Cormac O'Flaherty from Boston with his purple hearts or Pepsi lids or whatever it was they decorated them with.

My what, Kathleen thought, my second cousin? Or was it third? She remembered him in Claghan one summer with his brother and parents: a redhaired boy in jeans, younger than herself. There had been a big row with Pakky because the

Yank O'Flahertys had stayed in McCormack's hotel, and after
the row they never went near Quarry Street again but spent
the rest of their visit out in Claghan Bog taking the Murphys,
who were some sort of cousins too, touring the country in a
hired car. She had been ashamed of her family because the
whole street had its ears flapping, listening to the row. She
vividly recalled her shame, the sudden shocking end to her
bragging about Yankee cousins, Yankee uncles. She'd intended
taking the boys to St Ronan's school one day to show them
off, but after the row she never saw them again. Now she
pictured that eight-year-old face rising out of jungle camouflage,
driving a helicopter, spraying death over some busy little
Vietnamese village. Over Quarry Street, over Boharnamuc, over
the Bog Road. Old Sarah Morris running with her hair on fire;
her father with his fist raised at the sky, then exploding in
flames; thirteen wee Murphys scurrying like young pigs, their
skins sizzling . . . Her cousin, Cormac O'Flaherty, waving his
sword, keeping the world safe from something or other.

She scanned the marching faces mechanically, without hope.
Now that the revolution Eric used to talk about seemed to be
there for real, now that millions of young people all over were
down in the streets holding hands in solidarity, demanding a
better world, she was more aware than ever of the value of
what she'd lost. And more aware now of *why* she'd lost. Read
the papers, he used to say. Come aware Kathleen, there's a
world outside Claghan, you know! But she'd never found
anything to read *in* the papers then, never found anything that
spoke to her imagination. It was all droning on about who'd
succeed Nye Bevan, who'd take over from Hugh Gaitskell,
CND coming apart in petty squabbles, the significance of
working-class culture and its influence on . . . But now there
was Vietnam, the great central monstrosity, and all the little
famines and tyrannies and squabbles and injustices fell into
place around it. With Vietnam Kathleen felt that she had
entered into possession of herself. She was no longer an island
bounded by the polluted seas of Quarry Street and her parents

and Canon McGinty. If she met Eric now for the first time she would be his equal. He would take her hand and offer her a flower and accept her, as the wispy boy with the American accent was accepting her. A human being, a real person, not just "our nights they're great Kathleen but . . . "

The American swung her hand gently and she was ready to love him because he was awake and strong, as Eric had been awake and strong. Not one to be fooled by the fathers and the grandfathers and the generations of lies. Kathleen looked coolly and reasonably at the memory of those two young redhaired cousins, brought to Claghan long ago to gape at thatched cottages and crumbling gravestones in order, no doubt, to develop their consciousness of "the place from whence they came" (as the Irish pop star, Cuchulain McCool, sang in his recent highly publicised appearance live on stage in St Ronan's Hall, Claghan). They'd been dragged by the hand to Quarry Street in their jeans and cowboy belts to see the house (two doors down on the right from O'Flahertys') from which their ancestors set out long ago on a weary voyage to the promised land and been dragged away again after about twenty minutes because their father and Pakky O'Flaherty had begun screaming incomprehensible words like "betrayal" and "gombeen men" in the name of an old hate.

Kathleen looked coolly and reasonably (as she often did nowadays) at the image of the promised land where the descendants of Cormac O'Flaherty (*A Forgotten Hero* by Peadar MacEighire NT and would you learn that wee book by heart daughter and make your Bible of it) had been brought up and pampered by adoring parents and given toys and bikes and religious instruction and peanut butter and child psychology and the family car and trips to Europe and then suddenly wham! A president said forget all that, guys, the party's over! And dumped them in a hot wet diseased jungle to kill, go mad, die, be crippled disfigured blown apart. And they'd gone, unquestioningly, and their adoring parents were delighted—as

Kathleen's own father would have been delighted if *she'd* been dragged out to massacre people in the name of Ireland. She saw quite coldly the lunacy of it and saw that if everybody else could be got to see it, it would stop. Eric had seen it years ago, and Eric was by now probably involved very deeply in everything that was happening in the world. Even if physically he was still in Claghan. Even if . . . Maureen heard from Eric and his wife every Christmas but she naturally never discussed the letters with Kathleen, because Kathleen wasn't supposed to know the McLeods. It was incredible that Eric should keep in touch with someone like Maureen who was OK, quite kind, tolerant and all, but who had no time for causes or ideals or indeed for anything except making enough money to buy clothes and be trendy and. "My best friend that I live with," she said, "thinks all that matters is getting asked to the same party as Lord Snowdon's latest girlfriend."

"Crazy," the bearded American murmured. "Too much. And does she?"

"Does she what?"

"Get asked to the same party as whoever?"

"She did once. Or maybe twice. But she's quite nice really," she added guiltily, because what would she have done a few years ago without old Shanco? "Are you thinking of an abortion?" Shanco had asked. "Because if you are I know of this old biddy at Turnham Green. I've not *been* to her, mind you, it's not exactly my thing, but I've heard tell she works miracles with a knitting needle. She seems to have quite a success rate. Mind you, I wouldn't have heard about her failures, she wouldn't exactly advertise them!"

"Christ Jesus! Get myself butchered! No, I'm keeping it, I couldn't face . . . "

"Right. You're keeping it. You might as well move in here then, we've got a couple of spare rooms. Anyhow, it's no big drama nowadays, is it? You'll get fifty-nine and sixpence a week off the National Assistance—our Brendan's in the dole office, that's how I know. So consider yourself in clover, Kath!"

No sentimentality about Shanco. And how could there be? Poor Maureen had Boharnamuc to kill off and the McCormack one's cast-offs and being the school laughing-stock and that shit from Kilrush who gave her the push just before she married Trevor. That's why she bothers with me, Kathleen thought, that's why all the big hospitality. She needs me as a witness. Oh, she probably isn't *aware* of it even but she has me for an audience. I'm supposed to be sitting there in the front seat and applauding, I'm supposed to be the whole town of Claghan applauding her success. And if *I* need *her* it's because she keeps in touch with Eric. We're like a couple of old cripples holding each other up, like old Sarah Morris and my Granny O'Flaherty. They couldn't stand each other and yet they'd be hobbling to Mass every Sunday like a friggin' three-legged race. It's sick, she thought. I can't really stand Maureen and I can't stand Claghan and I haven't even the courage to cut myself loose from either of them. Paul was right, she thought, if I'd gone to Paul's friends instead . . . A nice posh abortion in a private nursing home that's what they'd have fixed me up with, I'd be . . . But I'd probably be here, I'd probably be doing exactly what I'm doing now, marching in a demo, it wouldn't have made a blind bit of difference to my life. And I never really *wanted* an abortion, I'm *glad* I've got Sarah. Who *wouldn't* be glad to have Sarah, she told herself.

The American, Jack, remained with her as the demo trailed off, and they walked aimlessly away through wet-smelling spring streets. It had not once happened in five years that she walked through a London street holding a man's hand. She tried briefly to torture herself with the thought that the last hand she'd held had been Eric's, but it didn't work because Paul had held her hand several times after that Sunday morning, and she had in fact clung tightly to both his hands in the departure lounge at the airport. The American's hand felt rather like Paul's, gentle and sexless and demanding nothing of her.

She was happy to be walking with him through London. She supposed they would stop for a coffee someplace before she had to get the District Line back to Richmond, and then she supposed they would drift back to wherever he lived and she would drift into his bed or his sleeping-bag and it would be gentle and kind and without violence. Her life would for a time have this gentle bearded shape in it, sheltering her from the knowledge of loss. Then she thought again of Eric's child and knew that she would never again be allowed to drift, or to forget. It seemed a treason that she had even wanted to forget. She swung his hand and smiled, erasing a small unexpected hate. "Did you burn your draft card?"

"I guess I didn't have to. I was in Europe and my old man wired me to stay there."

"He didn't *want* you to go to Vietnam?"

"No, I guess not. He's cool. Even sends me all the bread I need, care of American Express."

"I've got a cousin in the marines or something out in Vietnam and his parents are really pleased about it. They sit down and write to all their Irish relations every time he kills a Viet Cong."

"Oh, the Irish in the States, that's different. A different scene. Very straight. But I guess Ireland's a good place to be."

"Have you been?"

"Not yet, but I'm going. Next week. Some time. A bunch of kids I know live in this commune in Dublin."

"A commune? In Dublin?"

"Sure. Why not?"

"It's just hard to imagine," Kathleen said. "Maybe Ireland's changed a bit since I left. It can't have changed much, though. D'you know what's top of the charts over there? Not the Beatles. Not the Stones. Not even Joan Baez. *But* Cuchulain McCool from Claghan! That's my hometown. Sort of Middle Ireland if you like. *And* he's singing some grotty old ballad about my great-great-grandfather, of all people!"

"What was he, your old grandad, union leader or what?"

"Not even. He was some sort of Irish patriot. Died in a famine or something. Really ancient history. You know?"

"Maybe that's where it's all happening at, this Claghan," Jack said, and Kathleen laughed: "Nothing could be happening in Claghan. You should see it. Dead parochial Irish town. Two factories, a creamery, Catholic Bingo hall, Protestant Bingo hall, Catholic dance-hall, Protestant dance-hall, ninety-nine pubs and twice as many churches and chapels!"

"Groovy," Jack sighed, losing interest. "You dig coming back to the squat, Kathleen? We got some acid."

"I'd love to," Kathleen said, "only first I have to collect my daughter from the play group."

"You *married?*"

"No, I'm not actually, that's why I have to live with this friend. Landladies don't like kids much, in London."

"You on welfare?"

"No. I teach. I took off today for the demo. Supposed to be sick."

"You could always move in with us if you don't dig the friend so much. Well, I mean, it's up to you. There's a Danish chick, Krista, that's got a kid too. And a dog and hamsters. Like there's space."

"That'd be great," Kathleen said, seeing a lovely uncomplicated child's world of love and hamsters suddenly throw open its door in welcome. "Gosh, I'd love to, I'd really love to! Why don't we go back and collect Sally and go back to Maureen's and tell her and get my things?"

"Yeah, sure, why not?"

They picked up Sarah from the play group, and the other mums sniffed a bit and drew their mini-skirted toddlers away from contact with the longhaired couple carrying wilted flowers and heaven knew what besides. (You read of such people, they whispered, though not very often, thank heavens, in the *Richmond and Twickenham Times.*)

The three of them laughed all the way to Richmond Green, and then when they reached the house Sarah ran straight into the drawing-room where Maureen was being interviewed for her trashy magazine, and they heard Maureen saying to the reporter: "Kathleen lives with us now and helps in the house." Which sounded very hurtful and dismissive, especially in front of Jack ("Is that one of your women?") as if she was only there to scrub floors or something. A while later Maureen and the reporter came out into the hall and Kathleen did the introductions and Maureen smiled at Jack and asked, or rather stated: "You burned your draft card, right?" Her voice rising on the soft insider's ripple she always used when she was asking a trendy question and knew the trendy answer. Kathleen had often listened coldly to Maureen's ripple of "Polanski? Courrèges . . . ?" and now she listened coldly to "burned your draft card, right?" Glad that for once Maureen was wrong. But Jack grinned into Maureen's eyes and said: "Right!" and Maureen said: "You're coming to my party tonight," and Jack grinned again and said: "Yeah, sure. Why not?"

And all evening Kathleen, swallowing gin after gin up against the William Morris wallpaper, watched him being the token draft-dodger, token flower-child, being chatted up by boutique-owners' wives in false eyelashes and copywriters in mauve shirts, and getting asked to other parties to play the token draft-dodger for people to whom Vietnam was just another trendy brand-name. And it didn't help at all thinking back to Boharnamuc and thirteen wee barefoot Murphys in a zinc-roofed shack and Shancoduff with nits in her hair, because all that had no connection whatever with the Maureen who'd whipped Jack from under her nose just to make a party swing. The past was over. Old Shanco had climbed up with the Myrnas and the Carolyns and the nice safe winners, and Kathleen knew that Jack had forgotten her existence and she knew she was going to keep on standing there against the flowery wallpaper drowning herself in gin, making no attempt to remind him she was there. Just watching herself losing and losing and pretending it didn't matter at all.

CHAPTER THIRTY-SEVEN

MAUREEN IN CLAGHAN

"Well, Mary Brigid Murphy of all people! Are you long home? God, I'd hardly have known you!" Maureen rummaged in her memory for a name deliberately buried long ago: Campbell, Phyllis Campbell the grocer's daughter, teaching in St Ronan's, she'd heard, this four or five years. Why all the enthusiasm, she wondered, we could never stand each other. She was one of the worst: humiliating me, laughing at my mother's clothes, her endless pregnancies, her humility when she asked Mrs Campbell for credit. It was Phyllis who made up that song. "Do you keep the pigs in the parlour, Shanco?" one of her cronies would ask, to start the game. (Sometimes the crony was Kathleen.) And Campbell would lead the chorus: "No! No! No! The pigs are outside in Boharnamuc! All together now: The parlour's outside in Boharnamuc! The bog is outside in Boharnamuc!" They kept adding verses, supposedly descriptive of Maureen's home, her family's poverty, shabbiness, rural thickness, her parents' sex-life ("They do it outside in Boharnamuc!"), the food they ate, as evidenced by a sheaf of unpaid bills Phyllis stole from her father's office and passed round the dormitory on the first night of term: half-pound of bacon, five pounds of onions—"The Sunday stew in Boharnamuc!"—while Maureen wept, homesick and shamed, under the bedclothes.

Once, when Maureen was thirteen, a group of them surrounded her in a corner of the camogie field with raised sticks and forced her to join in the singing. Is eleven or twelve years meant to wipe all that out, she wondered? Are we supposed to be adult and civilised, shaking hands on a Quarry Street pavement, swapping innocent convent memories: "God will y'ever forget Fangs? And McGowan? And old Mother Imelda farting away at Legion of Mary meetings?" No, I'll never forget Fangs, I'll never forget McGowan, I'll never forget you either, you camogie-thighed bitch out of hell! You scarred me between the lot of you, she thought, you left me wounded. "Yes, I'm home for a few days," she smiled, secure in the knowledge of Courrèges dress and high white boots: local dolly bird makes good.

"In seeing the O'Flahertys were you? Listen, tell us, do y'ever run into Kathleen over in London?"

"Yes, now and again," Maureen said. "Actually she's doing quite well for herself. Teaching in this very trendy progressive school."

"Oh, that's great. Now I'm very glad to hear that. Only there was a lot of talk, you know."

"Talk?"

"When she never showed her face in the town this five years, not even home for Christmas. You know what they're like round here. The rumours! They were all saying she must be in trouble, y'know what I mean."

"She didn't want to teach in Claghan, that's all," Maureen said coldly. "Millions don't. It's hardly the summit of social aspiration, you know, a teaching job in St Ronan's parochial school."

"Oh, *I'm* quite happy there," the Campbell one said, "but I suppose it all depends what sort of background you come from. I mean, I can well imagine there's people would find it preferable to be as far away from Claghan as they can get. Well, as long as she's not in trouble. I suppose she had a row with the father and can you blame her? Tell us, Mary Brigid, is he all *right?* You know what I mean. Only they were saying . . . And I thought I heard him roaring at you a few minutes ago when I was outside the door. Honest to God, I hadn't even the courage to rap and ask for their contribution, the Canon'll kill me! Tell us, did he chase you out of the house or what?"

"Don't be absurd! Mr O'Flaherty has a loud voice, that's all. He was perfectly friendly. I was bringing them some presents from Kathleen, she'll be over herself in the summer . . . "

"Oh, that's great. Now I'm glad to hear that. Only, the rumours you hear about those people! It's Pakky O'Flaherty this and Pakky O'Flaherty that, this last while, honestly, you wouldn't know what to believe! Tell us is it true that he . . . "

"Look, I'm in a hurry," Maureen snapped. "Why don't you just drop in and ask him yourself, Phyllis?"

After twelve years she was still trembling, still about to cringe under some expected whiplash of small town contempt. And after twelve years it still seemed like a victory when she got away almost untouched. It's ridiculous, she thought, it's over now. You're free of them. But she knew she'd never be free of them as long as she kept coming back to Claghan.

I won't come back again, she thought, I'll make this my last visit home. Let my parents come to London in future. It'll make a nice change for them. This is the very last time in my life I set foot in Claghan . . .

"'Let her put that child in a home,' that's all he kept saying, Mammy. That's all either of them kept saying! I mean, a kid of nearly five that Kathleen's crazy about, that we're all crazy about, they just naturally expect her to be handed over for adoption while we all forget she ever existed. And not one *word* about what Kathleen must have gone through. They didn't even want to know if she was happy or unhappy or how she was after the experience or anything. All they could see was the disgrace to their bloody name. In this day and age! I'm sorry now I told them. They don't deserve to be considered. They're just not *human*, that crowd!"

CHAPTER THIRTY-EIGHT

MAUREEN AND KATHLEEN

"I'm sorry, Kathleen, but I did, I really did. I tried my hardest but they're just unreasonable. At least your father is. I think maybe your mother on her own . . . But even she! I mean she kept dragging the Canon into it. Going on about scandal and bad example and the legendary chastity of the women of Ireland and how you were a disgrace to your ancestors—no, that was your daddy said that. It was just real stage Irish, Kath: the heavy father, weeping mother, daughter in trouble, not to mention the ubiquitous priest. All that was missing was the whiskey bottle and I can tell you I wouldn't have minded seeing that appearing! No, but he just kept roaring at me. My God, I thought I was about fifteen again, in playing my Lanzas on your gramophone! Mammy was saying he's very neurotic anyway over this thing of being moved to a council house. I mean even *she* blames you for not being over there all this time helping them rise out of Quarry Street. She says it must be a terrible comedown for your father and the way he was reared getting pushed out now into a council place, and that it would have fitted you better to have bought them a house of their own instead of."

"You mean buy back Claghan Hall for them out of a teacher's pay? Jesus!"

"I can't see anyone short of a Rothschild buying Claghan Hall these days. You should see it, Kathleen. A real eyesore. The name picked out in neon, thatched stables, golf course crawling with Yanks. *And* they're planning a Celtic banqueting hall with the waitresses in saffron kilts. Your dad's going mad over that too. He even refuses to collect old McCormack's creamery cans. They say he's heading for the sack, Kathleen, and him with only a few years to retirement. He'll lose his pension and all."

"So I definitely can't go back? They won't have me back with Sarah?"

"Why do you want to go back? What's wrong with London all of a sudden? I thought you couldn't stand them. I mean I thought you were OK here with us. You're no bother, you know; the rooms are empty anyway. Or if you really can't stand us, if you want to move out to a bedsit or something . . . I mean what have I *done*?"

"You destroyed me with Jack, that's all. You didn't even fancy him, you were just trying to be trendy as usual. The one time I find a fellow I can be friends with, you went to the squat and everything with him. You ruined the whole thing for me. I wouldn't have minded you even sleeping with him if you fancied him but you just went up there like a friggin' tourist to play at smoking pot and."

"Your Jack was a knave, ducky! He was on the make. Christ, if you didn't realise *that*! And I *said* I was sorry. We've had this scene, Kath. Remember? That's why I said I'd go to Quarry Street for you. I'm a walking guilt complex. I'm in sackcloth and ashes, Kath! And you only knew him one *day*, God, don't let him drive you out of London!"

"I don't fit in, in London. You know fucking well I don't. I don't fit in with your friends, I just can't learn the jargon.

They think I'm a peasant or something."

"That makes two of us, *I'm* a peasant back in Claghan. And I've had to learn the jargon too, I wasn't born speaking like this. *If* you remember, ducky! If you'd stop being so heavy, Kathleen, you'd fit in like everyone else. I mean the *Labour* party in this day and age and socialism and Christ knows what! It's the swinging Sixties, Kath, who *cares?* And whatever possessed you to go on at that dinner-party about old Cromwell in Drogheda spearing all the babies on his bayonet? Well, I mean, you might at least have waited till we'd finished our kebabs!"

"It's not funny, Maureen. That Jeremy creep just disgusted me going on about the Irish. What does *he* know about."

"He was being witty, darling; he didn't *mean* anything. The English are often *like* that. And it would have been fine if you'd demolished him with something witty back, but *not* doing a Pakky O'Flaherty on him! Babies on bayonets, Curr-i-ist! This Vietnam thing you're into, that's all right! That's a pretty *now* thing, but all the rest! Will I go on about your parents?"

"Frig my parents. No, tell me, did you see . . . Listen. I suppose you saw the McLeods and all when you were over? Eric and."

"Well no, actually, I didn't get a chance this time. Why? You don't know Eric and Myrna, do you?"

"I know Eric. It was him that. We used to, well, I may as well tell you, Maureen, and get it over with. Don't have a heart attack. It was him that. He's Sarah's father."

"Jesus. Jesus Christ, Kathleen, give over. You're joking. Are you sure?"

"Well, unless it was the Holy Ghost, I never slept with anyone else. What do you think I am? What's he like now, Maureen? What does he do? Is he happy and all that? Is he still teaching? He used to say—"

"Look, I'm sorry, Kath, just leave me out of this, OK? I don't want to be mixed up in it. Just don't tell me any more. Don't tell me any of the sordid details. Don't ask me anything, right? Myrna's a friend of mine. She's happy. She's crazy about him. They've got two fab kids. I don't want you mucking everything about for them, Kathleen. Just drop it. Right?"

"Hell's teeth, Shanco, will you quit spouting out of one of your daft books. Don't panic. I don't intend to turn up on their doorstep in the snow. Can't you just see me? I'd just like, from a distance you know, just . . . Is he still on about revolution and all? Does he go on demos? The Vietnam war, things like that? What's actually happening round home now?"

"Revolution? You must be joking! What do you think they are, Kathleen, a couple of longhaired dropouts? They're a married couple, Kath, with kids. Very middle-class. They've grown up. The reason I didn't see them is that they're both up to their necks in the Claghan Conservation Society. Rescuing historic buildings. If you really want to know what Eric's doing nowadays, he's got up a Save Quarry Street petition. They're buzzing round the place trying to get people to sign it. They sent me a copy ages ago. I'm supposed to trudge round to posh Paddy places like the Eaton Square club and get Eamonn Andrews and Polly Devlin and Christ knows who-all to protest about your mammy and daddy's house and all the other condemned shacks being bulldozed by the council as soon as they're vacated. So now you know. I suppose you could *call* it a revolution if you really put your mind to it. It seems Quarry Street's of great historical significance. It was built before the Flood or the Famine or something. Some McLeod ancestor used to live there. Believe it or not, she was married to an O'Flaherty. My granny used to talk about them. I'm going to write a book about them one of these years. Did you think you were Tess of the d'Urbervilles, Kathleen?"

"I know all that. Eric used to go on about it when he. He always pretended that's why he noticed me in the first place. There's a country and western song about it now too, it's in the charts at home. I saw in the *Press*. And there is a book about it, do you not remember my father forcing you to sit down and read it one day?"

"Can't stand Irish folk-songs. What book? Oh sure, of course I remember. Pakky O'Flaherty knew all the details all right. But your daddy won't be signing that petition. Neither will mine. The only people who'll be signing it are people who never had to live in dumps like that. And just in case any Catholic might be tempted to join the conservation society the Canon's got them all steamed up over the St Ronan's restoration programme. They're going to decorate the chapel and rebuild the school. Now *I've* always thought that school the only decent building in Claghan but there it goes! You should see the plans. Picture windows, flat roofs, tarmacadamed playground where the master's flowerbeds used to be. There's parochial bingo twice a day, sponsored walks, kiddie concerts and, naturally, door-to-door collections by respectable members of our little community. I met one of them out on her rounds. Big Phyllis Campbell, her camogie muscles turned to flab. There she was with her mite-box, and her ears flapping away outside the door while your father was yelling your sins off the housetops. You'll be the scarlet woman of Claghan, Kathleen, you'll be cursed off the altar and Reverend Abe Clyde'll be burning you in effigy on the Twelfth of July.

"Christ! Claghan Claghan Claghan! I'm never setting foot in that place again! Not for you or Mammy or anyone. I feel I've got muck up to the ankles every time I meet one of the bloody natives. I mean, look at me, Kathleen, I'm arriving, amn't I? I'm doing all right, wouldn't you say? And yet every time I go back to that dump I run into some wee shopkeeper or schoolteacher or Civil Servant and they *patronise* me, Kathleen, they actually think they have a right to patronise me! I mean, they see themselves as great big successes, do you realise? And me as some poor emigrant living in Harlesden or wherever! Oh shit, why do I bother! Anyhow those are the twin obsessions at the moment, Save Quarry Street and Paint St Ronan's. Not a whiff of napalm in the air. Oh, and there's another one. Remember Dave Jenks from Lockhart Road, I went out with him a few times. Specs, spots and Trotsky? Well, Dave's into civil rights for Ulster's workers. He says it's the big new thing. He says Claghan's starting to move. Must think he's in Alabama. He's got his own personal Joan of Arc, guess who! Nuala McCormack, fresh from do-gooding with the Cherokees. And I hear she spent five minutes in Cuba on the way home, which naturally canonised her for old Dave! She won't look at him, of course, but he drifts around in her aura chanting slogans. Let's see, yeah: One man, one vote! A job and a house before creed and colour! As I said, it's Alabama at home. So that's Claghan, Kath! Still want to go back?"

CHAPTER THIRTY-NINE

THE YEARS 1968, 1969, 1970

D ave Jenks, unarmed civil rights marcher trying hard to keep fear at bay, put his head down and counted every dogged step he achieved between two rows of Reverend Abe Clyde's jeering taunting parishioners who lined the route at intervals between Claghan and Belfast.

Stones thudded and crunched on skulls and cheekbones and shoulder blades, sending gushes of blood over banners and jeans and anoraks.

Armed policemen stood by, not feeling they had any particular duty to stop a pack of Taigs and Commies getting massacred.

Eric McLeod counted signatures on his Save Quarry Street petition. Clifford Lewis and John Joe McCormack, walking through segregated Claghan graveyards, counted the number of recently dead who might temporarily rise and help vote them into Stormont. Harry Hale MP, standing in one of his own roadside fields with his friend the Chief Constable, watched the attack on the civil rights marchers and said: "Aye, you're right, Georgie, I wouldn't move the force in yet awhile. Let that pack of young bastards get a bit of a cooling first and they'll be in no hurry to go out protesting again for a wee while!"

The years of My Lai, of Charles Manson, of Huey Newton, of tanks in Prague, of the Sorbonne riots, of civil rights marches, of Bernadette Devlin. The years of barricades and petrol bombs and looting, of blazing Catholic homes. Of British troops in Ulster. Of the IRA's second coming.

Ho Chi Minh, Bobby Kennedy, Martin Luther King, Canon McGinty and Pakky O'Flaherty all joined the long list of the dead.

Nuala McCormack was fined several times for painting seditious slogans on Clifford Lewis's factory wall. She painted:

> To Be a Catholic and Conscious in Claghan Is To
> Be in a State of Constant Rage.

She painted:

> Che Guevara's Real Name Was Lynch.

Other hands added, variously:

> Lynch Lewis! Lynch Harry Hale! Lynch O'Neill! Lynch
> Lynch!

She painted:

> Cormac O'Flaherty's Real Name was Claghan.
> Claghan Lives! Claghan Marches! Claghan Demands!

But Nuala felt that the political education of the masses was just one step above knitting socks for the boys, and that—given the obvious ill-will of the ruling majority—offensive military action was the only real solution to the problems facing Claghan's Catholics. The masses, politically educated or not, could easily be coaxed or bullied into supporting it. When, in 1970, Sinn Féin and the IRA split into two factions, she was one of the first people in Claghan to join the Provisionals.

Doctor Martin McCormack attempted to join the Unionist Party, fastidiously distancing himself from his father's and his sister's distinct but equally brash brands of Republicanism. He deeply admired Terence O'Neill's quiet attempts to bring democracy to the north of Ireland and he honestly believed the future of the province lay in continued union with Great Britain. The Unionist Party turned him down, as a Roman Catholic and thus as a potential traitor, and he reluctantly allied himself with the non-sectarian People's Democracy party.

One-eyed Dave Jenks—scarred for life by a well-aimed stone during the civil rights march from Claghan to Stormont Castle—offered to stand as People's Democracy candidate in the forthcoming election. He was turned down because Nuala and Martin feared a Protestant candidate would lose the party votes in Catholic areas of Claghan. He stood anyway, for the Allied Workers' Socialist Party, which had similar aims to PD, and lost his deposit. The Reverend Abraham Clyde stood for the Free Protestant Workers' Party and won a substantial minority of votes—mainly from unskilled labourers who had hitherto, for want of anything more relevant, supported the 'Protestant Parliament for a Protestant People' conservatism of Clifford Lewis.

The Sunday before the election, Dr O'Donnell stood on a table outside St Ronan's green white and orange church, ordering Mass-goers to vote once again for their friend and benefactor John Joe McCormack, whose business interests had always created much-needed employment in the town and who was, furthermore, a Catholic like themselves. He reminded them that for well over a century Mr McCormack's forebears had been there to stretch out a helping hand to the people of Claghan in the darkest days of famine and oppression. Working-class people would gain nothing from voting for a Red Protestant schoolmaster like Mr Jenks, whose whole family was rotten with B-Specials and British soldiers from the dawn of time. And they'd gain still less, he laughed, from voting for a young strap in a mini-skirt, whatever slogan she was screeching! His audience, middle-aged, elderly, or lying over the road in the graveyard, laughed with him—it wouldn't have occurred to them in any case to vote for either a woman or a Protestant.

The two side doors of the church were held by John Joe's treacherous children who were busy urging all Claghan young people to vote for Martin's fiancée, Philomena Caiserbuill Ó Lorcáin, and help bring democracy and religious tolerance to Northern Ireland.

With the opposition split four ways, Clifford Lewis was once again elected with a comfortable majority. It didn't much matter. Three years later the Stormont parliament was abolished, the Six Counties were ruled directly from Westminster and Harry Hale became Claghan's only elected representative.

Five families living in a deteriorating block on Quarry Street were rehoused in the new estate. The cottages they left, though condemned as unsafe for habitation, were saved from demolition by the efforts of Claghan Conservation Society, founded by Eric McLeod, popular young master at Claghan High. A commemorative plaque was put on the house from which, 120 years earlier, Marianne McLeod set out to walk to the emigrant ship with her Catholic husband and their two wee babes. Myrna McLeod, opening the cottages to the public, spoke of "our common heritage" and felt sure that the work of restoring and preserving these historic buildings (as soon as sufficient funds became available) would do much to forge and strengthen bonds of goodwill between the two communities of Claghan.

The two communities disagreed. Working-class Catholics from the beginning saw Save Quarry Street as a deliberate attempt by big-shots to rub their noses in the squalor that had been forced on them by eight centuries of British occupation and by the callousness of successive Orange governments. (It was unfortunate that Eric and Myrna's effort to preserve the cottages should have been made at a time when Catholics were still wincing from the Prime Minister's well-meaning gaffe: "If you give them a good house and a good job they will live like Protestants.") Middle-class people of both religions who had signed the petition and given a shilling or two towards the plaque found it unnecessary ever to make the journey into a slum to inspect their common heritage. Since the murder of the Anderson boy, Quarry Street was known as a dangerous enough area and, in any case, the welcome that might be awaiting strangers there seemed to be spelled out very explicitly in the spectacle of St Ronan's parish church—recently redecorated—standing half-way up the mountain, shamelessly flaunting the colours of the Republican tricolour. Catholic professional people were embarrassed at what they perceived as a vulgar error of taste on the part of their clergy, and took their custom elsewhere. Protestants, whether bigoted or tolerant, saw St Ronan's colours as a deliberate act of provocation.

Both were wrong. One April morning, seventy-five years earlier, young James McGinty on his way to serve Mass happened to glance through the wrought-iron gates of a Protestant mansion in his native Tyrone. The sun was edging through dawn clouds, a lark sang. James was in a state of grace—and the park was covered in wild daffodils. Not golden, not tossing their heads in sprightly dance, not the stiff self-conscious things that grew in every shopkeeper's garden and were stood in uniform bunches of six on the high altar. *These* daffodils were just barely yellow. Pale drifts of cream, fragile and dew-damp with an air of careless privilege, they grew as naturally as daisies in the drenched silver-green grass. He never forgot that sight: until a week before his death it was to stand for the spirit of Easter, of Creation's first morning, of Eden innocence. During all the decades of his ministry in the uncouth poverty of St Ronan's parish he dreamed of bringing the essence of those wild daffodils to Claghan. Perhaps he was the only man in the Six Counties who had any inkling of the vision that may have floated through Terence O'Neill's mind as he made his notorious speech. To live like a Protestant . . . To live ankle deep in wild daffodils . . . He dreamed of transforming Claghan's grim old church into a symbol of that enchanted spring dawn. He saw St Ronan's standing on its hill, a wispy delicate edifice with sturdy roots, pale cream and shimmering silver-green: an image of the Resurrection, of purity, of eternal Easter. He dreamed for half a century. Then, with Cardinal Conway's permission, he embarked on the greatest fund-raising campaign of his long career. He begged, he promised, he threatened, he cajoled, he cursed, he blackmailed. He almost bled the parish dry . . .

Campbell and Son, Select Grocer, Hardware and Furniture Merchants, had little sense of nuance but they knew what colours grass and daffodils were. They undertook to supply the parish with hundreds of gallons of Duralite Weatherproof Gloss. Pius Finnegan, the contractor, recommended a wee touch of white, to pick out the doors and window-frames. Campbell's supplied that too.

A week after the job was finished Canon McGinty died, in great torment of mind, having wrestled for seven days and nights with the temptation to relinquish his life-long beliefs in Creation, in the Resurrection, in baptismal innocence. Quarry Street and district saw the newly-decorated church as a fitting monument to a great priest and a staunch patriot. No betther man, they said gleefully, for shovin' it up them Prods, do yous mind the wicked sermon he gave the time that . . .

The more enlightened members of the faithful began driving to Newry cathedral of a Sunday morning, or to the Redemptorist monastery at Portnafinn, or even away over to Crossmaglen where they had a fab chapel with this super new tabernacle designed by a trendy young Irish artist . . .

Lizzie O'Flaherty, up in the New Houses (to be transformed within a few years into a Catholic ghetto and christened Canon McGinty Park), had her own ideas about living like a Protestant. Through Campbell's HP services she bought a fitted formica kitchen, a lounge suite in uncut moquette and an English wall-to-wall carpet with a splashy pattern in violet, pink and turquoise—a recent mass-produced version of the colours in Maureen Murphy's drawing-room, which Lizzie had read about in *Her World*.

Her husband was another matter. For over twenty-six years, Pakky had looked on Quarry Street as a temporary degradation from which he would one day emerge to find his birthright and heritage miraculously restored. His daughter would succeed in life, marry well, claim back her ancestral home from the gombeen men and land-grabbers who had stolen it. The sordid transformation of Claghan Hall had shaken him, Kathleen's defection from virtue and filial loyalty had weakened him further and the vulgar suburban gentility of the new house destroyed him completely. He realised he was only an old man in a menial job, nearing retirement; that since the day his father beat him out of de Valera's army he had been living in a dream world; that indeed the world old Matt himself had been trying to re-create was nothing but a sentimental out-dated dream; that this concrete box with its nylon-curtained view of supermarket roses in a narrow municipal garden was the only future a descendant of Cormac O'Flaherty might expect in today's Claghan.

He knew he was finished and, sooner than sink into the final banality of senior citizenship in a council house, he decided to perpetrate one last crazy gesture of defiance. At midday on the fifteenth of August he parked his lorry-load of milk in the blazing Quarry Street sun, roared: "Fuck Caesar anyhow: *I'm* for God!" and went openly to twelve o'clock Mass in St Ronan's. The creamery supervisor, who'd received orders to keep an eye on O'Flaherty, came on the lorry and drove it to the creamery himself before the milk had time to spoil. Pakky was sacked. In the last weeks of his life he began drinking, and enlisted some sympathy around the public houses by declaring that the Protestant creamery sacked him for going to Mass on the feast of the Blessed Virgin. Dave Jenks's civil rights group briefly took up his case, but dropped it as soon as they heard the facts. His body was found one morning face down in a stream behind Claghan Hall. He had been drinking heavily the night before and the word "suicide" was never spoken, and indeed may not have entered anybody's mind but his wife's. Kathleen and her child were home for the funeral. Nobody paid much heed to them: for all anyone knew, Kathleen might have been respectably married for years and even if she wasn't, well, it *was* the late Sixties. Much as she was tempted to, she couldn't *stay* at home: late Sixties or not, no Catholic school would have employed an unmarried mother for fear of giving scandal, and it was out of the question, naturally, to look for a job in a Protestant one.

Lizzie was delighted to see them, and from then on little Sarah spent part of every summer in Claghan with her grandmother. For years this visit was the one point of certainty or stability in the child's life.

Every time she came home Kathleen haunted the centre of Claghan, hoping and fearing to see Eric. She did, once. He was in the shoe department of Gardiner's store with his wife and three children. His wife was dressed exactly like Kathleen in jeans and embroidered shirt, and wore her hair in a similar long plait. They were laughing with the salesgirl as she measured the children's feet. A nice modern couple, friendly. They didn't see Kathleen and she went away quickly, her heart thudding, her hand searching furiously in her shoulder-bag for the tube of Valium. He was no longer Eric, he had no connection at all with those years in Fitzroy Avenue, but that didn't stop her suffering.

Sufficient funds never did become available for the restoration of the five cottages, and within months of becoming empty they were briefly used as: an ashram, a Jesus People meeting-house, headquarters of the Claghan/San Francisco Brotherhood of Man faction, and the temporary homes of successive itinerant families. During the late Seventies and early Eighties they stood vacant, gently rotting away from the inside, then they stepped back for a moment into Claghan's violent history before collapsing, with tragic loss of life, in the autumn of 198-.

Little girls counted their skips in school playgrounds. Sarah O'Flaherty counted hers in Richmond, in Acton, in Notting Hill, in Battersea, in Kilburn, back again in Richmond—changing homes and schools and friends as Kathleen became disillusioned with lovers, friends, flatmates, squatmates, landladies; got depressed in sordid digs; fell behind with the rent in expensive ones; turned up endlessly on Maureen Murphy's doorstep with hair-raising tales of paranoid Poles, filthy Frogs, inquisitorial Irish, grisly Greeks, the flatmate whose dog chewed up all her clothes, the childless landlady who went off her head and threw Sarah downstairs, breaking her collarbone . . . All the tales were true—something in Kathleen's nature, Maureen thought, resisted happiness, resisted luck, resisted the simple banality of everyday existence—and Kathleen, the first shock over, recounted her miseries with such exaggeratedly hilarious detail that they always ensured her a welcome back in Richmond. If she still lacked wit and sophistication she had learned to buy acceptance as a friendly, put-upon and increasingly bawdy big clown. Trevor christened her The Slut which, he said, was only Cool Chick translated into Irish. Translated into *anything*, his wife retorted virtuously.

Maureen still went to Mass and the sacraments, in the delightful Spanish church up on Richmond Hill. Full of the most deliciously porno Crucifixions, she rippled to her friends, and instantly despised herself for pandering to their English paganism: her faith did actually mean a lot to her. Though still shocked at some of Kathleen's Quarry Street obscenities, she felt she owed it to the times occasionally to utter a four-letter word, and was surprised at the relief it gave in difficult situations. Her books sold less well as the innocent adolescent Sixties romped into the stridently sexy Seventies. Trevor's boutiques, full of Indian cottons and Afghan coats, of jeans and incense and patchouli and long silk scarves, did rather better. Kathleen bought all her things there. Maureen didn't. Her own jeans had designer labels and made her legs look much longer. Which was a relief too.

Sarah grew into a lumpish slouching child, which was a pity. When they came back to live in Richmond during Kathleen's crises, Maureen found it increasingly distasteful to cuddle or play with her as she had so delightedly done with the plump blonde baby of a few years earlier. Sarah reminded her relentlessly of herself at the same age, and she was as powerless to comfort or accept her as she was powerless to give comfort or acceptance to the memory of her own humiliated childhood. She had learned to be witty about the convent, to dress it up in anecdotes, but it remained there beneath her flippancy, bleak and ugly and riddled with shame.

She bought Sarah sweet flowery frocks from Laura Ashley as she would have done for a more graceful child, and she made a point of reading her Kate Greenaway and Alison Uttley, her rippling voice occasionally faltering as she glanced up and caught the blank pitiless gaze—listening? not listening? plotting? *judging?*—above the aggressive body so incongruously clad in folksy smocked cotton.

She thought it typical of Kathleen to sleep with someone as dishy as Eric McLeod and produce only such a rough beast of a child. Sarah must be a throwback, she commented, but a throwback to what? She was glad, on the whole, that she'd never run the risk of having an ugly daughter herself, because the poor thing would have had a terrible life of it. She would have dearly loved a child all the same. To put a stop to her mother's outraged sermons against birth-control, which grew more strident as Maureen approached thirty, she'd felt obliged to confess her irrevocable barrenness. A confession she immediately regretted as her prolific parents thereafter spoke to her and, she was sure, *of* her with a furtive sickroom courtesy.

She had often considered adopting. During the Seventies she daydreamed constantly of a tiny Colombian or Filipino or Bangladeshi orphan whom she would dress exquisitely in white *broderie anglaise* and ribboned straw hats, until Trevor reminded her rather nastily that small status symbols have a way of growing up and what did she want to do—grow fodder for the National Front bashers? Maureen suffered: she had not in fact seen an adopted foreign child as a status symbol and was hurt that even Trevor nowadays seemed to be taken in by the frivolous mask she hid herself behind. She worried in case the mask was growing deeply into her, like a corn, and as a protection cultivated the habit of thinking privately in the down-to-earth idiom of Boharnamuc, while her public image became more and more fashionably inconsequent.

She thought it unfortunate that her frustrated maternity could no longer be sublimated in caring for Kathleen and Eric's daughter. It was unfortunate for Sarah too. She had begun by conventionally worshipping Maureen and Trevor, who at first were generous with kisses and affection. As time went on and they stopped bothering, the worship turned to bewilderment, then to critical dislike and, as returning to live in Richmond generally meant abandoning yet another set of friends and teachers, she came to view her relationship with Maureen and Trevor as one more hated aspect of her eccentric life.

She knew it was eccentric because the little girls she made friends with at school had mums and siblings and grans and cousins and net curtains and china tea-sets and dads who watched football on telly and homes they'd always lived in and that smelled of lavender Air-fresh instead of dirty old incense. In some schools there were exotic dark girls called Precious and Tiffany and Yasmin, in others exotic fair girls called Charlotte and Victoria and Miranda, whose various life-styles might have made her own seem as normal as any, but she was so physically awkward and shy that she inevitably drifted towards the stolid unexacting little Lynns and Sandras and Tracys, whose accents and standards she adopted.

Kathleen was neither happy nor unhappy. She drifted, too. Reality was somewhere else. Reality was stuck, like a needle in a record, in the Belfast of ten years earlier. Her relationships monotonously repeated that one track, but in a lower key. The wispy marginal men she attached herself to were Eric diminished. She asked nothing else of them—which was just as well, for they offered nothing, neither passion nor a permanent roof. They promised no security, threatened no violence, made no sacrifices for her, burdened her with no guilt. They asked neither loyalty nor gratitude. They gave her an acceptance that was the mere opposite of rejection, and she found that easy to cope with. Sooner or later one relationship ended and another, similar, took its place. In the interval between the two she suffered, despised herself, doubted her own worth, felt that she was abandoned forever. During these periods she often achieved lucidity, became aware that she was missing much in denying herself a present and a future. From time to time she perceived Sarah only as the unattractive result of her obsession with the past and felt herself obliged to chastise the child for existing. She screamed at her, woke her in the night with long hysterical speeches about the failure of her life, about her forced exile, about injustice and betrayal, about her blighted passion, about the endless famine of her affections. Sarah listened with blank merciless eyes, and said nothing. Once safe in the pretty Richmond house Kathleen made up to her by spoiling her, buying her bright frilly dresses and cream cakes, jeans and milk shakes, riding lessons in Richmond Park.

Maureen always said: "Of *course* you can move in. Stay as long as you like." Kathleen had become a habit, as much a link with Claghan as the regular letters from Boharnamuc, and just as incongruous in the life Maureen and Trevor now led. "Kathleen's a delightful creature!" Maureen rippled to her friends, but rarely invited her downstairs when she was entertaining: bayoneted babies or Charles-Manson-looking boyfriends—it was best to forestall embarrassment. With friends who wrote or worked for television or were *engagé*, she could risk producing Kathleen: Northern Ireland was creeping into the news, from paragraph to feature to three-inch headline. Even Claghan was often in the news: the most unexpected people died there nowadays in the most unexpected ways. Though secretly glad to have cut herself off in time from such an extravagance of fanaticism, Maureen now began using an Irish passport instead of a British one: she explained that Ulster Catholics had double nationality, rather like English Jews. (Israel was fashionable then too.) She thought it a pity that she had no personal anecdotes about oppression by the Protestant establishment, the Protestants she knew in Claghan were most delightful people. It was rather the middle-class Catholics who had oppressed *her* but that was not the sort of thing one could get off with saying in the nineteen-seventies. The professional and business-class Catholics who used to taunt her about her parents' poverty, who used to talk about "down-and-outs" and "the lowest of the low" were now openly showing themselves binding up wounds in Quarry Street and Bogside and the Lower Falls, without even holding their noses.

Maureen thought once again of writing her historical romance about Cormac O'Flaherty but the time still didn't seem quite right. Perhaps later on, when the violence lost some of its rather unpleasant edge . . .

CHAPTER FORTY

LETTERS FROM BOHARNAMUC

21 July 1973

My dear Maureen,

. . . and wasn't it awful that poor policeman blown to bits in front of his wife and family. Honest to God, Claghan will soon be as bad as the slums of Belfast, they're going mad lately. It was all very well the civil rights crowd, you could understand them. We know there was always a lot of injustice about jobs and houses and the rent and rates strike done no harm to anyone except maybe Mr Heath but this latest carry-on of murdering an innocent man because of his job, sure they must know well that a married man has to take on with any work he can get these days. It's not the IRA that's going to feed the people's children for them and there's enough on the dole, God knows. And all the good it done is we have the army in Claghan now driving round mad in armoured cars and helicopters. There be's a lot of searches of houses in the town and a good few fellows were lifted on suspicion lately but things is quiet our way. They don't bother much with country people.

It's funny to think of you looking for a country cottage for the weekends, I thought yous were both real city slickers. I suppose you wouldn't think of buying a place round home? Though I'm sure Trevor mightn't feel too safe. There's an awful drop in the tourist trade this last lock of years, and it doing so well up to that with folk festivals and fishing and mountaineering and God knows what. Both of McCormack's hotels are half-empty this year, and when you think of the fortune he invested in that Claghan Hall one. Not many Yanks venturing over these days. I hope to God people comes to their senses soon.

Love from Mammy and Daddy.

1 June 1974

My dear Maureen,

Well, the Power Sharing Executive came to a speedy end, and everyone thinking we were going to get peace at last. The more fools we were, sure Catholics and Protestants were never fit to share anything and never will as long as there's the likes of Mr Paisley and the Reverend Clyde to keep them separated with wild talk and bullying. It was daft to think that Unionists would ever take on with treating Catholics as equals. They only had to mention sharing power and every Protestant worker in the country downed tools. We had no electricity or phones or anything, it was an awful nuisance. One thing, it showed which side has all the jobs!

Are you still keeping in touch with your Protestant friends? You used to be very great with them. They don't seem to be interested in politics anyhow, I do see her photo in the *Chronicle* sometimes all mixed up in some nonsense about Women's Liberation as if the country wasn't mad enough without that.

There's shocking rumours going round about Nuala

McCormack. They say every time there's a bombing or an ambush her car is sure to be parked nearhand and she was seen one time out on some lane with a mask on her where a lorry-load of soldiers was blown up, busy counting the dead and injured, and then got back into her car as cool as you like and drove away. Mind you, you can't believe every word you hear round Claghan but she must be mixed up in something all the same because she stopped all her mad protest marching and scribbling on walls and is letting on to be very quiet. She's a children's psychologist and goes round the schools talking to teenagers. Some say it's recruiting she be's at. Wouldn't you wonder and her so good-looking she didn't find some fellow to take her by this time, if she had a family it might settle her down.

How is the work coming on on the cottage? We hope you'll decide to take a run home soon even if Trevor doesn't want to come with you. Not that he'd need to worry. There be's bombs now and again but never anyone killed only soldiers and police. It's bad enough God help them but at least innocent people are in no danger and after near five years of this nonsense we're more or less used to it. You mentioned hearing about a bomb in Campbell's furniture store. I don't think you need worry as that is something you could expect at any time. A lot of the so-called bombs are planted when business is not going well. A lot of them are harmless but I suppose when you hear the news from a distance it must be frightening . . .

7 February 1975

My dear Maureen,
Well, we didn't get peace for very long, did we? It was such a relief when they called the ceasefire over Christmas and to be able to go in to Claghan and shop with no

worries about what might happen you before you got home. But now it's over and they're as bad as ever or even worse. Yesterday took out between explosions and machine gun fire. Your daddy and me were sitting having a wee cup of tea about 3 pm when one went off somewhere this side of Claghan and the back windows rattled that much we thought they were going to come in, the whole house shook. The soldiers are back out through the country night and day, you never know where you'd trip over one. The crowd we have stationed here now are very bad-mannered with the people but I suppose you couldn't blame them, they don't get much of a welcome. A few years ago you'd bid them the time of day when you met them but this last while there's none of that, you never know who be's watching or what construction they might put on it.

Do you mind poor Elly O'Hare that lived in that wee thatched house down beside the border? Well, she had a habit of giving a mug of tea to any of them that'd happen to be on patrol around there, I suppose you remember how she'd never let anyone pass on the road without offering them tea (I mind you giving out many a time about the nuisance she was!). I'm sure it was lonesome enough for her and she was glad to have a bit of a crack now and again, no matter who with. Anyhow, the boys warned her to keep her distance from the soldiers and she paid them no heed, sure she's over eighty years of age and has no television nor nothing, so one day when the poor creature came back from drawing her pension she had no house left to come back to, there wasn't one stone standing on top of another. They said she was giving information to the army and, God help her, what information would she have to give, any more than myself? So it seems you just have to watch what you say these days and who you say it to . . .

391

3 September 1975

My dear Maureen,

. . . Wasn't it the awfullest thing? I suppose you heard all about it between the papers and the television. The whole town is shocked, at least anyone with any decency is, though I heard a few of the neighbours making mouths of themselves within in Campbell's yesterday saying it was the stuff for them and a few more attacks like that would show everyone that Catholics wasn't going to lie down and be walked over like long ago. What I think myself is that it makes Catholics out to be real savages altogether but of course I didn't say that, I just let on not to hear them, it's the best policy these days. We all know that Mr Lewis is the greatest blackguard going and that he'd far rather shut down his factory altogether than employ a Catholic, but still and all if they had to assassinate him or old Clyde that he's so friendly with or even Ian Paisley himself I wouldn't have said a word, but to shoot down seven ordinary working men one after another at quitting time when they were leaving the factory, I don't see how anyone can condone it.

They lifted young Pascal O'Connor for it, he's not sixteen yet and still at secondary school, there's some say he's not too bright. His people maintain he was nowhere near the place but it seems a lot of the workers recognised the cut of him and I suppose the police and army won't be long beating the names of his companions out of him, human rights or no human rights. Most of the workers just panicked and stampeded back into the factory yard, that's what saved them, and the three gunmen ran. It's not O'Connor I blame at all, it's the smart boyos that put him up to it and put a gun into the hands of a young lad like that . . .

30 December 1975

My dear Maureen,

. . . but of course our Christmas wasn't as happy as usual
with such a tragedy happening so near us just two days
beforehand. It was really shocking and I think it spread
a gloom over every home and over Christmas for everyone.
There were six people killed in McCormacks' bombing, a
young student that had a holiday job in the bar, an English
couple that was the only guests (whatever possessed them
to come here for Christmas?), Pius Finnegan the painter
who had the misfortune to call in to make arrangements
for the daughter's wedding, that's one big day that'll have
to be postponed, God help the family, and two
chambermaids that were kept on through the winter to
make Celtic carpets for the banqueting hall. There was a
lot of people in that day and evening because of the
special turkey dinner and there was twenty or more badly
wounded. Mr McCormack himself was lucky enough to
escape with a broken arm and the wife and Nuala were
in another wing and escaped but it seems the whole
building was badly damaged. There was never luck on
that house even long ago. Your daddy was saying there
was shocking crimes committed there in his grandfather's
time, and sure the poor O'Flahertys never had good luck
in it either. They say it will be pulled down now altogether
and the McCormacks are already moved back to the town
house.

Jamesy and May and the children were on their way
back from Claghan when it happened, they were half-way
home when the bomb went off, two minutes more and
they'd have been in the middle of it. We ventured over
about ten minutes after we heard the explosion to see if
they were all right. I'll never forget that scene, bodies both
dead and injured lying everywhere. Jamesy was taking the
wounded to hospital, the ambulances were all busy with

the really bad cases. It was an awful finish up to an evening's shopping in Claghan. They brought the children in to see Santy and to get some things for the stockings. All the toys and sweets were in the car and had to be burned. It took some washing and cleaning to get the car in order again, May says she still feels peculiar sitting in it. I don't think they're over the shock yet, they were nervous enough coming home from Claghan because a car bomb went off there but seeing so many they knew just blown to bits finished them. I think everyone is scared now. As bad as the IRA are they gave warning but none from the other side at all. They claimed it was a reprisal for the murders at Lewis's factory. I wish to God it was all over. We used to wish you were nearer home but this last while Daddy says "If they were all settled in England they would be safer." I don't think they'll go all the same. You learn to live with it, what else can a body do?

Love from all at home and a Happy New Year.

15 September 1976

My dear Maureen,

. . . It's surprising the effect the Peace Movement is having in such a short time though there's a lot of people condemning it. I was on that Claghan march. We went right up the whole length of Lockhart Road to Kitchener Place and do you know I think it's the first time in my life I ever stood in a Protestant part of Claghan! Nobody took a bite out of me all the same and a lot of women of all ages came out of their houses to join the march, even from houses where they had big pictures of King Billy painted on the gables. They're not one bit different from ourselves when all's said and done and I suppose they're as fed up with violence as anyone on our side. It wasn't the ordinary people started this nonsense and please God if we all get together we can stop it.

Kathleen and her mother were on the march with us and they had Sarah with them. She's not a very friendly sort of a child is she, though I suppose at her age she's not too keen on hanging around with a crowd of old women. Phyllis Campbell led the Catholic contingent and Mrs McLeod and her mother-in-law were on the other side, so at least you can say your friends and enemies were all there even if you weren't yourself. It's an awful pity the way you cut yourself off from Claghan and there's no call for it, you're as well thought of as anyone else whatever ideas you have in your head! Anyhow, they all kissed each other on both cheeks up on the platform when we reached the centre of the town. The rest of us didn't bother with the kissing and hugging but there was a lot of friendly talk between the two sides all the same. I hope some good comes out of it. They say Nuala McCormack is taking good note of all the Catholic women goes on the march and that she intends to put pressure on us to stop it. The McCormacks is big heroes now since the bombing so I suppose there'll be plenty to listen to her. Whether or not, I have my plans made to be on the next march. Mrs McLeod was saying she's going to try and get Mairead Corrigan or Betty Williams to come and address the meeting next time.

The hot weather's continuing. Your daddy says that's why the violence has stopped, everyone's feeling too lazy to bother and a crowd of women marching has nothing to do with it. I hope he's wrong. I be threatening him I'll join Women's Lib next and then he'll see what effect women have!

You were talking about Dorset and all the people living off the land and weaving and baking bread. Well, I'm afraid the old-fashioned ways are not coming back round here, in fact as long as England sends over her dole and supplementary benefit nobody wants to work at anything. It is disgusting to go in round Canon McGinty Park and find a lot of loafers (girls as well as boys) lying around on the grass enjoying the sun. It's nearly too much to expect them to walk to the post office to collect their money. How long will this last, I wonder? And they're the very same crowd that's the loudest condemning England and standing up for the Provisionals and complaining about Catholics being denied work. Brendan was saying if he offered the likes of them a job when they went in to sign they'd think they were being insulted. I be telling him he's lucky not to be posted to Claghan dole office because he'd be making a lot of enemies. Not indeed that he'd have a lot of work to offer them, there's nothing at all here now, only it looks so immoral seeing them just lying about like that from morning to night. I hear there's a lot of dirty carry-on among the young people these days, things you wouldn't hear tell of a few years ago, not in Ireland anyway . . .

CHAPTER FORTY-ONE

Eric

The Laurels, Claghan, 31 December 1977, Your Excellency, I am deeply concerned . . . Though why bother to reread it? Read one you've read them all. He folded up the pages of polite protest, addressed a copy to the President, another to his ambassador in London. Now if you were let tell the bastards what you really thought of them . . . Eric had an instant's vision of someone like Amin Dada wiping his big fat arse with *Your Excellency I am deeply concerned*, and in the momentary awareness he saw once again his own youth sneering at him, cursing him, shoving two fingers up in his middle-aged liberal's face. Nearly thirty-seven years old, longish blonde hair slightly thinner these days but still the best-looking guy in the Parent-Teacher group, the Amnesty group, the People for Peace group. Not bad either in the staffroom at Claghan High in his khaki cords and Peruvian sweater, certainly not relegated to Old Fogies' Corner with paunch and pipe. Not yet. Not as far as he knew. But he remembered being seventeen. Being eighteen. Twenty-one. And now he was thirty-six. As we get older we do not get any younger. Will you still need me, will you still feed me . . .

And what did *you* do, Daddy, while Northern Ireland was falling to bits in everybody's hand? You what? You wrote letters? You mean you sat there and wrote polite letters to foreign generals asking them to be nice to their prisoners? Big fucking deal, Daddy! But what if his children were not as he had been? What if they asked no questions, screamed no angers, waved no banners of hate or of love? If at seventeen they would demand only a nice decent job, a nice decent home, a good solid marriage? What *you've* achieved, sonny boy, what their daddy's achieved. Dave would say. Did say. That's the direction they seemed to be heading, all three of them, and was it any wonder? Growing up within earshot of bombs weren't they very unlikely to see revolution as the answer to anything? They were not likely even to see action of any kind as an answer: over the years hadn't they witnessed plenty of well-intentioned actions wither to nothing in front of them?

And another due to wither shortly. Myrna was fed up now with the Peace Women. His mother and a few old stalwarts still kept soldiering on but that wouldn't last long. What had they been expecting, miracles? Superwomen? "That Corrigan girl's nothing only a silly wee typist," Myrna said after the Nobel interviews. "A fur coat! Isn't it just typical of the mentality!" Eric imagined the girl had been joking. He knew perfectly well she had. It was exactly the kind of thing he could picture himself saying if he was in her place: yet another stupid berk of a reporter shoves a mike in your face, now won't you tell all our nice viewers how you intend to spend your twenty thousand pounds Nobel Prize money? Well, like I wouldn't mind a fur coat! Tongue in your cheek, what the shite do they *think* I intend to do with it, hand it to Ian Paisley to buy guns? And the media *naturally* too thick to catch on. But Myrna claimed that someone in Mairead Corrigan's position had no right to joke. Joan of Arc didn't joke. Che Guevara didn't joke. Ghandhi didn't joke. Jesus

Christ was no great hand at the one-line gag. And for that matter the IRA didn't joke or the UVF either. Nobody *follows* people who make silly jokes, that was Myrna's reasoning. So it looked as if the Peace Movement was finished in Claghan. Oh, a few middle-aged women still kept vigil with lighted candles after every murder but that . . . That. Our feebleness. The best lack all conviction, as the man said. As Yeats said. And yet.

He recalled the passionate intensity of his youth. If there had at that time been any leader he could have borne to follow, if Ulster had taken a different direction. What else could he have done with his life the way things turned out? He was no believer in sectarian violence. He had hoped once, he had firmly *believed* once, that the two sides would get together and send everything flying. Send Clifford Lewis and John Joe McCormack spinning towards the stars. When that didn't happen he had been delighted, in the mid-Sixties, with the Prime Minister's gentle tiptoeing in the direction of reform. Civil rights for Roman Catholics slipped in like a dose of Guinness in the Bushmills and even the hardliners would have swallowed it down before they noticed. He still believed Terence O'Neill was the last good thing to have happened in Ulster. If he hadn't let himself be intimidated by a shower of thugs. If Paisley had not existed at that precise moment. If Reverend Clyde had never come to Claghan. If that young boy had not been murdered, starting a whole chain of sectarian hates. Yes, but how far back had you to go before you stopped iffing? If George McLeod had not been murdered a hundred and fifty years ago, if that girl hadn't let herself be screwed in the woods by a Roman Catholic jockey, if the potatoes had not failed, if the priests had been more enlightened, if the schools hadn't been segregated, if Daniel O'Connell hadn't let himself be intimidated like O'Neill, if nobody had ever dreamed up the Penal Laws or the Act of Union, if King Billy had lost the battle of the Boyne, if old

Cromwell hadn't been such a thick vicious bastard . . . If we hadn't fucking well come over here in the first place!

He thought of dusty barefoot roads, of palm trees, of crossing India in a cattle train, of being at one with the populations of the earth. Claghan had missed out on that lovely lotus-eating decade that might have dragged it out of its dark obsessions. He'd missed out on it himself. Funny that of all the people he knew Ian Lewis should have been the one to trek to Katmandu and Israel and Afghanistan, that Ian, of all the dirty-minded bigoted capitalist sods when they were at school together, should now be living penniless and celibate in an ashram in Amsterdam, genuflecting about twenty times a day among clouds of incense in front of a photo of some fat guru. His occasional letter, full of peace and love and satsun, that may have flowed sincerely out of his mind OK but that when you read them in a Claghan suburb sounded like a right load of old balls. It was going down to the American hippies in Quarry Street trying to score his fill of easy lays that got him hooked on gurus. Only for me, Eric thought, those hippies wouldn't have been in Quarry Street, those cottages wouldn't have existed. I was busy saving those cottages, he thought, while Dave and all the others were out marching for civil rights for the people who had to live for generations in cottages like that. I was somewhere on the outskirts of reality. That's when old Dave dropped me, and Nuala McCormack dropped me, and even Maureen Murphy, who you wouldn't think cared, cooled off a bit too, withered down to a Christmas card.

I took the wrong turning, he thought, I should never have got married. I should have gone hitching barefoot down the dusty roads while I had a chance. But then Myrna twelve or thirteen years ago, calm and cool and virginal, seemed to incarnate the dusty roads and the blue horizons and the search for wisdom and truth . . . Seemed all set to go marching off along the world's highways. We shouldn't have had children, he thought, that's where the mistake was. Because once you had children you were stuck, you were forced to place *them* in front of everything else. You couldn't very well ruin the stability of their lives, carting them round the world in rucksacks. It was unthinkable to let life damage them in any way you could prevent. Or so it had seemed at the time. Now he wondered. Wouldn't it maybe have been far better to have involved them in reality from the beginning instead of creating this lying nursery world of unfailing affection and reason and justice: what favour had they actually been doing the kids? Weren't he and Myrna just prolonging smug middle-class Protestant banality into yet another generation? Should he have sent the kids to St Ronan's then? Well yes, he should have, with his ideas that's exactly what he should have done. Maybe not St Ronan's, there were other schools, all Roman Catholics didn't live in the slums. But he should have done that, should have pointed the way. Taken one big brave step towards equality. Towards peace on earth, good will to men . . .

But with the best will in the world (and God knows he and Myrna were all for integration) you couldn't put three innocent lives in danger for the sake of a principle. Could you? OK, maybe it was wrong to overprotect them, but how could you know for sure? There was no way you could know unless you singled out one of your kids and had it reared differently from the word go, deliberately rubbed its nose in the shit and compared how it turned out. You'd have to be crazy to do a thing like that. Away back in the Sixties, when Elizabeth was born, he and Myrna had decided that the only way to change the world was to start in your own home and your own town. You started by letting your children grow up in an enlightened liberal atmosphere where every slightest potential was given its chance to develop. You kept up an honest meaningful dialogue with them at all times, you carried that honest liberalism into the school where you worked and the community you lived in. In a place like Claghan you built bridges across the centuries-old abyss.

So why did none of it work? Why were Liz and Carol and Bryan just as whining and conventional and spoiled as any other kids in the street? As for his teaching. Why had not even *one* of his past pupils manifested him or her self at any time in the past eleven years to spread a little of that so-called enlightenment through Northern Ireland? Why did the bridges just rust away? Did they build them in the wrong places? Or had they used the wrong materials? Last Easter he and Myrna marched down Quarry Street with the Peace People and as they passed the five cottages he listened to a group of Catholic women behind him saying God wouldn't you think the council would have pulled down them oul' shacks years ago and if God hasn't said it some poor passer-by will get killed, they're ready to tumble, but sure what does them Orange blackguards in the council care what happens in Quarry Street? He fell back into step along with them and tried to explain the significance of the cottages in Claghan's history. He knew far more about Claghan's history than they did—they hadn't been aware that those cottages dated back to the end of the eighteenth century, that the slate quarry behind them had been used to provide relief work in one famine after another, that in the Great Famine many of the workers had been so weak with hunger and disease that they'd fallen dead on the spot, that the town hero, Cormac O'Flaherty, had lived there for a time in the last of the five houses. He'd explained that the houses were all that remained of the original shanty settlement that grew up on the outskirts of Claghan to house evicted families in the bad old days of landlordism. The women had listened with smiling courtesy because smiling courtesy was the banner under which they were all marching, Catholic and Protestant, through the back streets of Claghan in 1977 to protest about a sectarian war that might never have begun if famished workmen had not been allowed to fall dead over their picks and shovels quarrying unnecessary slate to earn a few pennies to tide their families over an unnecessary famine.

He stayed beside the women as the procession moved out of Quarry Street and into Lockhart Road, and he pointed out the long high wall that also dated back to the famine and that had been built by starving men and women to separate the estate of the Earl of Baudry from that of the McLeod family. The wall had not been any more necessary than the slate that came out of the quarry but the Earl's agent held the old Victorian belief that it was immoral to hand out money to the poor without making them earn it. Eric recalled how he'd got quite carried away telling the story, repeatedly lashing his conscience with "*my* ancestors and *yours*, Mrs O'Hanlon!" But he recalled too how uninterested they had been behind their courteous smiles. They had no awareness of Irish history except as a series of emotive key-words: famine, Cromwell, landlords, evictions, tyranny. They'd heard about Cormac O'Flaherty because of Cuchulain McCool's hit record, but for all they knew he was a contemporary of the Black and Tans or King Billy, or even of the original Cuchulain.

The Save Quarry Street campaign had been a total failure. Far from bringing the two communities together to drool over their common heritage, the preservation of five historic buildings for the people of Claghan was perceived as another example of Protestant indifference to the welfare and safety of the town's Catholic minority. And wasn't it? Wasn't that all it was? Had he or Myrna ever tried to imagine how humiliating it must have been, trying to bring up a large family and keep them clean and warm and decent in one of those houses? As for heritage! Those cottages didn't in any way express the tastes or culture of a people: they expressed only the squalor that had been forced upon the conquered natives of a British colony. Rehoused or not, the inhabitants of Quarry Street would certainly prefer to forget the cottages ever existed: they

didn't give a shit about historic stones but were totally obsessed
with historic injustices. And could one blame them? He deeply
regretted not having gone on any of the civil rights marches
years ago. At first he hadn't taken the movement seriously,
he'd seen it as a frivolous attempt by Dave and Nuala
McCormack to ape the Martin Luther King business. After all
how could Roman Catholics expect anyone to believe that
their grievances were on a par with those of American or
South African blacks? They had grievances OK sure—well
there was plenty of job discrimination about—but compared
with what was happening elsewhere Ulster's RCs were in
clover. You only had to look at Nuala herself. And her friend
Kathleen had seemed a good example too, stinking with
boring old middle-class notions and not letting anyone forget
she'd been to a snooty old private boarding-school. The worst
sort of petit-bourgeois phoniness. It came as a considerable
shock, that's the only way he could put it—no, he thought,
let's be honest Jesus he was knocked fucking sideways, when
he heard the same Catholic women on the march saying that
house there is where the poor O'Flahertys was moved out of
and did you see the Kathleen one home on her holidays from
London with the daughter? So apparently there had been
nothing petit-bourgeois about Kathleen's background at all,
she *didn't* come from the top end, the "good" end of Quarry
Street, as she'd led him to believe, but from one of the little
grimy cottages along the old slate quarry, and *why* hadn't he
ever been interested enough to enquire about the families
who were moved out of the cottages? *Why* had a heap of
stones covered with thatch or slates meant more to him than
the people who'd lived their lives among those stones? He
hadn't even known the names of the people who'd moved
out of his museum. He'd just put a plaque on the wall:
Cormac and Marianne O'Flaherty lived here 1845-1847. (All
around the plaque now, he'd noticed, were obscene scribblings
and limericks about what Cormac and Marianne got up to in

the cottage. He didn't really care.) But *Kathleen* had lived there.

O'Flahertys must always have lived there and he hadn't even known. If he'd ever had the courage to walk her home or see her during the holidays he'd have known the middle-class background was all put on to impress him, Christ, the stupid bloody bitch, what a phoney, what a pseud! No wonder nobody had ever taken RCs seriously, when they were cringing away ashamed of their heritage one minute and singing their drunken bumptious songs about it the next. Why couldn't they wear their oppression with a bit of dignity like other races; then they might never have been driven to violence! There's nothing turns you off like an inferiority complex, that's what was wrong with Kathleen, must have been what made her so empty, a lovely big earthy woman to look at but when you tried to get behind the window-dressing, Christ, nothing. A flimsy lace curtain drawn across an empty room. He remembered saying that at the time, he recalled being proud of finding the ideal description of her. But. A flimsy lace curtain drawn across a thick black shutter maybe? And behind the shutter what chaos? What pain, what ugliness, what deep shame? You could never get through to them. They hid their minds away from you, hid their wounds till they festered, then shoved them up under your nose for vengeance. He compared her with Dave Jenks: look at Dave; same background only with the courage to wave his poverty like an angry red flag. Yes but then. For one Dave, how many Lockhart Road Protestants were there hiding away as bad as Kathleen, hiding behind the wee geranium in the window and the Orange sash and the bowler hat and voting Unionist and half-starving themselves to throw big boastful fivers into Abe Clyde's collection-box and pretending like mad they had something in common with the Clifford Lewises and the Grand Masters and the Harry Hales and the.

Yes but Kathleen. If he'd had a bit of courage that time

he'd have brought Kathleen to The Laurels and introduced her first go-off instead of making a big shameful secret of her with his parents as if she was a scrubber (was that a wound too, to be hidden away behind lace curtain and black shutter?) and he'd have gone to Quarry Street and probably preached revolution, the way he used to, to her poor old father, and the two families would have been forced to recognise the connection between them whether they liked it or not. It would have been all out in the open, Christ, they *were* related; they were the same race after all, the same tribe! Talk about building bridges! He'd missed his chance to build that one all right. But then, when he thought about it, there was no way he could have brought Kathleen to his home without deeply insulting his mother and father. And from the few hints she let drop about her own father he'd have been booted out of Quarry Street far quicker than he came into it. If he was lucky . . . Yes indeed, if he was lucky—the whole world knew what happened to Protestant fellows who went courting down Quarry Street in the Sixties! Don't dramatise, that was ordinary street violence those two murders, hooligans teds mods rockers what-have-you, only it got twisted and manipulated until. No, but there was *no* way, he thought, that he could have gone on a civil rights march that time without landing his poor Uncle Harry (who was one sleazy bastard but still and all married to Aunty Margaret) in the shit with the Orange Lodge and a general election coming up. And to bring Kathleen home he'd have had to be a fairly crass determined sort of person like, say, Ian Lewis or even Dave. He could imagine either of those two, if they fancied a girl, just shoving her up in their parents' faces and to hell with it, it was *their* life, wasn't it? Yeah, he could imagine. But. A guy like Dave or like Ian would never have started chatting up a girl at a party just because he'd fallen in love with the idea of her years before he met her. Before he *really* met her, because he didn't count that time Maureen brought her to the club, he'd hardly got a chance to notice her except vaguely. Though wasn't it that "vaguely," that vague impression of a healthy big earthy peasant girl that made him start rereading Marianne McLeod's diary? And wasn't it the diary that made him fall in love with the rightness of such a love affair, such a denial of his parents' narrow Ulster Protestantism? Kathleen was Ireland, the holy land of Ireland. And I was Marianne, he thought.

Jesus, I had myself cast as that poor man's Jane Austen. Papa Freud would have something to say about that! But why do I try to desecrate everything, why am I sneering? Is this being middle-aged? I was OK then, he thought sadly. I was new and clean and pure, reading that diary, seeing myself as some fantastic rebel riding off into the sunset with a tough sexy peasant. I was alive then. Only Kathleen wouldn't play. Kathleen refused to see herself as a tough sexy peasant. So there were no outraged parents, no hardship, no famine, no martyr's death. Just Eric, hitting forty before too long, sitting at a mahogany desk where his father sat before him, killing the time before a dinner-party with a bottle of J&B not too far away, typing nice polite letters to a shower of foreign thugs. And to crown it all, that pretentious prick from the Claghan museum was refusing his offer of Marianne's diary. Most probably not authentic, the little shit told him, most probably written years afterwards. By some joker of a great-uncle round the turn of the century, it seemed, an old Charles McLeod whose sins had always been just on the point of catching up with him. Old boy who'd died scandalously in Capri. Yeah, Eric had heard of him all right, but he didn't believe a word about the bastard forging a young girl's journal, I mean why *bother*? He'd have had to be nuts. Maybe he was and all.

Fuck the past anyway. If I'd married Kathleen, he thought, I might have had a martyr's death all right. Some of her crowd might probably have put a bullet in me. It happened. Oh, several times it happened. Were there any mixed couples

still living in Claghan, and if there were, what sort of a life
had they? Had their kids? He had an instant's appalled vision
of Claghan, of Ulster, of Ireland, after an IRA victory: a fascist
military dictatorship, a fashionable lost cause for well-heeled
outsiders. Nice middle-class people all over the world working
their way down the whiskey bottle on New Year's Eve while
they wrote letters of polite helplessness to the faceless mindless
Provo leaders. No, it worked out far better the way he went
off Kathleen that winter stuck in Claghan with nothing in his
vision only Myrna's guitar and Myrna's long straight hair and
Myrna's cool clear eyes full of wisdom and truth . . . He
wondered who Kathleen got married to, what sort of a guy.
He was glad she was settled down anyway and with a daughter.
He wondered if she'd ever done anything interesting with her
life, if she'd ever travelled or anything, or if she'd just drifted
into some nice safe marriage in a ghetto, a semi-detached in
Kilburn or someplace. There was no one he could decently
ask, and when it came down to it, he wasn't all that interested
in asking. He hadn't been all that interested at the time either
when he rang up and the Lily one said she was away to
England this five or six weeks, gone away to the airport in
a car with one of the blacks. Lily didn't know which black,
said she could never tell the difference between them. So he
asked Lily out for a drink and they ended up in Maxims at
the Civil Servants' dance of all things and he took her upstairs
to the bar and poured rum and coke down her and she kept
asking him if after all that time with Kathleen he never thought
of turning Catholic. And to show her exactly what he thought
of Kathleen and the Pope he started singing we'll kick ten
thousand papishes right over Dolly's Brae, and Lily tried to
drown him out with 'Faith of Our Fathers' and then a wee
bouncer with a face like a coffin came up and threw them
out. He tried to screw Lily up an alley behind the City Hall
but rum or no rum she was intent on hanging on to it—
typical bloody Taig saving it up—so he left her back at

Fitzroy Avenue and went and hung around Amelia Street, wishing to Christ he was in Soho or someplace, realising that all the fairy-tales he'd always believed about Amelia Street being full of brothels were a load of old cobblers and if holy puritan Belfast had a red-light district he wasn't about to find it that night and the sooner he and Myrna got married the better before he started growing hair on the palms of his hands and that bloody bitch Kathleen running out on him, Jesus, Jesus, with some black, Jesus, and in the end he went and banged on Nuala McCormack's door and she poured a bottle of whiskey down him till he passed out on the sofa before he could even get a grope, crafty bitch but at least civilised about it not like the Lily one, you take your dirty Protestant hand out of there, boyo, or I'll screech for a policeman.

Nearly fourteen years ago. He saw Paul at a party once and asked about Kathleen but Paul didn't know where she was, just London, no actually she never wrote, never got in touch, too bad old chap, and turned back to the long cold blonde he was chatting to. Where was Paul now? Dead in the Biafran war? For all he knew, the bastard was at the head of one of those African juntas, they used to say round Queen's his people were millionaires. He imagined the pampered ironic eyes skimming over *Your Excellency I am deeply concerned* and alighting with an amused eyebrow on *Yours sincerely Eric McLeod.* Except that Paul, unless he'd evolved beyond all recognition, would never dream of reading to the boring end of a letter of boring concern from a boring stranger. That was the problem: when you translated the possibly-open-to-persuasion faceless head of government into somebody like Paul Achebe you did, you had to, what else could you fucking do only, become aware of the total hopelessness of trying. Except that in fourteen years or so people did often evolve beyond recognition. Himself. Oh Christ, himself. Happy with his wife, three nice kids, good job with a pension, nice house well outside the barricades. And whose life *wasn't* full of frustrations? Who ever did travel in one pure clean straight line from eighteen to thirty-six to sixty to the grave? Ian Paisley, he thought. Probably the Reverend Ian's the only man in Ulster that can look back over his life and see it opening out nicely from the beginning, like a bloody bud opening into a bloodier flower, nourished on the compost of all the corpses from the battle of the Boyne on down through Cormac O'Flaherty and George McLeod and evicted peasants rotting on their feet from hunger, right down to Clifford Lewis's machine-minders and John Joe McCormack's chambermaids spinning in a thousand pieces towards the stars . . .

Who in their senses, he thought, could regret standing aside from the mess that's been Claghan's history, and Ireland's, and the world's? *Votre Excellence je suis navré . . . Mi general estoy muerto de pena . . . Dear Paul it has been brought to my notice . . . Oh has it old chap, and what do you suggest I do about it, eh?* Letters of courteous concern to Pinochet and Mobuto and Paul Achebe and the Shah of Iran and Mr Botha and the Emperor Bokassa and Hitler and the Red Queen and Cayo Bermudez and the Enormous Crocodile and . . .

"Happy New Year to the human race," said Eric raising his glass as Myrna put her head round the door.

"Oh, *Eric*, you're going to be reeling again by dinnertime! What are you doing, sulking in here by yourself? Your Aunt Margaret's just arrived, and Uncle Harry. Come and get them a drink at least, while I see about the vegetables."

On New Year's morning, 1978, Harry Hale, Unionist MP, slid in behind the steering wheel of his car, tooted impatiently on the horn to hurry his wife, switched on the ignition, and lived through one last, eternal instant of disintegration.

The Hales' daily woman, Mrs Brigid O'Hanlon, had stopped

as usual to leave her bicycle in the garage. She took the full force of the explosion along with him.

Bricks, glass, metal and pieces of human flesh were scattered about the yard, orchard and paddock. The dwelling-house was badly damaged. Margaret Hale, her daughter Judith and Judith's husband were all seriously injured.

The Provisional IRA claimed responsibility for the execution of Mr Hale, and offered sympathy and sincere apologies to the widower and five young children of their second, accidental, victim—adding, however, that Mrs O'Hanlon could quite easily have found work elsewhere than in the home of a known enemy of the people. Mr O'Hanlon, who in the past eight years had been unable to find work anywhere in Claghan, pondered the naïvety of this comment but, in the circumstances, thought it better not to contest it.

It proved impossible to separate the two bodies completely, so that minute parts of Harry Hale were buried with full Catholic rites in St Ronan's graveyard, while similarly small pieces of Brigid O'Hanlon made their way, unremarked, into the Hale plot in the Protestant cemetery. This was the only contact between the two communities in Claghan that year. The Peace Marches were not resumed. Friendships made across the barricades in seventy-six and seventy-seven were discreetly allowed to fade.

Harry Hale's was the first of several executions. "Things got shocking bad altogether this year," Mrs Murphy wrote to Maureen the following Christmas, "I think poor old Claghan's away in the head this last while!" To illustrate her point, she enclosed Rev Abe Clyde's two latest pamphlets: *The Return of the Borgias*, inspired by the deaths, in suspiciously close succession, of two Popes of Rome, and *Red Smoke Over Babylon*, which rejoiced at the election of a communist from behind the Iron Curtain to the papal throne—an event which, in Mr Clyde's opinion, would go far towards weakening the power of Rome throughout the world and lead eventually to the total annihilation of the Scarlet Whore. He seemed only slightly confounded when, some months later, the Whore's vicar seemed to be on the point of coming to confront him on his own ground. "If yon boyo sets foot in Claghan," he thundered in a television interview, "troth and he won't be kissin' the ground, he'll be bitin' the dust!"

CHAPTER FORTY-TWO

LETTERS FROM BOHARNAMUC
(1981)

10 January 1981

M y dear Maureen,
. . . and we heard from the Yank O'Flahertys as usual at
Christmas. Cormac is stationed in some part of Central
America now. He is a military adviser, giving instructions
to the army of that country, tactics he learned in Vietnam
I suppose. Isn't it great how well he got on? It seems
there's a lot of communism there all the farm labourers
wanting to take the big estates away from the landlords
and divide them up into small farms. Honest to God,
people seems to be going mad everywhere these days,
nobody's contented with what they have. Wasn't the world
far better off long ago when ordinary people had a bit of
respect for authority? 'Deed and I'd like to say that to your
friends the McLeods. They're going mad round Claghan
lately with petitions to be signed for these red Indians or
whatever they are. Of course nobody's paying them a bit
of heed, have the people of Claghan not troubles enough
of their own? No, but it's a shame Maureen now I hope
you won't be misguided enough to sign anything they

413

send you. The Yanks said in their letter that even some of the priests and bishops out there is turning communist and encouraging the workers to go on strikes and marches and join co-operatives—I'm thinking they could do with a visit from His Holiness. Joanne and Tommy are worried about Cormac but of course very proud of him too and he's as well out there as over in Iran or someplace, that's another wild spot. Tommy himself is kept very busy collecting funds for the families of IRA prisoners. It seems a lot of them are very badly off with the wage-earner sometimes in jail for years. Noraid is the name of his organisation, maybe you'd like to send them a wee donation sometime? Isn't it great the way they keep in touch with their homeland the whole time. No mad Yankee nonsense about them. He's talking of visiting Ireland soon to organise meetings . . .

1 June 1981

My dear Maureen,

Well what will you surprise us with next? I don't blame you for wanting to leave England. It must be a very depressing place to live in this minute with unemployment and strikes and rioting. The time was you could have looked for a place round home but I wouldn't advise it these days, much as we'd love to have you both near at hand. Times are very upset here this year with all the protest marches and hold-ups, not to mention the hunger-strike. Isn't it the awfullest thing? I was never a supporter of the IRA but when you see how that bitch sat there and let that poor young lad die, has she no nature in her at all? And if God hasn't said it she'll let them all die sooner nor give in. No wonder the English is called bulldogs, no harm to Trevor but they're a thick-witted race and too stupid even to realise that all they're doing is recruiting for the IRA the way they're behaving. I'd join it myself now if I was a bit younger and your daddy the same.

I see Sally O'Flaherty is away back to England. Did she get a job? She stayed a brave while with the granny this time but according to your Aunty Agnes the chief attraction was some wild crowd of youngsters she got in with. She was seen out round the country with them the time of Bobby Sands's funeral protesting and shouting slogans and painting on the road and it seems she was in and out to McCormack's lounge bar and her not eighteen yet. Poor Lizzie has no idea what she be's up to and won't hear a word against her. It's Kathleen I blame, has she no control over her at all?

Well, I hope you find the sort of house you're looking for and that you don't have to pay a fortune. Anyway you'll have a good holiday going round all the French estate agents.

Love from Mammy and Daddy.

P.S. I tore this bit out of *The Irish Times*. Would it be of any interest to you?

Going For a Chanson

. . . and prices are surprisingly reasonable. Due partly to *la Crise* and partly to the continuing trend towards the more-easily-run restored farmhouse as *residence secondaire*, there are several bargains to be found in bigger properties, especially those which, through unsuitability of size or location, are not likely to be snapped up for institutional use.

One such 'find' is the very interesting Château de Lapire-Vacherie, a late-seventeenth-century gentleman's residence set in eight acres of parkland on the outskirts of an unspoiled Breton village. The house itself needs much restoration work, as all but one wing has been shut up for many years;

but the structure itself is sound and the roofs have been maintained in good condition. A suite of eight rooms has been partially restored and is suitable for immediate occupation.

The château has an interesting Irish connection in that the nineteenth-century Earl of Baudry, a notorious absentee landlord who owned a large tract of south-east Ulster, was married to a member of the Lapire-Vacherie family and lived there for many years.

The present owner, Mme Antoinette de Lapire-Vacherie, is anxious for a quick sale and will consider offers in the region of eighty thousand pounds—a near-incredible price for anyone used to the exorbitance of the Dublin property market!

CHAPTER FORTY-THREE

SARAH (1)

Horse-hoofs skittered and slid, pawing the iced forecourt. Sarah sat on top with her stirrups too short, nose whipped stiff with the cold, eyes sore and watery, every inch of her dragged up tight with sleep and nervous boredom. Riding-school dream translates to reality, she couldn't even laugh—no one to bleedin' laugh with. If Aitch-Pee, fed up as she was herself with hanging about, took a notion to belt away down the dawn road with its half-awake motorists, juggernauts coming from the ferry with their all-night-in-the-bar slobs of drivers, or even empty, an empty skidding road with a bolting racehorse—where would *she* be? With her leathers tightened up foolhardy, thinks she's Piggott where would *she* be on a bolting racehorse?

He kept moving. She could feel him moving away seventeen hands down, half a mile down, muscles and sinews and long splinters of legs so smashable. And how, even if she herself survived the head-first scrunch on to the tarmac, how could she face old Gotherby, Aitch Pee put down, and how could she face his owner, how could she face the dishy millionaire? All her own fault, no proper experience, and back you go to

Ye Olde Jobbe Shoppe, a nice clerical? You must be joking, miss, you and three million more. Daft nonsense but Sean the old sod was making a right meal of it this time chatting up the woman in the smokes kiosk looking down her dress. At seven in the morning, I ask you! Make you want to throw up, thinks he's a bleedin' cowboy. Aitch Pee sliding and slithering and little Tony beside her snooty and silent up on Daddy's Boy daydreaming or stoned. The fool!—at this hour of the, miles away, oh come on, come *on* . . .

"Feelin' a wee bit yalla were ye, luv?" Sean turned Irish Rover towards home. She fell in behind him; he turned round in the saddle and called: "Fancy a nice bitta gallop up the grass verge then, Tony?" Her insides turned to a pool of sick ice. A gallop, is he mad? You never galloped out on road-work, nice gentle trot, that's all the reason they trusted *her* out on a millionaire's investment, couldn't go wrong with a nice gentle trot. Tony's half-witted wink and giggle. Having her on, the sods! What did they think she was, some bimbo? The sick ice melted, flooded her, turned to a tidal wave of rage. What do you think, bastards, what do you think I? She gathered herself into a crouch, kicked Aitch Pee, kicked again, swerved him astonished out round Irish Rover. All those lessons in Richmond Park long ago. Thought you were great, didn't you, up on riding-school ponies. Well look at you now thanks to bleedin' Trev and Maureen. Talk about having your bluff called! You'll break your neck, you'll damage their horses, you'll never stick it, Sal. Going to get the sack, nearly had him in the ditch, that'll learn him; and away up the grass verge crouching, clinging, praying . . .

She waited for them at the foot of the avenue. Sean was white. He would be. His fault, his responsibility, head-lad and everything. "Effin' bitch, you won't last five minutes when I report this lot. Better start packin' yer kit."

"Ah sod off, who'd believe you? Said we had to gallop, heard you saying it. Tony heard you and all, right Tone me old love? Tony's too dopy to tell a lie, right Tone?"

"Friggin' whore, you don't watch it you'll finish up with a knife in your back you will."

She unsaddled Aitch Pee, handed him to Tony and marched off to dump the tack. Tony the daddy's boy looked after her with the respect you give a suicide, poor cow, you don't threaten Sean. Sean'll keep it in for you. Sean'll do you for this. Eff Sean! She was going down home to London tomorrow and if she felt like it she needn't come back. Eff the lot of them, horses and all. She didn't owe them anything, did she! Hip-hip-hooray! She leaped up, grabbed hold of a saddle hanging on its hook, swung herself backwards and forwards: I'm gonna be, I'm gonna be . . . Whatja gonna be? Gonna be a jet-set beauty. Punk star with purple hair. Urban guerrilla pom-pom-pom and up the lot of you! Homesickness went through her like pain, homesickness for Claghan, for the crowd. For Malachy Ó'Lorcáin. What am I doing here? Why don't I just go back to Claghan? I can always go back to Claghan. That's where my home is, not London . . . Ah go in and get your breakfast, you daft cow.

Dead casual in khaki cords and out at the elbow chatting up Mrs Jay beside the Aga (poor old hag like a beetroot, her perm all steamed up) this hunk noticed Sarah coming in and waved the teapot: "I've made you a nice cuppa cha m'dear," in inverted commas lowering himself to her level like. "Shall I be mum?" Big ballsy Porsche waiting outside to roar him down to London to spend the day broking stocks or whatever but first this simple country lad needs his uninhibited canter before breakfasting with innocent simplicity (stew up your own tea!) in his trainer's kitchen. Shame there are no photographers about, she thought, and wouldn't you think if he can afford cashmere he could pay someone to darn his elbows? All the same . . .

"Wouldn't say no to a slice of that," watching him lope away across the yard.

"He wouldn't give you a tumble, my girl, 'e only takes out Sloane Rangers, dintja read it in Nigel Dempster? So where does that leave you?"

"Oh Mrs Jay, Mrs Jay with your nice cuppa tay, not jealous are we? Or is that a hot flush?"

"Cheek! Eh what did you do on our Sean? Face on him like a boot just now. Oh and before I forget, the missus wants you in the house this morning."

"Ah no, none of that lark, I'm cleaning tack today, she can take a running jump." Nice and homely in the tack-room, couple of beers, smokes, daydream, chat up poor Tony for want of something better. "She think I'm a maid or what? Bleedin' middle ages."

"Willing to help out occasionally in topsy-turvy manor-house, that's what it said in the ad. Just the kindness of their 'earts I reckon, leaving you to piddle around in the yard all this time. Just because your dad used to know the missus . . . "

"Old Trev's not my *dad*, thank you very much! Yeah. We're all a bit mad here, it said. Thought it was, you know, a joke, one of them jokey ads, Curr-i-ist, I never thought it was for real! Oh gawd, here we go again. Forgot the effin' colts."

Two by two she led the colts down to the meadow. They breathed warm steam on her, bumbled their long silly jaws against her face, snuffled and slobbered among her hair, they were delicate and awkward and lovely. I wanna be, I wanna be . . . Wanna stay here forever walking colts to the meadow. She slipped their halters inside the gate; they stood still for an instant, then were off with graceless grace over the crisp iced grass, blowing steam, whinnying, throwing back their heads to bite on great freezing mouthfuls of liberty.

The missus was in the drawing-room in a Jaeger dressing-gown, puff-eyed, playing Beatles records, crying. Scrapbooks and photo albums on the floor, ashtrays overflowing on the dirty Chinese carpet, right old mess. Boozy cow, flamin' cheek and all, what does she think dragging help in out of the yard, where does she think her old man gets his loot then? "Sarah, oh Sarah, please come and talk to me, I'm so lonely, there's no one to talk to in this dump. I'm not a rural person, Sarah, these yokels! Nothing but English yokels, Sarah, I can't bear it. All these years and I've tried and I've tried and I can't bear it. What goes on in their minds, Sarah? Have they minds, Sarah? In Connemara as a child I ran wild among the peasants, they were alive, Sarah, but these . . . "

Oh gawd, here we go again. Picture yourself on a boat on a river and blah blah blah. "What's become of me, Sarah, where have I gone to? We were the beautiful people. We mattered, Sarah. A great big party, the whole world was just one super big party. You're too young, Sarah, you missed all that, *how* can I describe it? Oh God, Sarah, where have they all gone?" All the lonely people, all the lonely people, calm her down and get out of here quick. Potty, bleedin' potty. "Yes, I know, Mrs Gotherby, it must be awful for you stuck here in the wilds after London. Mum and Maureen used to tell me and all. Bet it was fantastic London them times when you were all. Tell us about it Mrs Gotherby, what did you used to do when you were young in London?"

"*Do*, Sarah, *do*? We lived, we were real, wasn't that quite enough? We stood for something. We were the spirit of an age, Sarah. Can you understand that, can you? Everything was happening then. Beauty and love and flowers, Sarah, flowers everywhere. London was one vast garden, Sarah, look." Photos and more photos and magazine cuttings. Old-fashioned blokes with long hair got up like gays in frilly shirts, girls in wigs and minis and high white boots, Mrs G serving in one of Trev's boutiques ("Just a fun thing, Sarah, just for a giggle."), wrapped in about ten feather boas drinking in nightclubs. "Sybilla's! Annabel's! What's become of that girl, Sarah? What's become of me?"

You married an old slob for his money, that's what. Only

she couldn't bring herself to say it, Mrs G wasn't Sean. You could nearly feel sorry for her if you let yourself. If you weren't sick listening to the same whine ever since you left the cradle: what I gave up, Sally, the chances I gave up to rear you. I could have been anything, Sally, could have gone anywhere, could have travelled the world if I'd been as callous as some. India Cuba Israel, only I put you first, Sarah. I wanted you to have a good life. But I was pretty you know and trendy when I was young, Sally, could have gone anywhere, could have married anyone. But I wouldn't do that to you, Sally, I always put you first, I wanted to make a good life for you, Sal, and I did. Didn't I, love? Didn't I? And the old photos and the laments and the gin bottle and then, just as you were ready to kill dragons for her, the slap across the face: I must have been mad, Jesus, I must have been stark raving, Maureen knew an address and all, she'd have lent me the money, I'd have got over him and lived my life, if you hadn't been there I'd have got over the bastard, God, I'm sorry, Sarah, what am I saying? What am I saying, Sarah? I don't mean a word of it, love . . . Only, she meant it all right. Half-way down the gin bottle Mum stopped fooling herself, the truth started crawling out and you were nothing again.

"If I could only go back, Sarah, just for a week. I'm not *old*, Sarah, forty's not old nowadays, just a week to recapture . . . Oh God, what's the use? We had a flat, Sarah, four of us, just off the King's Road. The parties, Sarah! Look, there's Robyn from New Zealand. You'd have adored her, her people owned thousands of miles of sheep, imagine, but we've lost touch. She married some dreary man and went back home. And there's Philippa the blonde one there. She's married to a cousin of the Spencers, actually. What a cow, Sarah, what a ghastly cow that girl's turned into! And that's poor Rosemary, she was Irish like me, my very greatest friend, Sarah. We were at Kylemore Abbey together. She took an overdose, Sarah, do you realise? I've just had a letter from her husband.

She took an overdose and I never knew. I kept writing and writing to her and I never knew, Sarah, I never guessed. I kept writing letters and she wasn't there, she didn't exist. What shall I do, Sarah, what's going to become of me, what shall I *do*?" Search me, Sarah thought, arming herself, send a Mass card why don't you? But all the same it was rotten about the friend, you had to admit, God, imagine if . . . But catch me going on like that! Hell, even if it was my mum popped it, even if it was Malachy, I wouldn't go over the top like that. People die all the time, what were they, couple of old lezzies or what? "That's terrible, Mrs Gotherby. I'm really sorry. I wish there was something I could do to help, honest I do, Mrs Gotherby, I—"

"What could *you* do? Oh God, that's all I needed, she's sorry for me! I used to have real friends, beautiful amusing friends, real real people and all I have now is poor plain Sarah from the suburbs with her dyed hair and her spots and she's sorry for me! Well, I don't need your pity. I don't pay for your pity. What are you doing anyway, lounging around the drawing-room at ten in the morning? Go and help Mrs Jay."

"You sent for me, Mrs Gotherby."

"Yes. Yes, actually I did send for you. I sent for you because apparently poor little Matthew hasn't had his riding lesson for several days. It's just not good enough, Sarah, don't forget I only took you on as a favour to Mr Watts and you're on three months' trial. Have you an explanation to give? No? Well, take the child out *at once*. And then straight away afterwards come and help Mrs Jay tidy up this ghastly mess. It's like a fifth-rate suburban house in here and there's an owners' meeting tomorrow."

"I'm leaving tomorrow, Mrs Gotherby. My mother and Maureen are coming to fetch me. I don't have to give you notice when I'm only on trial, right? Oh, and I thought I'd tell you, *he's* dead too. John Lennon's dead, were you forgetting?"

"Get out, you fat soulless cow. Bitch, suburban bitch!"

Don't satisfy her, Sal, don't slam the door. Only—yeah, think of her poor drunkard's head and do slam it, hard. Lucy in the skah, Lucy in the skah, Lucy in the skah with dahmonds bee-uk!

Spoiled brat Matthew in the paddock lying on the ground chewing his fingers, drumming his heels, hating her out of green haunted eyes. "I shan't get up. I shan't get up. You have no right. You can't make me. I'll tell my mummy if you hit me. I'll tell my daddy!"

"Frig your daddy. Bet he'd love to know you're a cowardly little prick, wouldn't he? Worse than your mum even, scared to get up on a Shetland pony. I took pity on you the last few days and you have to go blabbing it all over the house. Tell-taleing little prick!"

"You mustn't call me that, it's a bad nasty word. You're not paid to call me names. My mummy says you have a filthy tongue, she says you're as common as dirt. Bog Irish bastard my mummy calls you, so there. I'll tell my daddy to sack you, so I will."

"Right, here goes. I'm going up the yard to get Sean and Tony *and* the jockeys *and* the drivers to come and see you pissing yourself afraid of a Shetland pony. And Mrs Jay, she'd laugh herself sick at you, wouldn't she?"

She was stuck with it now, she'd have to leave. And dead right and all. God, if Malachy and the crowd knew she was crying over a dump like this, they'd say she was off her head. She would be and all if she stayed. Like the missus. Daft ever to come here. Daft ever to leave Claghan. The one time you find a guy that fancies you, and you have to run home to Mum! OK, so he's on drugs, so what? Who isn't? Doesn't automatically make him a junkie, does it? Doesn't automatically turn him into a half-wit like poor Tony here. All right, so his mates, Kieran and that crowd, so they're not exactly the most savoury of, but what's that to you? He doesn't want you to sleep with his *mates*, does he? So why run? Why run away like a, like a Victorian maiden or something?

She trailed round the rooms after Mrs Jay, scraping a mountain of yard-muck off the good carpets. Nobody cared except the owners. She supposed when they came they liked to see their trainer looking half-way prosperous. The old man never once changed his boots when he came in and the missus never noticed: "I'm not a mere housewife, Sarah!" Or maybe she did notice. Bet he never changed his socks either. *Or* his drawers, filthy sod—drive anyone to drink. Poor Mrs G all the same, stuck with that in her bed and her face all gone to hell from crying. She dusted the sitting-room where the owners met, dragged the armchair with the broken spring to a prominent position. Mustn't forget to guide Mrs Hall-Egan to it tomorrow. Treat you like a servant, that cow. "No need to be nice to her, Sarah, her father was only a coal-heaver in Liverpool!" Snobbish old bitches, the lot of them. What's a coal-heaver anyhow when it's at home?

"This ex-deb who used to work for Trevor, imagine, she's advertising in *The Lady*, Sarah, needs someone for the horses. Since apparently you've gone off Claghan . . . We don't *mind* you here, don't think that, Sarah, only wouldn't you feel better earning some money? Paying your way for a change?" Of course they minded, she gave Maureen the creeps. She'd always known that. And she couldn't stay in the flat in Kilburn—Mum had found herself a man again. Divorced ecologist with a wispy beard. Trust Mum to get picked up by a cliché. Well, not picked up exactly. I don't *want* to be tough, she thought. I don't *want* to be all nasty and scathing. In fact this guy, Colin, what's wrong with him? He's a supply-teacher at Mum's school, he's all sincere and nice. Mum drove round the country with him in a Landrover that time, National Wildflower Week, sowing weeds in farmers' crops. So what? If that's what turns her on. Who am I to judge people?

She dusted round the trophies, the wall of framed photos: Aitch Pee winning at Kempton, Korrigan's Pride taking the last, old Gotherby's sleazy face grinning up at the Queen

Mum, the missus drinking champagne with the out-at-elbows millionaire Sal fancied like nobody's business, oh Christ . . . She was supposed to be going down to London for Maureen and Trev's farewell party, that was all. So if she apologised nicely. That was a joke, apologise for trying to sympathise with the daft old bag. It wasn't worth it to her to stay. God if any of the crowd in Claghan knew! A glorified skivvy in a madhouse, and the money! You were better off on Benefit. Forty's not old, Sarah, who are you kidding, missus? Forty's a hundred, forty's eternal, forty's my mum and Maureen, forty's my old bastard of a dad wherever he is. Whoever he is.

They were asked down to Sean's bungalow for supper, Mrs Jay and herself, it was settled days ago. Sarah wasn't sure about going after this morning but poor old Kath might take offence if she didn't. Kath was about twelve months pregnant and as sick as a dog most of the time. Mrs Jay said old Gotherby forced Sean to marry her. Sarah thought that a daft remark. It wasn't the middle ages and how could your boss force you to marry someone if you didn't want to? Mrs Jay said the guvnor knew plenty about Sean and if Sean left here he couldn't get a job elsewhere with all the muck old Mr G could spread about him. Kath was an amateur, riding in point-to-points before Sean got her up the spout and she could have done a lot better for herself. She must have been right and green, Sarah thought, to let herself get caught like that. Unless she did it deliberately, maybe that was her big turn-on, the thought of a lifetime with Sean's Irish freckles and dirty fingernails. Everyone seemed a bit flawed around the place, as flawed as she was herself. Tony was another Malachy only worse: got chucked out of his public school because his brain had gone all swimmy from dope, so Mrs Jay said, and of course Mrs Jay herself, according to the Gotherbys, well *waaow!* Some chick Mrs Jay in her time, said old Gotherby.

Sean was as nice as anything to them during supper, sloshing the booze around like a Pools millionaire and joking about the baby. "Makes you think, dunnit, few weeks' time and I'll be the proud daddy wheeling the chisler out in its pram. Might even take it fishing. Use it for bait." They all laughed a lot except Kath who had a face that length and looked ready to drop her foal there and then. Sean slapped her on the back and said, "Cheer up, woman, with all that gin you pour into yourself he's bound to be a dwarf. 'Prentice him on the Flat and he'll keep us in comfort for the rest of our lives." It was all very cheerful but when Kath dragged herself into the kitchen for the apple tart Sean followed her in and they could hear him yelling at her to for fuck's sake be a bit more entertaining and then they could hear him knocking her about. Sarah wanted to go in to her, she was pregnant after all, but Mrs Jay held her back: you mustn't interfere between a married couple, luv, it's not done. So Kath came back with her eyes red and a mark on the side of her jaw and no one mentioned it and they all drank a few more beers and said just a week or so, Kath, bet you'll have poor old Sean driving like a madman to the hospital at three in the morning.

The lights were all on in the front of the house like a party though there were no strange cars in the yard. "Awh-awh!" Mrs Jay said and sure enough when they went in through the side door and into the kitchen they could hear old Gotherby yelling: "Mrs Jay, Mrs Jay, is that you, Mrs Jay?" In a right old panic he sounded and all. So they ran through the dining-room and up the front stairs and there was the missus crawling about on the landing in a daze and old Gotherby in a pair of soiled Viyella pyjamas: "She's killed herself, Mrs Jay, she swallowed the whole bottle, what's to be done, Mrs Jay?" Matthew standing at his bedroom door chewing his fingers to the bone, staring with green haunted eyes at his mother crawling about on the landing.

"Get that kid back to bed, Sal, and go and ring the doctor, Mr G, didn't you ring him yet? Come on, missus, come along now, luv. I'll try and make her vomit. *She* won't pop it, there was only a few left in the bottle. Come along now, luv; don't be naughty, open your mouth. That's right, over the basin now, that's it. Was she drinking?" Was she what? "Come on to bed, Matthew, good lad."

"Is she going to die, Sal, my mummy?"

"Well, of course she's not. She's only play-acting to annoy your dad. Having a tantrum, that's all, like you in the paddock today."

"You sure, Sal?"

"Course I'm sure, cross my heart."

"I'm not a cowardly prick, am I, Sal?"

"Course you're not."

"Why did you say then, why did you say? You're not paid to call me names. Mummy can't stand you and Sean can't stand you. Mummy said you're a lazy big lump and not worth your keep, I heard her, to Mrs Jay and Mrs Jay said—"

What was the bleedin' use? She wasn't paid to sing him lullabies, was she, to tell him life was sweet and his mum and dad were flippin' saints and he'd grow up happy ever after. "Serve you right if she did die and all, you slimy little tale-telling coward," she said, switching off his night-light as she left the room.

Late next morning the missus in dark glasses arrived briefly to greet the owners and offer them a drink before they drove up to the gallops. Mrs Hall-Egan, discreetly trying to shift her big buttocks on the broken chair, was going on as usual about the lovely place you have here and are they real Tudor those beams? She asked if it was true that Dick Francis had written one of his novels there. "Sarah, darling, be an angel and show Mrs Hall-Egan the garret where Dick wrote *On the Bitch.*" The missus once said that Dick Francis was the Queen Elizabeth's Bed of English racing stables. If he'd written a book everywhere he was supposed to he could have bought up Aintree and indeed the whole of Lancashire by now.

Sal led stout asthmatic Mrs Hall-Egan at a gleeful gallop up three flights of stairs and along a mile of freezing corridors to an attic at the far end of the house. Go on have a heart attack, you bloody old snob, *go* on, panting and puffing up against the real Tudor wall. "There it is, that very table and chair. Sorta consecrated-looking wouldn't you say Mrs H-E, worth coming up for, like?"

"Oh, oh yes, how very delightful," stammered Mrs Hall-Egan uneasily through numb lips and then Sarah led her, at a gallop, puffing back to the sitting-room. The missus removed her dark glasses to give Sarah a bloodshot wink and went off to drink black coffee with Mrs Jay in the kitchen. "You're going for, what is it, two days, Sarah? Enjoy yourself, darling!"

They arrived while the owners were meeting, swinging the new Mercedes in through the gates to join the Volvos and Rovers. "Well, you're doing all right for yourself, Trev, must have a few pee left, stately home or not."

"Château, Sally, château. And call me Trevor, do you mind?" They had expected to be asked in to have a drink with the Gotherbys but Sarah explained about the owners' meeting and tried to hurry them away before anyone came out. Trev's sheepskin coat looked very camp with sort of horse brasses down the front and all the seams inside out, not at all the sort of thing the Gotherbys would ever be seen in. Maureen was wearing jodhpurs and cowboy boots and poor Mum as usual looked like a retired hippy who wasn't quite sure whether or not it was time to retreat, beaten, into a C&A Better Dress. She had a hangover and smiled at Sarah with wan affection.

Sarah tried to get them back into the car with all possible secrecy but of course Trevor insisted on being taken round to see the horses. "Where's this famous Horn of Plenty, then? Lost a packet on that three-legged sod the other day." Sarah led them to where Aitch Pee was swinging his beautiful bored head back and forth across his half-door. "Got it in for you, ye daft bugger ye!" Trev said in one of his funny accents, shadow-boxing playfully. Sarah died quietly with her back turned as firm as an ostrich towards the house windows. "Aren't they pretty, ooh aren't they sweet!" Maureen was rippling away, blowing kisses up at Irish Rover as if she suspected there was an admiring audience of her Faithful Readers crouching in the manger or someplace. "Wish I'd brought some sugar. Do they really let you ride them, Sally? Bet they're insured for a packet though!" Oh God, please make them come away. Please don't let the missus come out. She could just see Mrs Gotherby with her puffy amused eyes and her ironic drawl being kind to them, offering drinks, displaying them to the owners: "Little Sarah's people, darlings, in the rag trade . . . " Making fun of Maureen's jodhpurs, of Mum's awful folksy sweater. Sending them off to some garret to be told lies about famous jockeys. And they'd be thrilled. They'd never know they were being laughed at. Oh God, please make them drop dead.

She'd always felt slightly ashamed of, and protective towards, her mother, but she couldn't get over herself being ashamed of Maureen and Trev who used to be the glossiest, most infallible, most frightening adults in the whole world. Imagine seeing them so inadequate. So like foolish helpless victims, people from another age. I must be growing up, she thought, I don't need them now, I don't need their approval, it's not these people I need any more. They can go where they like, they've got nothing to give me. I've got Claghan, she thought. I've got Claghan and my granny and Malachy and a place where I know for certain I'm really wanted.

She herded them into the car at last and away down the drive. Maureen looked back at the big half-timbered house dappled with winter sunshine behind bare trees. "Su—perb! Sally, you know you're a right little liar. You do pile it on a bit, don't you? I mean, we came rushing up here expecting

Wuthering Heights at the very least. Falling apart, you said, a crumbling ruin and just look at it. God, isn't it perfect!"

Look your last on it, Sarah thought, because that's it. I've left. I'm not going back. If you can't see it's rotten, if you can't see everything's rotten. Your old books, your old château, Mum's old Wildflower Genius, your protest marches, all those posh sisters at Greenham Common, what are they for, what are they *for?* Only Claghan's not rotten, she thought, and my gran: she's somebody who actually loves me. Who's actually sitting there counting the days till I come back. Who's glad I got born . . . Claghan's real. And Malachy. I could marry him even. Move into that big warm solid family of his. Have wedding-presents and china tea-sets and a house to decorate and sit around with the kids of an evening playing ludo and taking them riding and. People do. Most people do. That's how people live, isn't it? I could be calm and happy and ordinary for a change . . .

"How long have you got?" Trevor asked. "When do you have to go back?"

CHAPTER FORTY-FOUR

SARAH (2)

A nd his face lit up like a Christmas tree when she got off the bus in the town centre. Claghan houses so mean-eyed every time after London, after the lovely Tudor village where the stable was, and the ghastly Claghan shop-fronts, ultra-modern. I'm not a rural person, Malachy. You'll die when you hear it. Three months, nearly three months I stuck it, well I had to work at something, but I couldn't wait to get back to Claghan. And to you, of course, well naturally, you twit!

And to the long long litany of her grandmother's life, funny old people in stiff narrow dresses, with stiff narrow minds, the holy pictures on the wall, all the old values wrapped up safe in mothballs: "So you didn't like living with Mary Brigid Murphy and the man? As tough as an old boot that one, nothing in her head only film stars and fashion, and when you think how she was reared out on that bit of a bog . . . "

And listen, listen to this, I've found us a place Malachy, the ideal place for us to go, all quiet and tranquil and no busybodies peering through net curtains. Half the street's been condemned for years, we'd be on our own. We could squat, Malachy, just move in with a camping stove and. No, it's *not* sordid, it's far from it. Just come and look love. It was a sort of folk museum years ago—you must have heard about it? Got old-fashioned beds and tables and chairs and a bellows wheel for making fires. My granny used to. She said that's actually where Mum was reared. There's about five tiny houses. They lived in one of them for years and years, imagine. Someone made a museum of it later. No, twit, not because of Mum! Because of all those old heroes, *you* know. Heroes and whatever, that used to live there. Making love by candlelight in a Quarry Street cottage, just think of it. Like my ancestors. And *yours*, Malachy, Gran says your people came out of Quarry Street. The old Kaiser Bills. No I'm only joking, don't yell at me like that, of course I believe you. Oh I'm so happy to be back you couldn't imagine . . .

And McCormack's Singing Lounge. The lights changing, darkening, dazzling, their own corner: Oh *you're* back are you, the hair dyed puce, ye huer ye! Why don't you stay in England if you want to play the tart? In a home they should have put you. That's what I said at the time. Oh and *I* told the solicitor. I said to Mr Ó'Lorcáin I said just take a look at the company your son's keeping, drugs and everything I told him. Puce hair, living on your poor grandmother, have you no shame? Aye and I'll tell him this latest, *I* see what you're up to, crawling in and out of that house in Quarry Street like your huer of a mother. I'll tell Mr Ó'Lorcáin what sort of a slut his son has trailing round Claghan after him. I'll let him know so I will . . .

"What *is* he, Malachy, why does he go on like that? My big uncle Jim, Gran said. What is he, a lay preacher or what?"

Lying dead in some trench or another, she said, and no one to bury him, the Kaiser Bill does be saying its pure slaughter in them trenches . . . Though Gran says she doesn't expect anyone even remembers he was in the. "In the *army*, Sal? You sure? The British army? I never knew that, I never knew Malone was in the. Hey, Kieran, Sean, Emer, come and listen, guys! This you gotta hear! This you gotta spread around! Tell them, Sal, *go* on, tell them!"

"And here's my mother and father, Sal. Mammy, Daddy, I want you to meet Sal O'Flaherty from London. We're engaged, at least we'll be engaged when I pull myself together and get a job." The faces. Their faces, set in stiff royal icing. "Oh yes, we've heard all about your London friend. We've heard."

"Sal, this is my aunt Philomena, and her husband, Dr Martin McCormack." The faces. The faces.

"How dare you, Malachy, how could you dare to do this to your poor mother and father? Bringing a girl like that . . . "

"And this is Nuala McCormack, Sal, the famous Nuala McCormack." Cool blonde statue. The faces. "They think I'm dirt, Malachy. Their faces when you said." Except Nuala: "I used to know your mother, Sal." Smiling like a real friend. "And my father? My father?" Face shut tight then like the others: "I have no idea. Someone in London, I suppose." I'll ask Gran, this time I'm going to force her, twist her bleedin' arm so help me . . . The faces. Well, at least it wasn't one of this tight-arsed crowd, Christ, if it had been one of them with their nice grey suits and their ties and their wee frosty jumped-up faces. Kaiser Bill! The Kaiser's crowd, that's what Gran calls them. The faces—you'd think I smelled, you'd think I had BO. A student teacher, that's all Mum ever told me, that's all she ever let slip. Very left-wing. As if that made it any better. Well, for her it would, she'd hate me to think she went round screwing the National Front! If she'd got married to him and stayed in Claghan, both of them teaching and respectable, I'd have been OK. I'd have walked into this shitty crew like an equal. And Jesus why not, even so? In this day and age. Wouldn't you think in this day and age? The memories they have, they all just live in their dreary old memories.

"Who is this Nuala, Malachy? . . . Yes, I know, but why? What does she do? Why is she so important? Why are you all on your knees in front of her?"

The hooded body of a man discovered on a border road early this morning is thought to be that of Mr James Malone who has not been seen since he answered the front door to an unidentified caller late on Wednesday evening. A section of the road has been cordoned off and traffic in both directions is being diverted, as it is feared that the body may be booby-trapped. Bomb-disposal experts have been called to the scene.

I can see him standing there with his wee brush of a moustache leaning up against the window: sure, what trenches, woman? God forgive me, Sally, we were reared together and still and all I never liked him. But an informer? An informer, Sally?

Lured from his house, jostled into a stolen car, tried by a People's Court, executed at dawn. It's easy, Mal, it's one big cliché, you could do it with anyone, I mean! I mean, was he giving information? Was he a spy? I mean, we all know he was a big mouth but. You could get rid of anyone. Like the Mafia or something. No one to stop you . . . How do you mean, the boys would get you? I bet they wouldn't bother. I bet lots of people, lots of old grudges . . . Well, of *course* I don't care what happened to him. What was he to me? Bleedin' old nuisance was all . . . She did. Yes, she did, she never liked him she said, but she cried a bit all the same, you know what old women are like. Then back to the eternal reminiscing!

"Yes, but *why* did his dad beat him out of de Valera's army? I mean, you'd have thought he'd have wanted him to fight for Ireland. I mean, being so proud of his ancestors and all, you'd think . . . Old Cormac O'Flaherty and that, so why?"

"Old Matt wasn't too interested in all that side of it. It was the other ancestors he cared about at first, when he came back from America. From what Pakky's mother told me. She lived with us for years you know, in Quarry Street, after old Matt died and the place went, and she used to talk to me. She wouldn't talk to anyone else. She kept herself well above the street. I could understand that. She was a Yank you know, and used to playing the lady all her life—a servant girl and hired boys, it must have been a shocking comedown. It seems old Matt married her out in America. He was doing well at the time and her people had money, and he used to tell her he was connected to this big family of English landlords. So back they came to Claghan and he offered a fortune for Claghan Hall. Some drunken old gambler was all the McLeod that was left in it. Matt thought all he had to do was announce himself to the rest of the family that was big-shots in the town, saying he was their Yankee cousin. Wasn't he innocent when you think of it! Sure, they wanted nothing to do with him. What was he only a rough-and-ready Yank with a bit of money. The grandson into the bargain of a known murderer that was supposed to have shed blood in the very family itself, what could he expect? So he did all in his power to make people forget that side of it and most of his children took after him. All except Pakky, the bad blood must have come out in poor Pakky! It was only when Matt saw he was getting no-place with being made an equal of that he turned back to Cormac O'Flaherty and his Catholic history."

"Who are these McLeods, Malachy, that Gran's always on about?" "Eric McLeod? You must have heard of Eric McLeod! The town joke! Ban the Bomber, Peace Person, Samaritan, Bleeding Heart for South Africa, you name it. You must have seen him round Claghan, you couldn't miss. Long hair going a bit grey, beard, anorak; still thinks it's about 1968. Oh, and plays the guitar and all, takes parties of mixed schoolkids

camping in France, wee Taigs and Prods living it up around
the bonfire. He tried to get elected to Westminster but even
his own crowd wouldn't have him. His wife's always on local
radio going on about something or other: Ethiopia or
endangered species or Nicaragua, I mean who cares? She
looks like an endangered species herself! What do you want
to know for?"

"Oh, Gran was going on. They used to be quite important,
she says. They got her a job one time."

"Well, they're not too important now. Times is changed, tell
your old gran! They're schoolteachers. I'll show you their
house sometime."

Château de Lapire-Vacherie
6 Jan

Dear Myrna and Eric,
Thanks for the lovely card. So sorry—we just didn't send
cards to anyone this year, up to our ears as we were
chivvying workmen etc. (Fierce blue-clad workmen with
heavy moustaches and wicked black eyes.) I was mad
enough at first to offer them a cup of coffee in the kitchen
as you'd do at home and they thought I was inviting a
pass! Started getting all smarmy and nudging. At my age!
Culture shock. I've a lot to learn about "Le Continent."
Well, we finally got settled in and looking ship-shape—it
took the best part of three years, but at least we can offer
to put you up if/when you decide to pay a visit. We're
loving France. Even with the socialist government and the
randy brickies it's a fantastic change from Thatcher's Britain.
To think we actually voted for her!

I'm writing, in fact, to beg a favour. Having acquired
Lord Baudry's château with all its Claghan associations,
I've decided to get down to work on an historical romance
that's been flitting around in my head for some decades—

437

the story of your beautiful ancestor Marianne of course, and her connection with the Irish hero all Claghan cut its teeth on, Cormac O'Flaherty. I've been wanting to write it for ages but these last years haven't seemed quite the best time to glorify Irish violence! However, now that things are quieter over there I think I could risk it and, given the level of public consciousness about Ethiopia and so on, the Irish famine might even go down rather well. (Let's hope it does—*Scent of Hibiscus* didn't exactly sell a bomb!) I remember Eric talking about the journal that fascinated him so much as a child: any chance of getting it photocopied for me? I'll pay all expenses, of course. Also any other relevant documents???

Not, of course, that it's all that quiet, as I'm well aware. That poor old man who was found shot last year, Big Jim Malone, was very much one of the figures of my childhood—he had one of those everlasting Irish engagements with my aunt Agnes, but it never came to anything. The pair of them embodied romance for me when I was a kid, seeing he fought in the war and all. I suppose that's really why they murdered him, an ex-soldier would be automatically suspect. I just can't imagine him being an informer. Though again, how can one ever tell? And, of course, all these kidnappings too! I'm so glad I managed to escape from Claghan and all that narrow fanaticism!

Well, I do look forward to hearing from you, and to getting a look at the Journal. Lucky you, having such ancestors!

Lots of Love to you both,
Maureen.

CHAPTER FORTY-FIVE

SARAH (3)

"He rushed off and married that cow while Mum was expecting me! Do you realise the humiliation? He didn't even want to know! Just because Mum was a Catholic, Gran says. Do you realise? I'm going to do that bastard. They all wanted to put me in a home she said. In an orphanage. *Me*. She'd have let me grow up in a home and thought nothing of it. She wouldn't even have missed me, she'd have preferred! That's what she said, that they were all in favour of just wiping me out—just forgetting I was ever born. Do you realise, *me*? *Me!* I'm going to kill that guy, Malachy, I swear I'm going to do him. I'm going to fucking do the bastard for this."

"Calm down, love, now come on, come on, calm, ca—it's over, love. It's all in the past, it's history by now all that, it doesn't mean anything. And your mother kept you, didn't she? She didn't wipe you out, you had a nice life with that old writer and all. It's over, Sal, you've got *me* now, we're getting married and all. Nobody's wiped you *out!* Come on and I'll buy you a drink, love, that's what you need, Sal, a few drinks down you. Don't keep on like that, Sal. *Please*. You scare me when you're like that. Honest! Come on now, calm down!

That's it love. We'll go up to McCormack's, get a few drinks. They've got Cuchulain McCool tonight, big special evening— the whole crowd'll be. Come on, Sal."

They were sitting there in McCormack's and it was hours later and Malachy had his arm round her and she was all woozy with Pernod, not drunk or anything but her eyelids weighed about a ton, the lights whirling changing dazzling, this old man on the stage with a guitar, about forty but not bad, sort of mournful dogs' eyes and a beard. "My old grand-dad must have looked like that when he walked into Matt O'Flaherty's kitchen: 'I'm Patrick the son home from England!' Poor Gran, she was only fifteen, Malachy, imagine, can't imagine Gran fifteen, can you? "

"Shut up, can't you, Sal, and listen to McCool, the seldom time he comes back to Claghan. He's famous, Sal." From the pleasant bay of Portnafinn the *Mary Jane* set sail. "Why? *Why* listen? Can't stand that sort of old. When *I* was fifteen Trevor made a pass at me. Up there in that twee little flat they gave us at the top of their twee little house, helping me with my maths and then. Next thing his hand. I told Maureen. Not that I minded or anything but just. Just to see her face, to try and hurt her, I suppose, and all she did was laugh. She said I was a right little liar and she shoved me up in front of a mirror, who do you think would make a pass at you, Sarah? Adolescent fantasies, just look at yourself. Go on go on, she said, take a good long look. I did look sinister, Malachy, gross and stupid you know, and sort of blank. I could have died when she made me see. But he did try, it was true. I'd hardly have imagined it!"

"You look great now, Sal. Like a cover girl off *The Face* or something. Hard rock star gettin' pissed in a pub! So stop worrying."

"But *The Face* didn't exist when I was a kid, Mal. You had to look sweet and folksy. Mum looked sweet and folksy, all plaits and fuckin' embroidery, 'Suzanne takes you down to her place by the river,'" that's what she used to sing to put me to sleep when I had nightmares, Jesus, poor old Mum took everyone down to her place by the river. 'Wearing rags and feathers from Salvation Army counters,' she used to sing. They all used to sing. All these embroidered guys and big flopsy women with no bras dropping in on their way back from hitching to Katmandu or someplace, and the room stank of incense and grass, Malachy. That's why I used to get nightmares, and yeah sometimes they even sang that thing up on the stage there: 'His father was a cruel man he turned them from his door.' It's my great-great-grandad, Mum used to say. It's about my great-grandparents give or take a great, who cares? Laughing herself sick, don't give *me* Irish history she used to say. Mum was the only one never hitched to anyplace. Hitched on the spot. Or maybe she was waiting. Hoping for. Hoping Eric McLeod would drop in some night, looking for his 'tea and oranges that came all the way from China.' I bet she was hoping that. I'm going to do that bastard, Malachy, I'll kill him for what he."

"Shut up love, shut up! We're going to get slung out! Shut up and listen to." God's curse was on you George McLeod for the homes you did.

"They all looked like that, they all looked like him, like old Cuchulain up there, all the nice gentle men with beards. I used to wake up in the morning and there'd be someone all quiet and peaceful sort of praying or meditating or just drifting about eating wheat-germ or. There was one took me to school by the hand for months and months, never said a word only smiled, and his hand was all warm and dry and sort of permanent. I told everyone he was my dad, I put him into my essays and all: 'How I Spent My Weekend.' I'd imagine him taking us to see the crown jewels and for picnics down to Kew Gardens and doing the pools and all and yelling at Mum if dinner was a bit late. He'd have died if he knew. I actually thought that all that was normality! Well, it was the way all the others seemed to live. And then Sandra, my friend Sandra, said he was only a dirty hippy, and her mum wouldn't let her come to my birthday party because we were freaks and probably on drugs and giving the district a bad name and it wasn't right, her mum said, I ought to be in care—a kid growing up like that. She was going to talk to the social services about us."

"Shut *up*, Sal!"

"He disappeared one day, just walked off, sort of like absent-mindedly with this Swedish girl and Mum freaked out for a bit, went on the booze and all. Of course it was my fault, all my friggin' fault. If I hadn't been there she could have gone with him to Afghanistan or wherever, could have done anything, gone anywhere. Always my fault when she was on the booze. It brought out the Paddy in her do you think, Mal? The Biddy. When she was stoned she was different, it was all 'heroes in the seaweed and children in the morning,' sick too but different. She wasn't always like that, I mean most days she used to drag herself in to school to supply-teach and all. I mean, she wasn't a *dreg*. Only sometimes the world used to sort of cave in for a bit. And then after a few days of that we'd get on the train and back to Maureen and Trev's. Back to Claghan, I suppose that's what it felt like to Mum. To wait. To get her strength back. No incense in Maureen's, Malachy. She used to even spray the cat with Dioressence . . . "

"Ssh, would you, old McCormack's *glaring* at us!"

The old songs drifted across her and she remembered the white perfumed cat. Maureen used to take it up in her hand and squeeze it into shapes, all long hair and tiny fragile bones, carry it everywhere. When she was very small the cat used to live on Maureen's knee or on Maureen's shoulder; once when she gave a party she wore the cat in the pocket of a long black silk dress like a brooch, with only its head visible. When it was a tiny kitten Sarah used to remove it from Maureen's knee and climb up herself and live there safe against Maureen's stomach for hours until her mum came back from wherever she was. Maureen was happy to have little Sarah on her knee while she wrote or chatted or just sat looking peacefully around her beautiful room. Mum's knee was uncomfortable because she clung to you and talked and asked you intense silly questions or showed you off. Waved you like some sort of flag. Or sometimes cried and told you terrible stories of when she was small herself, about her daddy and her little brother and being beaten until she bled. Then one day Sarah lifted Baby Roo off Maureen's lap but he didn't want to come. He dug his claws deep into Maureen's knee and hung on, and Maureen gave her an immense belt across the face and yelled in a voice that was quite unlike her usual voice: "Ye big awkward glunthakamay, ye have me ruined, so ye have! Get to buggery out of this and give my head peace, would you, you're too big for knees!" And then her soft rippling voice came back and she said: "Poor Roo! And did that big jealous Sarah try to tear him away from his mummy?" Sarah was eight years old. Her mum was not home so she went out into Richmond and wandered about the evening streets crying. She cried because there was no knee to sit on, and because she had wanted very much to tell Maureen how her dad had gone away with a dirty huer of a Swede, and because there was no longer a calm smiling person to lead her gently through the traffic with a warm permanent hand holding hers . . .

"Sing it again, Cuchulain!" someone called. "Go on, sing it again, give us a few bars of O'Flaherty!"

But there was someone now when it was far too late, someone rootless and smiling and as flawed as herself, ready to lead her wherever she asked him. A hero in the seaweed, drowning in the Claghan pubs, floating in and out through the violence, bumping now and then against the hooded corpses. "Listen, Malachy," she whispered, "I killed Baby Roo."

"Baby who?"

"A cat."

"Shut up, Sal. A cat, for Christ's sake, I'm telling you shut up. I'll listen later. You're drunk love, you're completely pissed."

"I took the little bastard up in my arms—come on Roo come to Mummy then—and I shoved him up purring under my mohair poncho one of the flopsy women wove for me, shoved him up happy among the llamas and the grinning masks—come on Baby Roo we're going for a walk—and I walked through Richmond in the sort of half-dusk, all the cars coming from work, walked for ages right over to Kew Bridge and I let him out among all the traffic—go on get lost Roo— whiff of Dioressence rising out of my poncho. He hadn't a chance, a raindrop in hell, and I walked back home and old Maureen was in hysterics and for once Mum was consoling *her*. Never occurred to them, never once occurred to them. I mean, you'd have thought it was obvious wouldn't you? To me it would have been obvious . . . What else would I have done? Who else would have done it? You're going to help me, aren't you, Malachy, you're going to help me?"

"Give over, love, you're pissed. You're crazy. Just give over and listen to the song."

"That song? May their children's children keep in mind, Jesus! You said we'd talk about it, you said it was possible. So what are we doing here instead, listening to that old has-been? It's got nothing to do with anything, that old song. What's *history* got to do with anything? I swear that's it, Malachy, if you don't. We're finished. You'll have had it, no more Quarry Street. No more nothing. OK, so I'm crazy. So what are you? You're hardly the most normal human being around Claghan, you're hardly the big solid citizen. It's the easiest thing in the world, Malachy, you said it yourself, it won't even occur to anyone, they'll all think it's the. I just want to see his *face*, Malachy, just want to see the shock . . . "

CHAPTER FORTY-SIX

ERIC

He woke thirsty, on his side, facing green paint. The walls were running with damp. If his hands had been free he could have reached out, touched his palm to the film of moisture, wet his lips. His head ached. He had slept minutes, woke, slept again. His arms ached. He moved his head. It seemed to be early morning, there was a grey light in the room. The girl sat upright beside his bed, a gun in her lap. He closed his eyes. He could hear others breathing elsewhere in the room. He gathered that they did not intend to kill him. If they had, why would they have brought him here, to this house, this town he'd spent hours of the night vainly trying to identify from its traffic noises. If they'd wanted to they could have shot him at once standing there by his car. They could even have booby-trapped his car as they'd done to poor Uncle Harry and so many others. Only, why should anyone want to harm him at all? Who had they mistaken him for? Had they simply picked him at random, a token Protestant? A reprisal for . . . For what?

He tried to recall the past week's news. Had there been a sectarian murder? A Roman Catholic killed? He didn't think so, but couldn't be quite sure. And is it not a shameful thing, he thought, to be unsure? I am part of this province. I am not English or French or German. I wouldn't mind being sometimes but I'm not. I'm part of this mess that's Ulster so I should know and care what happens here. They're not worth caring about, he thought, what kept me here anyhow? I should have cleared out years ago. For an instant he saw himself sandalled, rucksacked, walking lightly on a sand-coloured road, under a blue sky. The old cliché-dream of his youth. A helicopter passed over the house, quite close, another and then another. Which meant they hadn't brought him across the border. After they stopped him, driving to the airport, had they turned right or left? Gone further north, or south, or where? Names of towns flitted through his head, telly names, names out of a Jack Higgins thriller: Lisburn, Derrylin, Carrickmore, Crossmaglen, Dungannon. A town with soldiers, fleet of helicopters. A biggish town to judge by the lorries that passed, rattling the little window. When it got really light they'd have to open those curtains, to look natural. When they removed his gag he would shout. People would be passing on the pavement outside. Nice normal people. The silent majority, but surely not silent enough to leave a man in obvious danger? A cod: it wouldn't be so easy. Must be what they so melodramatically called a safe house, in a safe street, or they'd never have dared. They'd shoot him and to hell with it if he once opened his mouth.

Were those helicopters searching for him? Would he have been missed yet? When he didn't turn up in London last night . . . Myrna and the girls might just think he'd missed the plane. I *have* missed it. His car would be found on the airport road. To stop like that, just to stop like that for a fake accident, woman lying on the roadside . . . An absent-minded reflex. Good Samaritan. Let yourself be knocked over the head on a main road, shoved into a van. People must have passed. Cars must have been passing all the time, driven on past and not given a fuck. Been scared. And why not? What could they have done, some commercial traveller or wee tradesman, chuntering along home? What would they have stopped for? Roll up roll up let's all go together. Solidarity was the word but no one's that daft. Drive on, see nothing. They could have stopped later on though, at a call-box, reported it. Or not. Afraid the phone might be booby-trapped.

Odd that the IRA would act so publicly. Take such a risk on a main road. What for? He was no Ben Dunne, there'd be no big ransom. Maybe *not* the IRA. Maybe some gang of cowboy killers. Torturers. Jesus! Jesus! The Shankill Butchers years ago used to kidnap RCs and chop them slowly to death, Jesus! No, they wouldn't have . . . Why were they letting him sleep? Wasting time? Maybe someone reported. Maybe all over the province they were going mad searching for him at this very minute. So why? It was crazy, letting him have his eight hours as if. What were they waiting for? *Who?* He saw British soldiers crawling through fields, inspecting cattle shelters, smashing down front doors on the Falls Road, tearing up floorboards, getting spat on, jeered at, meeting glares and stony faces, waking up babies, dragging old crippled pensioners out of bed, putting a rifle butt through the glass of a sideboard, smashing wedding-present china, ripping through easy-payment upholstery. Come on, come on, missus. Tell us what you know or we'll bleedin'. For him, a man of peace. That was a laugh.

In a few hours' time they'd be converging in their thousands on Trafalgar Square, under banners and pickets, carrying their broken crosses, and he'd be lying here on a stinking mattress with a gun peering at him. The British army combing the countryside for one lost man with a CND badge, while another lot of deadly missiles was sent on its inexorable way to another base in England, and the crowds marching as helpless as he was, as gagged and as bound as he was, whatever they might think. As helpless as the motorists who drove past an ambush last night, as unfit to interfere. Nobody could stop the nuclear build-up except the shower of cynical bastards at the top, and *they'd* stop it whenever it suited them to. Whenever it paid them to. They'd stop the whole thing tomorrow as cynically as they started it if they thought there was any profit in it for them. But they wouldn't stop it otherwise, however many millions wore their feet down to the bone marching. Poor Myrna. Poor me, what a time to get such an illumination! Deathbed conversion. Christ!

One of the shadows on the floor said: "What are we waiting for, Sal?" Accent not northern, not southern. Educated Claghan maybe? But the girl, surprisingly, was English. Not that it meant anything. London-Irish certainly. Kilburn or Camden Town. Weaned in the singing pubs of some tatty High Street. The woes of Erin and our glorious heroes and all the daft old self-pitying legends. Stupid friggin' bastards, he thought. We're in the nineteen-eighties; the planet, God help us, is arming itself for annihilation and this country is still sitting flat on its arse picking fluff out of its belly-button.

"I'm asking you, Sal. What do you intend doing with that thing now that you've caught it?"

"Put it on trial, what do you think! Isn't that the procedure? Isn't that what they do, all your mates? Or we could always play Happy Families with it, could just fancy a game of Happy Families after all this time."

"You're crazy. It's not funny at all. It's not a joke. You haven't even thought about it, Sal, have you? Never thought beyond the first blow. It was all in your head wasn't it? It was just some dream you made up, some mad obsession got hold of you all those nights lying awake in squats listening to your drunken old mother raving away about being betrayed every time she couldn't cope with things. Every time someone saw through her. Isn't that all it was? Well, you're not going to let *this* out into the traffic so easy. This here's no Persian kitten you've got shoved up your jumper, you're going to land us in the shit with this."

"*What* shit? Don't panic, love. It's between me and him, that's all. You can go if you like. Your wee mate Kieran's gone, so go on, *go*. I can cope with him on my own now."

"Cope? You're still pissed, the pair of us were pissed, we were mad to. Mad to ask Kieran of all people. That psycho. Kneecapped, do you realise? They could *kneecap* us for this. Bet Kieran goes off running to. *You* started this, Sal. Bet he'll be back with the whole. You have no *idea*, Sal, where it could end, could turn into a whole big. Taking that *gun* for a start! Nuala and Sean and everyone. It was just something in your head, Sal, and you've landed us in the, right in the friggin' shit you've landed us."

"It's not in my head. I know exactly what I want to do, I've been planning this for. Don't panic, Mal, don't be such a baby."

"Friggin' adventure story. Character in a friggin' *book* you think . . . Let's go, Sal. Why don't we just drop it and run before they all . . . "

Not the IRA. Not professional killers. Couple of lunatics. Drug addicts? Holding him for a ransom? Perverts? Bunch of weirdos? Jesus! The wee boy was scared witless, that was the most frightening. Nerves might go, might fling himself on you, might. In the growing daylight the girl gazed straight at him. "A gaze blank and pitiless as the sun." Knew he was awake all right. Knew he was listening. Making him sweat. The face of mindless violence, he thought, but not necessarily Ulster violence. Not a face lit with the blowlamp flame of a fanatic cause, of patriotism, of power. She had it in for him. For him personally. Why? Who the fuck was she? He never saw her in his life before, he could swear *that*. An empty punk face below the spiked ridiculous hair, an almost-identical face crouched on the floor beside her. How many more blending into the shadows beside the table, behind the door; how many more on their way? The Seans, Nualas, Kierans? And why? What did they want with him? What, according to the merciless nihilism their creed must be, what could *he* be guilty of?

There was early sun now through the small window, through the flowered curtain and, in an instant of unreality (This cannot *be!* This *cannot* be! God I must be dreaming), he recognised the room he was in, knew what house he was in, what street, what town. The deal table with its brown and yellow crock, breadboard and goose-feather. The dresser, the settle-bed, the crane and fire-irons he and Myrna had haggled over for days in a farm kitchen, the set of iron pots around the hearth. How extraordinary, he thought, that in all these years when the museum was left abandoned, that after a succession of gypsies and hippies and squatters of all descriptions, those old artefacts should still be there! Should not have been stolen. Had they not been worth stealing? Had they passed through here, the hippies and the tourists and the gypsies and the lovers and the crazy religious sects and the homeless and the squatters and the vandals and had they not even noticed that there was anything to steal, anything to desecrate? The only change, as far as he could see, was that someone had covered the whitewash with green gloss paint which was now peeled and blistered and blackened with damp. Even the nineteenth-century black and white dogs still stared at each other from opposite sides of the fireboard. That was rich. God, that's really rich, McLeod, he thought. The one thing you achieved in forty-five years of life, the one project you took to heart and really worked on, your one big contribution to Claghan's history—and even the local vandals didn't think it worth desecrating! He laughed and a sob came out instead, shaming him.

The girl heaved herself off her chair and stood over him. "Good morning, Dad!" she said. The scared loony-faced boy beside her sniggered. That's about all it was worth, a snigger. The old old cliché. The generation gap. Anyone over thirty just fit for the scrap-heap: dad, grandad, old fogey. The clichés of his own and everyone's youth. We're gonna change the world so we are! Oh yeah? Just take a look backwards sometime. She turned and glared at the boy, he blushed scarlet and straightened his face. Funny sort of relationship. Betsy Trotwood and Mr Dick? Suitably Dickensian to go with the surroundings. When Marianne and Cormac lived in this house would Dickens have been sitting in comfort in his study writing *David Copperfield*? People *lived* here, actually lived. What did it do to them, living here? How were they shaped by it, twisted by it? How long will *I* be let live, here?

She was a big thick lump of a girl, nearly a six-footer, but with something undernourished in her face. Something wanting. Not attractive. Slouching, in baggy jeans and leather jerkin, purple hair spiked and jagged. A girl of her time. Born in euphoria, growing up as the euphoria screamed itself into madness. The same age as his own children. We didn't give them much in the long run, he thought. We promised them everything, we promised them Utopia, and then . . .

"Good morning, Dad," she repeated. "And what have *you* been up to all these years while the world was falling to bits in everybody's hand?"

CHAPTER FORTY-SEVEN

LIZZIE

. . . Dispersed peacefully and the convoy was allowed
to proceed through the village on its way to the
missile base.

Now, Northern Ireland. A young man, believed to be a
member of a paramilitary organisation, was shot and killed
this morning as he ran away from a derelict house in Claghan.
The man, who has not yet been named, is said to have
ignored repeated calls to stop and be questioned by security
forces. The area has now been sealed off and bomb experts
have been called in to investigate a block of houses near the
scene of the shooting. Mr Seamus Mallon, deputy leader of
the SDLP, has once again made a strong protest against the
shoot-to-kill policy which, he claims, has now become routine
in Ulster. The Northern Ireland Secretary, Mr . . .

"I don't know at all, Lizzie, sure we were sleeping in our beds,
it was the middle of the night, and the next thing that awful
hammering at the doors. It put the heart across me, and they
said come on we're evacuating the street, it's not safe for you

they said. So I threw on a few duds and came out, and that's all I know. I'm here since. They said an hour or so, but . . . "

"A bomb or something. And there was shots heard."

"Maybe that Protestant, the one that disappeared the other day, maybe that's where he."

"Th'oul' famine museum as they used to call it. That'd be a laugh, sure wasn't he the playboy that started it? Years ago."

"Your own old house, Lizzie. I'd say that's where it is all right, that's where they have the lorries in front of. Aw bejay, if poor Pakky was alive, Lord a mercy on him, that's the man would have had something to say to them! He wouldn't have let no British army heel *him* out of bed in the middle of the night! Haw, the right oul' stock!"

"He'd have put up with it like the rest of us, what else can the people do? I hope it takes a notion to fall in on them! Them old houses were always rotten. Do you mind that storm?"

"The time poor Sarah Morris . . . Oh yes, that lower end of the street was neither fit for man nor beast. If they had to knock it down at the time . . ."

"Some nonsense about history. Well, the poor blackguard must have his bellyful of history by now if the boys has him in there. Mind you, no one claimed it yet . . . Let's hope they get him out anyhow without any damage done. Did you see his poor wife on the television?"

"Oh, it's likely just some bomb scare. There'll be nothing in it . . . Awh-awh, looks as if they're coming to move us out of here next. Must have found something. Must be serious . . . Th'oul' faces of them covered with boot polish! No harm to them, and this crowd's nowhere as bad as the Paras, but they'd give you the creeps looking at them, wouldn't they?"

"You know, I wouldn't spread this round—you never know who's listening—but there was a lot of activity round there this last day or so. If you know what I mean? Certain people was seen, oh aye, well-known people, naming no names. In and out that wee back way past the slate quarry . . . And in a certain wee dark-coloured van, late at night, the night that . . . You see what I'm getting at? I wouldn't say it in front of poor Lizzie, but . . . "

"A couple of shots wasn't there, too? Yes, they were saying . . . "

. . . this Thursday lunchtime. Police and army are still surrounding a house in . . .

She sat at the kitchen table trying one station after another but there was no further news, no details, so she made herself a pot of tea and sat there thinking of old times. At four o'clock she was just going to try the news headlines again when she heard the big rumbling in the distance and the sirens going. She grabbed her coat and handbag and walked quickly off the estate and round the back lanes towards Quarry Street. She pushed and elbowed her way through the crowd and she heard someone saying: "They're digging for bodies . . . " Was it an explosion, she asked, was it a bomb or what? But nobody answered her and she kept on pushing her way to the front, elbowing her way towards the barrier where soldiers were trying to hold people back. "My daughter," she said, "my poor wee daughter's in there, what did yous do on her?" When she came to herself again she was being carried to an ambulance; you fainted, they said, you'll be all right now, missus. Just you sit in there now and you can be with her as far as the hospital.

The priest was there, and Doctor McCormack and old Doctor O'Donnell, they all knew her. She supposed she wouldn't have been let go to the hospital otherwise. She only wished she'd had the time to tidy herself up a bit, it didn't seem respectful to poor wee Sarah . . . Caved in on itself, she heard, that whole block of houses just caved in on itself. Just the one survivor so far, she heard them saying.

CHAPTER FORTY-EIGHT

KATHLEEN

She left Trevor sitting stunned at the breakfast table, left Maureen hurling herself at the telephone. Booking a flight? Checking with her old mammy that Kathleen hadn't gone completely off her head and unloaded a shower of sick fantasies on them? And if she *was* booking a flight, which funeral would she feel she had to go to? Now that was a fascinating question for anyone that was interested: where were Maureen's loyalties? Would even old Shanco be able to split herself in two to that extent? And if she went to Eric McLeod's funeral would someone put a bullet in her? Nuala or someone? Was Maureen *worth* a bullet? Would anyone even recognise her if she went back to Claghan? They'd probably take her for Thatcher or someone and put a bullet in her anyhow. She'd got it all, down to the neat soft waves and hooded eyes and synthetic voice, real old Tory lady these days was Shanco. And Trev, Jesus, Trev. How did they live with each other? Old Shanco, at the age of forty-five, taking herself for a great big success story, not even *realising* that she was still visibly kicking and struggling and fighting her way out of Boharnamuc. Fighting her way out by way of château and landscaped park and avenue of ancient elms. Except that the elms all withered the year they moved in. Trevor must have polluted them with his Cockney breath. Maureen was shattered when the trees died. Maybe she did realise? Maybe she thought it was symbolic or something, the whole place rejecting her? Was that why . . . ? Maybe that explained her old novel. Kill Claghan off and have done with it.

Nineteenth-century Claghan, though. Just far enough into the past to take the edge off any unpleasantness she might be called on to describe. Any batterings to death, for instance. Any kneecappings. Booby-trapped corpses rotting on roadsides in the name of liberty. Famine victims vomiting their guts up. Maureen's faithful readers would trust her not to serve them up the *One O'Clock News* disguised as light fiction. So, old grandad Cormac as a piquant hero: cross between Tom Ripley and Mack the Knife and Romeo. Montague and Capulet sinking their differences in a pit of blighted potatoes. A hundred and fifty years was enough to wash away the blood. So Maureen would have been thinking. She must have got the shock of her life just now when I came out with it about. When I told them about Eric and Sarah. Cormac lives OK. Mouth wide open, the pair of them. Not a word to me. I thought people were supposed to—I don't know—to comfort me or something. Sympathise. Sorry for your trouble, ma'am, and all the old formulas. But no, she made a bucklep for the phone. Lifeline to Claghan. To the Irish mammy. Thought I was still drunk? Or maybe she just went into shock. That's it, if I'd stayed, if I hadn't charged out through the French windows like that, Trevor with his mouth hanging open, crumbs of toast on his chin.

Am *I* in shock, she wondered. Is that why it doesn't really matter very much? Why I can't seem to think about . . . about anything except where to go. Where *am* I going, where the hell does this blasted avenue lead to? Poplars they planted when the elms died. They grow up quicker, Trevor said.

Country gent. Be years all the same, they'll both be dead before. What's at the end of this long bare avenue, where am I *going?* Where was there left to go? Not back to Claghan. Claghan did not exist. There was no Claghan. There never had been a Claghan for her, not since the day she gave wee Gerry the shove that landed him under a car. The day that killed everything. Forever. The screeches the thunder the sky falling in, the taste of carvy-seed cake on her tongue, her mother away in the ambulance. Dead too, she thought. She had lived through her mother's death that day, and never afterwards was she able to accept her alive. Loneliness. Desertion. An ordinary day smashed into fragments. Her father with the belt raised to annihilate: get thee hence into eternal darkness. An ancient bearded God leaning out of a cloud, dropping them in casual handfuls into the pit of fire. Michelangelo or someone. That painting there came out of Claghan Hall, daughter, the only thing we were able to save, the only thing the gombeen men didn't auction. Destruction and the wrath of God and the flames of vengeance, that was all they saved out of Claghan Hall. So where was there left for her to go, where could she go now, feeling neither wrath nor vengeance, only emptiness? Where does anyone go with a load of emptiness?

She strode on down the long avenue with her head down and her hands in the pockets of her red parka, down between the two rows of saplings dropping their pathetic leaves, Maureen's *nouveau riche* avenue. Did you really imagine you'd turn into Lord Baudry, Shanco, did you really think it was possible? To do anything about changing history? She strode on blindly, off the avenue, into the main road without even noticing, down towards the village, blindly into the arms of this crazy-looking elegant old cliché of a French aristocrat waving a newspaper: "I have found you, Madame! The whole world fears that you are kidnapped too, or dead! Your photo is in all the papers, Madame, in your pretty red jacket and streaming hair, I saw you at once. How you have suffered, you poor persecuted little thing, how you must be mourning!" And Kathleen let herself go against the gaunt sympathetic shoulder—she *was* persecuted, she *was* mourning, she *was* in need of shelter—the first sympathetic shoulder that had been offered for as long as she could remember. She cried and cried, and allowed Madame de Lapire-Vacherie to lead her gently by the hand across the landscaped park and into the warm sanctuary of her cottage.

CHAPTER FORTY-NINE

MAUREEN

It's true, Trevor, it really is true what she said. Poor Eric's dead. It was Sarah. She was in the crowd that kidnapped him and, well I couldn't really make sense out of what Mammy said (talk about melodrama!), but it seems they had him in a house in Quarry Street, one of those old houses that were condemned, where Kathleen used to live, and there were shots heard, nobody really knows . . . I suppose what they did, they condemned him to death—you know how they do. People's court and all that. And then one of them got scared and ran out the back. That's how the army. So anyhow, all these tanks and armoured cars and that, they moved in and Sarah was killed in the general sort of. It seems Eric was already dead. The house collapsed, imagine, just sort of caved in on itself, Mammy said, and they were all crushed and buried under it. Probably the noise and the heavy vehicles and all.

The whole town's up in, well anyway the Catholic side, riots and everything. They reckon Kathleen's been kidnapped in reprisal. *Think* of her, just turning up as cool as. What should we do, Trev? Do you think we should, I don't know, ring up the papers or something? Though if she came to us it's because she needed. Because she wanted to be away from it all, I mean she wasn't necessarily being callous or. Should we let her stay, do you think? Might we get into trouble? The Yank O'Flaherty's in his element it seems. Trust him to be on the spot, bloody old scawl-crow! He's planning to give Sarah a military funeral, with paramilitaries carrying the coffin, volley of shots, well that's what Mammy heard . . . Only, the IRA hasn't claimed responsibility, so who?

What will we *do* about Kathleen, it's. I can't get over it, Trev, it's stupid and senseless, Eric was about the most tolerant of, and poor Myrna, should I ring her or write to her or what? Should I go over? No, I'd better not go over. If I went to Eric's funeral and not to Sarah's, or the other way round . . . They probably wouldn't want me at Eric's anyway, a Catholic, and I'd probably get shot or something if I did go. Mammy says feelings are very. But why go to Sarah's and not his? I mean, they've been my friends for years and I never could stand Sarah. I always said, didn't I, that she was half-cracked, that she'd end up . . . You know, I don't think even *Kathleen* could stand her lately. It's a dreadful thing to say but I think Kathleen was scared of her. Only, that's where my place would have to be if I did go over, isn't it? At Sarah's funeral with the Yank O'Flaherty and all the gunmen and all. Because I'm a Catholic.

Lord Baudry's château stands on its little hill above a prosperous farming village. The room that used to be Lord Baudry's office has three tall windows, overlooking church spire, creamery and neat electrically-fenced grazing. In 1841, Emma Watterson stood in this office, haranguing Lord Baudry about the misery of his tenants and getting laughed at for her trouble. The descendants of those miserable tenants are today's prosperous farmers. They wear sheepskin jackets and drive German cars. Their houses have been tastefully restored and enlarged while preserving as much as possible of their traditional architecture. Dishwashers and microwave ovens are discreetly hidden inside solid oak presses. On the *fête de village* young women often dress up in lavender-preserved nineteenth-century Sunday best. Their folk-memories are of the gentlest—*fest noz* and procession and the picturesque gaiety of the yearly washday at a public *lavoir*. Never hardship or injustice or a great-grandfather transported in chains to Cayenne for attacking a *régisseur*. Maureen thinks they must have an extraordinary talent for self-deception because, even granted that their bedtime stories were not of dead men in bogholes, they must surely be aware that their ancestors—living on black bread and getting regularly raped and horsewhipped by Lord Baudry's agent—could not possibly have owned solid oak presses or lace coifs or enough clean sheets to go a whole year without washing them?

Or did they? *Did* they have all those material things and still get humiliated? And could it be possible that they didn't, and don't, *care*? The local history society can't enlighten her: they specialise in Roman remains. The crimes of the Romans are safe in the very distant past, beyond hate and beyond vengeance. Madame de Lapire-Vacherie can't enlighten her either: no, she doesn't recall her grandmothers ever telling her stories or even mentioning the past. They had been, in any case, much too busy. *"Vous comprenez, Madame,* the position of women at that time! The cooking, the washing, the housework, the children, the knitting, the sewing! And my grandfathers always exhausted from their work, coming home to be pampered, to be cared for. How do you expect, Madame, that these women should have bothered themselves with history?" Of course, the down-to-earth hard-working French, the lazy impractical Irish. Ethnic clichés. Maureen drops the subject.

It is a pity. She had been intending to transfer the story of Cormac and Marianne to Lord Baudry's estate in nineteenth-century France. It is no longer possible to set it in Claghan, at least not if she wants to be truthful about it, not if she wants to reject the pious old legend. And she does want. Maureen in middle age feels she has had enough of lying pieties, whether about love or about history, she sees herself as perhaps evolving into a serious novelist by the time she's fifty or sixty. Look at Mary Wesley, she tells Trevor, and Trevor who never reads anything but the *Financial Times* says sure love, you go ahead, you beat them at it! But she won't write about Claghan. Since the tragedy, the O'Flaherty family is on a pedestal, once again perceived as a romantic mixture of victim and hero, as it was immediately after Cormac's own death. Sarah's story is as full of ambiguities as Cormac's: Maureen is prepared to swear that that lazy great lump was never a heroine and if anyone was an innocent victim in the business, she insists, it wasn't our Sarah! Sarah was half-cracked, she repeats, idle and paranoid and a monument of egoism. Do you know, Maureen says, she actually killed *my cat* out of sheer jealousy when she was a child? Or out of revenge, because she thought I rejected her. Because I did reject her, you'd have had to be a saint not to! I guessed it immediately, she was transparent in many ways, and Kathleen guessed it too, though she pretended not to. But then Kathleen spent a lifetime fooling herself.

What I think is: she reckoned poor Eric had rejected her, Kathleen or the old grandmother must have told her about him, told her some bitter fantastic version of what happened. Knowing the pair of them, that would have been it, and Sarah just struck out the way she always did strike. Instinct, paranoia. Talked that boyfriend of hers into? He must have been as mad as herself. Unless they were really in the IRA? No, Mammy says he was half-daft anyhow, a bad breed the old Kaiser Bills. Claghan judgements. Claghan memories. But Mammy says Nuala was seen round Quarry Street that day, that maybe Nuala had a hand in it. That it's *Nuala* the army was watching, and just stumbled on the rest . . .

Nothing's ever that simple in Claghan. For months after the

incident they were saying all sorts of things. That a big cache of guns was found in the Quarry Street house. A big cache of heroin. That Sarah was blackmailing Eric. That Nuala was blackmailing him. That Eric dealt in drugs, a longhaired hippy type like that you wouldn't be surprised, they whispered round Claghan . . . That the famine museum was some sort of headquarters and poor Sarah came on it. That Nuala already owned three hotels across the border and where did the money come from? Blackmail, bank robberies, protection rackets? That Quarry Street was Nuala's headquarters, her recruiting office, her bomb factory. That Eric came on it when he was round checking his museum. That an explosion was heard seconds before the house collapsed. That . . .

They'd say anything round Claghan, Maureen agreed. But gradually the sensational stories were forgotten and the Yank O'Flaherty's version accepted: Sarah as heroine and victim. Sarah, direct descendant of Cormac O'Flaherty, striking a blow against the cynical McLeod who, years before, had her family evicted so that he could construct a monument to the glorious memory of Protestant landlordism. "But everyone in Claghan knows that's just not true!" Maureen protested. "Weren't they all agitating for years to get out of Quarry Street? Evictions, in this day and age!"

"Well, to be sure, they all know it's not true," her mother said, "but that won't stop them believing it. In a few years it'll be gospel. And you can't deny, Maureen, now I'm not saying a word against poor Eric, Lord a mercy on him, but you can't deny that them McLeods was always a bad breed. God Almighty, the stories your poor grandmother used to tell me about the way they made their tenants suffer! Hardship and slaughter and starvation and whole families turned out of their homes to die . . . You could hardly expect the people to forget. It's all right for you, Maureen, you're away . . . "

But how far away *am* I, she wondered, putting down the phone, how far away did I actually *get*, after all? Recalling with shame her instinctive pandering to traditional loyalties the time of Eric's death. But then, as her mother said at the time, what else could she have done? If she wanted to come back to Claghan she need have no outsider's illusions about choosing sides. The sides had been chosen centuries ago. And you couldn't be in Claghan and not have a side, however implicit the support you gave it. As indeed poor Myrna had pointed out all those months ago when she was sending the diary.

So Maureen had stayed in France through all the mourning and recriminations, the prayers and the protests and the riots. She sent a wreath to Eric's family with a rather stilted Interflora card, and a Mass Bouquet to Lizzie O'Flaherty. The two women replied with almost-identical notes of formal acknowledgement: Maureen realises that her long friendship with Myrna McLeod is over. As for Kathleen . . .

For some years now, Kathleen has been living happily in Madame de Lapire-Vacherie's cottage with a fifty-year-old Palestinian who lost wife, children and possessions during the bombing of a refugee camp in Beirut. She feels that she has finally come home, that gentle stooping Sadek pottering in the organic vegetable plot is an Eric survived, an Eric come safely through the fire, purified and understanding, wise with disillusionment and loss. She is certain that they will end their days together in this cottage attic, content in the simple anachronistic existence their patroness has imposed on them. Sadek himself could ask for nothing better than to continue sleeping and waking and working beside this warm peaceful big Irishwoman: her resigned emptiness, her complete absence of will, her passive abdication from the blood and screeches of reality, are now the most comforting qualities he can imagine in a lifetime companion. But he knows he will not be allowed to stay. Already hints are filtering down to Brittany from his compatriots in Paris; soon the hints will be replaced by suggestions, the suggestions by orders, the orders by threats. He has begun to consider which is the most effective way a woman like Kathleen can be used in the merciless war against the infidel that is inexorably preparing itself.

Madame de Lapire-Vacherie watches over her collection of national dolls with authoritarian benevolence. Most of them resent her attitude to them, but the life is easy, the food excellent, and they are in shelter. They find it more comfortable to act out their roles with good grace: Madame has made it clear that she will tolerate neither criticism nor impertinent displays of individuality. Occasionally, one of her protégés rebels. She has found foxglove leaves in her salad-bowl, a year's output of day-old chicks mutilated under their mothers' wings, an explosive device in the coal-bucket. Once her entire living-room furniture was silently hacked to pieces in the night. At each new outrage she calls the refugees together, turns on them a blast of aristocratic rage—this she will not accept! This she will never tolerate! Her vengeance will be terrible!—and afterwards privately interviews the culprit in her office, soothing him with gentle tact, reassuring him of the sincerity of her regard, offering him selected privileges and delights if he will promise never again to disturb her peace. This arrangement has worked for many years now. She hopes it will continue to work. She sees no reason why it should not. Arrogantly innocent, she is unable to visualise a time when one of her guests (maybe Sadek, maybe Kathleen, maybe someone quite different) will, through stupidity, madness or calculation, judge that the total destruction of Madame de Lapire-Vacherie is of more value to his cause than any privilege she has in her power to bestow . . .

Maureen and Kathleen meet from time to time, have a stilted drink together for old times' sake, and go thankfully back to their separate lives. That friendship is over too.

Finally, Maureen has realised that she will not set her book in France either. It seems a pity to waste all that material, but the story needs hate, and there is not enough memory of hate among Lord Baudry's old tenants. Not enough memory. Listening to her village neighbours, she knows she could never hope to create believable French peasants. The mentality is too alien. She thinks of the Yank O'Flahertys and how they pounced on Sarah's death, built on it, furnished it, whitewashed it, thatched it with shamrock, made of it a shrine to attract more hate, more money, more guns, to continue a sequence that began centuries before the McLeods came to Claghan and that can have no foreseeable ending, because there will always be more victims, more heroes, more memory. While insisting loudly that she deplores this mentality, she is uneasily aware that she finds it more natural than Madame de Lapire-Vacherie's comfortable amnesia, than the compromises and bargains and stratagems that allow her to survive and prosper. More understandable. Maureen has begun to be aware that she never did fully escape from her childhood, but is no longer sure that this is a matter for regret.

"Why don't you write the thing anyhow?" Trevor asked. "What's Sarah's death got to do with anything? And who cares what's said in a book for godsake?"

"The Yank O'Flaherty might care. And Nuala McCormack's crowd. Remember their old slogan: Cormac O'Flaherty's real name was Claghan? That's what started them, that's what got the people behind them. So imagine if I go around saying that Cormac was a great big nothing. They'd go *mad*. And I'm not even sure now myself that he *was* a great big nothing!"

"Real typical Paddy, aren't you, love? Don't know whether you're coming or going. True story of Cormac O'Flaherty, that's a laugh! I was getting quite interested in it and all. As the man said, we'll be dead and buried . . . "

"Everyone in Claghan will be dead and buried before the true story gets told. There *is* no true story, it's just a mess of ambiguities and lies and more or less guesses. And it doesn't matter, it doesn't change a thing. Claghan will make up whatever truth suits it. Don't we all?"

But Trevor has long since lost whatever interest he had in Cormac O'Flaherty. He is kept increasingly busy these days, making money. Selling off all the barns he bought during the Eighties, at lovely fat prices, to the insatiable stream of English buyers looking for holiday homes. Maureen finds all this exciting too—it reminds her of the old days in Carnaby Street when they were both young and full of ambition. She decides that she might as well cash in herself on the British occupation of west France, and has already written the first chapters of *A Decade in Brittany*, a good-humoured account of an English couple's life in a picturesque old French village.

Tidying her desk one day, she comes on the almost-forgotten stack of documents about Claghan and, looking wistfully at the useless jottings for her Cormac O'Flaherty book, she wonders if Dr Martin McCormack, the historian, had been down the same road before her and if that was all he meant that day on the phone, and if that was why he retreated, decades ago, to the safety of ancient monuments and defunct Gaelic families.

She wonders, too, what to do with the photostats of the diary and the old documents, and decides that it would be unnecessarily melodramatic to burn them. So she files them away under "Claghan" along with thirty years of her mother's weekly letters and the one completed chapter of her novel. Frost in a thin sun. November. All that may perhaps come in useful one day, in another context.

Also by Poolbeg

Nothing Like Beirut

by

Briege Duffaud

These are stories of exile and return. The lonely but liberating distance of London, Amsterdam and Paris is compared to the stultifying closeness of Irish family life. In *Innocent Bystanders*, Helen, who has committed the unforgivable sin of divorcing and remarrying, returns to Northern Ireland from Amsterdam to see her ageing Catholic mother. At first Helen thinks that Ireland and her mother have changed. A Mills and Boon novel jostles the Rosary beads on a shelf. Her mother watches *Dallas* and *Crossroads* on the telly. She is cocooned in a cosy dream-world in a border town whose name is synonymous with terror. But Helen discovers that her mother hasn't changed. She is still the image of Mother Erin, "that poor unwilling battered wife with her trials and tribulations, exalted by suffering to a monumental egoism, obsessed to the point of neurosis with the terror of being in the end betrayed by her faithless ungrateful offspring."